For my family, Heather, Freya and Georgia.

To Tony Dawes, my father, for allowing us the freedom to explore and misadventure across the world unimpeded. Always with me.

B. M. Dawes

LIFE ACCORDING TO BRIAN

AUSTIN MACAULEY PUBLISHERS™

LONDON * CAMBRIDGE * NEW YORK * SHARJAH

A CIP catalogue record for this title is available from the British Library.

ISBN 9781528938228 (Paperback)
ISBN 9781398411593 (Hardback)
ISBN 9781528969475 (ePub e-book)

www.austinmacauley.com

First Published (2021)
Austin Macauley Publishers Ltd
25 Canada Square
Canary Wharf
London
E14 5LQ

I would like to thank my mother, Shirley, Daniel and all the crew that made these stories possible.

Invictus

Out of the night that covers me
Black as the pit from pole to pole
I thank whatever gods may be
For my unconquerable soul.

In the fell clutch of circumstance
I have not winced nor cried aloud
Under the bludgeonings of chance
My head is bloody, but unbow'd.

Beyond this place of wrath and tears
Looms but the horror of the shade
And yet the menace of the years
Finds, and shall find, me unafraid.

It matters not how strait the gate
How charged with punishments the scroll.
I am the master of my fate:
I am the captain of my soul.

– William Ernest Henley (1849–1903)

The Beginning

Flicking through an enormous book, God, who do we have today? Ah yes, here we go, one of the Dawes family. 'Charles, my good man, you might want to start polishing some of your awards and you're going to need a much, much, bigger cabinet.'

Darwin, wearing a chef's hat takes a sponge cake out of the oven.

'Smell's delicious Charles, is the kettle on?'

'Yes, my lord, we could sit down and discuss my book again?'

God sighs, 'We have been discussing "The Origin of Species" ceaselessly since you knocked on my door in 1882! Anyway, we have a much more important task, bring over the tea-trolley and sit.'

Charles makes himself comfortable, pours the tea. God speaks a long-forgotten language and a chessboard appears. God smiles at Darwin, 'Let's play. I've got a nagging feeling we won't be disappointed!'

White Pawn moves forward…

1

Family Living, Zambia, 1970s

My earliest memory, Zambia, Ndola, 1976. We wake up Shirley (8), Daniel (2) and my good self (5). Dad is in a rage, screaming down the corridor with his famous white Y-fronts on. We have been robbed, they had cut through the bars on the window entered our bedroom, stole Dad's keys and made a break for it. Three hours earlier, my mother, 'Tony, I'm sick of those bloody dogs barking all night, go and lock them up.'

Dad gets out of bed, 'Yes dear.'

Dad now has a problem, Zambia is dangerous and he knows this. They have his keys, they can steal the car, gain entry to the house; the rest doesn't bear thinking about. However, Tony is an electronics expert and doesn't suffer fools or extremely dangerous robbers lightly. *Dad was no average man or father, for that matter. He was much more than the sum of his organic parts. His old Cumbrian nickname "The Firecracker" had been tested and proven many times.*

Dad wires the car up to the mains electrics, a shrill scream a couple of nights later, the car still in situ, problem solved. It's Africa in the '70s. That's the way it was, you couldn't take any chances or you wouldn't survive.

Many years later in Bahrain, over a few beers, Dad tells me…

'One time, we had just finished a tough mission. They were a team of six raiding an arms cache, which turned out to be a bush hut occupied by three goats and a chicken that was evidently lost.'

Dad continues explaining, 'I was exhausted and had fallen asleep on a makeshift chair. I woke up to one of the crew whispering, "Tony, do not fucking move! Look down but stay still." I looked down and joining me for my afternoon siesta was one of the fastest and deadliest snakes, a Black Mamba, coiled fast asleep between my legs. Eventually, my colleague managed to coax the snake away with a stick. On the trip back with bollocks intact, I was ruthlessly mocked with innuendoes that could only be expected by having a large black serpent between your legs. So having scared three goats half to death and repatriated the chicken back to the local village, I thought to myself, Tony…only in Africa.'

However, I reassured him the snake infestation was just as prevalent in Queensland and that I was never falling asleep ever again.

Before Africa, we were living in Western Australia, where I was born. One of Dad's jobs was the installation of ground satellite technology that could monitor Chinese Atomic weapon testing. Dad was at Aldermaston, at the AWE. The Atomic Weapons Establishment, responsible for the design, manufacture and support of warheads for the UK's nuclear deterrent. So there had always been a suspicion that Dad's postings had been a front for many "other" jobs. But he quite rightly would never reveal anything. He wore many hats.

Shirley screams, 'C'mon Brian, you can climb it, it's easy.'

My beloved sister is about 10 feet up the tree. I'm struggling to get up the trunk, suddenly Shirl has shaken a branch and a massive snake has dropped not one foot away from my feet. Fortunately, the Zambian gardener, Samuel had seen my sibling's attempt on my life, comes sprinting over and with a rake held overhead and after several strikes later, kills the venomous beast. I look up and realised that Shirl must have taken a life insurance policy out on me. The ink hadn't even dried and the first attempt had been made. Do the deed, make the claim, and buy lots of sweeties. Her addiction was getting out of control.

I would have to be on my guard from now on. Not accept free ice cream, unless it has been tested on Daniel first.

For work, sometimes Dad would have to travel out to the mines on a small plane, being flown by an eccentric World War 2 fighter pilot. Who had long forgotten the war was over. Dad and his colleagues used to dread it when visiting dignitaries came to visit. As this was the perfect excuse for the handle-bar moustachioed airman to relive his air battles against the dreaded Hun. Most were sick as he did the loop de loop and death roll. Dad and those in the know would numb themselves with a few stiff drinks before the flight out. Sometimes the whole bottle was required, especially if it was someone really important.

Dad's stuck in traffic; it's hot, very hot. The African sun is beating down. Dad winds down the window and sighs to himself. His secretary has been sexually molested and robbed again, in the local township. Happens most days; as soon as she finishes work, she's attacked. Dad horrified, offers a team to go in and sort it out, the secretary refuses; 'They're gangsters, so many…you will all be killed,' she says.

As the warm air starts to circulate through the car, a man runs over and pulls a weapon. He's being car-jacked. The gangster jumps into the passenger seat and says, 'Take me to your home.'

Dad utters 'No problem' and starts to think. The large gate is locked, so Tony tells the bandit, 'You will need to get out and open the gate.'

As the man opens the car door, Dad gives him a push and floors the accelerator, smashing the man and the car door into the side of the wall. Problem solved, the man escapes bleeding and badly injured.

One month later, we leave Zambia; within three years our garden wall grew from four feet high to reach twelve feet, accompanied by guards and dogs. Such is the quick descent of an African country.

After we left, the next resident and his family, also from Dad's company, were murdered in a most heinous fashion in the very same house three months later. Revenge a possibility, or just Africa, no one ever found out. That was the risk all the expats and their families were taking every day. Sometimes you paid the ultimate price for seeking adventure.

Zambia was starting to rapidly crumble, the local population, with the usual government assistance, was turning against the expats. Leaving immediately was a good option, especially if life preservation was important to you.

As the plane left the makeshift dirt runway, we would say goodbye to Zambia one last time. I was quite relieved not to have been killed by either the marauding machete-wielding locals or my plotting sister…

…after all I was quite keen to "see in" my 6th birthday!

2
Rearranging Mother's Wardrobe, The Mystery Gang Returns

Charles contemplated, 'You know rearing children can be a rewarding, if not a never-ending task?

For example, take my 10 kids, my lord, when they come to visit, are they not an absolute delight?'

God sighing, 'Yes, that's certainly one word for it; Pavlov the terrified dog may have a few others!

Well Charles, my dear friend, it's time to play, we have only just started. Is the kettle on?'

Suddenly, there's a thundering noise from outside, a whip-like cracking sound and horses rearing in anger.

God looks at Darwin raises a brow, 'I think we are about to meet one of the greatest ladies and generals to have ever graced the Earth. Now, remember Charles she suffers no fools and only has allegiance to her lord and her countrymen.'

A beautiful lady enters, crisscrossed with battle scars; there is a savage sword at her side. She is covered in blue tattoos all dancing and playing out a never-ending battle, live on her body.

'Boudicca, my most gracious Warrior-General, what do we owe the pleasure?'

'My lord, and good man Charles, I hear on the chariot-vine that you are playing with some of mine. As you know my lord, I am honour bound to protect all my blood kin, since AD 61.'

'Please sit, my lady.' Charles offer's a horn of English honey mead. 'Let us play.'

Boudicca's delicate hand of steel moves the Black Knight takes a White Pawn. They all look down.

Mum lays out brand new clothes as she gets ready for a party in-house tonight. It looks like fairies hallucinating on LSD, let loose with a whole paint pallet have designed the dress. Dad with massive side-burns, frilly white shirt with its buttons undone has his hairy chest exposed proudly. It was the '70s, they looked sharp, and they both knew this.

'Pour me a Campari and lemonade, dear,' Mum said as they sat around the bar in the living room. Every expat house has an in-house bar. Bahrain is a party place and lots of fun; alcoholism is the norm.

It's about 11 pm, the party is in full swing, and I need the loo. Bob Dylan is playing another suicidal track, I take a sneaky peek. It looks like some mad religious cult, all psychedelic, sideburns and bright blue eye makeup galore.

On the toilet, door locked. I can see Dad's Beretta, that he always swore unconvincingly was a replica, on the window ledge. Next thing the door just disintegrates. Dad piles in, all sideburns and hairy chest. 'Damn! I thought it was stuck,' he proclaims.

Spots me on the loo, 'What are you doing still up? Get to bed!'

Next morning, Mum arises first, Campari hangover dial on max. Mum looks out of the window.

'Tony...Tony!'

Dad answers back, 'What is it, Maggie?'

'I don't believe it, a whole load of Arabic women from the village have just walked past.'

Dad grunts back, 'And?'

'Well, I'm pretty sure the village ladies are wearing my clothes.'

'Can't be true,' Dad mutters as he gets up.

'Look, there's another one.' Yes, you can just catch glimpses of Mum's clothes under the Abayas; the scarfs and tights more visible.

Mum rushes over to the wardrobe and flings the doors wide open. 'It's empty, not again! I didn't check yesterday, as I'd just bought a new dress for the party! Those little barstools! Kids...KIDS!' Mum screams.

Bursting into the bedroom she asks, 'Explain why the local village is running around with my wardrobe on?'

Mum is confused, but not as confused as the local men returning from work seeing their ladies dressed in the latest psychedelic '70s fashion. *A thought occurred to me, maybe to balance the odds we could sell Dad's clothes next time, create an underbelly Bahraini hippy community. Looking at Mum's face...maybe another time?*

'At least, Mum, you can buy a brand-new wardrobe,' we both piped up. Shirley 11 and myself 8, Dan (still too young for covert operations) 5, we couldn't hide our excitement at the thought of the new stock arriving, Mum clocks us.

'Tony, I want you to put a lock on that wardrobe.'

Dad runs off, exasperated 'I will go get my drill, damn it!'

Mum's shrill voice, 'Is that vase still missing from the living room? Check if the TV is still there too? Tony (Mum starts to weep softly) ...and the fridge!'

'Yes dear,' Dad replies.

A couple of days before the party, Shirley frustrated, 'This pocket money sucks, we need to find a way of making more.' Our gang's Goal was to keep Mr Habeeb's corner shop afloat, purchase sweeties on an industrial scale. All funded by daring entrepreneurial feats. We are sitting in the Mystery Gang (Self-named)

Hut. Current membership, three; Shirley, Jackie and myself. We were always trying to make money. Alan Sugar would have been proud, even if some of the practices were highly dubious.

'Well, how are we going to do it this time? We need something to sell.' I enquired of the other two gang members.

'Yes, that would help.' Says Jackie. Shirley (an idea starting to form), 'We also need to be able to get our hands on it for free? Yes?' both Jackie and I look at my sister.

'Well, isn't it obvious?'

'No?' came the two replies. 'Our house is full of free stuff, just sitting around. Why not sell it and buy sweets?' The realisation dawning on our young minds. It was right under our noses the whole time. We couldn't believe how stupid we had been.

'Right, let's hatch a plan; we need Mum out of the house. Dad won't have a clue. They're having a party Friday night. Why don't we tell Mum her dresses are looking a bit tired. Why not buy a new one?'

Plan hatched; now for the operation.

Mum confused, 'Really? Don't you think I'm the height of cutting edge 70's fashion?'

'No, your outfits look a bit tired, Mum. Why not buy a new dress? Phone Joyce, your shopping buddy, and take the day off; Dad can look after us.'

'Yes, that sounds like fun, I will give her a phone.'

Forty minutes later, Mum has left. We have a large cardboard box just outside the wall of our house. We know the local village always passes by at this time. We set up a stall. The word spreads like wildfire through the village. You can see a mass of women jostling for position, running towards us, yelling in Arabic. We sell out in eight minutes. The hoard runs off with Mum's finest fashion. Wow, what a result! We should do this all the time.

We have made about 10 dinars (£12) for a wardrobe costing at least several hundred more. Proudly, we start to calculate how many sweets and what type we can purchase. Fill out the gang ledger, off to Mr Habeeb's.

'Right, that's it! You two are grounded for a week. No Dairy Queen or slush puppies and definitely no sweets or visits to Mr Habeeb's. GOT IT!'

'Yes, Mum.' Aw, we've just come off grounding!

A couple of days later, bored from being grounded and suffering sweet-anoxia, we are having a fight. Shirley is half-way up the stairs; me at the bottom. I chuck a clog (all the rage back then), Shirl ducks. It goes straight through the window. We stop fighting to inspect the damage. Damn, there are about six windows from the floor to the ceiling like a ladder. We need a solution and fast. Mum had already chucked a wooden spoon at us today. Shirl and I conspiratorially, *What if we knock out a few more of the windows, they will all look the same. Mum will never know.* We bash out a few more windows, step back and look admiringly at our handy work. We clear up the evidence and hide in our bedroom. We hear nothing for ages; it's now night time. We head cautiously downstairs into the living room. Suddenly, Mum comes tearing down the stairs.

'Tony! TONY!'

'We've had a break-in!' Mum gushes horrified. 'Someone has smashed the stair windows in.'

Dad races off, roaring angrily up the stairs, ready to fight any intruder. Mum, looks at us, we look back. 'Maybe, just maybe, that Vase wasn't you two after all?' She mutters. We look back angelically. When Mums' back was turned, I ask under my breath, 'How much did we get for it?'

'400 fils (60p),' Shirley whispers back.

Spotting Mum's confusion and an opportunity, 'Can we get some sweets then?'

A week later, grounding over and malnourished from a lack of sweets, the gang is back on the hut floor planning strategy. There is a large block of flats opposite, 'Let's go play.'

By the flats, we discover a whole load of pots, vases and statues all broken in bin bags. Shirley's entrepreneurial mind at work again, 'Why don't we glue these back together and then sell them door to door; we can buy sweets.'

Two hours later, we have salvaged about six pieces, meticulously glued together. The obvious place is the flats next door; more people, more sales. We bang on a few doors, no answer. We ring a doorbell it opens, it's an expat.

'Hello missus, we have some fine statues to sell, would you be interested? 500 fils each (75p).'

The woman, crisp English accent, picks up the first statue, looks at it closely eying us warily.

'That's funny, this looks very familiar. I'm sure I just asked my husband to throw this out yesterday. Hey, you're the kids that live in that hut, aren't you? Did you paint those bright Red 6-foot letters on the wall? M-I-S-T-U-R-I,' she starts to spell out the graffiti. Suddenly, the bottom of the statue drops off and bounces off her foot. We look at each other. Run. Run! We scarper, foiled again, no sweets today.

We escape to the gang hut, back to the drawing board for the threesome. 'What about car washing?'

'Yes, we could do that. Let's set up a car wash business.'

First customer, local Bahraini about 500 yards from our house, Mr Yousef. 'OK, 1 dinar it is. *Shukran* (Thank you).' We have stolen Mum's Fairy Liquid and a couple of buckets. Using Mr Yousef's water supply, we start. We manage to lift ourselves onto the bonnet and then the roof. We are barefoot as we had gone feral after living in Zambia. The car finished, actually looks OK, we congratulate ourselves. Ring for Mr Yousef, he inspects the still wet car. Satisfied, he pays and we run off to Mr Habeeb's.

Next day in the gang hut, we can see his car circling slowly around the compound, looking very, VERY angry. His whole car, from bumper to roof, is covered in 1000 small footprints and handprints, one part even looked like it had been licked. Once dry, funnily enough, it looked like three kids had trampled all over it. We hid out for a few days whilst Mr Yousef cooled down and took his car to an authorised car-wash and body repair shop.

'Right, let's have a break from business and have some fun. What about knock down ginger?'

'Yeah, great idea.'

Terrorising expats and Bahrainis alike, we came to one door. I got on Jackie's shoulders and rang the doorbell; this had been the 5th time. The door swung open immediately and my comrade in arms, Jackie, ran off. Sprawled on the floor, the very angry Bahraini swore at me and grabbed me by the arm. 'Tell me where you live.'

'No,' I retort.

'Well, then,' he says and starts to twist my arm. 'OK,' I agree and we go outside. I lead him all over the place. Getting suspicious and angrier, he starts to really twist my arm backwards.

I spot Shirley on the other side of the road on her bike. He shouts over, 'Do you know him? Is he your brother?' (We look almost identical). Like true comrades in arms, my dear sibling replies, 'No never seen him before in my life,' and rides off.

Eventually, arm at 360 degrees, I take him to our house. Mum answers, still wearing her one and only dress from the other night, flies are starting to circle.

'Yes?' she answers in her strong Glaswegian accent.

'Is this your son?'

'Maybe?' Mum is glaring at me, still angry at the entrepreneurial flash sale of her entire wardrobe the week before. 'He has been ringing doorbells and running off! Very bad!'

Mum, not known for her filter replies, 'You get in and you, PISS OFF!' She shuts the door, once again, restoring Arabic-Expat relations for good.

Grounded, one week, no sweets... 'Aw, Mum, I've just come off a grounding!'

3
Four Fools Go Poaching — Escape from Alcatraz

Noj whispers, 'Have you packed all your kit, Brian?'

'Yes,' I replied, conspiratorially. 'Have you hidden all the fishing tackle and rods?'

'Yip.' *Right off we go lads.*

Noj, Big Daz, Rimmer and I are all imprisoned in boarding school, in deep dark Cumbria, England, called Alcatraz. We have just been deemed mature enough to go on our own camping weekend. Away from the prying eyes of our always suspicious teachers. Their unfounded, misplaced trust would soon be rewarded, at the tribunal.

I have packed 60kgs of weight not realising it's a five-mile hike to the site. Abandoning most of my clothes on the way, I arrive at the campsite in my underpants. We have enough fishing gear to decimate Lake Victoria. Responsibly, we have also smuggled in vodka too. Setting up camp, we pitch ourselves in the farmer's field, directly opposite his main livelihood. It's a trout farm, Rainbow trout to be precise. We know this because Noj and Rimmer, a year older than me, had camped and poached here successfully the year before.

Fully prepared, we wait for night time. We sneak over to the fish farm, it's too easy; the fish pools are 6 feet away. We just cast over the fence and catch immediately. Massive Rainbow trout, the farmer's pride and joy. We catch nine, two each and one promised for Monyers, who was deemed too irresponsible to go camping.

We crash out and are woken up at 6 am. Tent zip opens, 'Good morning lads,' it's ONLY bloody Lippy, the Housemaster of Alcatraz. This is the lunatic teacher who drags us up mountains to see the sunrise at 6 am, gets to the top and starts doing press-ups. He should be sectioned, we all know this. However, we are under his jurisdiction and he also knows this! He's called Lippy because when stressed (at least 300 times a day), he does this weird pursed lip thing and vigorously simulates washing his hands. Like I said, completely bonkers, but our jailor nevertheless.

Lippy is delighted, 'Right boys, thought I'd do a surprise visit on you. You do have form after all,' he grins viciously.

'Don't know what you mean Sir? Nothing to see here.' Lippy looks suspicious. 'Sir, we are proper matured out now and can be fully trusted.' The lips start to grimace and the vigorous hand washing starts. Unconvinced, he carries out a thorough internal inspection. Fortunately for us, we had hidden all the kit in the woods and the fish under the tent. How he didn't smell the offending contraband, I still have no idea.

'Anyway boys, looks all good here, must admit I thought I'd catch you lot up to something.'

'No sir, really mature, like really,' our shrill voices answer back in unison. 'Well, OK then,' with suspicion and general madness written all over his face, he does five press-ups and jogs off.

Damn, that was close…so close.

Noj, baffled asks, 'How did he not smell the fish?'

'No idea. I think his olfactory system must have teamed up with all of his other senses to wage war against his wonky grey matter,' I replied.

'I think the grey matter has soundly won, he is bonkers,' we all agreed. Stark-raving mad. Big Daz, shaking his head, 'Definitely a good choice to run a boarding school of 200 reprobates. Couldn't possibly speed up his mental deterioration or suicidal tendencies, at all!' We all agreed he should have been a dishwasher, with those hands.

'I think lipstick tester,' I added. 'Imagine trying to paint on those waving lips, hilarious.'

'Anyway,' says Noj, 'Let's cook some trout up for Brekkie, keep an eye out for that farmer too.' Everyone knows he has a wild temper and that no one would dare poach any of his fish? Especially not mature 13 years olds!

Satiated, we packed up and said goodbye to the relieved fish still swimming about. *See you next year?* Laughing at our hunting prowess and cunning we made our way back to Alcatraz.

Noj's dad was in the armed forces, as was Rimmer's and Daz's (who himself would later end up in Afghanistan, with the Royal Marines) and mine was out in the Middle East. That's how this motley crew had been thrown together. We were best mates. We lived side by side, shoulder to shoulder, day in and day out.

After leaving school, I would return and catch up with Noj and Big Daz. On my last visit, we went on a drinking binge and as always ended up in a bike shed. This time, however, it was 'surprisingly' next to the girls' house. Mrs Martin, the headmistress, ever vigilante of the girls' modesty and reputation, ended our not-so-subtle soiree. As she commando rolled into the hut with full cam-cream on, I was told to leave and never return. They had heard I was in town and had posted sentries around the different houses. Noj and Big Daz ended up with a week's suspension for their efforts.

The last thing I remember was Mrs Martin doing star jumps, 101, 102, 103…proper mental those teachers were. We, however, were saints and completely normal, except for Monyers. He was certifiable.

We were a tight crew. Monyers was also part of the crew. Monyers talking quietly, 'How did it go? I heard Lippy, the mad bastard, did a surprise raid on you. I thought you were so busted!'

'Yeah, close one! He's a sneaky git, for one so insane,' I tell Monyers.

'Did he do some push-ups?'

'Yeah, five.'

'If he does 10 then he has really lost it,' Monyers whispers conspiratorially. 'Yeah I know, he once did nine, when we got caught the last time; I thought his head was going to explode!'

Monyers muses, 'He should be a dishwasher or a lipst...'

'Yes, we know.'

'Anyway, did you score me a fish?'

'Sure did, matey.' We hand Monyers a fish and he scurries off delighted.

Now, we were a little light on the logistics of our little caper. We now have 12 Rainbow trout, native to North America and definitely not Cumbria. We have just been camping next to a Rainbow trout farm. It doesn't take a genius to figure we have a problem.

'Right, boys, we need to refrigerate them, how do we do it?' We all looked at each other, in unison, 'Mrs Brambles.' Now, Mrs Brambles was the kindest, most caring teacher to ever breach the walls of Alcatraz. We all loved her and she did her best to keep Lippy as sane as possible. She, we thought, was not the sharpest tool in the shed and therefore perfect.

We arranged a meet up and handed over the fish to Mrs Brambles, problem solved. What could possibly go wrong again?

Prep time, (where everyone has two hours of silent homework) usually with Lippy prowling over our shoulders like a sentinel.

'Brian, can I have a word?'

'Yes, sir, anything sir.'

'So, Brian, I have just spoken to Mrs Brambles and she has informed me that you have had a very successful haul.'

'Haul, sir? I don't understand?' The lip starts to quiver, the hands slowly writhing. Thinking to myself this is defo going to be a 10.

Sighing he says, 'The fish, Brian, the fish languishing in Mrs Brambles's freezer?'

'Ah, that haul, sir, yes, I can explain.'

Lippy on scale 4 now...'Go on.'

'Well, we had travelled for about six hours over two mountains, through two, no three rivers until we came to this stream filled with trout. It was dark so we couldn't possibly find it ever again, if you were thinking of catching some fish for yourself, sir.'

Lippy snarling, level 9. The urge to start doing press-ups was almost impossible to resist. That was a masterclass in deception, I congratulated myself.

Lippy sighs, 'Sit down, Brian.

David (Noj), come over here. Can you tell me where you caught these fish?' Noj, steely back (I knew we had got this), 'We poached them, sir.'

I couldn't believe it; we were going to walk this one. If Lippy had followed my directions he would have ended up ice fishing in the North Pole, we would have been home dry. Lippy hits 10, 'David, sit down.' Ranting, hands on full rinse cycle now, 'Mr Fruit, take over, I need to de-stress.'

'Boys see me in my study first thing in the morning,' he says as he jogs off.

We enter the study next morning, number 4567, 4568, 4569. 'Sir, you asked to see us?'

He gets up from the floor. He looks terrible. 'I've been up all night destressing because of you imbeciles. I have phoned your parents, they are furious. I have also decided we are all going back to the farm and each of you will personally apologise to the owner. Also, boys, you will pay for the stolen goods, mark my words.'

'Sir, he does have a reputation.' I offered as an escape clause.

'Silence! That didn't stop you lot! Mature, responsible, what was I thinking…never, EVER, again! After that I will think of a suitable punishment, be afraid, very afraid,' laughs insanely, hands start up again. 'Now, get OUT!'

As we look back, he lies on the floor and starts to push, 4570, 4571…

Jase, (another crew member) catches up with us. 'You boys really knocked it out of the park this time.' Jase laughing, 'If Lippy doesn't have a mental breakdown after this episode, it will be a bloody miracle. Plus, if he does any more stress press-ups, we should enter him into the Mr Universe contest. Win some cash.'

We go back to the farm. We are standing about 30 metres away with Mr Fruit, who is playing nervously with his false tooth again. Quickly catches it, as it pops out of his mouth. Looks at us, greasy hair and black nails.

'Hah boys, finally caught you, you are in for it now!' The last word is drowned out by the farmer with bright orange hair going absolutely mental at Lippy. 1 cm from his face, Lippy is almost bent over backwards. The choice language would have terrified hardened sailors. Mr Fruit quickly takes cover behind us; his false tooth falls out for good this time. Lippy eventually regains his colour and hands over £12 for each boy, the cost of the haul. He walks silently over, 'Get in the minibus now,' he hisses.

'But, Sir, I thought we were each going to apologise?'

'Get in the bus, NOW!' We drive back in silence. Mr Fruit is sweating profusely. However, Lippy is shaking with anger, he is livid. 'Camping banned for 100 years,' he mutters angrily to himself! 'I was just trying to do the right thing…'

This isn't going to end well for us, we all agreed. But, as fate would have it, Lippy was so outraged at the treatment he received and the language used, that he went light on us. We had to weed the huge front patio in front of Alcatraz with a small fork. Our parents turned up; I could hear Lippy recalling all the events, which was met with silence. I waited, a few minutes later, they had all started laughing.

'I couldn't believe it!' Lippy to the parents, 'I could have offered everyone some nice Rainbow trout for lunch. But the fish went off, as the boys hadn't cleaned them before hiding them in Mrs Bramble's freezer.'

Sighing, they all looked over at us weeding and rolled their eyes.

Meanwhile, a few days later, the boarding school had to be evacuated and then fumigated. The stench was unbearable. Monyers, the genius, once he had got his trophy and scurried off, had the same dilemma. Where to store his fish? So the obvious place in Monyers head was his own locker. Yes, Monyers stored his un-gutted, rotting fish in his locker for a week! We all got sent home for the weekend. Result…Monyers was a HERO.

Lippy, 6790, 6791…

4
Half-Term Mayhem — Saving the Family Name

'Right, that's it boys, just got off the phone with my 80-year-old gran. She has the keys for Mum and Dad's house (they are away in Bahrain) and she's expecting three of us.' A week before (at school), 'Half-term party at mine (in a small village in the Lakes). All invited, folk can come and go as they please. We'll be there for the whole week. Let's party.' 15 of the first tranche travel down on the train.

'Yes, Gran, absolutely best behaviour, yes just refurnished, reputation to uphold, trust me, all will be fine.' The three of us are collecting the house keys from Gran.

'Right, Brian,' says Gran cheerily, 'enjoy your half-term. I will be up in a couple of days to see how you are getting on. I have baked apple pie and made your favourite jam. I see Niall is with you, that gives me some reassurance, such a lovely respectable boy.'

'So true, Gran,' I gave Niall a nod of approval.

'Yes, yes, anyway you three boys have a good time, remember early to bed and don't drink too much Shandy!' My little Gran waves us off, 'Toodle loo!' She closes the door.

I two-finger whistle and call out, 'Right boys, you can come out from behind the garage.' 12 boys exit. 'Well, you heard my Gran, no trouble. These villages have ears and burning pitchforks.' We move silently, every curtain starts to twitch…We'll have to go incognito. 'Stop, you boys wait under the bridge until dark, then commando-crawl into the house.'

Darkness arrives, the party of 15 successful in this stealth operation, start to unpack all the booze. We have 15 cases of beer for Gran's Shandy, eight bottles of Tequila, and six bottles of Vodka. Niall concerned, 'Do you think it's a tad light?'

'Most certainly,' I said, 'but we can get supplies as we go along.'

17 years of age, we settle in for some serious drinking, escape from Colditz, Scotland (my second boarding school). We were proper crew, shoulder to shoulder, day in day out we were all growing up together. We had the art of camouflage mastered. Doggedly determined, either to smoke cigarettes or hide the homebrew under the school floorboards. We were expert at getting away with things.

2 am, 'Right boys, as is tradition, we need to jump off the bridge into the local river. Remember, no trouble and if you are drowning, do it quietly. My Gran lives only 100 yards from the bridge.'

'Have you done this before?' asks Chris nervously. 'No, and not at 2 am and definitely not in November.'

Team confidence restored, we walked into the -3°C night in our swimming underpants. Curtains eager to twitch had no owner to comply; the silver surfers were fast asleep. I took note of this, most of our work must be done after 2 am. I tell Nugi, who was our scribe, 'Take note of that, no "curtain twitchers" after 2 am. You'll learn something on this adventure, my good man.' Nugi in his underpants, starting to shiver, is scribbling madly away.

As we hit the freezing water, anaphylactic shock is only six seconds away. That's the survival window in order to reach the river bank and live. We all make it, 15 ice blocks slide back to the cottage. 'That was a genius idea,' I mumbled weakly as we cuddled around a firelighter.

'Please can someone just set me alight already,' say Ricardo.

'Us too,' 14 voices reply back.

'Tell you what boys, as is tradition, get a bottle Vodka out of the freezer and I will light the fire. We can sing some rugby songs.'

'Where do you switch the fire on?' enquires a voice (sounds like Timothy), 'I can't find a button?'

'Hurry up,' say's another voice (sounds like Chris). 'It's fucking freezing, pitch black and my wet undies are rubbing!'

Sighing I say, 'Sit down, Tim, it's coal, there's a bunker outside. Electricity only arrived last week and the post is still by carrier pigeon. It will only take me 4 hours to get it to light. Be grateful, before you had to burn the local sheep to keep warm.'

'I bet that smelt delicious that heat and light source,' says Ricardo, licking his lips. I acknowledged this font of wisdom and the rumble in his belly. 'We should bring it back as a "protected" tradition,' Ricardo continues. However, I curbed his enthusiasm and appetite; the burning herbivore might make everyone ravenous. 'Think, if you ate the only light and heat source, then you would be back in the dark, frozen again: Catch-22. Farmers, I ventured, would be none too pleased either. They have general anger management issues at the best of times. This would definitely not be helped if we set their sheep alight...just to keep warm.'

Needs must, however; paper, scissors, stone. Sheep or coal?

Coal, thank God for that! I didn't fancy being back in the dark, freezing but full, 30 minutes later.

I wound the TV up, seeing if any music could be found. The news in black and white was on, Germany had just invaded Poland. Switch it off, the news in the small village was at least 50 years behind and none of us fancied our chances against the Nazis. Especially not in our wet undies. As the sun started to dawn, hearing a cockerel warming up with excitement, we went to bed.

Next morning. 'Right, boys, as is tradition, we have to have a Toga party. Raid Mum's new bed sheets. We have bright pink, blue, green and yellow. Form an orderly queue, receive designated Toga. Right Niall, king size. Dan, single. Timothy, queen,' Timothy starts to protest, paranoid from alcohol abuse.

'No, it's not a reference, see it's on the label, Queen.' Still protesting, he walks off in a bright pink sheet with a pillowcase on his head, muttering angrily about dignity.

Team Toga, we set up a garden tea party. Fill the teapot with 140 proof alcohol and in our new Togas we throw some shapes on the lawn, it's 10 am. Bemused hill-walkers are strolling past. I heard one say, 'I'm sure I just saw a six-foot pink smurf pour a cup of tea.'

'Don't be silly, dear!' came the reply.

Merrily, we wave them on their way. The curtains in the valley are starting to go into over-drive. I could see smoke signals emanating from the chimneys, a sure sign the villagers had clocked us. One curtain twitched manically and then fell silent, heart attack no doubt. The average age of 104, meant mortality was being fought on a day to day, hour by hour basis.

At least we were getting the averages down on this jaunt. Thinking evolution, survival of the fittest, the village stock would be much stronger after this week. Get them through the winter. I expect chocolates and flowers would arrive posthumously from grateful relatives. However, their gratitude would have to wait. We had a situation on our hands. Gran would surely see the SOS signals and come with Apple pie to investigate.

Time for a team talk. We huddle together, rugby style. 'So far we have stayed out of trouble and we have followed all the traditions to the tee. I think we can afford to let loose a little bit. But, do you see that smoke signal?' I look up. 'Which one?' says Nugi.

'The big arrow one pointing at us, that one!'

'Oh yeah,' Nugi replies looking up at the arrow pointing at his head.

'Well, that's my gran signalling to my 503 relatives all around this valley that we may need surveillance.'

Dan, thinking aloud, 'Oh shit, didn't Granddad pull out all his good teeth in one sitting too?'*

'Yes, now imagine how strong the woman who married him was.' 14 blokes back, 'Oh shit!'

'Yes, so we have to be proper Colditz-Cunning if we are to survive this and party all week incognito. Also, we are running out of booze.' Everyone gasps, Timothy starts crying uncontrollably.

'Niall, slap him for me.' One slap later, right so they know now. Gran will be baking furiously, I mused.

'We need a plan. Neil any ideas?'

Neil conspiratorially suggests, 'What about we barricade ourselves in and hide under the bed.'

'What for a week? What about the booze run?' Niall says panicked.

'We could grab a bottle of Vody each and ration,' Neil offers. Good, but not good enough.

Ricardo says, 'What about camouflage? We could dress like the locals, go undercover.'

'I'm not wearing a flannel checked shirt,' says Timothy indignantly. He starts crying and runs off.

'Is he transitioning again?' I ask the group. 'Yes, looks like it,' says Kristian. 'I wish he would make his bloody mind up.' *However, he has given me an idea. Mum's got a wardrobe full of clothes, that's a cunning disguise for sure, cross-dressing in the Lakes, absolute bullet proof.*

'Now, Nugi, my good man, take some notes. Let's re-evaluate our successes so far.

For starters, we have gained the trust and respect of my suspicious 80-year-old Grandmother. We have also learned that the river is life-threatening and loss of underwear is a near certainty. Not ideal when on average we have packed one pair each. Neil is sharing his and Rob spotting a business opportunity, is renting his pair out. Toga parties in the morning attract unwanted attention. Communication across the village is by coal-fired chimneys, not burning sheep. We have probably been busted and Timothy is transitioning again!

So, Nugi, my good man, when you do grow up and finally run Sri Lanka, as is your destiny, there is still a lot to learn from this tour. One thing, family respect and its good name must be upheld at all costs.' Patting his shoulder, I continued, 'Especially for the elderly members. Keep the family honour intact.'

First disguise, Toga time again. Our bright green, pink and yellow togas should have been a dead giveaway but I was confident that Cumbrians were colour blind; Grandmother wore reading glasses after all. Thank God it was a full moon, that would definitely grant us enough cover. Silently, we crept out. Hiding amongst the sheep, we could see the pub. We just needed to cross two fields and one river.

Suddenly, a thunder-flash bunny explodes not five feet away. I could see Gran riding on a stag. God, she looked magnificent, no time to admire the scene. Happy hour was about to start; using hand signals we make a pincer move. We outflank Gran and two of my aunties, Jan and Sue riding on badgers. Head to the pub, just in time as the starting bell had just rung. We were safe for now, they couldn't follow us in. The White Lion pub was hallowed ground to the village and family.

I go to order at the bar. My cousin, Jonas, saddles up.

'Hey, what's a good-looking lady like you doing here?' He looks down appreciatively, slow whistle, 'nice legs.' I take the pillow slip off my head.

'Hi Jonas, it's me, you fucking idiot.'

'Cousin Brian, what the HELL! I thought some new talent had arrived. Got my BLOODY hopes up,' Jonas mutters as he furiously storms off.

1 am and pleasantly drunk, we clean off in the river and head home.

Next day, there's a holler from one of the sentry's posted in the large oak tree in the front garden.

'It's your gran!'

'Oh shit! Can you see what's she's holding?' I yell at the sentry.

'Why?'

'Just DO it?'

'Looks like one Apple pie and one jar of Strawberry jam.'

'Phew, she's not too angry then. Right, there is supposed to be three of us, Dan, Niall and myself. You lot, hide in the coal bunker, quick now.' 12 blokes jump into the bunker. We close the heavy lid.

Just in time…knock, knock! Resisting the urge to shout 'Who's there?' I'm about to open the door…

In the background, the TV is droning on 'One small step for man, one giant leap…' some dodgy baked bean can has just landed on the moon. 'Turn that drivel off,' I say to Dan. 'It's sooo boring.'

Opening the door, Gran, at four foot eleven enters the cottage and starts to investigate with vigour. Into the kitchen, fast as a ferret, opens the washing machine door, nothing. Cooker, nothing again. Her suspicion starts to lose faith. With one last try, she flings the microwave door open and looks for footprints. Empty. With her curiosity finally satisfied, she says, 'I've brought you some lovely Apple pie and some Strawberry jam. That should keep you out of trouble. Remember, we have a reputation to uphold in the valley.'

'Yes, of course, Gran. Thank you for the lovely pie, this should last the 3 of us, a good while.' I smiled back gratefully. 'Let me help you with that walking stick.'

'Toodle-loo. I'm off to bake some more pies and pick some fruit for more jam making.' Out of earshot, Gran says to herself, 'There were so many, where are they? I will call in reinforcements, Uncle Peter and Uncle Paul (two hardened mountain men, with hunting and tracking skills). We'll catch them this time. The village will start talking soon, family honour is in peril.' A curtain twitches as Gran makes her way home.

We finally prize the bunker lid open. All we can see is 24 eyes blinking back at us. Everyone is covered in coal dust. That gives me an idea, I hatch a plan.

Under the cover of darkness, we have rubbed coal all over ourselves. We make a break for the pub, suddenly a badger barrel bomb rolls down the hill. Only two experts in the world have this type of country warfare knowledge. Cursing, it's Uncle Peter and Uncle Paul! We dive into a ditch to gain our composure. 'Shit,' I tell the boys of who our new adversaries are, suddenly a burning sheep thuds next to us. My uncles are using mortars now, we need to move fast. 'Everyone into the river,' we make our way downstream, using the diamond formation we outmanoeuvre the huntsman.

We use Timothy as a decoy, he runs off in the opposite direction.

Timothy as a decoy would definitely work. If the beauty was caught halfway through his transitioning, the huntsmen would be so confused, they would lose their focus. That would give the party the time needed. It was desperate; happy hour was 10 minutes away. The plan has worked, we reach hallowed land. The glorious pub.

'Brother Peter, what mockery of mankind is this? Murder most foul, tis a hideous beast.'

'Aye, *The Bogan* for sure, Brother Paul. Pray to thy GODS!' The uncles have caught up with Timothy.

Timothy, purring, 'Hey boys! What are a pair of cuties like you doing in this here sheep field?' Timothy is twirling a curl in his hair, blows a kiss to both hunters.

'Brother Paul, I think I've found God again, we must pray.' They both kneel, spotting his chance; Tim makes a break for the pub too.

Back in the bar, Cousin Jonas is lamenting, 'Y'know there is a serious shortage of women in the valley. Even Cousin Adam is faking homosexuality just to get some attention and a cuddle.'

'What about the sheep, Jonas? Plenty of those willing beasts?' I offered in consolation.

'Yes, we tried that but the local restaurants banned it.' Points to a sign on the window. There is a symbol of a sheep sat at a candlelit table with a fork in one hoof and a glass of wine in the other. A big red circle with a cross through. 'So damn unfair,' he sighs.

'A few of the boys even tied the knot. Didn't work out. No romance and the language barrier led to many divorces and break-ups. They even went en-masse to a home economics class in desperation, to learn how to boil an egg.'

'The locals?' I said sympathetically.

'No, you idiot. The sheep.'

'Sorry. Hey Jonas, I've just had a genius idea. If you can wait a couple of days, we have Timothy who will have fully transitioned by then. He'd be very keen to test the new pipes out, no doubt. Ripe fruit for the plucking,' I promised Jonas.

'I love fruit, especially blueberry jam,' he muses.

'Think more lemon curd,' I said patting him on the shoulder. 'He's our decoy for the night, look there he is.' Timothy crashes through the door, a woman screams 'Tis the Bogan!' a dog starts to growl. A pitchfork suddenly imbeds in the door just above his head. 'Stop,' a shout from outside is heard. 'Stop, tis hallowed ground.'

Cousin Jonas gives me a dark look. Has another look at Timothy. Tim's black pudding mascara is smudged and his ketchup lipstick is all over the place. 'I said shortage Cousin Brian, not a full-blown FAMINE!' he bellows and storms off again.

No pleasing some people. I buy Timothy a well-deserved Pina Colada.

The next morning. The sentry hisses over, 'It's your gran, she coming back again. She's carrying three Apple pies and two jars of Raspberry jam!'

Damn, I could tell she was losing her patience. The situation was becoming more precarious. If she came with Gooseberry jam, we were screwed. Gran had already had the local shop ban us from booze. So we had to travel further for supplies.

'Everyone, back in the bunker!' Wind TV up. *JFK has just been shot, I repeat…* 'Turn that drivel off!'

Knock at the door.

'Hi Gran, what an absolute pleasure. More pie, the three of us haven't even managed the last one yet.'

Gran enters with "Spot", Granddad's fully trained half-wolf, half-sheepdog, who was now moonlighting as a police sniffer dog. Full inspection ensues, under beds, in wardrobes. Gran climbs up the ladder into the attic, almost everywhere, except for the coal bunker. Gran leaves, muttering to herself about tradition, the deteriorating family name and leaving the valley for good.

'Nugi, my good man, I hope you have taken lots of notes. Remember, when you become president, how honour and family tradition are of the utmost importance.'

Nugi putting on one of my Mum's dresses,

'Yes Brian, of the utmost,' he acknowledged.

'Where are we off to?'

Confused, I replied, 'Back to the pub, where else?' We have been proper busted, so now we have to be even more cunning. Time for the secret weapon, Mum's new wardrobe. No one will ever suspect, just 15 ladies going for a quiet drink at the local. Pass Gran's house, no need to hide as she will never suspect. Just pray she doesn't have her reading glasses on.

'Sounds perfect, where did you put the Lippy,' Nugi asks straightening down Mum's designer dress.

'I don't think there is any, here use ketchup.'

'Brother Peter, LOOK there he is on the brow of the hill: flash of floral.'

'Tis nephew Brian,' cries Peter, 'Hurry, before he reaches hallowed ground. Cometh the hour maketh the man, Brother Paul. Look at him go! Tis Brother Tony *the firecracker's* son for sure,' marvels Peter.

'He's quick even in those tights. Just like his father,' they announce proudly, 'Except for the dress, high heels, handbag and ketchup.'

We successfully reach hallowed ground. Go to the bar and order a round in. Tap on the shoulder, 'Hey you little beauty, what brings you to the Lion?' It's Cousin Jonas again. I pull my wig off.

'Jonas, it's me, you fucking idiot.'

'Damn it to HELL cousin Brian, what are you trying to do to me? There's not been any girls in the village for 45 years, damn it. I've just phoned all the boys because we heard through the smoke-vine that 15 lovely ladies were walking through the village. Some have even brought engagement rings and dowries, just in case!'

Cousin Jonas stops the monologue for a second,

'Wow, just wow!' Jonas is distracted. 'Look at that beauty,' he says, looking at 6 foot 6 Ricardo. Who would later clear Sandhurst as an Officer, was certainly no gentleman tonight, not in those heels. Bending over, he exposes his white buttocks.

'Oh hold on, he's one of yours, isn't he? I recognise your mother's wedding dress (now a mini skirt).'

'Sorry, Jonas.'

Jonas hollers over to the expectant grooms queuing outside the pub, 'Call it off, fellas. It's cousin Brian and his school mates.'

Large groans come from the group.

'That's the drought back on,' one local sighs deeply.

I gave Ricardo a dark look, 'Hand back that engagement ring, right now!' I scolded him. 'You too, Neil!' Pair of bloody chancers, anything for a snog.

Jonas clears his throat, 'Ahem.' Holds out hand, questioning look. Damn it, I hand my ring back too. 'Beautiful zirconia that,' I sigh.

I pat Jonas on the shoulder sympathetically, 'You boys need to get out more, at least travel to the next village. I will send you a photo of a woman to realign your perceptions, not hit on drag queens or family members. FFS.

Anyway, the reason for the dubious disguises Jonas is that I'm trying to have a party with some crew from school and I don't want Gran finding out.'

'Oh, why didn't you say so? I thought it was a bit weird when I witnessed Peter and Paul sharpening the dogs' teeth on the stone grinder? Then checking and cleaning their shotguns, I thought a hunt was on?'

'It was, Cousin Jonas, it was…'

No visit from Gran the next day, we had been successful. As the week drew to a close, we had managed a 7-day party. Gran had also managed to get all alcohol banned from every shop in the surrounding valley up to a 10km radius.

Our last night was upon us. One last dash to the pub. We would have a full battle thrown at us. Adder snake tripwires, flaming squirrel arrows and hedgehog mines. But we were determined not to fail. In a ditch, Dan exclaims horrified, 'What the fuck is that?'

I look up it's hideous. 'I think it's a Bogan,' a Cumbrian creature of myth. Think Haggis but on two legs, all pointy teeth covered in hair with red eyes and poisoned talons. Fear starts to grip us. It staggers over, we prepare for death.

'Oh, hold on a second,' says Ricardo, 'it's Timothy in the final stage of his transition.'

'Bloody HELL Tim!' We all said terrified. 'You scared the crap out of us, at least put some lippy on.'

'Wow, it's like the transformation of a butterfly,' pipes in Neil.

'More like a moth,' grunts Niall. We make our last attempt for the pub…to find that we have been barred for life, under strict orders from Gran.

We head home, 14 blokes and Tabitha (nee Timothy), to watch the Berlin wall coming down on the telly. Outraged at the wanton destruction of a perfectly good wall, we crash out.

Nugi, in the morning, has finally enough material to run Sri Lanka in his later life. I looked forward to his inauguration, knowing that his training was now complete.

Back in Colditz, we have taken loads of photos. I have taken the films to Mrs Apple, the matron (lovely 67-year-old lady), who as a favour would take them into town and get developed.

One week later, all hell has broken loose. Once the shop (Boots) had seen the photos they had called the police. They had thought that Mrs Apple was some kind of child pervert and she was taken in for questioning. We were summarily called into the Headmaster's office for explanation and general abuse. Eventually, scarred for life, Mrs Apple was acquitted and the whole thing was hushed up by the school. The press would have had a field day, the school's global reputation had to be preserved at all costs; just like my Grans good name.

Mrs Apple, a devious sexual predator? Disguised as a caring Matron? What a disgrace! Such a poor lack of judgement on my behalf! I berated myself. I couldn't believe that I had trusted the photo processing to such an evil twisted viper. Who knew, she seemed so nice too, that lovely Grandmother of six.

End of term arrives. Dan and I head back home to Bahrain. Dad is waiting, 'What the hell is this?' he hands me a letter. It's from the school, detailing yet again the disgrace I had brought upon their treasured institution and my family's honour.

'Dad,' I comforted, 'don't worry this is a storm in a teacup. They have totally overreacted, yet again! Look they even wear top-hats (they don't) and play cricket.'

Dad sighs, 'Cricket? Hey, that is a bit posh.'

'Exactly,' I continued, 'so you can imagine how they would totally lose it, over a few boys having a couple of beers, right?'

'Yes, I guess so, no harm done then. They really do go completely overboard! Couple of lads having a few beers, in my day…' Dad starts to monologue about country life on the farm as a young man growing up…

I interrupt, 'Really quite boring Dad, the whole week, nothing happened. Gran baked her famous Apple Pie and the three of us watched TV mainly.'

'No Gooseberry Jam?'

'Nope!'

'Thank God for that! OK then, no harm done. Try and stay out of trouble Brian, just for once.'

'I do try Dad. It's just not one of my strong points.'

'However, no more letters threatening your expulsion! I had to pull every string so the school wouldn't throw you out. Sometimes I don't know why I bother. As usual, you are on the opposite side of a good idea, Brian! Remember the family name for once.'

'Yes, Dad, it's a top priority for me.'

The phone starts ringing.

'Oh, hello Mother,' he covers mouthpiece and whispers, 'It's your gran, she says she has something very important to discuss, matter of family honour…'*

'Oh, really? I'm heading out now, no need to wait up.'

'Taxi! Taxi!' I jump in, '*Yalla, Yalla* (Go, Go) to the airport I say in a shrill voice.' Dan opens the door and dives in, 'Me too! Drive!'

*Granddad suffering toothache (with one tooth) went into town one day and had every single tooth pulled out in one sitting, replaced by wooden dentures. His reasoning: didn't want to waste any more time with dentist visits. Farm work was more important, no teeth no dentist. Gran said some years after when talking of the past, 'Silly man he had great teeth too.'

*Gran bless her, didn't tell Dad about the smashed front door window, broken toilet/general plumbing (blocked by newspaper, unblocked by Neil and then professionally by my uncle), kitchen table destruction (used for dancing, everyone), empty fire-extinguishers (Ricardo) and the 500 beer cans and empty bottles of every description we had consumed over the week. Gran fixed it all with no fuss (as was her style).

5

The Big Send Off, Bare-Faced Cheek

God, perusing the globe, 'Where is he now? Ah yes, we should have guessed, Bahrain.'

Charles starts to hop up and down, super excited, 'Oooh I love that place, it's proper mental.'

God replies, 'Yes, they certainly know how to enjoy themselves, highly entertaining.'

'What's that noise?' *There's a strange melodic, haunting music playing.*

Darwin quizzical, 'I'm sure that's a Kurdish tambour?'

'Ah,' says God, 'His eminence has arrived.' A large man in glorious blue, with pure silver chainmail enters, his chiselled features and proud stature attest to his infamy. Charles mutters, 'Wow, he's magnificent.'

'As-salamu alaykum, my gracious lord and Charles, my good sir.'

God, 'Peace be upon you too, my lord. Thank you for coming, you received my request?'

'Yes, your Excellency, I have to play the game of chess, keep all of Arabia safe from this marauding crusader.' Saladin sits on a cushion and inhales from his Hukka pipe. The warrior-leader accepts a small glass of hot black tea from Charles.

'Let us play.'

Black Castle takes White Castle. They all look at each other, oh dear…

So, I wake up to laughter, look down and see Lars (Dutch mate) pointing at me. I'm on the top bunk, no mattress, completely hungover with my family jewels hanging indignantly through the bed slats, causing Lars mirth. Dutch Bastard! I look around we are in jail, there are four of us. I have absolutely no idea how this has happened. Two are wearing fancy dress, yellow and pink Hawaiian outfits all flowers and gaiety. Big Mike is wearing formal attire (all black); who I was pretty sure, after attending his leaving party last night, should by now, be safely back in the UK?

I look down; I'm in full formal attire, that's good, except for a hideous bright blue pair of boxer shorts. On closer inspection, I noticed they were covered in little Huggy bears, that's bad. And where the fuck are my trousers? I've been robbed. I tell the boys this, they all start laughing.

'You don't remember, do you?'

So I get a phone call, it's Stu, 'Get suited and booted, Big Mike is heading back to the UK and the crew need to send him off. Tomorrow, Senor Pacos, 7 pm. Don't be late!' Stu hangs up the phone.

Senor Pacos, eight of us boys, all dressed smartly. Tequila slammers and whisky chasers for starters. Mike's flight departure time is 11 pm. No problem, we will easily make that. One of the boys receives a phone call, there's a Hawaiian fancy dress party at the rugby club. More crew to catch up with, let's go. Jump in taxis, plenty of time.

Partying at the club, another mate, Jim says, 'Look, I'm picking up my mate from the airport, it's his first time in Bahrain. Why don't we kill two birds with one stone, drop big Mike off, pick up my mate, all sorted.'

This is running like clockwork. Nine of us jump into the jeep, four boys and five girls (including three girls we had never met before). Seven are in Hawaiian outfits and Mike and I are wearing formal attire.

In the airport car park, Anika (Lar's sister), says no way can she go in with these fluorescent blue Huggy bear boxer shorts on. Thinking irrationally in a Muslim country, in an International airport, I said no problem, I'll wear them. We swop clothes. What could possibly go wrong again?

So we rock in. Lars, Mike, Jim, Anika, Sharon, myself, and the three girls no one knows. I have a formal black shirt on, black socks, smart shoes and the blue Huggy bear boxer shorts on. Something strange is going on, the airport is packed full of people wailing and screaming, all in black. Anika on one side, Sharon on the other…they pulled my shorts down to my ankles. I took a while to realise that I had just displayed my "tackle" to the whole, very upset airport and fell over trying to get them back on.

Big Mike, 'Shit Brian, you better run. You just mooned the whole of fucking Bahrain! LOOK!' points Mike, the security is coming over with their sub-machine guns drawn…

I run out and hide under the jeep. Not five minutes later, the security guards grab me and take me back in. Poor camouflage technique. With those shorts on, I could have been spotted from outer space. As we are being led away, Jim spots his mate (first time Bahrain) coming through arrivals but can't get his attention. We are taken upstairs to the security room. Leaving the newly landed guest, stranded in the airport…expectantly waiting on Jim's "pick up".

We were made to sit and wait…then this guy marches over. Tough, with a no-nonsense attitude, an obvious military man with mirrored 'Aviators' on, it's dark outside. I start taking the piss, 'Look at this guy, who does he think he is? "Maverick" from Top Gun? Or more like his dad?' I continue on, making sure that any chance of not being incarcerated or killed by "Maverick's dad" was rapidly disappearing. I later found out that he is Colonel Jack Jones, head of security, Bahrain intelligence and one of the most dangerous men in the Middle East. Rhodesian ex-special forces, black ops et cetera. Probably several hundred confirmed kills under his belt, with one more to be added shortly. Oh, and 100% not to be taken the piss out of, like EVER! The Colonel is also a good mate of my dad's, "Quelle Surprise," which I would only learn later.

As Jack Jones marched over, I could only admire my beautiful boxer shorts gleaming back at me in his mirrored Aviators. So gloriously bright. He growls at me, 'I have just spoken to your father and he is furious! You know we have a situation here and you turn up with your bollocks hanging out. The Pakistani President has just been shot down and the place is jammed full of mourners, all flying back for the funeral. Did you not hear and see all the wailing from the 1000 strong funeral party?

Plus, your dad, Tony says you are supposed to be seeing a mate off at "Senor Pacos". Not streaking naked through the fucking airport!' Jack Jones' lip starts to twitch uncontrollably. Metaphorically, I know he has his hands around my neck, squeezing.

Found out later. 'Tony, we have a situation, your son has turned up with a few mates, and you should see the bloody state of them! One looks like a peacock! But your son takes the bloody biscuit barrel; he has hideous bright blue bear shorts on. Which he then whipped right off in front of 1000 mourners. We arrested them for their own safety. We're lucky we didn't have a riot on our hands. If the Pakistani government finds out Tony, there may be consequences.' Dad, furious 'That bloody son of mine. If only we could lock him up for good!'

'What do you want me to do, Tony?'

Dad in anger replies, 'That's easy, teach the idiot a lesson, once and for all!' Colonel Jones, 'No problem. The pleasure is all mine!'

'Maverick?!' the cheeky bastard, they both laugh.

All of us are in the back of a security jeep; the first stop, breathalyser. Seriously, a mere observation would have sufficed. Then we were separated from the girls and chucked in jail, fluorescent blue Huggy bear boxer shorts and all. Our jail was fine, however, the girls had been thrown in one of the worst prisons Bahrain has to offer. They told us afterwards that the local jail population (mainly prostitutes and junkies) were very interested in communal showering. Which they politely declined! Missed opportunity, I say. The three girls that no one knew must have been beside themselves by now.

A couple of days later and a lesson taught, we were released. Like fate, the last parent to come and pick up their kid was my dad. He was like, 'Bloody HELL Brian, fluorescent blue bear shorts, really Brian? REALLY!!!'

Dad continues, 'You told me you were going to the Mexican restaurant to see Michael off and funnily enough I have just passed him and his furious looking dad in the corridor.' Mike's dad was the CEO of the Bank of Germany. The second most important representative from that Teutonic country, in Bahrain. The six-foot five captain of the industry was now officially the joint second angriest dad on the Island, along with the five other girls' furious parents.

At least my dad (now a respected Managing Director), was resigned to it. Dad in monologue, 'Oh and by the way you do know who Jack Jones is!'

'I do now,' I mumbled weakly.

Driving home, Dad heaves a big sigh, thinking to himself, *where had it all gone wrong? Looking at me, had he even come out of the right exit? The local priest hadn't been so sure? What about 'that' christening? We had been expecting three wise men on donkeys! That's it! I would have to look again for the "mark!" Fly to Jerusalem, collect those seven sacred daggers. Do the deed and save mankind. At least I'll pick up some air miles, silver lining and all that,* Dad smiles.

Musing to myself, I would put Dad's mind at ease. *I really don't know what all the fuss is about with family honour and all that moral compass stuff! Let's face it, mine had been spinning anti-clockwise ever since those four hooded horsemen had gate-crashed my christening. Bestowing that "mark" on my inner forearm was adding insult to injury, the cheeky bastards!* I look over to see Dad smiling.

Spotting my opportunity… 'Anyway, Dad, that full-scale riot and probable international diplomatic incident, technically wasn't my fault! Firstly, not only had I not pulled my own shorts down! But they weren't even mine in the first place!'

'Dad,' I continued, giving him a serious look… 'I'm the victim here.'

'Son,' another big sigh, 'just don't! For starters, you look like a badger's arse…'

Back home ring doorbell, Mum opens the door.

'Hi convict, you must be starving? Lunch is on the table.

It's true then,' Mum looking down. 'Nice shorts, son!'

Later I found out that some of the dads had gotten together when we were incarcerated, had a few beers and a laugh at our expense. That'll teach them, they thought it was hilarious. Such is the expat mentality of what constitutes as fun. At Court a week later – the charges: drunk and disorderly, indecent exposure and disturbing the peace in an international airport. 300 dinar fine (about £500) and some serious disapproving looks from the presiding judge. Especially after hearing details of the sordid case.

So, Big Mike missed his flight. Jims' mate was stranded at the airport for two days, not knowing what the fuck was going on and if anyone was ever going to pick him up. Even, if he was in the right country, let alone the right airport? The wheels had proper fallen off this caper! Rolled down the hill, never to be seen again…

My learning – don't trust your friends ever! Don't be taught a lesson from Tony Dawes ever! And whatever you do, definitely don't take the piss out of Colonel Jack Jones EVER!*

…and who were those three other girls?

No one ever found out.

*I bumped into the Colonel a couple of years later at the British club. Only to be told he was still watching me and still disappointed.

6
Off a Balcony, Without a Drainpipe

'Mr Dawes, his Excellency the Prime Minister will see you now.'

The phone rings…

'Sorry, excuse me sir (the secretary interrupts), there is a phone call for you, says it's urgent.'

'Who is it?' Dad enquires. *This meeting is very, very important.*

'Mr Mustafa, the Bahrain Yacht Club manager,' the secretary replies.

Dad (long sigh), 'Can I take the call in a private room?'

'Yes, of course Mr Dawes. Sounds serious,' the secretary says looking concerned.

Mr Mustafa almost in tears, 'Yes, Mr Dawes, both your son and daughter have turned up with three taxis full of American soldiers. What should I do?'

'Christ, let them in, we can contain them there. I have a meeting with the Prime Minister, so I will be there as soon as I can. I'm so sorry, Mr Mustafa.'

'Please hurry Mr Dawes, I'm very scared,' Mr Mustafa, starts sobbing…

My sister, Shirley is dating an American GI called Ray. Ray is a Texan and is as cool as they come. We get to know the army boys really well and become good friends. Party hard.

'Right, let's get the troops together and have a party at the Yacht club.'

12 of us rock up to a tearful Mr Mustafa. With a little tear running down his cheek, he opens up the barrier and stifling another sob, lets us in. A couple of hours later, Ray and Shirl are dancing on a table. When a lady with a crisp English accent comes over and orders them off.

Ray cool as ice, in his Texan drawl says, 'Fuck off, ma'am.' I could see the confusion on the poor lady's face after being told to 'Fuck off' so incredibly politely. Her genetic makeup meant that politely she would have to comply and she walks off confused.

We head away from the gathering angry club members and head down to the bay. Jim* aka "Walter Mitty" is reciting one of his many colourful tales. Think more Barney Rubble with wispy blond hair and moustache, than Rambo. 'Did I tell you guys (Jim in monologue, yet again) about the time that I jumped on that live grenade and saved that family from instant death?'

'Yes, Jim,' we all sighed.

'Wasn't that a pineapple on your all-inclusive Cancun holiday?' I quip.

'Yeah, you guys can joke. But did I ever tell you the time I single handily took out a jihadi base with a penknife?'

'Yes Jim, two days ago,' the group replies.

Jim warming up to himself, 'And the time I blew up that Tank garrison with my cigarette lighter.'

'Yes Jim,' a few GI's start groaning.

'Don't forget,' says Jim now in full "Rambo" fantasy, 'that I also killed half of those Vietcong in Nam. Just by looking at them,' Jim jumps up for effect.

'Too far, Jim.'

'However, Jim,' I said, 'if you had made them sit down and listen to your stories, I could believe that the Vietcong would indeed have surrendered. Such suffering was inhumane.'

'Damn it, it's all true!' Jim storms off.*

We all breathe a sigh of relief. 'Bat shit crazy that boy!' Johnny, a soldier from the Bronx says. We all nodded in agreement…*sure is!* 'Must have been dropped on his head as a baby?' Johnny makes a credible assessment of Jim's mental constitution.

'Right, you boys must have some good military songs? I have some good rugby ones. Let's have a song-off.' Beginning of a beautiful cultural exchange program.

The usual American perception of all Brits being directly related to the Queen, and therefore more sophisticated than themselves…well that bubble was about to get a great big pin through it!

I start to blow the perception balloon up…reach for the pin.

My turn first, *'Tie me kangaroo down sport, tie me kangaroo down. Bestiality is best boys, Bestiality is best, shag a wallaby'*…ditty carries on, *'Stick your rake in a snake boys, stick your rake in a snake, shag a wallaby…stick your pole in a mole boys…'*

The soldiers once over their initial shock, are howling and hollering with laughter. *From one of Queen Elizabeth's relatives too, they nudge each other.*

Back and forth, it goes.

'A man jumped out of a coconut grove, he was the meanest muddafukka, you could tell by his clothes. He wore a two double piny and a three-double stitch, coz he was a whore licking muddafukking son of a bitch.

He ran through the jungle with his cock in his hands, singing hey muddafukka's I'm the king of this land.

(Ditty goes on another four verses)…

Now who was this man you may all ask?

Ends… *'No one knew, coz he fucked soooo fast!'*

Loud BANG! The balloon explodes into a thousand pieces.

Few more and we are all singing together. The songs would now traverse all across the mainly poor areas of America, as is the US military recruitment target market. From the Bronx over to Compton, the British rugby songs would find new life. Eventually, end up in the rap charts.

Johnny exclaims, 'Wow, there is no way you are even related to her corgis, let alone the Queen! Those songs are so messed up. Have you seen a psychiatrist, we have one at the base?'

'Perfectly normal. They're learnt at private school,' I replied.

'Parents actually pay for you to learn those songs?' Johnny says incredulously.

'Yes, I believe it's called gaining a "good" education,' I informed Johnny from the Bronx. 'They should ask for a full refund,' he replies.

Johnny now shaking his head, 'Anyway, more importantly, not all related to the Queen? Wait till I tell everyone back in the hood.'

As poor as they might be back home, the boys were on three separate salaries in the Gulf. Normal pay, overseas pay and danger pay. Although I thought Jim would have to return the last cheque, as the only danger he posed, was to himself and anyone with ears. The army boys also had one of the best party pads I'd ever seen. Ray stands up, swigs from a bottle of Bacardi 151, 'Let's party back at ours,' he declares.

All jump in taxis; we pass Dad, screeching down the road swerving through traffic at 130 mph.

Now the army boys' pad is on three levels. Level 1 is bedrooms, level 2 is a pool room, bar and dance floor. Level 3 they have a roof pool and Jacuzzi. The place was made for a party, so we felt compelled.

At about 1 am, Scotty decides to have a psychotic episode. He jumps off the bar and screams, 'I'm going to kill me all the AYRABS!' Puts a hunting knife between his teeth and rushes out of the building to start Gulf War 3. We run after him, this is so not a good idea! Firstly, he would give Jim ideas and secondly doing the maths, he couldn't possibly kill all of them. A car screeches to a halt, you can see the skid marks. Scotty has jumped on the bonnet and is threatening an 85-year-old Sikh and his family with instant death. Ethnically confused, Scotty screams and runs off into the night.

15 minutes later, the US military police with their *infamous* white helmets come bursting through the door.

'Where is he?' They have their pistols drawn.

Looking down at the bottle. I think I will lay off the Bacardi 151 for the next 60 years, avoid a psychotic episode and the general desire to kill the entire local population, single handily.

We never saw Scotty again; he was whisked off the island faster than a speeding bullet. His arse didn't even touch the ground. The whole episode was hushed up. Shame, he was a really nice guy, bar the psychotic killing spree bit.

'Right boys, return the favour, party at ours. Next Friday. Starts at 2 am. There are only two conditions: you have to bring a bottle of spirits and a Lillo. We'll get all the crew (GI's and expats) together. Downstairs in the pool area. Mum and Dad won't suspect a thing.'

So, we live in an apartment block on the first floor. Below to the side of the building is the swimming pool and social area. That is where we are going to party and keep out of trouble. Under no circumstances are we to enter the apartment, NONE. We had already got a bollocking for the last party and the ones before that…

On entry there is a 60-litre bin, where you pour your bottle of spirits in, make a lethal punch. That is your pass to join the party. 2 am arrives. We have a full mix of expats and US soldiers, all having a ball. We have set it up so there are flotillas in the pool, so you can grab a floating beer (whilst in or on your inflatable). Stu sails past on a windsurf. Some neighbour had foolishly left this tasty morsel to play with. A few days later, they must have thought a hurricane had whipped through the indoor pool and ravaged their vessel.

Guys and gals are all having fun. Talking Heads' *Burning down the House* is playing in the background. I swallow dive into the primordial soup.

I say primordial, as a few years earlier I had lost my virginity in this very pool to a girl called "Clingy Claire." Thank god, you only have to lose it once. The floor of the pool was made of very slippy rubber. So as Claire mistook my survival noises for pleasure rather than drowning and as I tried to get my footing, she started to up the tempo. I was taking in water fast.

'Are you out of breath my darling?' Claire excited, whispered to my submerged head. She was met with rapidly diminishing air bubbles.

I couldn't get the image out of my head, the baby alien monster fully wrapped around me, squeezing with pleasure. Hence the "Clingy Claire" title. *I had imagined the title to be an emotional one, not an actual physical reality!* I should have brought a crow-bar to prize Claire off.

At least Ripley, in those 25 (and counting) Alien movies, had a gun to battle those misunderstood acidic beasties. Next time I'll arm myself with a spoon and survive drowning by enthusiastic sex.

I spot Jeff, a good mate since childhood. I owe Jeff; he pranked me good the week before. I nod to Stu sailing past again and point at Jeff, he nods back a big grin. We start to creep up on Jeff.

Jeff spots us at the last minute, squeals and runs off into the shower room. He's holding onto the shower pole. I have one leg and Stu has the other, both pulling. The whole pipe comes away from the wall and the full water mains start to flood the shower room. Jeff makes a break for it. I just catch his swimming shorts and they start to tear, Stu joins in. Jeff's last valiant struggle breaks free just like his shorts. Runs off naked.

'Battle stations, after him!' I shout.

Jeff races across the pool and makes a break for the apartment block, we are in hot pursuit. Up the stairs, through Mum and Dad's apartment, along the veranda. Now, the balcony stretches the width of the apartment. There is a drain pipe at the end, which you can climb down onto the roof of the pool. There is also a large hole in the pool skylight that you can jump through into the pool. We had done this once before, so we knew about it.

Jeff is hurtling along the balcony, shimmies down the drainpipe onto the roof. I'm not one minute behind him, screaming…

I leapt onto the drainpipe, that at this very moment decides to no longer tolerate my existence and comes away from the building. Now, if it goes straight back, I have a 50-foot fall onto the cars parked below. *Probably land on dad's new car!* I scolded myself. It sways a couple of times. I can see Jeff's horrified face. It's all in slow motion, the pipe makes a cracking noise and the whole thing comes away from the building and I land squarely on my back...on the swimming pool roof, 20 feet down. Jeff is by the skylight still naked, absolute shock all over his face.

Relieved, I can't feel a thing. Not through paralysis, but through the consumption of three litres of 100 proof punch earlier. I'm still holding the drainpipe, I jump up, 'Come here, you skinny bastard!' I shout at Jeff.

Jeff exclaims, 'NO FUCKING WAY! I thought you were dead?' Yelps and jumps through the skylight, 15 feet into the pool. I run after him, follow him through.

Meanwhile, there's a formal letter of complaint being typed: Dear Brain, we the collective vital organs, nerves and blood cells would like to draft a formal letter of complaint and relieve you of any formal duties!

Jeff has disappeared again; I head up to the totally forbidden parents' apartment. Jeff, stark bollock naked is sitting on Mum's couch, an arm around Michelle and Kelly's shoulders.

Seeing me, he says, 'Oh, excuse me.' Pulls a tissue from the box on the coffee table and covers his privates. He then puts his arms around the girls again. Cheeky bastard! I would get him later. There are 12 of us in the lounge when Dad comes thundering through with his famous white Y-fronts on. All teeth and hair.

Everyone, 'Oh shit! It's Brian's Dad.'

'Right, you lot! Get out, it's 4 am and I have work in two hours. Jeff put some bloody clothes on! And you Brian get the FUCK to bed now!'

Now, I knew this was serious. Dad never swore.

A few days later, Mum closed the door on the next-door neighbour, asking if we had seen her son's windsurf. She swore she'd left it secure by the pool.

Mum, shaking her head, 'That woman is obviously insane, using a windsurf in an indoor pool?'

Dad and I are on the balcony, he's furious, 'Look at that! What a damn mess! I'm going to call the management; this place is falling apart!' he says pointing at the drainpipe strewn all across the pool roof.

Looking down at the carnage, sipping my coffee. 'I know Dad, it's a BLOODY disgrace!'

*Ironically Jim would survive a grenade attack unhurt, in a nightclub some months later. So finally, he had a real story he could re-tell over and over again. On reflection, I wonder if it had been 'friendly fire' in a vain attempt to silence him for good!

7

Plain Sailing, Dad's Birthday Treat

Led down into a darkened room, deep in an underground basement. The CIA team had gathered to hear Tony Dawes' assessment on the upcoming first Iraq war. The four field men, with masking tape crudely cut over their eyes, to disguise themselves, start to fire questions at Dad.

Meanwhile, in the corner, a Brown Trout is strapped to a board. It has a muslin cloth over its head and every now again water is poured over it. Dad, to the nearest American (all conveniently called Hank) raises an eyebrow. Hank responds, 'New technique you limey bastard, called waterboarding, simulates drowning.'

Dad confused, 'But doesn't a fish live and breathe in water? So in effect, it's very relieved every time you simulate drowning.'

'OK, you clever limey bastard,' says the leading Hank. Signals to another Hank, 'Go fetch me a mammal!' The other Hank runs off. Back five minutes later. 'Hah limey bastard!' Straps a penguin to the board, starts pouring.

'Where did you get the bird from?' Dad asks confused. Hank replies conspiratorially, 'Santiago Zoo. We had a surveillance team operating. Heard the "Ruskies" were going to steal Boris, their "dancing bear" back. Came up with the penguin idea.'

Tony, 'How long have the team been there?'

'Since Khrushchev,' Hank proclaims proudly. Then quietly, 'We lost four men.' Tony sighs, 'To radiation poisoning? Novichok?'

'No, old age. The Russians never showed.'

Dad rolls his eyes. 'Anyway, about this invasion of Iraq. Do you want me to address the special forces of what to likely expect and have you spoken to all the tribal elders?'

'First one, yes, second one…what tribal elders? We have bombs like freaking loads of them. It won't be a problem for Uncle Sam, you Limey bastard.'

In the background, the penguin is squealing, clearly delighted with every pour. He's going to teach this new game to his mates on his zoo return.

Door bursts open, 'Mr Dawes, sir. Sorry, you have an urgent phone call, (sighs) on the red phone.'

'Red! Damn it to hell. Must be important. Is it the Ambassador?' Dad enquires.

'Err, no, it's the manager of the Bahrain Yacht Club, Mr Mustafa. He sounds very upset; I think he's been crying.'

'Hello, yes, sorry Mr Dawes, sir, we have a big problem. It's your son; he's turned up again with his friends. They have been sailing on your boat again. It's just crashed into the rocks, in the Marina.'

Dad groans, 'Is anyone hurt?'

'No, that's the thing; there is no one on it. Except for a case of Fosters!'

'Just like the *Mary Celeste*,' Dad muses. 'Have you checked the bar,' looks at his watch. 'It's happy hour, isn't it?'

'Yes sir, I will be right back.' On return, 'Yes, they're there all right.'

'That's it! I promised myself last birthday I would do it. This time I'm going to follow it through. I'm going to kill him.' Looks over at the ecstatic penguin, flippers going mental.

'Gentlemen, I've just had an idea!

I may have a more worthwhile subject for your waterboarding. An uncontrollable animal that can't hold its breath underwater for three days!' Dad announces, looking at the penguin.

'Damn it limey, why didn't you say so.'

'Hank, my good man, it just came to me. Give me a couple of hours. I will go and get him.'

Hanks in unison, 'Who is it?'

'My bloody son!'

'What waterboarding a real person? We hadn't thought of that. That's barbaric, we love it! Go get him, you limey bastard.'

'Be right back,' Dad runs off.

Eight of us are on Dad's Hobie Cat 16 (his beloved catamaran sailing boat), that should nicely fit only two. Four cases of beer are strapped to the trapeze.

We are barely afloat, 'See boys am I a genius or what?' Freddy impressed, 'Must admit *Mr Dawes*, this was indeed a pretty genius idea!' With Freddys' stamp of approval, some doubt should have started to creep in. Off to "Bird-shit" Island, a 40-minute trip, should take two days. Drink beer to lighten the load and get there faster. Two minutes into the trip, we manage to pole-vault 20 yards off the beach, beer cans and bodies floating everywhere. We can hear jeering and laughter from the shore.

'Too much weight, let's drink some beer first and improve the ballast. Start again. Pure physics boys.'

Jeff, 'You sure your dad doesn't mind, especially after the last time?'

'It's cool Jeff, he doesn't know. I will give him a call when we all arrive safely back in one piece, sometime next week.'

Jeff, halfway to the island decides to surf under the boat by hanging on to the T-bone tramline. As he jumped down to catch the bar, his timing could not have been more impeccable as a nine-foot shark came up to greet him. We managed to quickly drag him back on. He would have had a very quick speedo change if he hadn't already lost them jumping on the shark.

'Err Jeff, I said in one piece, not several. Rip some cardboard off the beer box and cover yourself up, this is a Muslim country after all. Show some respect man!' Jeff complies, looks like a very dodgy Robinson Crusoe. We sail along at -1 knot, we would have got there faster going backwards, I mused.

We finally land on Bird-shit Island and, as its namesake implies, is covered in birds all having a poo. We set off to explore and drink most of our ballast, get back quicker and in time for happy hour. We'll save one case of Fosters for later. Genius boys.

We arrive back at the club, with no more life-threatening mishaps. I will give Dad a call after happy hour. Quite a few beers sloshing around was dimming my natural instinct to make good judgement calls.

'Freddy, release the *sheets* mate, I'm off to the loo. All that beer matey, I need to go!'

We all catch up in the bar and get stuck into happy hour. We're enjoying ourselves; Jeff has bribed one of the waiters to lend him some pants. We have decided to coin him "shark-bait" from now on.

'Well, boys,' taking a sip of my ice-cold Fosters, 'that was another successful trip, methinks.'

'First class Captain Dawes! Faultless,' the boys all agreed.

We are sitting on bar stools, looking out to the Marina, when a very familiar sail goes shooting past. Wow, someone is really nailing it out there! Must be practising for next week's race. I'm so going to enter it, ask Dads' permission to borrow the boat. He'll be absolutely delighted.

The boat goes shooting past again. There is a metal bar obscuring our view.

It looks so familiar, 'Boys do you recognise that boat?'

Seven voices back, 'Yeah looks really, really familiar.'

I stand up; each boat has a large identifier numbers on its sail. I start to read 4562...shit! SHIT! That's my dad's fucking boat, just as it smashed into the rocks on the other side of the bay.

We sprint out onto the beach, where the Hobie Cat should have been safely sitting.

'Freddy, I told you to release the sheets, so she wouldn't catch the wind.'

Freddy bleary-eyed answers, 'I thought you said you were going for one! That's why you went to the loo.'

'Freddy, sheets you fucking pillock, the ROPES.'*

Rob sighing, 'Do you think your dad is going to be cool about this?'

'Yeah, of course,' I said confidently. 'He's pretty chilled. It was an easy mistake.' The wind catches the sail again, pulls Dad's pride and joy off the rocks and the mortally injured boat starts to limp off over the horizon. Look at her go, what a beauty. Dad would have been so proud of her...

I was deeply upset, that the case of Fosters, still strapped to the trapeze had managed to escape unharmed. Life was so unfair at times! However, I better inform the coastguard. I sure hope they have a submariner department with underwater boat extraction equipment.

Back in the bar, the manager's head pops through the door. He looks delighted.

'I'm on the phone to your father, and he is coming straight over!'

Runs off, I could hear the glee in his voice, 'At last, at last!'

'Right boys, fantastic my dad's coming over, he can get the next round. Catch the last of happy hour. Now there's a result,' I grin.

Freddy pipes up in a rare moment of clarity, 'We should leave like right now! Like really right now!' *Freddy might be onto something there. We need to go into hiding for a few days, wait for the coastguard to retrieve what's left of the boat.* 'Rob, your dad's away. Let's hideout at yours, till he cools off. Remember the last time!' We all shiver. 'He even managed to get a shot off.'

On the hill, Tony loads the dart into the chamber. A trickle of sweat runs down his temple, it's 40 degrees. There he is! 15 minutes of happy hour left, I knew it. Concentrate. Inhale, slowly exhale. Now, squeeze the trigger…

'Hold on, lads, still have 15 minutes of happy hour left, get a quick one in?'

Suddenly, Mr Mustafa comes bounding in, super excited. 'Hah, this time he gets you! You no longer disgrace name of best yacht club in world.'

He stops in front of me, makes a little groaning sound and face planks onto the floor.

'Is he praying?' asks Jeff.

'He's so pious, Mr Mustafa,' we all marvelled. The manager responds by snoring loudly. We look down to see a six-inch dart with a bright red feathered plume, sticking out of his back.

'Shit, it's your dad! Run, everyone RUN!'

Annoyed that I had missed out on a free round, we fled, just as Dad was reloading another dart.

Dad exasperated, 'Damn it to Hell Tony! I will have to wait until my next birthday to treat myself.'

A week later, after the boat had been recovered and sent off to the repair yard, Dad had started to chill (after I had just bought him his eighth can of Fosters). I explained the mix up with the nautically challenged Freddy.

'So Dad, in summation, technically it wasn't my fault.' Dad reluctantly puts his beloved Fosters down. Sighs, 'That's the problem, Brian. It never bloody is!'

*By not releasing the sheets/ropes the wind had caught the sail, spun the boat around and it had flown off the beach across the marina, onto the rocks.

8
Dhow Trip. Venus Aligned, Love Conquers All

Charles, in a contemplative mood, 'Why do we fall in love?' God smiling, that's an easy one, 'Love is the strongest passion and most magical gift, it bonds and divides in equal measure. But ultimately for those who find it, it is the greatest reward.

Let's face it Charles, the number of times your jaw has dropped when VIPs and dignitaries have visited; you really could do with a girlfriend! It's getting embarrassing. At the very least you need a makeover Charles. That beard is not only touching the floor, but is evolving a whole new species! Just like your book. What was it called again?' God smiles.

Charles baited, replies indignantly, 'You can talk!'

There is a magical sound, *is that a harp*? Charles looks at the door.

Charles, now super excited, 'Is it who I think it is?'

God smiles, 'I think so, we are in for a treat.'

Charles, scrambling over a chair, 'I'll answer it.'

Nymphs and fairies are cascading, dancing over the floor, small flutes playing the most magical of tunes. Venus, the Goddess of Love enters the room, a small harp in her hand. Charles nearly faints. God catches him, Venus smiles. 'My lady Venus, what a delight!'

'My lord. My good man, dearest Charles.' Charles faints.

The fairies put a pillow under his head. God sighs, 'He will be out for a while; it's all too much for him.'

Venus nods, the most beautiful, lyrical voice enquires, 'I hear you are playing chess. As you know love, even unrequited must be answered.'

'Yes, he has been trying so hard, it's painful.'

'Yes,' they both wince.

'Maybe we can solve this?' Venus, the most beautiful of all the gods, sits down.

'Let's play.' Black Pawn takes White Knight.

'Oh dear! We didn't see that coming?' They both groan.

So I get a phone call, it's Stu again; Bahrain. 'Right, we have partied on rooftops, pools, beaches, the desert, houses, flats, tents even the odd palace. But we have never partied on a Dhow!'

'Oooh! I like the sound of that.'

'Namir has a second cousin who has a Dhow business, if we promise to behave. Then he'll sort it for us.'

'Exactly how many second cousins does Namir have?' I enquired curious.

'401 at the last count,' came the reply.

'Give him a ring.'

I'm thinking this is the perfect chance to charm Susie, a girl I have been shamelessly chasing for what seems like an eternity. I tell Stu this.

'Give it up, mate, she's not interested.' Encouraged, I would give her a phone and invite her along.

Offering to pay off her credit card debt, she agreed. I knew she couldn't resist me.

Right, I phone around. We have 25 crew all willing, including my younger brother Dan and his best mate, John. Time for the pep talk. 'Right, you two, this is an honour that the two of you can come and party with us (both underage). Ground rules, none. With one exception, I have been pursuing this girl Susie for ages and I'm so close…'

They look at each other. Sighing, 'Yes, everyone knows.'

'Shush, anyway I do not want you two getting drunk and making a disgrace of yourselves. Do not screw this up for me. Got it! I really want to impress her. I think at last she will be mine.' They both nod un-reassuringly. 'Good talk boys,' I walk off confidently.

As the Dhow's plimsoll line drowned under the weight of the 15 cases of beer, 20 litres of Vodka and 10 bottles of Tequila, plus 1 bottle of Campari (that would return back with us, another vain attempt to get rid of it), we set off.

Destination: an island that only appears for 3-4 hours each day and then disappears under the Arabian/Persian Gulf waves again. The trip takes two hours, we start drinking. I start my charm offensive by getting stuck in the "Thunder box" (small wooden box, hangs precariously off the back of the Dhow, which with a hole in the floor, is the loo). Rescued 20 minutes later, I knew Susie was concerned. My plan was working.

We arrive on the island. I start to demonstrate my excellent husbandry skills, by cremating the sausages, chicken and steak. Susie nodded encouragingly. Scraping the sausage, I offered her the best morsel. Declining demurely as she had already eaten.

The heat and alcohol are mixing to a toxic effect. It's summer, the heat is nearly touching 50. The island starts to submerge, time to leave. We pack up the BBQ and grab the last plastic chair before it floats off, as the sea once more consumes the small Island.

On board, everyone is enjoying themselves; we are all having a great time. Eight of the crew are sitting in a circle, we start to sing: '*Tie me kangaroo down sport, tie me kangaroo down…*' I look back and can see the two old Arabic men steering the boat. The two elderly Bahrainis, respectfully glaring back at us; they were going to kill Namir when we got back. Worry beads being manhandled at a furious pace. Double praying when they got home.

It's idyllic. Susie in a bikini looks stunning, me glistening with baby oil and white speedos looking heroic. We were the perfect match, we both knew this.

Let's play 'Fuzzy duck,' I was an unchallenged legend at this game. *'Fuzzy Duck, Fuzzy Duck, Dozee? Ducky Fuzz, Ducky Fuzz…Dozee?'* It goes back and forth until someone makes the fatal call, *'Fuck he does!' or 'Does he fuck?'* Then you have a drink punishment/penalty, for screwing it up.

The blazing sun, the swaying boat, the pheromones and the eight beers and 12 Tequilas swilling around me, I knew I was on top of my game. Susie was finding me irresistible. My master plan had borne fruit; Susie was ripe for the plucking.

Susie is opposite me, suddenly I screwed up. Double Tequila shoved in front of me. They start to sing. *'Here's to Brian, he's a blue' he's a piss-pot through and through, he's a bastard, so they says and he'll never go to Heaven in a long, long way…Down, down, down.'* They chant. I neck it.

Not two seconds later, the whole day's food and drink, burnt sausage, chicken et al had decided to say hello to the circle, with a special mention for Susie, opposite me. As her screaming died down, I knew now that Susie, after playing the long game, would succumb to my love; victory was sweet. I was at my very best, invincible. As the last piece of burnt sausage (that I had offered previously) bounced along the deck and landed on her foot; I passed out in-between my good friend Jacquie's thighs.

My last recollection, *as my unconscious head was about to invade Jacquie's dignity*, was seeing my impeccably behaved brother and his mate John, look at each other and roll their eyes. *Damn them to hell!*

Carried off the boat by the good Arab family, I knew love knew no boundaries. Sobbing tears of joy, Susie fainted in her father's arms (who had come to collect his beloved daughter). He shot me a grateful look and swore. I waved them away, 'Godspeed my love. Call me, my darling.'

Unceremoniously dumped by the gracious Bahraini family and a '*Mafi Mukh*' (No Brains) later, they wandered off to find and kill Namir. '*Shukran,*' (Thank you) I shouted after them. I left, with a little skip in my step, requited love so sweet.

Caught up with Dan and John, 'Well I think that went well! Definitely a second date boys. 100%.'

'Yes,' says Dan, 'because vomiting on a prospective date is 100% bulletproof.' John sighing, 'Brian, have you ever thought about writing romance novels? You're a natural.'

The two cheeky bastards then walked off…

9
Filipino Dance Off, the Incredible
Mr Singh

God to Darwin, 'Look, Charles, it's about Perception versus Reality.'
Darwin, 'But surely if you perceive something, then that is your reality, bit like religion.'

God sighing, 'Don't be facetious, Charles'

'So did you create me or did I evolve?' Charles retorts.

God under his breath, 'Here we go again,' rolls his eyes.

There's a large bash at the door. Charles, 'Oh no, it's the Norse Gods! Do you think they have been drinking again?'

God, 'Probably. Non-stop party that Valhalla.'

Large smash…the Norse Gods pile in. God groaning, *the day that those visiting deities ring that doorbell!*

God, 'I will have to get John the carpenter to fix that door again. Just like after your last unannounced visit.' Odin, big grin, 'I like to make an entrance. Anyway, shush we come on important business. We hear on the God-vine that the God of the Christians is playing chess with Beardy boy Darwin, with one of ours!'

Loki interrupts, 'Hand out any awards this year, Charles?'

Odin continues, 'So, we get to play. Have a go at his demise.'

God exasperated, 'What are you talking about?'

'Let me explain, you see, Loki created him. Who else would put a Glaswegian and a Cumbrian together, with mad Irish genes on both sides? Have them born in Australia, and travel like a fool all over the place intoxicated.'

Loki sniggers, 'I thought it would be fun.'

'He never stood a chance, did he?'

'Not one little bit.'

God, 'Look, there are too many deities to play chess, what about Mah-jong; anyone know the rules?' The question is met by silence. 'No, it's a mystery to me too.'

Loki leans over Gods shoulder, 'My turn.'

Black Pawn moves forward, 'Watch this…'

One eyeball wakes up, I'm in agony, every muscle is sore. In bed, white chinos still on, one black suede boot on, one on the floor. I could see my favourite shiny black silk shirt (shut up it was the fashion back then) crumpled on the floor with a Hawaiian Ley over it. As my other eye woke up and I realised I was bi-focal...I was staring at an award on the bedside table. I peeled myself off the bed and started to read, Bahrain National Filipino Da...Oh fuck, hold on a second?

So I get a phone call, it's Paddy. Fancy going out tonight new place just opened. I hear in the background, 'Patrick you told me you were never going out with him again, EVER!'

'I know honey, he says it wasn't his fault the last time.' Missus back, 'That's what he always says.'

'Honey, sweetie, he is wearing his favourite shirt...' *they both snigger.*

'Oh, go on then, but you have to promise to tell all on your return.'

'So, you up for it?'

'Sounds great Paddy, count me in, what's the address?' As I put the phone down I thought, did he say a time? No worries, I will go early get a few drinks in.

I pitch up at 7 pm; about 30 folks are in, no crew. I order a drink and sit at a table. Five minutes later, this stunning modelesque Filipino lady asks me to fill in this form and sign. I comply, must be some sort of team quiz or something. I think nothing more of it. The crew start to turn up on time...*they snigger* and sit down. We order Tequila slammers. I tell them about the lady and that we might be in a team quiz or something?

Namir says, 'Really doesn't look like a quiz type of place with the mirror balls and stuff.'

'I know, but look at the crazy places we have been and look at what happened in the end?'

'That's undeniable,' Namir grunts.

It's now 8 pm, the model goes on stage. Microphone in her beautiful hand. 'Now, ladies and gentlemen, we have the Bahrain National Filipino Dance Championships, with an awards ceremony afterwards.'

The curtains draw back, big banner, flashing lights everywhere. The contestants are, starts reading out names, I have to stand, everyone claps. I sit down and look at the crew opened jaw, they look back at me. 'I thought it was a bloody quiz?'

'Before we start,' the vision of beauty declares, 'Let us look at last year's winner, Hose Fernandez, who will now demonstrate the dance.'

The wailing starts *I pluck my eyes out with my sword for the love I have for you*...Hose's bright blue sequined shirt writhing and tossing like an eel with its head cut off. Eventually, the dance finishes and we can hear again. The crew look at me and say in unison, 'You've been dancing like that for years.' I nod confidently, 'I know, I've got this.'

'20 contestants, five round knock-outs. Will the contestants make their way to the dance floor.' I look back at the crew; at least I have my favourite shirt on. As I turned my back on my sniggering friends, I made my way to the dancefloor. The presenter with a microphone, 'Hello pretty man, tell the audience how long you have been practising Filipino dance?' I reply over the mic, 'All my life!' Not a dry eye amongst the crew.

As the wailing started, *I smash my head in against the wall for just one kiss*, and the third Tequila began to kick in. I started to writhe, thrust and rotate. I was at the top of my game. Everyone knew this.

The agonising song finishes. I head back to the crew. I survive to the next round. Big Mike, 'Wow, that was insane we have so got this, someone towel him down. Get a Tequila into him.'

Namir, 'Dude, some serious Bollywood moves there, we can do this!'

Round 2 begins with the lyrics about slaughtering a small animal to prove another undying true love sacrifice, I start to sway in the melody.

I over thrust, there's a high-pitched scream and a woman in the audience faints. I don't know if that is a point scorer or not. I continue, *The salt I pour into my eyes for just one look.* The beautiful love song finishes. I'm sweating…into the next round, five folks are left.

Back to the crew. Susan exclaims 'Bloody hell Brian, did you see that woman scream and faint.'

I said 'With excitement?'…*silence.*

'It was more of a curdling scream,' Sighs Susan.

'Damn it!'

Paddy my new dance coach, 'You're over thrusting, we will lose points, reign it in FFS.'

Semi-Finals. The pressure is on. We eye each other wearily, worthy dance adversaries. The wailing starts *I will throw myself off the highest cliff for just one glance*…another thrust another curdling cry for help, reign it in…the table full of Saudi men are going mental. One screams and faints and is quickly carried off. Damn it, another fan lost! I almost pull a hip out with my last move, it's a crowd-pleaser.

Back to the crew.

'What do you think?'

Anika, 'It's tight but maybe…just maybe…someone towel him down, get a Tequila into him.'

'And now, ladies and gentleman, after a long-fought, torturous battle we have our two finalists.

Will you make your way to the dancefloor for the final of the Bahrain National Filipino Dance Championship; Mr Singh and Mr Brian Dawes!' The crowd goes wild, except for the Filipino table muttering about cultural misappropriation.

I look at the crew, 'What do you think about Mr Singh?'

Crew, 'He must be late '60s and top of his game, a true pro.'

I looked at Mr Singh in awe, 'I know, he looks sharp. I love his shirt. It's going to be tough for sure. He has so much respect he doesn't even have a first name, just Mr,' I muttered, concerned that I would be out-danced.

Mr Singh and my good self are on the dancefloor, we eye each other admiringly. He is wearing a shiny white silk shirt and I knew then that he, like myself, was a man of immaculate taste and clearly ahead of his time. As the audience stopped sniggering, we began the greatest dance-off.

The screeching starts, *I will slice both my ears off, so that I will never hear a bad word against your name.*

With my thrusting under control and every disco dance technique that I had mastered coming back to life. All those accusations against my favourite shirt, shining in all its glory, now snuffed out. Well, look who's laughing now baby! We swirled and swayed, I knew he had the years and was a true pro. But I had consumed 10 Tequilas, no match for any mortal man…the dancing stopped, it was over. We collapsed into each other's arms crying. Both knowing, we would be comrades for life.

As I made my way back to the crew, sweating and limping, I knew at that very moment; I was at the pinnacle of my dance career. I sat down, towelled off…we waited.

'Wow, ladies and gentlemen, now that the two patrons have recovered, we can announce the winner of this prestigious award.'*

Both contestants on stage; 'The Winner of the Bahrain National Filipino Dance Championship is… (drum roll) …BRIAN DAWES!' The vogue model puts a Hawaiian ley over my head and hands me the award. The crew go wild, thumping the table!

Ten minutes later, I say, 'Do you think it's too early in my career for autographs?'

Crew back, roll their eyes, 'Probably.'

As we are heading out, Namir starts laughing uncontrollably.

Everyone, 'What is it? What is it for God's sake?'

He says, 'Look, LOOK at the flyer!'

We all look.

7 pm Registration and Sign in for the Bahrain National Filipino Dance Championships.

The crew look at me. I look back.

'DAMN IT! I was sure it was a bloody quiz!'

*My 'Award winning prize' was a year's membership to one of the dodgiest hotels in Bahrain. I went for one day to the pool and was solicited fifty times by Saudi men.

10
The Italian Job — Death of a Salesman

Charles excited, 'Where is our Pawn now?' God, *perusing the globe,* 'There he is in Italy. That's my domain, for sure, every time one of those crazy Italians straddle a Vespa, I expect that doorbell to ring!'

Charles observes, 'Probably why they pray so much.'

'Indeed, so pious our Latino flock. Right is the kettle on Charles? Hopefully this time we will get to play without any interruptions from visiting dignitaries or marauding deities!' God let's out a big sigh, 'Usually lost, looking for directions, after a few too many Viking brews at 'that' Valhalla bar!' They both look at the door, nothing. The pair both pleased. 'Let's begin, my good man Charles.'

Suddenly there's a 'Rat a tat-tat' at the front door, then silence, then a 'Tat,' long pause another *'Rat a tat-tat'*...Even longer pause. God and Charles look at each other. *'TAT!'* God exasperated, 'NOT AGAIN! Fifth time this week, and it's only Tuesday!' God gets up to answer the door. A few moments later...Large angry booming voice, 'FOR THE LAST TIME, GO AWAY!' A few moments later, 'Yes, I do look exactly like the God on your poster, but that's not me!' Darwin can hear the muffled conversation in the corridor. 'What do you mean I should start praying then? THAT'S IT! I'm going to fetch my "Taser Crucifix!"' BANG! The front door slams shut. *The "God squad" terrified, flee with their little poster.*

Re-enters the room. Charles a quizzical look, 'Well...Italians?'

'No!' God has a thunderous look on his face. 'Those infernal Jehovah's out witnessing again!' God exhales slowly, 'And now relax! "Channel" my good friend Buddha. Now that I've "shooed" them away to bother some other poor deity, let's grab our chance and play. Maybe Charles we can find the "enlightened path" and get one of your awards handed out?'

White Bishop takes Black Queen. 'Oooh, that's a powerful move.' God smiles, 'I know, watch this.'

So I get a phone call... 'The job is yours, can you get a one-way flight to Milan, next Friday?'

I'm 19 and broke, just back from Bahrain with my sister. My kiwi girlfriend (Gulf Air stewardess *cue* small sob) has gone to London to become my ex. We are in Glasgow, I need a job, badly.

'Shirl, I've just seen this ad,' I said…

Travel to Italy, learn a new language, good career prospects. Interview tomorrow at 1 pm, Carlton Hotel.

'Well, you better take this money; buy some smart clothes as you can't turn up in Hawaiian board shorts.'

'Good point, Shirl.'

Go to the interview. Get a phone call the next day, scored the job. Shirl, 'What's it for?'

'You know what, I have absolutely no idea? I think it was to teach English, mentioned students and some other stuff.'

My sister, frowning, 'But you can't speak Italian?'

'Yes, I know, *Mein Frau.*'

'That's German, Brian.'

'Yes, but it's not English, so that's got to be close right?'

'Yes, Brian.' Came the exasperated sigh.

'They mentioned a one-way ticket to Milan.'

'No worries 'Bruv,' I've got some money.' At the airport, we embrace.

'Take Care!'

'Don't worry Shirl, what could possibly go wrong again?'

Shirl, 'Hmmm, I'm guessing probably everything.'

Arrive Milan; get picked up by a guy called Mark. We will spend the next few months together.

'Right, this weekend we need to start getting you settled, explain what the job is about and what to do. Oh and learn some Italian too.'

'That sounds great,' I say. We head to a hotel in Milan for the weekend, met by the owners, a French couple, who state training will begin first thing in the morning.

Saturday morning arrives.

'Right, here are four sides of A4 in Italian which you will learn off by heart and be able to recite by Sunday. The rest is on the job training, you may begin.'

Sunday night, pretty much got it learnt. Right, Monday off we go, Mark and myself, who is now my manager and coach, head north to the Italian/Swiss border. The North consists of small towns such as Lecco, Lipomo and Cantu. The job is to work one town per week, then move onto the next.

'So, here's the deal, you will be selling business cards to small businesses and local shops/merchants. It's 10 hours per day, six days a week on foot, the company pay for all food and accommodation. After six months you will be paid 5000 Ecu (pre-Euro currency) if you hit your targets.'

The rest including what we were actually saying was never explained and other details were vague if not opaque!

Anyway, nothing ventured nothing gained, right? I was here. Northern Italy was beautiful. The people were super friendly, the local girls stunning and the food was superb.

It was tough and exhausting, *'Bonjourno, devo polari con il titilari per fevore?'* (Hello, is your manager/owner here, please?) the call would start, if the customer came 'of piste' and free-styled their own language, I was generally screwed.

They then couldn't understand the blank expression staring back at them, after I had just completed a 30-minute pitch in fluent Italian. Puzzled, how could I not understand their questions? Tumbleweed would roll past as we stared at each other.

The company had been very clever with their script, which I was to find out later. I got better but it took time.

Mark was a great guy and we became close. He used to be a drummer in a band and had an Italian girlfriend who lived in Bergamo. So about a month into the job, he says why don't we go down and visit her and her friends and I can play in the band down there, next Saturday night. Sounded good; we needed a break.

Nerves shredded from constantly swerving to avoid the suicidal Italian drivers and their desperate attempts not to drive in a straight line or indicate, we finally arrive at Bergamo.

We head into a pub/café/music venue; Mark is chatting away and knows all this crew as he had worked there last year. Next thing his Italian girlfriend and her four mates turn up, now it gets weird. The friends come straight up to me. I've had one beer and then one after the other start snogging me, no talk, no chit chat, just straight in. Now, this on paper sounds great, except it was like your first snog at 12 – full tongue. I couldn't breathe and was in general shock. Even went I went to the loo, I came out and was accosted by another girl; it was insane. My mouth was starting to feel bruised and my tongue lacerated. I needed to make it to the bar without being assaulted. No eye contact, make a dash to the counter, order a Tequila. I tried to hide in the shadows as the girls prowled Terminator like, with their eager tongues.

We eventually left, Mark was driving back in the Cinquecento 500.

Mark queries, 'What did you think?' Me, mouth all swollen, tongue stuck to the roof and refusing to come down.

'Yeah, very different,' I muffled.

I fall into a deep sleep.

Suddenly, I'm jolted awake by a massive smashing, grinding noise. Mark has crashed into the central reservation; the whole side of the car is bashed in.

'What happened?'

'I fell asleep,' Mark in shock.

'Shit, are you OK?'

'Yes, let's get back. Maria (the owner) is going to kill me.' I said, 'Don't worry, we will come up with a story in the morning.'

However, I can't believe that out of all the insane Italian driving I've witnessed, we bloody crash! We blame a mad Italian driver running us off the road, (in the morning) to a sympathetic Maria.

So, we are in Lombardy, really pretty Italian town. We are working there for a week. Every day we go to the same eatery for lunch and get to know the café owner quite well. One day, it was the *Festival de Morte* (Festival of the dead); we go for lunch. The owner comes up and explains that he has set a little room aside as a little treat for lunch to celebrate the festival (at that time in Northern Italy everyone invited you everywhere).

So we sit down. A waiter enters and we are poured a glass of Grappa (80 proof rocket fuel). Now this is a lunch I could get used to. So I ask Mark, (I'm picking up the language bit by bit, three months in), 'Can you explain the sales pitch to me please?'

Mark starts to decipher the sales call, 'So, we are saying that we are students travelling around Italy to learn the language and culture.'

I interrupt, 'Why are we always writing numbers on our hands and putting a line through them? Also, the interview was super vague. I thought I was coming to Italy to teach English?'

Mark says, 'That's the intention.'

'Why?'

Mark starts to fill in the blanks, 'Because, once you are here you are kind of stuck and have to get on with it. That's why they don't pay you for six months and provide food and accommodation only. Paying you would give you choice and freedom, they would lose control.'

Mark clarifying, 'The sales pitch is designed to tug at the heartstrings of the Italian good nature. If you knew what you were saying to the customers at the beginning; most people would walk. They know that.'

I gave Mark a puzzled look, 'So just WHAT exactly are we saying?'

'In a nutshell, we are telling them that we are a group of twenty students from the UK, travelling around Italy to learn Italian culture and the language. And that, in order to continue to study we have to accumulate stars, once we reach 3000 stars we will get a prize of 5000 Ecu. That prize will allow us to continue our studies and travel in your wonderful country. Generally, the Italian response is "That's fantastic! We are so honoured to have you. How can we possibly help you?"

Well, in order for us to accumulate stars we have to sell X amount of business cards. We have a bronze, silver and gold package. The better the package you purchase, the more stars we will win. This will help me achieve my dream of studying in your beautiful country. You then show them the numbers on your hand with lines crossed out, showing how you are striving to achieve this target. You then ask them, if out of the kindness of their heart, can they please help you. This is also filled with lots of other clever little details to manipulate the customer, hence why the pitch is so long.'

'But,' continues Mark, 'The business card side is legitimate, just not the means to get the sale.'

Fuck! I needed some time for all this to sink in. I knew something was up. Mark after the crash trusted me, otherwise, he would never have told me.

The food arrives. Bonjourno! A steamy bowl of stew arrives, along with another Grappa. It's absolutely amazing. There are loads of floating things and something that looks like spiralled spaghetti and triangle shaped things that I assume to be pasta. We finish. The owner comes back and we thank him profusely for his hospitality. We then ask him what the delightful dish was.

Cassoeula, a local dish from Lombardia.

'What's in it?' The owner explains with lots of gestures. Pig trotters' points at feet, pig snout points at nose, pig ears holds his ears out (the triangles) and then the finale, pointing to his crotch…pig's penis (the spirals). As the colour left our faces, I did wonder if we had been had or it was some part of the *Festival of the dead* graveyard humour.

Anyway, I had a lot to think about after my chat with Mark.

About two weeks later, as my sales dramatically declined, I just lost heart conning all those really friendly, trusting people; I ran into some trouble. I had entered a car wreckers' yard, *not thinking to myself what moron goes into a car yard in Italy, to sell some dodgy rip-off story?* Well this idiot does! Had I not watched the Godfather like a hundred times!

I was doing the usual pitch when this heavy-set guy turns to the other monobrow and starts getting angrier and angrier. Then in broken English he says, 'You work here last year, Marco says he not get cards. You not students you thieves…if we see you again…' he finishes as he makes a snapping noise. Everyone knew everyone in this small town. I was like, *Shit Brian not good, really not good,* as I made my excuses, they chased me out of the yard.

Even 'organised crime' needs a business card, I guess? I could just imagine the title and offer*:*

> *Franco and Marco's Body Disposal Services.*
> *We crush your rival, with a smile. Special offer: Two bodies for the price of one. Acid Baths currently 10% off.*
> *RSVP your corpse today.*
> *Ciao Ragazzi.*

That was the final straw! I didn't fancy sleeping next to a horse's head. I had to escape. I had no money. I needed a plan and fast. I worked another week, in which I checked the train times and other routes. I hatched my plan.

Time to operate…so I duffed myself up a bit, split lip and a decent black eye, some general bruising, enough to look like I'd been mugged (sorry, Italy). I then staggered back to the hotel, told Mark I had been robbed. Not pretty, I know, but a scam was a scam and it was going downhill rapidly. I wanted out.

I had the next day off (due to the 'mugging') and I was in the possession of a customer's cheque, paid to the company for a completed sale (a couple of days before). We had been staying for about a week, so the hotel manager knew us quite well. So as not to screw the customer, I asked if they could photocopy the cheque for our records and could they cash it for me. They did…I had some money at last. I justified it by saying to myself, that the customer would still receive their goods…but these bastards still hadn't paid me in months.

I went upstairs, wrote Mark a letter explaining my actions and the photocopied cheque and made my way to the station. I had just enough to get to Dover. I bought a loaf of bread and a chunk of cheese, my meal for the next 48hrs. I then phoned Dad with the last of the monies and explained the situation.

Dad (on the phone) sighs, 'Brian, you always leap before you look! Do you need me to make a phone call? Those heavies are still not about, are they?'

'No Dad, I'm all good (other than my black eye and sore jaw). I will catch the train down to Milan, then make my way back over.' *The train would then double back up through Northern Italy (oh great), through Switzerland, then across to France.* Dad I said, 'Finally, I'll catch the ferry over to Dover, from Calais.'

'OK, I will arrange a pick-up at Dover.

Bloody HELL Brian, your first career move! Maybe you should go to university before you get yourself killed in the real world.'

'Dad, I think you might be onto something there. I will see you back in Blighty.'

'Good,' say's Dad, 'I will come and get you in a few days, when I can get back over (from Bahrain). I will ask Tim to pick you up for now. Take care and be aware.'

I catch the train to Milan.

11
21st Birthday Party, The Passing of 'Sally'

So I get a phone call. 'Hi Brian, it's Niall. How are you getting on? How's your gran? We haven't spoken in ages, matey.' Niall was another partner in crime at my old school (Colditz), where we were the trusted keepers of the school home-brew black market racket. It had been passed down through the generations. We were endlessly doing our best to get expelled, usually through alcohol or idiocy. But to our mutual disappointment, we had both failed and left as free men.

Niall is talking, 'My brother, Martin is having a 21st Birthday bash, up in Glasgow. Go up, get trashed, party hard!'

'Sounds good, when is it?'

'This weekend,' Niall replies, 'I know it's short notice, but you've got to make it.'

'Shit, damn it, I can't Niall. I'm working on the (Lakeland) steamer boats this weekend. It is the most important date in their calendar. Full of VIP's and shareholders and they can't operate without me.' *I had been working all summer as crew on the boats and without sufficient staff, they couldn't sail safely or legally.*

'Don't worry,' Niall says, 'I will catch up with you on Friday. Go for some beers and we can discuss.'

Friday arrives. Niall had just been travelling around Africa on a six tonne, four-wheel drive monster truck. I was jealous, the pictures were awesome. I wish I'd gone. But for both our mortalities, it had been a wise choice to stay working on steamers in a contained lake. Keep Africa safe. Few more drinks were had, and Niall's travails through Africa were making me yearn for a bit of real adventure.

Niall, with persuasion dial on max, says, 'C'mon, this 21st party is going to be proper kicking, loads of girls too!' After being in the Lakes all summer, as beautiful as it is, I was party-anaemic and easily persuaded. Cousin Jonas was right; there was a major shortage of dateable girls in the village, not even a lonely transvestite. I had been eyeing up the local red squirrel population in desperation and had even been on a few speed dates, but all they were ever interested in was storage logistics for the upcoming winter. It was forecast to be a harsh one, so the little buggers were shitting themselves. So Niall had hit the Achilles heel. Career shortening box ticked once again…

'Right, fuck it, Niall, I'm in!* We'll deal with the aftermath, if we survive the party. We need to hatch a plan, it has to be so unbreakable and so believable that no one could question it. Let's put our heads together and work this through, think of all our past escapades.'

I start, 'What about chest pains tomorrow? Feign a heart attack; tell Mum I need to go urgently to the hospital to receive life-saving surgery.'

'No,' Niall sighs, 'wouldn't work. Your mum would phone the hospital and come visit her dying son. Which would be interesting, as we would be in Glasgow, getting drunk. Not Carlisle Hospital on life support. Also, you're 19 not 90 remember?'

'Damn it to hell, good point, Niall.'

'Wedding?'

'No, not good enough, no notice and not serious enough.'

'Your wedding, Niall? Is that serious enough?'

'Nice try, I'm way too young,' replies Niall indignant.

'What about my wedding?'

Sighing, 'Wouldn't work either,' I acknowledged. 'Mum would bloody kill me. So we would definitely miss the party.'

'Damn it, tougher than we thought. What is really, really serious?' We both looked at each other, connected, in unison… 'A DEATH!' Yes, of course it was a no brainer, no one could argue with death, it was so final! *But who and how, we pondered?*

'Let's do the "who" first?' I suggested.

'It needed to be someone close. But not close enough that they would have to be resurrected a month down the line when they came to visit. Just imagine Mum's face. "Hi Dave (Mum speaking), I thought you were dead, struck by 15000 volts of lightning whilst playing croquet." Dave, with a quizzical look on his face, "No, never been fitter thanks…croquet?"

'"Brian…BRIAN!' So, no close friends.'

'What about family?' I tried again.

'I think they would know,' said Niall shaking his head, 'Especially if they then received an invitation to their own funeral. Family reunions would give the game away for sure. "Uncle Tom, I thought you were dead. Eaten by army ants after breaking a leg in the Amazon?" Tom, looking confused, "No, never been fitter thanks…Amazon?"

'Brian…BRIAN!'

'Damn it! No family allowed then. So, who?' I was running out of people.

'What about an old girlfriend?' Niall grins.

'Niall you bloody genius. Let's do rock, paper and scissors, see who the lucky candidate is. God, if only they knew? They would be so excited, being chosen for such a noble cause.'

'I know the super fortunate bugger,' agrees Niall.

'Who you going for, Brian?'

Sighing, 'Sally, she was always such an emotional wreck, this might do her some good.'

'I'm going for Kim,' says Niall. 'She always wanted to be chosen first for bloody everything, now's her chance.'

We look at each other, 'Let's go…rock, paper, scissors.'

'Yes!' I whooped. 'Paper beats rock, I win, "Sally" it is. She will be so excited, we should text her.

Niall laments his loss, 'Shame, Kim* will be completely inconsolable, poor girl. Not first this time.'

'Just don't text her,' I tell Niall. 'Cheer her up.'

Grinning at each other, 'Anyway, how exciting. OK so we have the "who," but not the "how."'

Niall starts. 'Sally, the poor emotional girl was electrocuted in the bath by a falling hair straightener?'

'Sorry, won't work. I won't be able to stop laughing at the mind-picture I have of Sally's frazzled hair. Ruin the mourning process, Mum would be immediately suspicious.'

'What about if you could picture her being crushed by a large animal escaped from the zoo?' Niall offers.

'Like a Rhino? That could work Niall, but it would be front-page news. They would also have to shoot an innocent Rhino dead and there is like two and a half left in the whole world. I can't abide any animal cruelty and what was Sally thinking of crossing that road in the first place? That terminal hospital treatment on the other side could have waited a little longer?'

'Silly girl. Yes, she was always so thoughtless,' Niall acknowledges.

Hmm tricky this, I was always so good at Cluedo too? Take a mental note for the next party excuse, real accidental imaginary deaths were much harder to design than first imagined. Typical, now that we needed that sticky beak Miss Marple's advice, she was missing in bloody action.

'What about a Great White shark attack, proper Jaws hit,' says Niall excited.

'What in the UK? Lucky to get sucked to death by a goldfish,' I shake my head.

'Sally could be on a dive holiday to Dyer Island, South Africa,' Niall enthused.

Admittedly, it did have some merit. She was dippy enough to dive at the most notorious shark island on earth, dressed as a seal. So, that could be a possibility. 'However,' I informed my partner in crime, 'it would take too long to find all the pieces, put her back together again, and then fly her back for the funeral in time. The party is tomorrow, remember?'

Niall sighs, 'Yes we need to act fast. Should we text her see if she has any ideas?'

'No, we don't want her worrying about her own funeral, that's inhumane.'

Niall musing, 'Could we not just make up a fictitious girlfriend?'

'No, because I'm going to have to act out of my skin on this one. It will have to be a mash-up of *Watership down* meets *Plague dogs*, meets *Marley and Me*.'

'Stop, you're making me well up, I loved that Marley.' Niall wipes away a tear. 'Still can't believe the mutt's gone.'

'I know Niall, they were proper tough movies, those poor bunnies too. Makes me so angry, those murdering bastards!' I growled.

'What about Bambi?'

'No, just makes me feel hungry.'

My last attempt. 'Right, we need to get this sorted. It's Sally, she needs to die in a very serious fashion, without having endangered any innocent animals or having a really bad hair day.'

'Yes, in a nutshell,' Niall confirms.

We looked at each other, 'What about a car crash?'

'Yes, it's simple and she really was a hopeless driver, so it's authentic. But not into another vehicle, we don't want any innocent people getting hurt, do we?'

'Absolutely not!' I protested. 'She really is so selfish at times.'

'WAS,' says Niall.

'True. Poor girl, I'm going to really miss her.'

'Me too,' Niall mumbles upset. 'All that charity work! True trooper, not just donating one kidney but two to that Romanian orphanage.'

'However, she also had her faults too, her driving for one,' I said. 'But to die so horrendously. Sometimes makes you not want to believe in God,' we both sighed.

'Amen to that,' I muttered. 'The lord often works in mysterious ways.'

'Right, Sally drunk on two bottles of Vodka and high on Cocaine after a lottery win, runs through a level crossing and is hit by a train. Survives and escapes the wreckage only to be killed by a horse and cart from a travelling circus. Sound good?'

'Flawless Brian, my good man. Let's high five, seal the deal.'

'Excellent, let's get back to mine. Niall, you sneak out in the morning from my parent's house. Phone my 80-year-old Gran* who lives down the road from the red phone box. Explain the tragedy and that we have to meet for a wake in eight hours' time, up in Glasgow. Reiterate that it is essential that Brian, as her old loving boyfriend, is there to read the eulogy and console her deaf parents.'

Gran in the morning shaking, 'Oh my God, that is horrendous, the poor girl, her family must be devastated.* The horse was OK though?'

'Absolutely fine,' Niall down the phone sobbing.

'Thank God for that, lottery gambling is the devil's work.'

'I know,' Niall wails.

'Anyway, I will rush up and let his mother know. She can break the very sad news to him gently. He is such a gentle soul; he will be beside himself with grief. Oh dear! I've just thought, Brian has that big important, "vital to the existence of the steamer business work" day on. They have been preparing rigorously for months. Such tragic timing,' says Gran distraught.

Niall, holding back another sob, 'I'm afraid this is so serious he will have to miss that. By chance, I am in the neighbourhood and can take him to the "wake".'

'Oh, that's so very fortunate and good of you. God bless and speed your journey, my dear.'

Niall, sniffling, 'Amen to that.'

Niall now has to sprint back to mine, climb in through the window and pretend to be asleep in the next room.

Mum comes into my bedroom and sits on the bed, 'Gran has just come over, the poor dear has just received a phone call from one of your old school pals. I don't know how to put this? Do you remember a girl called Sally?'

'Sally? Yes, she was an old girlfriend. I loved her with all my heart. The most beautiful girl in all Christendom. She was to be the mother of my children until she donated those two kidneys.'

'Sally has died in a tragic accident. Killed by a travelling circus. The horse is fine, and the train was only slightly delayed.' I start to wail, rocking (inside my head in a Shakespearian voice, act god damn you, act). I thought of Marley and those fateful last days and sealing it off with a mental picture of the rabbits in Watership down. I gave the performance of my life. I was assured of an Oscar nomination later that year. I could hear the crowds going wild. Beautiful, just beautiful, I congratulated myself. Poor Sally, how utterly tragic.

'Leave, just leave. I need to be alone right now.'

Mum continues softly, 'There's more they want you to do the eulogy and speak to her deaf parents; about all the wonderful moments you shared together.'

I stifled another sob, 'When is that happening?'

Mum patting my shoulder softly, 'Tonight, in Glasgow my dear.'

'So soon? What about my job, the big day, the VIP's?'

'Brian, sometimes in life, it is more important to do the right thing. Go to Glasgow, do the right thing.'

'Amen to that Mother, you are so right.'

'Did Niall know her too?'

'Yes…they're cousins.'

'Oh my word, he will have to drive you up.'

'Yes, you're right. I will pack my suit.'

'Poor Niall, how dreadful.'

'Don't worry Mum, I will look after him.'

Sobbing and holding each other, we jump into the car, Glasgow it is. After we clear the village, driving along the road (I am hiding in the back), we pass all the VIP's and dignitaries who are heading to the ship. That would remain moored for the weekend. After all, death was a very important thing you couldn't be late for.

We partied for two days, enough alcohol to make sure I had stripped out all my serotonin. I felt so hungover that it was possible to believe that I had died and not Sally. I would have to write my own eulogy at this rate. At least mourning for two weeks would take minimum effort, I felt so rough.

I arrived back home. The main boss had come to the house looking for me. Oh crap, I will need to mourn for at least two weeks extra then. I faced the accusatory looks and derision, but I was made of sterner stuff. After all, Sally was more important than their "special day" saving the company from those creditors and imminent bankruptcy.

Mum, did eventually become suspicious. I think talking to Sally's "deaf" parents and coming back with a Hawaiian lei wrapped around my forehead was a bit of a giveaway. Anyway, they should be thankful. Sally was still alive and doing very well at law school, not trapped under a horse cart facing a drug conviction.

'However,' I said to Niall (over the phone), 'The lord sure does work in mysterious ways…just glad that horse wasn't badly hurt.'

'Amen to that brother.'

*I would like to offer my sincere apologies to my mum, Gran and the Lakeland Steamer Company's management and shareholders. With a special "sorry" to Sally and her family and to the dry-cleaning company that I dropped that suit into after the "21st wake party."

*Niall would like to apologise to Kim for not making "the cut".

*Gran on meeting Niall a couple of years later, 'Such a shame about your cousin, Sharon wasn't it?'

'Sally,' I corrected Gran. 'Yes, we miss her dearly, the shock when her family saw the obituary, they had no idea.' I didn't have the heart/guts to reveal the sordid truth. Apology no. 3581.

12

Australian Gangsters' Paradise

Darwin to God, "*Sale of indulgences*" to the poor in the 16th Century? What the hell was that all that about?'

God, furious 'I know Charles, the chancers, the damn lot of them! Selling my poor brethren fake certificates to pass through purgatory, in the vain hope that they too will knock on my door. Well, the last laugh is on those snake oil salesmen priests; I've trapped THEM in perpetual purgatory hell. Ironic, don't you think?'

'Indeed, you reap what you sow' Charles replies.

'Anyway, I am so excited,' Charles rubbing hands…opens cabinet, several awards, await their engravings. 'We have been so close, so many times. Please! Oh please, this time.'

'Charles, my dear friend, you are going to polish the enamel off, calm your exuberance down. There's a very good chance we can get him sent to purgatory too, this time. Let's play. Charles, be a good chap and put the kettle on, is there any of that Mr Kipling cake left?'

'Let me check, my lord.' Charles rises to go have a look…

A strange wailing, clicking and stomping noise starts. God, 'I really need to get that doorbell battery changed; better give Edison a call next week.'

Darwin looking curiously at the door, 'That's not a bell, that's a didgeridoo!' They both look at each other. The Elder aborigines pile in.

'Hey God, how you doing, bro? Mr Darwin, love the beard, fella. If you tanned up with some good Aussie sun you could pass for one of us.'

Darwin, 'I always wear Zinc factor 50, it's a Galapagos Island thing. I got badly burnt.'

God, 'What can I do for you, my "Eminent Elders?"' Elders in unison, 'We come on important business. We hear on the "Dreamtime vine" that you two are playing chess with one of ours…'

God under his breath, 'Here we go again, we are never going to get a shot.' Darwin sighs…

'Well, fellas, he was born in Australia, so we're claiming him too! So we get to play.' The Elders gather around the board… 'Like a Roo a Knight can too…' The Black Knight jumps over a White Pawn takes the White Bishop.

'Watch this!' The didgeridoo starts playing. The Elders start to dance…

Dad offering advice, 'Brian, I think you should explore somewhere else?'

'Where do you have in mind?'

'Australia. You were born there after all. Go to University, get an education. Try and keep out of trouble and, if possible, stay alive.'

'What could possibly go wrong again?'

The greatest adventurer, in return sighs, 'Probably everything son.'

I arrive in Sydney. I've just travelled for three days.

London MLK flight to Amsterdam was delayed 24 hrs. Next flight to Delhi, delayed 24hrs. Singapore only had 20 passengers left after multiple suicides.

At the desk, 'Sorry sir, we have lost the flight.'

I'm exhausted, 'How can you lose a plane FFS.'

'Yes, sorry, definitely lost.'

Day 3. I look back at the other dishevelled passengers, one now starving; Rummages in the bin.

I cheer them up by threatening to blow up the airport and kill the MLK chief executive. With the mood lightened, the last survivors (after re-booking) travel the fantastic Singapore Airlines into Australia.

Arrive in Sydney. It's old school. I love it. Everything is proper laid back. I buy a pack of smokes for $2.30, light up, buy a beer for $2.00. A smoke ring later, Dad was right I'm going to enjoy this place.

Get a pick up from Mum's relatives (Glasgow crew tearing up the city for the last 20 years). Stay with Mum's cousin. I've hit the worst jet lag ever. Fucked, I go to the beach to chill. Lying on Maroubra beach, I start to cook. One minute later, I'm bored. Fuck this; I spot an open bar, Bikie gang drinking. I'm having some of that. Share a few drinkies with the "Angels of Death".

'G'day mate. Where ya from mate?'

'Scotland, my good Angels of death.'

20 blokes answer back, 'Awesome mate.'

We start to party. Playing pool, shooting tequila, I thought to myself, *Dad you truly are a genius.*

Back to bikie's house. The biggest bong I've ever seen turns up, being polite to the motorcycle gang so as not to be murdered, I take a toke. One second later, I'm stoned. Day two Australia, this is going well…

I have to get back to my Mum's cousin. What fucking bus was it again? Who am I? Was Michael Jackson really married to Bubbles? God, I could kill for a chocolate bar right now!

I arrive stoned, with a desperate hunger for anything sweet. Dinner at the table, Glasgow full chat starts. How's your Ma, et cetera. 20 years of chat catch up starts. Oh crap. 10 hours later, I feign death and crawl to bed. All I can think about is a nice bar of chocolate. I fall asleep.

The local family are as feral as could only be expected by our gene pool from East Glasgow and great fun. I have a few mad days, then it was time to move on.

I was heading to Queensland.

I arrive nicely exhausted into Brisbane, after a short bus journey of 16 hours. No idea where to go? I'm not interested in city life. Overhear a bit of chat, a coastal town called Surfer's Paradise is mentioned. Sounds good, Surfers Paradise it is! Now the fun begins...

"Surfers" is cool; great beaches, beautiful people endlessly bored, looking beautiful at each other. I'm not adventuring for vanity, I'm here to party. Meet a couple of Canadian dudes, Todd and Jim. We start to party hard but we need survival money. Jim comes up with a genius plan, start selling cans of cold coke and ice creams, bought at half price in the local supermarket. Sold for twice the price on the beach to fund the booze bank. Sorted. After getting super fit from running away from beach security, with 2 cool boxes in each hand, we call it a day. I enter the local iron man competition with my new found skills. Disappointed not to win, we head back to the backpackers.

A week later (at 6 am), I'm dragged out of bed by the local backpack owner. Seriously not happy about a neighbour complaint at 2 am. The complaint being; *A furious fight breaking out, in the swimming pool, after an English boy decided to head-butt me.*

I protest by not being floored. A Cumbrian no less, surprise not over, I go get my frying pan. A culinary battle ensues. I get chucked out. The Cumbrians packed up and fled the hostel in the morning and the other co-owner, who I know well, apologised. But I still had to leave.

Saying bye to Todd and Jim, I started the mass migration. Like the marauding wildebeests, I moved 500 yards to the next backpackers.

'G'day, sign here, you are not that fella, Brian from up the road?'

'Don't be ridiculous, I'm David!' I exclaimed outraged.

I'm visited by my Canadian crew two days later, when I had sobered up. Looking up from the floor, I said aloud, "Has the party started yet?" "Brian, it's Sunday, you idiot!" came the not very helpful reply 'Put the frying pan down, the party is definitely over.'

'Damn it! I always miss the best bits,' I replied indignant.

So, I had met some local Ozzy crew whilst trying to spread the good word of God in the local bars. The Australians have arrived! Then landed, and THEN set about destroying everything! Drinking like mature idiots, we know all the local reps who have the booze-cards (free grog coupons for backpackers). We become mates and drink for free for a couple of months.

Kaz (Karen) asks casually, 'There can't be many backpacker hostels in Surfers you haven't been banned from?'

'I'm still looking,' I answer her.

Kaz looks me in the eye, 'Brian, you are so blacklisted! We have a flat, share the rent? Stay safe. Two mattresses on the floor, we can share a room?'

Kaz had the propensity to stalk and then shag random drunk Irish, English and Scots backpackers with or without a pulse. I would often have to help Kaz drag an unconscious one back to her boudoir by their ankles for servicing. Kaz was a certifiable nymphomaniac and a good friend.

'Damn it Kaz, has word spread?'

'Yes, everywhere,' Kaz sighs. 'Fiji has stepped up border patrols and brought in a pack of hungry wolves.'

'Damn it to HELL, wolves? What about Vanuatu?'

'Nope, they imported Cholera.'

'Nauru?'

'Sorry, the elders introduced a height restriction policy.'

'Seriously! I thought I was being so incredibly discreet?' Kaz groans, 'Let's move on, are you in?'

'Yes, although I do have Bible school on Sundays.'

Kaz sighs, 'Yes, Brian.'

'Well then…I'm 94% in.'

So the flat is in a block of six. I'm staying with two girls, three locals in the flat underneath and two Irish boys next to them and the rest are randoms.

Partying, we all become great friends. Our average arrival time back to the flats is 3 am. Bible class is 9 am, I make it most days.

We are staying on Whelan Street, unbeknown to my good self, has one of the worst reputations for just about everything. So while I had been jumping naked at 2 am into the multiple pools (coined pool hopping*), getting backpacker life bans, the local gang-bangers had been plying their trade. I was now living in their receiving flat.

'Help me, help me,' the Irish backpacker whispers over, stifling a small sob. 'It's been four hours already.'

Kaz looks back, 'Is that emotion mate?' she accuses. 'Shush,' I whisper to the backpacker, 'Or she'll call the Q.E.S.' *The Queensland Emotional Squad, a ruthless Queensland Police squad that would clamp down on anyone exhibiting any signs of emotion, such as kissing or holding eye contact for more than five seconds. See "Leap of faith" for the full horrific explanation.*

I looked at my watch after having been woken by the desperate plea. 'Anyway, you're still on foreplay time mate. Kaz will let you go after 48 hours. If you run out of gas follow the scratch marks to the closet door. Kaz has a spare in there.' I point to the sign on the door. Reserve Backpackers. KEEP OUT. I whisper over, 'Gunter, you OK mate?'

There's a German voice from the closet, 'Ja, Ja, I'm goot Ja, but very hungry can you bring me a nice sausage?'

'Yes, and for you Seamus, a fine potato?'

'Smashing, that'll be grand,' the Irishman replies gratefully.

'Hang in there mate, chin up and bum down,' I encourage. 'I will bring those supplies on my return.'

'What did I do wrong?' The Irish boy stifles another sob. 'I didn't even chat her up!'

'Well, Seamus my good man no need for a chat that's for time wasters, being Irish you probably drank yourself stupid and passed out mate. That's where you fucked up.

Is everyone else OK?'

Six voices back from another closet, 'Si, Oui, Aye, Da, Ja…Konichiwa.'

Oh hold on a second, Konichiwa? Crap, Kaz has borrowed one of those perpetually confused Japanese folk again. He probably thinks it's part of that authentic Australian tour his mother booked online.

He clears his throat, 'Excuse me, but when is the Dolphin trip starting, please?'

That's it! I would insist Kaz release him, so he could catch up with his real booking. I hear a whisper from the chest of drawers; it's Gavin from Wales. A small note is pushed through the gap, it has an email address written on it. 'Can you send a message to my mother in Cardiff, tell her my flight has been delayed for a week.'

'No worries, do you want me to bring you a Leek in the meantime?'

'O'boyo my favourite food. That would be magic.'

'Anyone else?'

Kaz looks up, her voice hoarse from all the activity and pheromone overload, 'Can you get me a jar of Vegemite and don't worry about a spoon. I've got me own.'

'Right, boys, I'm off. See ya later Kaz.'

'See ya later Brian (Kaz a bit breathless), you proper Pommie Bastard.'

I would wait 24 hours, when Kaz would go for her smoke break, to have a quiet word with her. Not only was her addiction getting completely out of hand but her 24/7 recreational pursuits were making sleeping in that "den of iniquity" unbearable as the temp was touching 55°C with all that action. I was losing two pints in sweat just by existing. I would have to install a water machine or at least pull the garden hose through the window to keep us all cool.

I would often wake up after Kaz had shagged another random bloke and find strange artefacts in the living room. *Dickinson's Real Deal* the antiques television show, would have had a field day. 'Now, what have we here?' Dickies getting excited. Once, two 6-foot chess pieces both red, both knights had come for a sleepover. I look at them, red and red. Only bloody Australians would have the audacity. Confused as to how the same colour could beat each other, I made a coffee.

Later that day, the master chess player arrived. Six foot four tattooed from eye to arse, heavily scarred.

'What do you think?'

'Well, gangster dude, where are the rest of them, and why are they both red?'

'They're both bloody red, you Pommie Bastard because it's Checkers!'

As I enlightened my good gangster friend of the intricacies between Chess and Checkers, acknowledging his newfound knowledge, he would consult the gang "capo" …who would have me killed in the morning.

I ask, 'What again?'

'Shut up, you Pommie Bastard,' he replies, shaking his head as he leaves to terrorise the local neighbourhood.

Mutters to himself, 'I told Shaun he was bloody insane.' I shouted after him 'And you'll need a board to play on, at least a forty-foot square one.'

So I wake up, I've been in hiding for three days. I go for a long-needed shower, it's 40 degrees. In the shower, shampoo on. Five minutes later, my hair starts to fall out. I check it, too late. *Shaun you Australian gangster bastard, hair removing cream in the shampoo bottle!*

A few weeks earlier, Shaun enters; he looks like a typical Surfie dude, long blond hair, stocky build. He's the gang leader and a good mate of mine.

'Right, boys, we have a job to finish. Back to Marco's tonight get the rest of those Checkers pieces. Prank Marco.'

'Shaun, have you boys not thought about stealing cash or Rolexes rather than miss-identified board game pieces?' I offered as a more lucrative pursuit.

'Don't be a fucking drongo mate, where's the fun in that!' Shaun replied indignantly.

'You're coming too this time, you proper Pommie Bastard!'

'Shaun mate, you know my thoughts on sharing a cell as Big Bruce's from the Wagga-Wagga's new girlfriend. I'm not particularly keen on being jail bait. Can we not just go to the beach like normal fucking Australians?'

'Live some mate, don't be a coward.'

Vlado the Serb pipes in, 'He can't be a coward.'

'Why not?' Shaun asks.

'Because he's fucking insane,' Vlado offers.

Shaun (with his persuasion dial on), 'Think of us as a "Surfers Robin Hood" mate.'

I said, 'That's a bit ironic because you are "robbing the hood".'

'IRONING Pommie Bastard! That's for Sheilahs and Pooftas mate!' Shaun declares outraged.

'I tell you what boys, the "International pool hopping championships" are a fortnight away, and I need to practice. I'm only going if there is a pool I can practice in? I'm an athlete you know. Quite famous, here let me show you.' I rummage around in my backpack, 'Here it is *Pool Hoppers Weekly*.' I thumb through, 'Yes, there we go.'

Title, *Backpacker-owners outrage at late night marauding of mad Scotsman.*
Article continues, *Outrage and disgust amongst hostel owners and Christians. Insane Scotsman terrorises local swimming pools at 3 am. When the law enforcement arrives, runs off claiming practising for a very important International event. Public warning, do not approach as the Pommie Bastard may be unarmed and probably naked.*

Emergency meeting to be held in the Town Hall: Friday, 2 pm.

'Damn it, that's the wrong magazine. That's *Hostel Owners and Christians Weekly Alert*.

No time now anyway, I will go and get my kit.'

Shaun, 'Balaclava and crow-bar mate?'

'No…swimming cap and speedos.'

Vlado adds, 'See, Shaun mate, I told you he is fucking insane.'

'We will go over to Nico the Greek on our way, pick up some kit.'

Vlado the Serb, 'We should bring Sammy the Samoan too.'

'Yes, he's handy, those Checkers pieces weigh a bloody tonne.'

'Err, can I get a gang nick-name, please? What about Brian the Scot, I said thumping my chest?'

They look at me with admiration, roll their eyes. 'Shut up, Brian the Pommie Bastard!'

'That'll do,' I exclaimed, delighted.

'Christ, I hope Nico has that dog locked up?' Shaun says worriedly. We all shudder, that ain't no dog. It's a beast that would scare Satan himself, a Pit-bull the size of a lion. If it sets off, we are all dead.

'Remember boys, don't show any fear.' Shitting ourselves, we head to Nico the Greek's place.

Pick up Sammy first, the heavily scarred giant Samoan. 'So, Sammy when did you boys stop eating people?' I enquired politely. 'Thursday mate,' he growls. I thought of a Samoan getting together with a Glaswegian and the offspring they would create. Suddenly panicking, I would inform NATO first thing in the morning of the impending threat to mankind and Christians. I couldn't shake the image of a drunken eight-foot, 40 stone terminator causing absolute havoc after missing happy-hour. The genes must be kept separated at all costs; the whole of humanity was at stake.

Sitting on the sofa at Nico the Greeks, the beast from hell is softly nuzzling my crotch, looking for a scratch. I'm ashen, the dog's one-foot-wide head is covered in teeth and muscle. The dog stands on my foot and it's like the weight of a grown man. *Don't scream, breathe, just breathe. FFS.* 'Nico mate, can you call the dog over, I need to piss,' I squealed like a man.

'"Cuddles"'…come here boy.' The beast wanders over to his master.

'Is there no sane restrictions on the type of dog you can have in Oz, Nico?'

'Oh yes, but Cuddles is completely illegal.'

'He's in good company then,' I muttered.

'Yeah, he got in a fight with another pit-bull that went for him, when I was walking him last week. Took me 30 minutes to prize them apart. Bloody bent my new crow-bar.' A dog bigger than Cuddles? I'm never leaving home ever again.

'Oh, that's a shame,' we all nervously laughed. I used the opportunity as a cover for the tears that had been welling ever since Cuddles had fallen in love with my crotch.

Tripping over each other to get to the bathroom and escape the impending canine slaughter, Nico stands up, 'I'll put him outside.' We all have a quiet sigh of relief. Nico leaves the room. With the monster gone, the room now fills with the smell of fear.

'Fuck Brian, he was right on your bollocks,' Vlado hisses over.

'I know, I think we might have to stop at our pad again, I need an undie change.' Crew back, 'Not wrong mate, us too.'

One thing is for sure, Nico the Greek is never going to get robbed, we all agreed.

'Where the hell have you been?' Shaun is carrying a large chess piece, looks like a bishop. Sammy the Samoan, eight foot ten, heavily tattooed, was carrying another piece. 'Sorry, I had to jump in the pool, remember?'

'Really, you need to practise now?'

'It's very important to me,' I explained upset. 'Anyway, I managed to steal this Lillo.' Chest full of pride, I showed him the pink Lillo. 'FFS, Brian the Pommie Bastard, could you not even get a Pawn?'

'Pool attractions are more my speciality, Shaun,' I replied indignantly. 'Anyway, whose gaffe is this, it's massive?'

'It's Marco the Sicilian's.'

'Err Shaun, did you say "Sicilian", as in the mafia? He doesn't by any chance own waste disposal businesses too?'

'Several actually, don't worry we are just pranking him,' Shaun pats me on the shoulder.

'Crikey, if we had followed your suggestion and nicked his Rolexes, we would all be wearing cement thongs.'

'But pranking the mob Shaun? You sure that's OK?'

'Yeah, because that's fun mate,' Shaun replies as a matter of fact.

'Right, I will be five minutes, just going to nip back and return the Lillo with a box of chocolates and a sorry note.'

Back in the van, all huddling Chess pieces. Excitedly I say, 'Crew, I think we should create a rap song for our Posse? Let me work on it for a few days, get back to you boys,' I informed the gangsters.

Vlado, 'He's insane Shaun mate, I keep telling you.'

Back home there's not much room, we now have five six-foot chess pieces sharing our rent.

'So, you boys are right into pranking?'

'Yeah, for sure mate.'

I started to hatch a plot, pranking a gangster what could possibly go wrong again. I had an idea, Shaun would love it.

Off to the chemist first thing, purchase my goods, plan hatched.

'Shaun mate, you fancy a coffee?'

'Yeah, go on then.' I make a very strong coffee, add the secret ingredient, stack load of laxatives enough to kill a horse. Beforehand, I have hidden all the toilet roll from the whole block of flats. Shaun finishes the coffee, 'See ya, I need to do some shit.'

'Some shit?' I say expectantly. Shaun leaves as his belly starts to rumble.

24 hours later, Shaun stumbles in crawling on all fours. 'What the fuck, I think I have Salmonella. Call an ambulance, how the fuck can the whole block run out of loo roll? How is that even possible!' Bone curdling scream, 'My guts are bleeding,' rolls on the floor in agony.

'Well,' I said, 'it's not supposed to go on for that long?' I'm looking at the back of the pill canister. Shaun stops writhing for two minutes, 'What Brian the Pommie Bastard is not supposed to go on that long?'

'The Laxative effect. I put 10 tablets in your coffee yesterday as a prank. Said one on the packet, why skimp I thought…Shaun deserves so much more in life.'

Shaun furious, 'You fucking Pommie Bastard idiot! I've been trapped on the toilet for nearly 16 hours, tripping out of my head on acid. The hallucinations will stay with me for the rest of my life.'

'Well, Shaun,' I said perplexed, 'I didn't know you were going on a drugs fest, and I can't believe you can't see the funny side of this. I even hid all the toilet roll. I'm very disappointed Shaun. Plus you do know drugs are bad for your health?' I scolded him.

Shaun looking up from the floor, with clenched teeth (just like his buttocks) … 'YOU! You Pommie Bastard are a danger to my health! I'm going to kill you, you Bast…argghhh' (drowned out by another wracking cramp).

'What kill me again, Shaun?

Anyway, I'm off to the shops, buy some new speedos. The final championship is around the corner. Do you need anything?'

'Yes, fucking loo roll and a gun to kill you,' Shaun screams from the floor.

Back to the present. So, as my hair fell out from the shampoo-switch, courtesy of Shaun. I wondered whether a comb-over with my last three strands would suffice. I had to applaud Shaun, what a marvellous prank. Jealous, I wish I had thought of it. Maybe I'll try it on Kaz, she's game for a laugh. I would ask her in-between shags.

Later, I found out that the shampoo switch was Shaun's dad's idea (says it all really).

'Shaun, my good man, now that is a prank.' Looking like I had leprosy, I bowed to the master. The remaining strands fell to the floor. 'Reminds me of when, back in Edinburgh, my Scottish mates and I decided to shave each other's eyebrows off after we passed out. Only shaved one, left the other, for maximum effect,' I informed Shaun.

'I started the prank and swore I would never pass out. Two boys down, I had this. So after the 3rd mate got caught out, I proclaimed myself the winner and immediately passed out. Walking down Princes Street with three mates, not one of us had a full set of eyebrows. We had a council meeting and called a truce.'

Shaun is delighted, 'That sounds brilliant, Brian. Who should we start with?'

'What about Kaz?' We listened to the banging from the bedroom.

'Nah, she's busy right now. What about me?' I volunteered, 'but I will have to pass out first and that's never going to happen.'

Vlado, excited runs off, 'I'm going to the bottle shop to get some booze in.'

Shaun runs off, 'Me too!'

'Boys try to buy it with cash or a card this time rather than an armed hold-up,' I shouted at their departing backs. Too excited to listen, they ran off.

When they came back, I told them, 'Boys, I have come up with our gang rap song it's a mix of Belinda Carlisle and Bobby Brown.'

'Shit, Vlado you were right. He is insane!' Shaun exclaimed.

Last story on Shaun: it's New Year's Day, Shaun says, 'I'm going out to buy some smokes, be back in 30.'

A couple of weeks go by, 'Anyone seen Shaun? Where the fuck did he go?'

Vlado says, 'I've looked everywhere. Marco the Sicilian has got over the prank, Checkers returned, say's nothing to do with him.'

Another two weeks go by. I'm practising hard for the *World Pool Hopping Championships*, there's "wanted" posters of me in speedos nailed to every post. It makes me so angry when such a talented sport doesn't get the recognition it deserves. All that training and mental strength, totally wasted. I should write to the Australian Olympic Committee in the morning, demand an inquiry and an apology from the Queensland Backpackers federation.

Thought to cheer myself up, I'd go to the speedo shop and buy a new pair. Gold, just like the Olympic medal I desperately wanted to win. Walking to the shops a man is coming down the road with massive grin on his face, completely bald.

He gets closer, it's Shaun! 'What the HELL! You said you would be back in 30 minutes, not 30 days. What happened?'

'Oh, I got in a fight with a bloke.'

'Why?' I asked not wanting to know the answer.

'I wolf-whistled his missus.'

'You know that is so 1980s, right?' I informed the gang leader.

'Shut it Pommie, anyway, I got pulled and I had pending violations as I had skipped parole. So got 30 days in the nick, shaved my head.'

Putting my arm around Shaun's shoulders. 'Right, well let's get drunk! I have to leave for Uni in a few days.'

'Sounds like a plan mate,' he then looks at my eyebrow with anticipation. 'You thought about passing out yet?'

'I'm working on it Shaun, my good man.'

'Excellent let's get started,' Shaun slaps my back.

Next morning, 'Right, Kaz, I'm leaving town now.'

The banging from the room stops. I hear a muffled voice say, 'Crikey, get me some water. I'm as dry as a lizard's gizzard.' Looking at each other in the living room, 'Wow, she has some stamina,' we said admiringly.

Vlado pipes in, 'She's as fit as a butcher's dog.' We all nodded in agreement. Water arrives, 'Ahhhh that's better. Right, see ya later, you proper Pommie Bastard.' *The knocking starts up again.*

Shaun's gives me his parting words of wisdom at bus station. 'You know we're all insane, right?'

'No, I had no idea?' I said to his bald head, glistening in the Queensland sun. 'I will visit sometime; send me your parole dates mate.'

On the bus, one eyebrow left (after passing out again), no hair and a gang scar called a smiley from Vlado (that I still have to this day) as a keepsake. Now looking like I had just vacated in Chernobyl, I thought to myself, *you know what Brian that trip could not have gone any better, no Sir!* I even scored a silver medal at the *International Pool Hopping Championships*. I would beat that South African bastard Johan next year!

*Pool Hopping, a self-named "sport" whereby I started at one end of Whelan Street and jumped in every pool along the street, climbing over walls, fences, over roofs and anything else that got in my way. With a pool entry of can-openers, bombs and belly flops, then a race to the end and on to the next pool. Then cross over the road and back again chased by backpack owners and those folk whose pools had gotten in the way (collateral damage). Think aquatic steeple-chase.

*Shaun did try and recruit me, they felt my British accent and penchant for misadventure could prove useful on their capers. I was introduced to one of the scariest guys I have ever met, a six-foot four Islander, every inch of his body heavily scarred. I could sense the fear and awe of the others. The gang had many tentacles unknown to me. It was definitely time to leave. As *the web's we weave, when we first start to deceive* came to mind. Also, forget the gang, my dad would have bloody killed me. I could just imagine the conversation; Dad exasperated 'Son, I thought you were going to get a college education...not join a CRIMINAL gang?! Now son...run at my fist!'

13
Hervey Bay, "Pablo" the Accidental Farmer

I walk out, the sun is blinding; it's 40 degrees. Just standing is almost unbearable. I look at my teammates unconcerned about the 90 minutes about to be played in an oven. Halfway through, I can only see stars it's so fucking hot…deserts I'm used to, football Queensland style I am not. It's 1 pm, my heart has decided it's had enough, packed its bags and is leaving town on the next train. A ball is kicked over to me, next thing animals from everywhere run over the pitch. I stop; the forest next to me is on fire. I thought what would "Skippy" do in a situation like this? A Wallaby with its tail alight hops past at 100kph, answers my question. FFS, like it needs to get any hotter. That's it! My two kidneys were packing their suitcases too. Join my heart on that train.

As the pitch started to catch fire and the ball started to melt, I stopped playing. Soon all my vital organs would be on that train. I should run catch up with them before I became a mixed grill. Wild-eyed, I scream manically, 'Run for your lives, fucking RUN! Everyone save themselves! Help, SOS, mayday, murder; someone save me, anyone? Hello?' I start to make a lifesaving break for it.

Queenslander team looking back at me like I'm insane. 'Shut it, you Pommie bastard, pass the ball we can win this.'

Afterwards, a teammate is lamenting, 'You know what is so annoying Pommie Bastard?'

'Er, the tragic loss of wildlife and my eyebrows?'

'Nah mate, the beer's gone bloody warm again.'

I share a beer that may as well have had a tea bag floating in it with Carlos, a fellow footballer. I get his life story, originally from Spain been in Oz twenty years, we become good mates.

A few weeks later, Carlos, his mate, Matias Ignatius Gonzalez the second (aka Matt), and I are drinking some homemade hooch. You could strip walls with this shit. I examine the sclerotic cloudy yellow bottle, looks like piss. Tastes like piss too, we all agreed. The kidney killer juice, finished. Open another, now delicious, Matt is relaying a story of when he was out in the bush, wild pig hunting. Matt's English isn't great.

'So, I'm on hands and foot.'

'You mean knees?'

'Yes, crawling big holes (tunnels) in bush, big porks (wild pigs) make run fast. I follow, then big porker chase me on knees and hands, my gun jam, no bang-bang. Big open, a tree, I climb up. Big porker, down below grunting; I wait till night, big porker go. I climb down, head on knees back to Ute (pick-up truck), next big porker back, chase me back through holes. I manage truck and grab what I can out of Ute's back and roll with pig, over, over, stab, stab. Kill big porker!'

'Shit, how big was the pig?'

'Maybe 200 kilos.'

'What was it you managed to grab out the Ute?' "Charades" starts; Matt is making a hammer-in-ground motion and then a sleeping noise and triangle with hands. Another swig of the yellow piss, clarity arrives…

'A tent peg?'

'Yes.'

'Plastic?'

'No, you idiot, metal,' Matt replies.

'You killed a 200kg wild pig with a metal tent peg! Were you on this fucking hooch by any chance?'

Oh FFS, even the Spanish had gone bonkers in Australia. This unusual behaviour could be squarely blamed on the local bushfires not allowing the beer to chill appropriately. I would inform the fire authorities in the morning. However, it did occur to me, I've learned a valuable life lesson, from now on start training with a tent peg, stay safe.

Carlos says, 'I need to go and visit my parents in Tin Can Bay (yes it does exist), about 100km south of here. Do you want to come?'

'Sounds good, mate.' Carlos is pleased, 'Great I will pick you up next Friday. I need to check my crop on the way.'

'Wow, I didn't know you were a farmer?'

'Yes, one of the finest in Queensland,' replied Carlos proudly.

He really was a multi-talented gent, I marvelled. Carlos arrives on his Honda 1000cc Flatbed motorcycle. I would ride shotgun. Now, Flatbeds have no trimmings, it's just a flat seat both people sit on. For the unsuspecting passenger, there is no obvious place to hang onto except for your mortal coil. I hold on to Carlos as he races off. He quickly brakes and asks me, 'What the fuck are you doing?'

'I thought it was obvious, I'm holding on for dear life.'

'No, don't hold me, no man holds another man in Spain, no, no, NO!'

'Does it matter that we are not actually in Spain?' I retorted. 'NO! You just hold under the seat.'

'There is nothing fucking there!'

'Just grip on with your fingertips,' is the answer to my very reasonable, life preservation question.

'Are you fucking serious?' I shoot Carlos a dark look.

'Yes!'

Now, holding on for dear life with my fingertips as the 1000cc bike roared down the Bruce Highway at 140kph, I began to wonder how Carlos had gotten into the farming game. Must be a family tradition from his homeland, probably oranges, I mused. Judging from the hooch, thank god it wasn't a wheat-based crop for distilling moonshine. I shuddered at the thought. We had nearly all gone blind the other night.

Roughly an hour into the trip, Carlos pulls onto a dirt track and we head about 30 mins into the bush. He stops the bike, 'Right you need to get off here, while I go check the plants.'

'Plants? Is it kale, corn, or maybe a potato of the tuberous species of the Solanaceae family?' I ask.

Carlos just laughs, 'You Scots so funny,' he then jumps on his bike and rides off.

Forty minutes, 40 degrees and still no sign of Carlos. I'm standing in the bush admiring the sunbathing snakes all around me, trying not to scream to arouse their hunting instinct. I begin to wonder if watching that half episode of Bear Grylls survival show would suffice. I can hear the bike, the snakes open up like Moses parting of the water, thank fuck. Carlos shows up with a big grin on his face.

He hands me a "rollie" cigarette. We have a smoke each, 'Bloody hell, Carlos, that's a bit strong!'

'Yes, it's from my crop, Cannabis Sativa from the family Cannabaceae,' he grins. 'Otherwise known as good shit, mate!

Sorry, I had to drop you off in the bush, but if I ever get robbed or busted by the DEA, I will always know it wasn't you.'

'No worries Carlos, I'm just glad you remembered to come back; normally I wouldn't even remember to pass the potato chip bowl on!'

Clarifying my Australian motives, 'Anyway, Carlos I am not in Queensland to be the next Pablo Escobar, I'm here to get a college degree, not join a cartel.'

He laughs, pats me on the back, 'C'mon let's go Pablo!'

On the back of the bike cruising at 140kps along the Bruce Highway, both the rider and passenger are completely stoned. It's a classic straight Australian road; I'm looking up at the clear expansive forever unchanging blue sky. The bush is whizzing past, the cramp in both hands from lifesaving clenching has finally been anaesthetised from Carlos's crop. I begin to really enjoy the experience, the scenery is beautiful. I can see nature in its true purity. Bob Dylan starts to play in my head. I hate Bob Dylan, change the track, Lou Reed, good but not perfect, then the Eagles' *Take it easy* starts, *perfect choice Mr Dawes*, I congratulate myself. I start singing into my helmet and just as I was about to fully relax, hit the high note and fall off the back of the bike, we arrive in Tin Can Bay.

I go to shake Carlos's dad's hand, but my hand is still a claw from holding on by fingertip. I wouldn't massage either hand; keep the claw position, so I could just clip my fingers back on for the trip back up tomorrow. I didn't think they would unclasp anyway. I wasn't sure whether that was from cramp, abject terror or both.

That night we had a few cold Tinnies (beers). Carlos reminiscing, 'Yes, I used to be a sergeant in the Australian army, loved it. My mum and dad were so proud until I got kicked out!'

'What happened?' Carlos starts to remove his boot, then socks. 'See!'

'You got kicked out for not wearing socks?'

'No *Puta*, see, look closer.' I look down, how could I have missed it. There covering the entire top of Carlos's foot is a massive tattoo of his favourite plant. The spiky leaves unmistakable, 'You got kicked out for this very subtle tattoo?'

'No, I got kicked out for smoking it, regular drug tests.'

'When did you get the tat?'

'When I was in the army,' Carlos is looking at me like I'm an idiot.

'Carlos, my good man, did you not think your choice of motif might have been a slight giveaway as to how you like to spend your recreational time?'

Carlos looks at me like I'm insane, 'I didn't roll my foot up and smoke it. FFS!'

'Don't worry, as a farmer you will make your parents proud again,' I reassured him. Nodding, he takes a draw, 'Yes, the best "Farmer in Queensland".'

A week later, looking at my still clenched digits, I realized my fingers were angry at me and were sulking. They would only unclench for a cold beer; that made me proper suspicious. That's when I knew the little bastards were at it. 'I'm part Cumbrian not Columbian!' I scolded them. My digits so moody…and completely shit at spelling?!

I promised them that I wasn't going to grow my own 100-acre Cannabis crop or become Carlos "second in command farmhand" or even change my name by deed poll to Brian Escobar and they finally started to see reason and relaxed.

After all, I had college in the morning and parents to also make proud.

Interesting end to Carlos's story. He was eventually contacted by Spanish lawyers (while still living in Australia), who informed him that he had inherited 3 houses in Barcelona from his mother's side. The lawyers had been trying to track him down for years. Unscrupulously his father had hidden the properties from Carlos and had been collecting rent on them for many years. So not only did Carlos head back to Spain as a wealthy man, he also had ten years of back dated rent due from his (always disapproving) father.

14
Having a Happy Moment — Hervey Bay, Queensland

Ernest Hemingway enters – square jaw, piercing eyes, arms of steel. Arguably the greatest fisherman to have graced the Earth.

Earnest in monologue, 'I've won every fishing competition thrown at me, caught record-breaking Marlin, arm-wrestled Great Whites...but I have never met two more worthwhile opponents such as these two, their reputation precedes them.'

God under his breath, 'You have no idea.'

'Loki, who I bumped into in the corridor, says they come highly recommended.'

'Really?' Both God and Charles look at each other and groan.

'Yes Ernest, Charles here has been trying to "catch" these two for his awards podium, for longer than I can remember. They must have eaten their own body weight in poisonous fish by now, with no ill effect.'

Charles exasperated, 'Students really can eat anything!'

Ernest rolls up both sleeves, 'Let me try...'

The greatest fisherman moves the Black Bishop takes the White Castle.

This has got to work. The Chessboard changes into a window.

'Look down there!' Earnest exclaims, 'Those kids on the jetty have just caught a "Happy Moments" fish, chew your own arm off...'

God and Charles, 'Yes, we know...let's have some fun and get those awards handed out.'

'Too right,' they all look down excited.

I wake up to loud snoring, Firthy hungover in the next bed. An empty bladder of a four-litre box of wine is being lovingly nuzzled. There's a sharp needle-like pain in my calf, I look down and see pinpricks all down my lower leg. What the HELL?

Fishing a couple of days back on the Jetty, Firthy and I land a fish. Excellent, supper caught, we are about to stick it in the bucket. Old fisherman strolls over, strong Queensland drawl 'Aw boys you don't want to eat that it's called a Happy Moments fish...because the "Moment," one prick of those spines gets you...you won't be happy until you've chewed your own bloody arm off – the pain's so bad.' Shaking his head, wanders off muttering.

'My God Firthy, is there anything in Australia that won't kill you?'

Firthy contemplative, 'Not to my knowledge mate.'

We quickly kick the fish back into the water, lucky escape. Crap, I wonder how much poisonous fish we have unknowingly eaten so far, tonnes probably. That would explain a few things, we both agreed!*

Right we need to catch "Tea". Hervey Bay is a small town on the Queensland coast, where we would stay as students for a year and supplement our meals by catching fish. As Firthy stated, studying was a mere possibility but fishing, was our everyday. We spend the money saved on boxes of 4-litre rocket fuel wine costing about five bucks.

Off to the bait shop we go, three of us including another good mate, Chris. We get some prawns and burley (fish guts/chum). Chris picks up some squid. Back to the flat we go to make fishing preparations.

We open up a prawn packet and feed our two huge (size of a hand) huntsmen spiders that are sat in the middle of a web that spans six feet across each window. They are named Sid and Vicious and they keep the beasties at bay, as their web acts as a massive fly screen. One on each window, sorted. Initially confused about how prawns were landing on their web, they soon developed a crustacean addiction. Overcoming their suspicion of foul play or sorcery, they happily munched on.

We make plans to go fishing later. Meanwhile, Chris is making supper. Supper arrives. Great, I'm starving.

'WTF, Chris?' Chris, chewing on a tentacle, 'What? It's all good; I cooked them in garlic…' Chris (now a respected banker), looks delighted with himself.

'Chris, mate, you can't cook and eat the squid bait. FFS!'

'Why not?'

'Because it will probably kill you for starters.'

'Yeah, but you two have been eating poisonous fish for at least three months,' Chris retorts.

'Yes, but WE didn't know. Anyway, if you start eating all the bait, how are we going to catch any bloody fish? We will all go hungry or worse have less booze money and you will be visiting the loo for the next two days…or the morgue if you eat any more. Sid and Vicious will be pissed too, eating all their dinner.' 80 eyes stare angrily back at Chris.

'Right, that's decided it, stand down student, you are not required on this fishing mission.' Chris shrugs and walks off.

'C'mon Firthy let's go and Chris, don't eat any more bait; there's 400 packs of two-minute noodles in the cupboard.' Chris opens the cupboard quickly disappears under a mountain of noodles. Muffled voice, 'It's OK, I'm not hurt. Wait boys! I can't feel my toes…' Firthy and I look at each other, we wait… 'Oh yes I can…sorry.'

Sighing, 'Right Firthy, let's go…'

On the jetty, we start to fish. Two old Queenslander fishermen are sitting on two wooden crates; Captain Quint from Jaws could have been a cousin. Sun beaten, wizened and emanating respect, they looked at us and rolled their eyes.

Waving back enthusiastically, I knew the respect was mutual. Hemmingway would have been proud.

Back to fishing. Next to us, a couple of local kids have just caught a fish. I look down, 'Shit Firthy, is that a Happy Moments fish?'

'Yip.'

'Should we tell them?'

'Nah, they're local kids they'll be all right.' No worries we fish on.

Not two minutes later, I get these searing set of jabs in my calf, feels like a whole load of bee stings. The first thought in my head was *those little bastards have just pricked me with that Happy Moments*. The thought of now having to chew my own leg off, and possibly having Firthy join in to speed up the process, sent me into a meltdown. Practicality took over, should I marinade the leg first, and would it really taste like chicken? Screaming down the Jetty, I began to feel hungry.

Sprinting down the jetty, hysterically crying, 'GET it off, get it fucking OFF! MURDER…Murder most foul, the little bastards have stabbed me with the fish. I'm going to DIE. Arghhhh!'

I collapse at the end of the jetty having screamed for 40 yards. Writhing, starting to foam at the mouth I whimper, 'Someone save me, is there an antidote? Quick good sir, I need mouth to mouth!' Shaking me off his leg, one of the old fishermen looks at the other throws me a look of utter admiration and states 'Bloody Pom!'

I finally look down, expecting to see a fish sticking out of my leg, but instead there's a whole load of little bait hooks in my calf, about 15. Oh crap. Damn it to HELL! I now wished it had been a Happy Moments, dignity (although without leg) would have been intact. We will never be able to fish here again. Shunned from the fishing community and all of humanity.

While on the jetty, another group of young lads were fishing for bait. It's is a line with 15 plus small hooks on, that you jig and catch small bait-fish on. The youth that had utterly crushed all fishing dignity, had jigged too hard, the line had come over his shoulder and bulls-eyed my calf.

Looking down, I pull out the tiny hooks. Firthy quickly puts shades and a cap on and tries unsuccessfully to blend his six-foot two body into the jetty. We catch up sobbing inconsolably. Hugging each other we make a dignified exit.

The two old men. Battle hardened, look at us sprinting into the distance. Shaking their heads,

'In all our 70 years.'

'I know mate,' in unison, 'BLOODY STUDENTS.'

Back in the gaff, we quickly draw the curtains. Firthy to me, 'Let's have a commiseration drink.'

Chris, in the background, 'Anyone hungry?'

Both of us, 'NO!'

'Oh, hold on a sec,' Firthy chucks a bag of bait prawns, 'we won't be needing these anytime soon.' Chris excitedly reaches for the garlic…

I sigh; *we can never fish in the daytime ever again. Only night fishing from now on, when there is no full moon…just in case anyone recognises us.*

Looking through a gap in the curtains, I switch the lights off.

'Any locals out there?'

'No, it's all clear,' I inform a mortified Firthy. 'Well,' I said to Firthy, 'all things considered, I handled that well.' Firthy groans, 'Impeccable mate.'

'Yes, not a disgrace at all.' I congratulated myself.

'No sir!'

A few moments later, 'I should leave town, right?'

Silence… 'Leave Queensland?'

Firthy back, 'Think bigger mate.'

'Bugger, the Pacific Rim?' Firthy nods.

'Damn it to HELL! You're right, I better start packing…'

*Stings from rabbitfishes are extremely painful (*Siganus* species; also known as spinefeet, Black Trevally, or Happy Moments), the patient should seek medical help immediately. In severe cases affected limbs may become extremely swollen. Occasionally the pain may reach the point of causing delirium in the victim.

15

Two Fools, Shark Bait

Darwin, 'Who will triumph at the 1991 awards ceremony? Will it be our pawn?' Is scanning the globe from afar.

Charles, ecstatic, 'You have got to be kidding me? There he is with his good friend Firthy, on that little rock. Oh we so have him this time, look at the sharks! Two awards for the price of one.'

God relieved, 'Thought I'd lost him for a while. He's a slippery character at the best of times!

Right, God clasps his hands together, let's get started, have you boiled the kettle, Charles?'

'Yes, my lord.'

'Two lumps as usual?'

'Of course.'

'Is there any carrot cake left?'

They both sit down by the Chessboard with two cups of tea and two plates of cake.

'Let's play, the winner gets (yet again) to choose the method of demise.'

'This is going to be so close,' Darwin whispers excitedly!

Suddenly, there's a strange rustling and a small twister begins in the corridor, then leaves, birds and all manner of animals enter.

'Is it? Is it?'

'Yes,' says God excitedly. 'It is "The One".'

They both kneel, granting full respect. Mother Nature enters the room and starts to speak in the most beautiful, melodic voice but it is tainted with a deep sadness.

'What have they done my lords? They have killed all my animals, cut my trees down, they are relentless there is no stopping them.' Mother Nature starts to cry softly as God rushes over to comfort her. 'Does mankind care nothing for the Paradise we granted them?'

God sighs, 'No, they haven't learnt anything as yet, they haven't even figured out the Gaia system.* It was supposed to be a loan, not a free gift to plunder at will.

Please my lady, without you none of us would exist, join us.' God looks up; the massive clock is still "ticking". 'Still, we may not be too late? Such sacrilege won't go unpunished, the Gods are furious!

Let's play some chess, my dear, take your mind off the destruction for half an hour. Charles bring her lady a nice cup of tea, plenty of organic honey.'

They sit down.

'Oh, yes my lord, I heard you and Charles had a game on, it's the talk of the universe.'

'Yes, it's a lot of fun, please, I insist' God points at the board.

'Oooh, this is exciting,' Mother Nature now with a small smile, stirs up a small wind which moves the piece forward.

White Queen takes Black Pawn. All three look down as the board changes into a looking glass.

I wake up, I'm exhausted…still have wet Hawaiian board-shorts on in bed and I stink of bait chum. An empty jug reeking next to me, is grinning viciously back. Oh' hold on a second.

So I get a phone call…*Let's have a party, get trashed. What's the excuse? None. OK, that sounds convincing.*

What could possibly go wrong this time? So we are partying, making a hangover somewhat impossible to avoid. I pull out my party trick, called the "Bushfire" (unsuccessfully copyrighted), which basically means setting some nether regions alight and watching the flames cascade upwards, just like its namesake. However, forgetting that earlier in the day we had been sunbathing on the beach. The lighter flame ignited the residual suntan lotion which combusted, creating a massive fireball. Quick thinking Eamonn rolled me out on the floor laughing his head off.

As my screaming died down and now missing both eyebrows, I thought to myself this party has picked up a gear. I was on top of my game, everyone knew this.

Eamonn still laughing claims 'That is one of the funniest things I've ever seen.'

2 am, two men are left standing (just)…looking at each other, I say, 'You know Firthy I have the best idea. Why don't we go fishing?'

'Brilliant idea Brian, first class, nothing could possibly go wrong again? Let's grab the rods.'

Big Firthy and myself mine sweep all the leftover drinks into a jug (shut up, we were students, studying very, very, hard). So the mauve, 120 proof jug came along for the Darwin Award ride, a certificate of achievement would be sent out posthumously.

'Firthy, let's grab the deck chairs too.'

'That my friend is fucking genius,' we grin at each other.

Now feeling inspired, 'Right, let's get all the raw meat out of the freezer, we have no bait.'

We remove three weeks of essential student survival food from the freezer. I knew my flatmates (Eamonn and Ronette) would understand, this was important fishing business.

Two drunken idiots, two deck chairs, two rods and a whole load of suicidal shark bait stumble onto the beach. So Hervey Bay is a small town in Queensland, next to Fraser Island, one of the most condensed Tiger shark breeding and feeding areas in Australia and also a massive tidal bay. Firthy and I, holding each other up, 'OK, so where are we going to fish from, the tide is fully out?'

Eyes squinting through the fog of alcohol, I can just make out a silhouette in the darkness, 'What about that outcrop of rocks way (way…way) over there?'

Firthy gazes into the night, 'That looks perfect my friend.'

About 2.30 am, another swig of the jug of death, we rock and we know it. It's pitch black.

At about 3 am, sitting on deck chairs on the outcrop of the rock, starting to chuck raw steak into the water along with Ronnie's favourite sausages and a pork chop for good measure (some fish may have a more refined taste after all?).

I say, 'Y'know what, Firthy, this is possibly the BEST fucking idea we have come up with yet.'

'I know Mr Dawes, First Class,' I could sense rather than see Firthy's big grin. 'On fire, my good man,' we both agreed.

Fortunately, the earlier burns from the attempt I had made on my own life were starting to fade…I was feeling much better now.

'Firthy mate, look at that star constellation up there, looks exactly like Charles Darwin.'

Firthy in his recliner gazes up, 'Wow, it so does, big bushy beard and all.'

One hour later, still no fish…

'Ha ha ha!' I joke, 'the sharks have probably scared them off.'

'No way' *slurs* Firthy, 'it's not even that deep!'

More time goes by that will never be recovered. Suddenly, we start catching big style, must be about 4 am…

'Brian this is awesome dude, we can eat for a week.' Maths not being our strong point, having used three weeks of "bait" to catch one week of fish. I thought on the little outcrop of rock in the pitch black, that the accountancy module next semester couldn't come quick enough.

Even more time goes by, must be about 5 am.

Firthy to me, 'SHIT…serious shit, have you looked behind us?'

'No, why? I can hardly see past my eyeballs this mauve juice is so lethal.' *The whole bay had filled up, we were now on a piece of 10-foot rock.*

'Can you see the land?' Firthy's voice asks from the dark.

'Not a bloody thing!' Oh crap.

So, we have just chummed the water for several hours, we have finished the jug of death and now we have to make a swim for it in infested Tiger Shark country. The icing on the shark baits cake is that it's their prime feeding time too. I bet Tiger Sharks love a nice pork chop, I berated myself. Not one week before, there had been a horrifying story in the news of a prawn trawler capsizing further North. Three men had entered the water and for over two days a Tiger shark had stalked and eaten two of them. The third, who when interviewed was a broken man, had only survived by being washed over a reef. The shark had stalked him for three days. I throw the last of the chum in; the hooch was distorting my sense of survival.

I could see the local morning headlines. Hervey Bay Herald, *Two fools commit suicide, by using themselves as shark bait.*

Firthy and me in unison scream, 'This is possibly the WORST fucking idea we have ever come up with yet!!!'

As we staggered into the dark water with two rods, all our caught fish, two deck chairs and a constant theme of Jaws on loop, we made our way back. Every now and again there would be a big swoosh in the water and our bladders would loosen again. Trying not to poo as well as pee in the water, assisted by the sheer terror and attract even more sharks, we struggled back. The sharks had probably approached but confused by the plastic deck chairs, foul-smelling liquor and strange swimming motion, were not going to take a chance. End up with chronic constipation. Plus in our favour, we had been drinking for 16 hours straight and were now highly toxic, just like everything else "Down Under".

Hervey Bay Herald, next headline down:

Tragedy strikes! Endangered 16-foot Tiger Shark poisoned by two USQ Students.

I don't know how long it took to get back as we lay exhausted on the beach, the sun was fully up, but we knew we had both made our mothers proud...yet again.

The next day, Ronette, my flatmate, who is a pretty petite Indian/Fijian girl with a temper like a raging Tsunami asks, 'Where's all the meat? I'm going to make a curry.' Eamonn sitting on the sofa looks over. 'Didn't you and Firthy catch a whole load of fish last night? We could have a fish curry?'

'Yes, enough to feed us for a week,' I replied.

'Well?' says Eamonn curiously.

'The bastard sharks ate them!'

Eamonn rolls his eyes...

Ronnie looks at the empty freezer, starts to weep softly. I rush over, have a look too. 'My God, Ronnie!'

'Well, Brian?' Ronette sighs.

'Ronnie, my dear, it's an OUTRAGE! We've been robbed! The thieving bastards!'

Ronnie holds back another tear, 'Ughh...not again, Brian.'

'Don't worry my dear malnourished Ronnie! I gave her shoulders a little squeeze, I will shout us a takeaway curry!' I said dramatically. *Third time this week! And it was only bloody Tuesday??*

Under my breath, 'As per usual Mr Dawes, generous to a fault!' I cursed myself.

16
Gone Bush – 21st Party, Meeting an Expert

Toowoomba, a country town in Queensland; Mick the legend (my flatmate and ex-horse musterer) announces, 'Right Brian, we have a 21st party to go to in the bush.'

Puzzled, 'I thought this was the fucking bush.'

'No shut it Pommie Bastard, four hours away farmstead, in the real bush.'

Mick tells me, 'One of my mates will pick you up.'

'Excellent, I will get my suit dry cleaned.' Mick rolls his eyes, 'Bloody Pommie Bastard.' Goes into his bedroom where his six girlfriends are eagerly waiting.

A couple of days later, a massive V8 beast car turns up with its engine growling menacingly. A six-foot-four cowboy gets out. 'The names Bruce, you ready to party?' Confused, I'm in a full suit, it's a dignified 21st Birthday party after all, isn't it?

'Get in!' the giant says, wearing a cowboy hat…AC/DC, *Highway to Hell* blasting out of the car. I am so in. Big Aussie says, 'There's Bundy rum in the boot, help yourself mate.' I open the boot; eight cases of Bundy are staring back at me, expectantly. Bundy rum is the staple diet of all true-blue Queensland farmers. I grab a bottle. The bottle chuckles, another victim enticed. The whispering starts after the first sip; *do it, do it.* Do what?

I start singing. The Aussie looks at me with a smile on his face. Bloody Pommie Bastard.

I explain to the cowboy, that the rum is talking to me. 'Ah, yeah mate, it does that, the little bugger. You'll see.'

Three hours in, the Bundy is on full chat. Bruce has not only my life story but my family history, going back to when William came over to conquer. I've brought my extensive photo encyclopaedia with me. 'So Bruce, this is Sammy my hamster,' I start to well up, 'he died last year.' Bruce's face ashen, frantically looking for his special button. 'Bruce, mate…what are you looking for?'

'The bloody ejector button, you Pommie Bastard. My ears are bleeding. One more dead pet photo or another ABBA song, and I'm going to kill myself. My brain is bleeding, mate.'

'I thought your swerving into the oncoming traffic was a local norm? Not an attempt to lessen this beautiful exchange of differing cultures.' Bruce let's out a groan and starts to swerve into traffic again. The Bundy bottle, near-empty, looks confused, *'Pommie Bastard should be fighting by now, not singing Super Trooper?'*

Satisfied now that I had Bruce's full attention and admiration, I would now cover my mother's family tree. In addition, I thought excitedly, I had the long sorry tale of Waldorf my pet newt and his long battle with depression to tell. That should cover the last hour and make this trip bearable for Bruce. 'How time flies,' I informed him.

Bruce, one hour later, has grabbed the Bundy bottle and is pouring the last dregs over himself, frantically trying to get the car cigarette lighter to ignite. I take the lighter off him and say, 'If you need a smoke you just need to ask?' I light us both up a smoke and blow a smoke ring, 'Good talk Bruce, good talk.'

We arrive. I leave Bruce crying in the V8, I knew Waldorf's story was a tough one. But had no idea Bruce would take it so hard. I must be more careful in the future, these cowboys were a sensitive bunch.

I go to a makeshift bar made of bales of straw.

'What have you got?'

'Bundy mate and fermented Galah's blood. We also do a Roo's pickled testicle punch?'

'Bundy, will be just fine my good man.'

Bruce finally pulls himself together and comes over, 'Mick has me as your charge, so you'll stay safe. The country folk on Bundy can be a little rough. Especially, if the Sheilah's get a skin full.'

We catch up with two more cowboys, both 6 foot plus.

Bruce introduces me. 'Bloody Pom, had my ears bleeding for four hours; won't stop talking, like a Jackrabbit on a wallabies arse. I even got wordy with a G'day mate how ya doin? That's twice my word count for the whole day mate.'

'I hear ya mate,' they consoled.

'What's with the suit, you going to a funeral mate?'

Feeling confident that I was now one of the good old boys, 'Let me guess, are you by any chance Mr Croc Dundee, that infamous crocodile wrangler?'

'Nah mate,' says the cowboy chewing on a gecko, 'he's my uncle three times removed.'

'Removed?'

'Yeah mate by crocs, mate.'

Mick with his entourage of girlfriends turns up.

'Mick mate, what's the story with this bloody drongo in the funeral suit?'

'Bloody charity mate, it's called adopt a Pom.'

'He looks like a bloody car crash mate, what's with the hair and missing eyebrow, was it an explosion?'

'Says it's called a bushfire mate.'

I excitedly chirp in, 'I will give you a demonstration later. I'm an expert you know.'

'Not with Bundy rum you won't, blow us and the farmstead to high heaven. You'd be as black as a wombat's bollock.'

Serving girl goes past chewing some straw, 'So you're the Pommie Bastard everyone's been talking about?' Offers me a hors d'oeuvre.

'What is it?'

'Dried koala nostril.'

'How quaint, sounds delightful.'

I look over and a man is crying with a near-empty bottle of Bundy in one hand and a 10-inch hunting knife in the other. I ask the boys about him.

'Ah yes, sad story. That's Nick, cutting himself up again over his Sheilah. They break up at least six times a day. It's gutting mate, not many Sheilahs out in the bush, plenty of snakes not many Sheilahs. It hurts mate. Mick has most of them sown up.' I looked at him, his selfless act of servicing so some many local ladies was truly admirable.

'Yeah, Mick's as randy as a dingo's dick.' Another tray passes, I grab a fruit bat wing BBQ'd in possum fat.

I commiserated, as Nick drew another 10-inch river of blood across his chest. Unrequited love was brutal and baffling, my love "Susie" never returned my 451 calls. I thought the sex change and leaving the country a bit extreme. It was after all only a minor misdemeanour on that Dhow.

I look past Nick, who at some stage would surely need the assistance of a blood donor.

'Hey boys, what is that?'

'The farmstead?'

'No, no,' excited… 'Next to it?'

'What the swimming pool?'

'Yes, the swimming pool.'

'That's John the farmer's 40 feet pool, complete with Lillo.'

'Excellent, I'm off, I will explain later. I'm still in training, have a South African to beat.'

They all look at each other, Nick even stops cutting himself. *What a proper Pommie Bastard, they all agreed.*

It's magnificent. I swallow dive in, my years of expertise and hard training kicking in. Next a bomb, then finally a can opener, it's a masterclass in pool hopping. I get out, waiting for the crowds to go wild. I've aced it, I congratulated myself.

The local band earlier with the guitarist strumming on a dried brown snake and the vocalist singing into a live Kookaburra. All backed up by the drummer wearing only a cane toad beating on a wombat's head, had fallen silent.

I took a bow. The respect was palpable. The audience was mine. We all knew this.

'Bloody hell Mick, your adopted Pom is insane mate. He's still got his fucking funeral suite on. Worse than that he's just bombed in big, big John's pool mate. Big John mate, we're fucked!'

Mick mutters anxiously, 'Shit, I didn't see that coming.'

'Nah, mate neither did we,' 100 voices back in unison. 'We should run!'

The farmstead door crashes open, the father of the birthday girl has entered the outside. Horses start to rear in fear, Roo's hopping all over the place trying to escape. Magnificent in full crocodile, I knew he was an instant admirer of my talent.

Meanwhile, back at the swimming pool ranch. I have to say I am delighted. I have just mastered one of the most technical moves, the can opener. Victory would be assured at next month's *Inter-planetary Pool Hopping Championships*. I start to make a speech to the adoring crowd.

A large shadow descends. No one told me it was a full eclipse. Massive hands grab my shoulder spins me around. I'm faced by a six-foot-eight giant.

'G'day,' he growls, 'I'm Big John.'

'Hi BIG John.' Silence…I can hear whimpering in the crowd, all hidden behind straw bales.

'Well, you Pommie Bastard, what are we to do with you?' He growls.

'Well sir, I do have an impressive bushfire that I was going to show the boys. Now would be the perfect time.'

'Silence Pommie!' The huge farmer growls.

'What were you doing in my beloved pool?'

'I'm in training, Mr Big John.'

'Training?'

'Yes, for the Universal Pool Hopping Championships.'

'Really?' Silence…I could hear Mick protected by a phalanx of his girlfriends, whispering *God no, shut up Pommie*!

'Show me.'

Dripping in my suit, I knew I could muster the courage. Big John needed to be impressed, we all knew this.

I stepped out of my black brogues. Took a deep breath and launched one full perfect can-opener.

Gasps from the audience, I come out of the pool. Big John, steely gaze. 'Not bad, Pommie Bastard.'

'Stand back,' he strips off the crocodile suit. Standing magnificent in Tiger snake speedos. Without a word, does a double flip can-opener into the pool. I'm stunned, no one has ever done a double; it's unheard of. I started to cry to see such a wonderful spectacle.

Big John re-emerges gives me a big hug and says, 'I was *Inter-galaxy World Pool Hopping Champion* five years in a row.' Stunned, all those non-believers and nay-sayers would finally be silenced, I started to weep again. I know, I know Big John was cradling me in his massive arms.

Mick and the cowboys, stone the crows. I'm as stunned as a mullet, mate.

Big John addresses the crowd, 'From now on Brian the Pom is one of us. Now go and enjoy yourselves.' A hundred Stetsons fly into the air, followed by woo-hooos and yee-has. The band starts playing *Once a jolly swag man*. Mick extracts himself from his bodyguards, so selfless again, a true gent.

'Mate, I had your back, fair dinkum. Let's have a rip-snorter of a party.'

I was shaking my head in disbelief, double can-opener, in all my days, I marvelled. Who knew?

Many drinks later, 'Let's call it a night, get up early tomorrow. We'll go catch some snakes for the BBQ.'

Snakes?

'Goodnight, Mick,' I shout over, so he can hear over all the giggling in his supersized Swag (Bush sleeping bag). 'Goodnight, Brian the Pom.' I hoped he would get a comfortable night nestled amongst those 12 boobs; he must be exhausted looking after all those girls.

'Goodnight, Mick's Harem.'

Six voices back, 'Goodnight, Brian the Pom.'

I had my own Swag and a little scorpion to keep me company. I wondered if Mick could lend me a pair of boobs for a pillow, get a decent sleep. Nah, I was just being selfish. Mick was keeping those vulnerable girls safe and warm…like a true gent.

I look up at the trillion bush stars. Goodnight, little scorpion, little rustle at bottom of the Swag, content I fell asleep.

I get a kick, 'Wake up you Pommie Bastard, it's time for brekkie.'

'Well, that respect didn't last long.' I muttered to myself or would have if the Bundy hangover would allow my tongue to detach from the roof of my mouth and my vocal cords to operate.

Fuck, this is the worst hangover ever, the pain intensifying to supersonic mach level 5 and counting, I was in mortal peril. Groaning, I get a mug of hot coffee from the campfire billycan thrust into my trembling hand. Mick, now dressed by his entourage, chucks me over a Stetson.

'Time for your bush training. We'll make a Queenslander out of you yet.'

I retrieve my still wet suit, which takes 30 minutes to wrestle on. A Ute with six good old boys in the back comes screeching along, country music blasting. Using a Wallaby as a speed bump comes to a skid in front of us.

'There he is, the Pommie Bastard. Big John says we have to show you around, get to know the 6000km square place like the back of your hand.'

On the back of the Ute, my suit is starting to steam as the massive burning sun starts to wake up, furious at being called on for another day's hard work. We are going at breakneck speed, I'm being rattled and my hangover has reached a new crescendo. As the Olive suit started to dry, it began to shrink.

'Stone the crows!' One of the good old boys says startled. *Christ, I thought to myself, not even the crows are safe?* The cowboy continues, 'The Pommie Bastard has turned into the Incredible Hulk, look at him!'

It's true, I have channelled the green superhero who kills everyone indiscriminately due to his untreated anger management issues. Just like my Olive suit, my complexion has also turned a nice shade of green. My suit sleeves just like my trousers have migrated halfway up my limbs. I'm stuck fast like the Tin Man and I think I'm going to be sick again.

The Ute hits another marsupial and we shudder to a halt. 'Look, Bruce mate…there's one.' Shouts a cowboy. 'Ya beauty!' They start to run towards an old barn. 'C'mon you Pommie Bastard, hurry, it will get away.' As I waddled after them, cursing that I hadn't packed WD40, they stop and I catch up.

'What will get away?' I knew this lot were suffering from heatstroke, so I prepared myself by switching on my insane button. A button that allows me to cope with the ludicrous as if it were completely normal (after this weekend I would need to change the bulb).

'Snake mate, bloody six-foot Brownie. Kill 10 men, mate. Look there she is, c'mon you can help catch it, and they're bloody good eating.'

I knew it, I bloody knew it. Obvious delirium, sunstroke the cause. The snake makes a break for it and much to my relief didn't have to prove that trying to catch it by hand, hungover to hell was an incredibly shit idea.

'No worries mate, plenty more where that came from.' I knew with my current five kph average sprint speed I would be the easiest Pom a Brownie had ever killed.

'Right, here she comes,' a massive Combine Harvester comes along. It's at least four times the size of a European one and had obviously been injecting steroids for some time. 'Up you go you Pommie Bastard.'

I go up the steps, past the wispy cirrus clouds and enter the little cabin 40 foot up.

Now the boys are going to show me how they plough a field. Hanging on with my ever-decreasing olive suit, I am taken on a Combine Harvester masterclass. Eventually, four days later we reach the other end of the field.

'What d'ya think, isn't she a beaut?'

'This, my good man, is the finest and most certainly the largest reaping, threshing and winnowing contraption I've ever seen.'

Grinning, 'I've no idea what you just fucking said, but yeah she's Bonza all right.'

Eventually back on the Ute, frazzled from the sun but at least the hangover like my suit has evaporated. We have a few Bundies back at the farmstead.

Mick looks at me concerned, 'Mate, you're as cooked as a BBQ'd Goannas gonad, better get a few Sheilahs to help you home.' With a two-finger whistle, three girls peel off from the entourage. 'Help this Pommie Bastard into the wagon, will ya?'

Grateful that now I had the respect of the Bushman and his adoring harem, I was hoisted onto their shoulders and bundled gracefully into the back of the Ute. Time to go.

I thanked Mick for his gracious help, he really was a true gentlemen.

'No worries, you proper burnt Pommie Bastard,' he thanked me back. One more wolf whistle later and the Sheilahs floored the Ute's accelerator…off home we went.

*Gaia principle, that the Earth is a complex system whereby all organisms and their inorganic surroundings are closely integrated to form a single self-regulating system, maintaining the conditions for life on the planet.

17
Leap of Faith. Flyer
Backfire, Queensland

'This is it, Charles, get those cabinet doors open, scrub that medal clean. I will print off the certificate.'

'Are you sure?' Charles replies, super excited. 'Absolutely, look at the tour flyer, it couldn't be more perfect. In fact, I'm so sure, I'm even getting my robe dry cleaned for the ceremony and the "Fairy Godmother" is going to embroider a new gold lapel on for me.'

God thoughtful continues, 'Yes, after so long, we finally have him. Quick bolt the door, switch the lights off, so the deities think we have gone shopping or 10 pin bowling again.'

'Genius my lord, let's play.'

Black King checks the White King. Woah, it's going to be so close, they high five each other.

As the two Balinese guests introduced themselves as my sister and her boyfriend, I was astounded at their authenticity to the small Indonesian Island's traditional fashion, straight out of 1960. They had obviously been exposed to too much culture and the sun. Insanity box ticked, they had bought an entire wardrobe from the local Balinese hippy community for $5. Happy with their misguided fashion sense, they had brought over a few outfits for me too. 'Too kind,' I thanked them.

Now fully dressed in Balinese "haute couture", the three of us made ourselves comfortable and I caught up with their travels so far, over a few drinks.

Suddenly, there's a loud knocking on the patio window, I recognise it instantly.

'Don't move,' I hiss to Shirl and Chad.

It's Ross, Chair of the Mews committee. She's peering through the window. Fortunately, the Balinese traditional dancing outfits have allowed us to blend in perfectly with the carpet and curtains.

'Brian, BRIAN! I know you are in there! We have important committee minutes to go over.' I start to tremble, a trickle of sweat cascades down my neck. Ross is a 70-year-old Queensland matriarch who looked like she had been prize fighting for most of her septuplet times 10 years. She had been terrorising me and my flatmates for two years. I had made the terrible mistake of letting Ross know that my family owned the mews townhouse, which was nestled in a housing complex in Toowong (a district in Brisbane). Unfortunately for my sanity, from then on, I was immediately drafted as an ally in the fight against generally everything in the world. She would visit every second day with committee updates that would last for six hours, without a moment's breath. How she wasn't rushed off to hospital with hypoxia was one of God's greatest mysteries.

I was surprised at the usual unannounced visit, as the last time she had arrived was at 4 am.

A few days earlier. 'C'mon Chris mate, it's my 25th birthday tomorrow, you have to come out?' I pleaded. Normally, there would have been a stampede to the bar. This was like a total friends' blackout, on my birthday eve too, the light weight bastards. Had there been a zombie apocalypse? Should I start packing two-minute noodles, find a survivor's camp. Worse, had New Zealand invaded?

I knew I would have to blackmail Chris. I start with a small sob. Chris horrified, 'No Brian please don't, just don't! I'm begging you.'

Another little sob, 'It's coming, Chris, I can feel it.'

'Oh FFS then, yes we'll go out you bastard!'

Drying my eyes, 'I knew you would come around Chris.'

A grown man crying or showing any emotion was a capital crime in Queensland, the punishment: a public flogging. An Echidna shoved in the mouth to stifle the scream, and then soundly thrashed with an angry Platypus. Chris would be guilty by association and shunned from society and his loving mother. He was snookered, we both knew this. Off out we went to celebrate. Chris brought hankies just in case.

Next day, hungover, but both relieved. We had avoided another phone call from the PTSG (Platypus Thrashing Survivors Group), it's about 4 pm. We both stifle a whimper as the hangover matured.

My flatmates, David and John have turned up. We have a few beers and it looks like it's going to be a nice quiet birthday gathering. Door rings again, four more people enter, this goes on for the next couple of hours.

Hold on, I finally twigged, it was like a "Downunder" surprise party, whereby you turn up first then everyone surprises you by being late.

David, 'Hey Brian, I organised a surprise party for you. Really Brian, do you think we wouldn't drink our own body weight and get trashed on your special day.'

'Chris,' David glares over, 'was on strict orders not to go out with you.' Chris, glaring back 'He started crying again.'

David, 'Christ! Blackmail again Brian, really!'

'Bloody hell David, you know Chris and myself nearly got beaten stupid last night by the QES (Queensland Emotional Squad) again, so have some sympathy, just don't bloody show it.'

The QES was a black-ops division of the notorious Queensland police. Armed with Australian wildlife they would give out random beatings to anyone displaying un-Queensland like behaviour, such as kissing or holding hands.

Crying was a thorough thrashing. Funerals had to take place in the dark for safety reasons and to protect the endangered wildlife.

'David, my good man, that explains the unusual reluctance of last night's drinking cowardice.'

'Sorry mate, I know, but we knew you would get hammered, end up in a tree or the river again. Or worse still, nicked by the QES and ruin the big surprise.'

Damn it he had a point. I had fallen out of a tree only last week.

We start to party.

At 4 am, David's lower body decided it needed some air, as the top half had already passed out. Opens the patio doors by falling through them, just in time for Ross to turn up, unannounced again. Delighted that for once she didn't have to 'break and enter.' Stepping over David, she declares the birthday party over, after all, it was the next day and we had a committee meeting in two hours.

Presently, the sweat is starting to gain momentum, 'Stay still her eyes are not that good.' I hissed at my Balinese guests. One more shout of 'Brian!' Satisfied that we had not been surprised this time, Ross wanders off.

'Right Brian, why don't you boys go out,' my sister is talking. 'You can show Chad, Brisbane…get to know each other.'

Excellent idea, we waved Shirl off as we headed into town with the taxi driver trying to converse in Malay. 'Well, Chad considering we are dressed in traditional Balinese dance costumes we should go to a club my Fijian friend, Ronnie, used to take me to.' *Mainly for Polynesian Islanders, Tongans, Samoans, Maoris and now two idiots.*

We'll fit in perfectly, as I had not disclosed to Chad that the general 6 foot plus, 18 stone of solid muscle Islanders had only stopped BBQing Europeans last week. I knew the two non-six foot whiteys would be perfectly safe.

I'm at the bar ordering us drinks, Chad is in the pool room. I scan the room to see if any of my new PNG brothers have travelled into town.

Back when I had a job in Mackay, I had entered into the New Guinean brotherhood, up in North Queensland. Thirsty, due to the insane heat, you couldn't go outside without 'sunnies;' it was so blinding. I had entered a bar with a local reputation that was unknown to me. That was to change rapidly as the barman grabbed my forearm and whispered to me, 'Be very, very careful. No white guy, except for me has entered this bar…ever! These boys are extremely volatile with a few drinks in them.'

'Don't worry,' I assured him, 'the Scots with a few drinks in them are much the same, perfect match. *'Tis better to live one day as a lion than a thousand days as a sheep'* I said unconvincingly. 'Christ good luck mate, you're gonna need it,' he reassured me back.

I head over to a table of New Guineans.

'Hey bra, take a seat, where you from?' We have a few drinks and exchange stories of our differing and similar cultures. It's fascinating, I tell them that the Scots go to war wearing skirts, they love this.

'Hey Bra, so tough they can dress like women, kill the enemy, use a baking rolling pin instead of a spear!' They joke with me.

The boys laughing together 'Hey Bra, you should come over to Papua, we show you around.'

'Hah,' I joke back, 'you boys would have me boiling in a pot, in no time, see if I tasted like Haggis.' They find this hilarious. 'Hey, you're all right for a white fella!'

Another group enters and my alarm bell starts to tingle, the mood has darkened. It's confirmed when one shouts, 'What's the fucking whitey doin here?'

'Hey brother, you better leave now, we have some bad blood. Maybe we visit Scotland, take about three years in the dugout,' he jokes.

'I'm in Brisbane, if you're ever visiting, look me up. There's a bar my Fijian flatmate goes to, the Kookaburra.'

'Yeah bra, we know it, maybe we catch up?'

Now, with the alarm bell on full blast, I head over to the barman. He whispers, 'I think your *lion day pass* has just expired, get out now these two groups hate each other. This is going to kick mate.'

'Here,' I hand him an imaginary pass, 'there's still a few hours left as a lion.' He grins, the 6-inch scar dancing across his face.

'Fuck yeah, no worries...I have Sharon.'

'Sharon?' I ask quizzically.

'Yeah mate, my sawn of Shotty, Sharon. She'll keep me sweet mate.'

'There it is!'

'What is?' asks the lion behind the bar.

'My cue to get the fuck out of here!' Resisting the urge to sprint and crash through the window bleating like a sheep, I make my way to safety. The last thing I saw as the shouting erupted, was the big barmen reaching under the counter...probably to wake Sharon up.

I hail a taxi and dive in the back.

'Where to mate?'

'Any fucking-where mate!'

Driving, 'What were you doing in that crazy bar?' he looks back.

'Going for a cold beer,' I replied. *I thought to myself, being a sheep would do nicely for a thousand days, try stay alive. Bugger the one-day lion bit!*

Back to the present, in Brisbane, I survey the club. There's no sign of my New Guinean brothers, probably still in that fight.

'Ah Bro, where are you coming from dressed like that?' Sammy the Samoan's cousin 40 times removed and covered in face tattoos is looking four feet down at my fine cotton sarong with bright pink flowers running through it. 'Bali mate, traditional wedding, very cultural and no misappropriation whatsoever.' The giant grunts, 'Were you the bride?'

'No,' I sigh, 'the bridesmaid.'

The giant rolls his eyes, 'Fucking idiot!'... walks off.

I take the drinks over. Chad is in a heated discussion with an immense Islander. Chad is accusing the huge man of cheating and that he obviously doesn't understand the Queens rules. I'm making cutting signs over my neck signalling 'SHUT the fuck up, or we're both dead, fool' moves. Chad, oblivious to the cannibalistic nature of his foe, carries on relentlessly.

Now, my first mistake was assuming that:

a. Chad, who I had just met, was normal

b. That he would not be a complete idiot after a few drinks

c. Understand the dire nature of pissing off Islanders.

Within half an hour, Chad had hit three strikes. The huge man strikes Chad, not too hard, just as a warning shot. I instinctively, sarong and all, jump on Jake the Muss' twin brother's back, ripped with muscles. I cannot help admire the sheer breadth of the man-beast. Both my arms were fully extended as he shook me off like a dog scratching a flea. Exiting quickly, after slamming face first into the wall and sliding down, we make a break for the stairs.

Followed immediately by our escort. Crawling up the stairs next to each other in our beautiful pink and turquoise sarongs, we are being slapped over the head individually, like a couple of naughty children. I was grateful the man-monster was just showing us the door for Chad's naïve disrespect. It could have been so much worse.

Outside, impressed, I thank Chad for nearly getting us both killed on day one of his visit. I would sit him down and educate him by watching *Once Were Warriors*, temper his death wish. 'Chad!' I said, as if scolding a naughty, demented child 'What the fuck were you thinking? Just one of his arms was the size of your whole body, and he had two of those beauties, just in case you hadn't noticed.'

I didn't think Shirley would be too pleased if I returned with Chad's head wedged up his own arse. The "Save Chad re-education program" would have to start immediately. At least enjoy day two of their holiday.

Back home. Let the lesson begin, ah here it is, my laser pointer. PowerPoint presentation begins. 'Here we have Jake,' my pointer lasers over the muscles for emphasis. 'He's a Maori, and with minimum effort, he will kill you. Here's a pic of my mate Sammy the Samoan, he will also kill you, let's be brief. The Tongans, Fijians and PNG boys can, and will, also ALL kill you.' Lesson over. Keep it simple. Avoid death.

Daniel arrives a few days later. I sit him down; put *Once Were Warriors* on just to make sure that the event a few nights back is not repeated. Especially not in a pink sarong. Jeans and a t-shirt would be just fine and running away screaming was also perfectly fine too.

Our first vacation stop is my favourite place, Fraser Island. The largest sand island in Australia. Only accessible by four-wheel drive. Beautiful freshwater lakes internally, surrounded by rain forest and wild dingoes. Four of us head off with another four backpackers. Three days, travel and camp, self-drive jeep.

The first night we set up camp and get to know each other through the "Can game", introduced by the two German backpackers. Who knew they had invented the eighth wonder of the world. Get all volunteers, the coerced and blackmailed into a circle, shake the can of beer, first time round hit the can same place with forehead once, second round twice, and so on. Eventually, after receiving the award for "most idiotic cause of permanent brain damage", the can splits and beer spurts all over the place. You then have to take a swig, hit it how many time the round is, then chuck to next brain damaged victim. When the pressure runs out, whoever it lands at pulls the ring, downs the remaining beer. Think pass the parcel for the mentally impaired. Dan and I stay up late, watch dingoes prowling on the beach, the early morning swim is discouraged by a 10-foot manatee with its whole back tail bitten off, lying very dead on the beach. This is Tiger shark country.

We stagger back in the pouring rain, pass out in the tent shared with Shirl and Chad. Selflessly leaving the tent door open so as to encourage flooding from the cyclone. Shirl and Chad eventually have to swim for safety. Dan and I, at the top, higher half of the tent, have a nice dry lie in.

Shirley, cursing her lack of preparation re: a waterproof sleeping bag, snorkel and flippers and poor choice of siblings, swears to never go camping again. We head off to Lake Mackenzie. Halfway there, the four-wheel drive jeep comes to a shuddering halt.

I start the engine and pump the accelerator a few times, nothing. We wait for about an hour, when along comes another jeep. I'm in the driver's seat and can't get a good look at the owner. I can hear the offer of help in a strong Queensland accent and a flash of a cowboy hat. A tow rope is attached. I put the jeep in neutral and then just on sand tracks, the annual Fraser inaugural four-wheel drive Rally starts.

The "rescue" jeep in front shoots off with six in the back screaming, Dan sobbing in the passenger seat and one idiot holding on for dear life to the steering wheel. We are dragged hurtling through the bush dirt track. About 40 minutes later, which feels more like 40 years, we stop by an old garage. The man who has just tried to kill us gets out and comes over to the driver's side window. I would have rolled the window down but I can't prize my hands off the steering wheel.

He opens the door. 'G'day…did you enjoy the ride!'

The six in the back finally thud to the floor now that the zero gravity has stopped. The six-foot four Australian lunatic is all hair and wild staring eyes. I stammer, 'Fuck, just what the FUCK?'

'Yes mate, Dwayne's the name. I used to pull the stock cars out at the races when they got all mashed up. Before that, I was a rally driver. Travelled all over Australia, desert rallies mainly. Now I own *Hillbilly's Towers* with my son,' nods at a smaller mini-me cowboy with the same crazy eyes and unhinged persona. 'We "rescue" rally cars out bush.'

I looked at his madness… 'No shit,' I said!

I thought Johnny from *The Shining* had only suffered a mild psychosis (with that axe) compared to Dwayne's general mental constitution. He was off the chart. I had seen that look somewhere before? I looked in the rear-view mirror. Ah yes, there it is…thanks to demented Dwayne's tow from HELL!

'What's wrong with him?' He looks over at Dan. 'He looks like he's had a Cane Toad shoved up his arse!'

Dan with fingers embedded in the dashboard. 'Don't worry about him mate, he's just in mid-scream.' Dwayne acknowledges the condition, 'No worries, seen it before. He'll be all right in a day or two.'

One of the Germans in the back starts to sob uncontrollably. The Queenslander looks suspiciously in the back, 'Is that bloody emotion mate?'

'Nah mate, no need to phone QES, he's a bloody German, still upset at the 2-0 war result.'

'Fair dinkum, we gave those Nazi's a good licking,' walks off happy. Jumps in the tow truck, then hollers over 'Toodle loo,' then speeds off on two wheels, to "save" some other stranded, soon to be terrified backpackers.

A couple of days later, after Shirl and Chad had qualified for their open water tent diving ticket, courtesy of the selfless acts of her brothers letting the tent "air-out" in the monsoonal rains at night, we headed home.

Leaving Shirl and Chad to recover from pneumonia in a nice dry bed back in Toowong, Brisbane, Dan and I head over to Surfers Paradise, my old hunting ground. We stay in a Backpackers that doesn't have a lifetime ban imposed on me. There, next to a faded old wanted poster of myself, is an invite to a waterfall trek, $20 all you can drink. I say to Dan, we'll have some of that.

The little minibus full off backpackers makes its way through the bush to the start of the Trek. Dan and I are concerned there may be one of those recurring Australian droughts and for survival reasons only, are making light weight of the cooking wine. Three litres each swirling around us, we arrive.

Eventually, the two of us, 40 minutes later, catch up with the other backpackers who have been running away in tears after our delightful minibus chat and rugby songs. Trust us to get the local Bible group travelling from Minnesota.

We head down to the lower waterfall and jump in the cool water from about 20 feet. Inebriated, my fear had packed its bags and caught a taxi back to the hostel, along with his good mates' sense and sensibility. They had been sent home by "all you can drink" wine.

I somersaulted in.

A niggling doubt had started to creep in, that one of the two parties had definitely booked the wrong trip. Had we just consumed six litres of their Holy Communion wine? Looking around at the scowls, I knew I was onto something. No worries, I would sing them a nice rugby song on the way back, cheer them up. Tell Dan of my vocal intentions. 'Superb idea!' he confirms. Musing to ourselves, singing really could bring people together. 'Stick your log in a frog boys…shag a Wallaby,' I started to practice.

I knew they would be touched. It would be a beautiful moment.

The trek leader then took us up to the top of the waterfall, where we have a few drinks and enjoy the scenery. Drinking the rest of the Bible groups' rations in case they strayed off the righteous path and discovered fun, I felt invincible. William Henley's poem *Invictus* came to mind. *I am the master of my fate: I am the captain of my soul.*

My internal organs worried about their fate and who was bloody in charge are furiously writing a group letter of complaint. The synapses fire and the letter duly arrives at the *out of order* sign on Brain's door.

The leader stands up and making a point of showing off, leaps off a small rock, feet first into the pool 70 foot below. Obviously done many times, this is his party trick. Something is definitely up. What I thought was a walking aid is a sceptre, he put down his six-foot cross that he had been dragging up the hill and when he had de-robed, his magnificent speedos were emblazoned with *Jesus loves you*.

I made a mental note to check that poster when we got back, the double vision from that Samoan slap last week was causing havoc.

As he made his way back from the near-perfect jump, the diving priest is not expecting his brethren to leap like lemmings into the pool of death too. Nor his insurance company for that matter.

Excited, I have stripped off to my underpants. Fortunately for all that is decent in the world and keeping the Americans' religious beliefs intact, I had been demonstrating the bushfire to some clients a couple of days back. A bikini wax was therefore not required. I looked glorious, my burn patches all over my body were starting to heal and my missing eyebrow was starting to grow back nicely.

The Father looked on, concerned. 'So, you jump off that little rock, keep your body straight, legs together if you want to have children in the future,' he instructs me. 'I really, really don't think you should mate!'

After convincing him that I too was a high cliff diving expert, with at least 40 jumps under my Y-fronts, he reluctantly conceded.

The group who had booked the correct trip start to pray, *thy lord is thy Sheppard*. The priest splashes holy water from a vial.

'Good luck mate, we'll pray that we hear a splash and not a splat.'

'Thanks, Father.'

Feeling reassured, I scramble to the little rock. I could hear Dan, 'Brian bro, I don't think this is one of your better ideas?'

'Dan, don't worry, I haven't made a good judgement call yet.'

I look down; the waterfall drops into a circular hole. I can't see where I'm supposed to jump or land. The expert hollers over, just aim about four feet out. Should be fine.

I launch, to Dan saying 'I really, REALLY don't think…' The bible group now five octaves higher chanting, *As he cliff dives through the valley of death…lord guideth theeee*. The last word is a shrill scream.

Down I go, the expertise of my pool hopping days forgotten. I'm going down on my back. I eventually hit the water like a nuclear bomb. A full back flop! It's like five of those Islanders have just hit me, with the biggest sledgehammer, full force. The air is knocked clean out, winded I'm immediately sober, feeling nauseous. I'm going to be sick.

I lie for a few minutes, floating on the surface like a stunned jellyfish, unable to move. I put my arm out and touch a large boulder sticking out of the water. I've missed it by about three feet.

At least my double vision has cleared either through the atomic impact or the fear (which now sober) has finally made an appearance. A bit bloody late for the show, I scold it.

You can talk, three bloody litres of Holy Communion wine, fear scolds back.

I straddle to a little pebble beach to be sick.

Learning lesson: Next time don't take an "all you can drink" tour literally, travel only with non-religious backpackers (so as not to consume their communion wine rations). Wax appropriately and stick to paddling pools from now on.

Oh and listen to Dan and don't let fear call a taxi, EVER!

Back at the Backpackers, the two of us are looking at the posters next to each other. If I hadn't been Quad-focal from that slap, I would have spotted the error of our ways.

First poster:
Baptism with Brother Mick, $20 donation, free complimentary glass of Holy Communion wine.
Lord be praised. Water Baptism in the Holy Trinity waters.
GOD BE WITH THY SOUL.
Newcomers welcome.

Next poster:
Backpackers night, $20 all you can drink wine.
Bring your togs ya bloody Gallahs. Diving compo in the pool.
GOD SAVE YA DRONGOS.
New Pommie Bastards welcome.

We look at each other. 'Damn it Dan, will we ever be on the "Right side of Right?!"

Dan in return, 'Nope.'

18
Thailand: Safe Hands, Act 1

God in a serious mood, 'Friendship is a very noble thing. A good friend, reliable, trustworthy and above all safe, is a true treasure. Take the Norse Gods, I would say Odin is a great friend, drinks too much for sure, but boy can we have a good time. Even Loki, if nothing else is highly amusing, so naughty stirring up all that trouble in the corridors.

Yes, it is truly a gift to have a friend who has your back, Charles. I've unscrewed the door buzzer so we can have a quick game; Odin is coming over later, more of a cribbage God than a chess one.'

'Brilliant!' Charles exclaims. They both sit down with two steaming mugs of Horlicks.

White Pawn takes Black Castle. They both look at each other. 'Oh dear, we didn't see that one coming?'

'Looking for obvious signs of insanity or dementia, could you repeat that?' I asked confused.

Chris (Firthy's mum), 'I'm just so relieved and happy that Andrew is travelling with you. I know he will be kept safe and well in your capable hands. I will definitely sleep soundly at night now.' Chris is thanking me profusely.

I thought to myself, you might want to get a prescription of horse tranquillizers just to be on the safe side. Thailand is our first destination.

That's it, I must look harder, there must be a sign, a nervous twitch, rolling eyes, frothing at the mouth, something? Had there been an outbreak of rabies, had Chris been bitten? I looked for bite marks, nothing. Chris must be having some mental relapse or at the very least suffering from amnesia. How could she have forgotten the mayhem and general criminal destruction of the last five years?

'That's very kind of you, don't worry Andrew is in safe hands.' Smiling, relieved Chris and Jim give us a lift to Brisbane airport and see us off.

'Now, remember Firthy, safe hands I promised your mum. Get the Tequilas in, it's going to be a long flight.'

One final check of the local papers, no mention of rabies. Relieved that Chris had avoided the outbreak, we get sailor drunk.

Bangkok is best described as utterly chaotic, think manic beehive with the Queen on her period, shouting orders outrageously drunk and high on LSD. General disorder is the dish of the day. Trying to figure out how it all works is utterly pointless; you have to go with the flow. It is definitely not for those inflicted with OCD. You would be sent back a gibbering wreck the very next day, marigolds in tow. Sectioned for life.

It's bonkers and that's exactly why it's a brilliant city.

The first thing that has never even occurred to Thai people is Health and Safety. If H&S officers ventured around Thailand, even just one small village, the paperwork involved would make the bible look like a post-it note. Mopeds with six family members and a pig, even in the middle of the city, is not unusual. Many times the pig is steering, the 2-year-old is on the brakes, Mum is putting her makeup on and Dad is reading the paper. Miraculously, they weave in and out of traffic without a care in the world. To try to drive in a straight line would end in disaster and screw the whole system up. If foolishly attempted, you would be arrested for following the Highway Code and charged with reckless sanity. A capital crime in Thailand.

Firthy looking at the guide book says, 'We should stay on Koh San Road, nice and cheap, plenty of bars.' We hail a Tut-Tut, greeted by an 80-year-old wizened man with one gold tooth. It's raining, the driver puts the wipers on and the blood starts to clear off the window. The tourist slides off the little bonnet, a couple of bumps later and we are off.

Koh San Road has the speedo dial arrow terminally stuck on full bonkers. It's heaving with backpackers, hookers, transvestites, lady boys, you name it and this road has it. It's like a mash-up of the bar in Star Wars. I'm expecting Chewbacca and Jabba the Hut to walk past at any moment, both looking at a tourist map.

The small street vendors are selling BBQ'd grasshoppers, sugared crickets and to my utter delight, dried gecko tongue. The noise is like a crescendo of drunk seagulls fighting over a discarded fish wrapper. The utter chaos and manic crowd is delightfully intoxicating.

'C'mon Firthy, let's get a room and then hit the bar.'

'Too right, this place rocks,' Firthy laughs back.

We book a room or more like a mattress enclosed in a cell. It's black and has obviously had more sinners on it than Hugh Hefner, judging by the body fluid stains of the last 20 years. We have sleeping bags, it's cheap so fuck it, we make a cross sign and enter. Drop rucksacks off, let's party.

At the bottom of this fine establishment is a large open bar, full of hookers. Unwittingly, we have booked ourselves into the largest whorehouse on the road. We sit/lie down in sunken seats next to a low table, order a half bottle of Sang hip whisky each. It comes with a little silver bucket full of ice, its $5.

An hour later, we are chatting with some German backpackers, who recommend this crazy bar on another street down a few alleys. Whisky bulletproof jackets now fully zipped up, we head for it.

It's a large open bar, music blasting; looks pretty cool. We order some more whiskies when suddenly this high-pitched screaming comes from the corner. Six wild banshees have spotted us and are throwing people out of their way to get their manicured hands on us. All high heels and definitely no knickers, we were in trouble. Firthy had been out in the bush for a while and the sight of six Thai girls making a beeline for us could only be a result. Hold on, one was about 6 foot 4; I was beginning to smell a rat.

The six beauties screamed to a halt in front of us, hysterical delight. The full medical examination could now start in earnest, every orifice was examined. I was really hoping to have my prostate checked in my 50s, not 20s. The huge hands were now examining my teeth to check for age and authenticity. I garbled to Firthy, 'Firthy I stink theeyyre meen,' the large finger still investigating my mouth, lip pulled back.

'Whaaat?' Firthy also in oral examination.

I half snarl, saliva dripping down my chin, 'I fink they men,' finger removed. 'Firthy, they're men, FFS.'

German Bastards had set us up. 'Are there any weapons handy to save ourselves and our virginity?'

We equip ourselves with a fork and spoon off the bar. Culinary utensils pointing outwards, fend them off back-to-back, a manicured hand with bright red nail polish tried again to break our defences, quick groin rush, all my training had to kick in. It was like the charge of the drag brigade. Firthy, starting to weaken. 'God, they look so bloody gorgeous.'

'Be strong, Firthy my good man, we can get through this. Don't look at their eyes look at their man hands and Adam's apple, not their new implants.'

We inch our way out of the bar, with significantly less clothes on than when we arrived. The Germans have followed us and are absolutely pissing themselves with laughter. 'Ja, willkommen to Thailand,' high five each other and march off goose-stepping gleefully.

'Bastards!' I shout, 'who won the bloody war anyway,' to their departing backs. Both of us stand there in our shredded boxer shorts, spoon and fork ready, covered in scratches. Firthy has a hair extension between his teeth and I, a false fingernail sticking out of my forehead. I wondered if we had really won that awful war after all.

Wryly I notify Firthy, that we are now part of the "Me Too" campaign, join the next protest march. Bloody Germans, General Montgomery would have been furious, we had been squarely outfoxed.

With our dignity of the highest order upheld, we hobble back to the whorehouse.

Few more mad days in Bangkok, time to travel to Chang Mai; we take the bus, it's cheap. The correlation between cheap and mortality in Thailand is a direct one. We get on the bus, with a load of other backpackers, the air-con has packed in and it's stinking hot. To aid his thirst and cool down from the heat the bus driver is drinking straight out of a half-bottle of Sang Hip whisky. He was about 60, his age was a comfort. The driver must be one of those Thai master drunk drivers that the monks are always praying in vain for. If sober, driving in a straight line would result in us all being dead. The driver…immediately arrested for code violations.

We fall asleep, it's about 1 am. Suddenly the whole bus literally jumps to the left, as a massive truck, lights flashing, hurtles past with horn on max. All the guys on the right are now sitting on the left passenger's laps.

Damn it Firthy, I knew we would be on the wrong side of right again. The bus swerves a few times, and then pulls over. Engine still running, we wait a few minutes, nothing. Firthy and I go have a look. The driver has passed out and is starting to snore; there are three empty half bottles of whisky at his feet. Shit, the prick has passed out and we are in the middle of nowhere. Sod it, we'll have to wait till he regains consciousness.

The whole bus sweltering to death waits for nearly two hours. We finally wake him up, splash some water on him and carry on with the journey. The next time we took the bus we came prepared with four kilos of Valium (happily supplied over the counter, at any local pharmacy); the trip was a dream. Not even a heart flutter, even after the second driver passed out at 80 mph.

Arriving Chang Mai in one piece, we had booked a tour. Joining us were two boys from London, who were now going to give the group of eight a masterclass in the rhyming slang of the cockney language, where everything has a rhyming second meaning, that no one understood? 'Oi Geezer, I don't Adam and Eve it (believe it)! I, is not getting me shiny white Dinky Doos (shoes), all mucka! Me plates of meat (feet) will feel like they're brown bread (dead). You're having a Bubble Bath (laugh). This can only lead to Barney Rubble (trouble) the cockney finished looking down at his brand-new white plimsolls and the swirling river we had to cross on foot. Firthy and I shot each other a sharp look of annoyance.

We had booked ourselves on a three-day hill trek, visit the local hill tribes and these two Cockney chancers had turned up in their finest club gear. It would involve elephant riding, rafting, jungles and crossing many streams, rivers, waterways et cetera, and these two peacocks had come fully prepared all in white with their plimsolls on.

'I'm a DJ,' he informed the whole of North Thailand.

'Is there a cure for that?' I replied.

'In Laandon, I'm a DJ.'

'Great, so what are you doing in Chang Mai?'

'Came for the Opium mate, hear it's rife.'

'And the trek bit,' I queried.

'What trek?' the disco duet replied baffled.

The rain started to come down jungle style, like a large bucket being poured out in one go. The blonde Cockney's perm started to frazzle and little coils of hair started to spring all over his head like little jack in the boxes. The large smiley icon on his t-shirt, which was obviously all the drugs craze back in Blighty, didn't look so blissfully pilled out in the downpour.

Fortunately, there were other backpackers; a French couple that I could just scrape by with my Franglo chat. Thierry turned out to be a Gallic madman, so we got on great, make up for the two half-anchors. One of which was now starting to cry, something about a lost washbag and missing teeth whitener.

Firthy and I, by this stage had gone full Vietnam, bandanas, cam-cream, spoon and fork at the ready. All we needed now was a pair of ornaments for our necklaces. I nudge Firthy pointing at blondie's ears. 'Those bobby dazzlers would be perfect when polished,' I confided. They clock our intentions and start crying again. Will someone please slap the DJs, a couple of slaps later we cross the raging river.

First Hill tribe, I'm squatting on the Thai equivalent of a 'thunder box' with gravity as the flush. A little hut with a hole cut crudely in the floor, which hangs 30 feet off the hillside. Looking down, I can see (in-between my knees) 300 years of green curry fertilising the lush jungle. I then look at the wall opposite my squat, a piece of newspaper is stuck on the wall, it's faded yellow, all in Thai hieroglyphics. I can see a photograph. It's a picture of Dwight D. Eisenhower. Looks like the Korean War. I look at top corner, 1953. Fuck me, the local villagers had been squatting here looking at the same piece of paper for the last 40 years. Wait until they see a full newspaper, their minds would be blown. Better keep the moon landing secret or we would be accused of witchcraft and burned alive. Quickly now, I tell the rest that we are now living in 1953, any mention of 1954 onwards must not be mentioned at any cost. We could all end up in a large boiling vat accompanied by chilli, garlic, ginger, fish sauce, coconut milk, galangal and basil.

No sweat for Firthy and I, we had just come from Queensland which was still living in 1853.

Next day, once the DJs had re-whitened their teeth and plimsolls, we headed down the river on the bamboo raft to the next village. The two-man raft consisted of 10 poles strapped together and generally under 10 inches of water at any one time. The torrential rain had washed all manner of debris and organic matter with it into the dark swirling mass. A bloated pig overtakes us, all four trotters bobbing in the air. We rise to the challenge. Pole faster, we beat it to the next rapids and high five each other. A thought came to me as the pig slalomed like a true pro down the rapids.

I would write to the local Thai Green party representative, "Use dead pigs to traverse rivers". Sit on the upside-down floating pig, use pole to cross river. Once crossed, you could then cook up the pig and eat it. Full re-cycling complete, zero-carbon wastage. I congratulated myself on my own genius. I would send a carrier pigeon to the party headquarters in the morning with a self-explanatory diagram. Excited, we poled on avoiding the flotsam and jetsam of empty Lloyd Grossman and Uncle Ben's Thai curry paste jars.

Next couple of days we would ride elephants, eat fabulous cuisine and the DJs would accomplish their goal of meeting Dr Opium. On the last night the DJs head off to get their hits with a wizened 900-year-old Thai with no teeth, eyes rolling, cackling manically, is well known as the "Doctor". I thought his deteriorating constitution was a great advert for the mental health benefits of Opium. Ignoring the obvious warning signs, the Londoners return absolutely wired.

'I fort it would be dead funney like if this diamond geeza and me had a compo on. I won at 23 hits Of Opium,' summarily throws up. 'Nice one,' says geeza two, 'he's been proper Moby dick.' Pushing my irritation buttons, 'What the fuck are you two half-anchors talking about? '

They crash out, snoring in between being sick. We all agreed, what a pair of "Moby dicks, they were acting like proper pricks".

Next day, they have to dye their plimsolls green in order to colour match their complexions. They moan and groan for the whole day. We return to Chang Mai, the two London boys look like they had been in a Vietcong POW camp for the last 10 years. It all went '*Pete Tong!*' (wrong) They commiserated. Crying, holding each other, they depart.

One more hell drive back to Bangkok, with all of the passengers screaming every few minutes. Firthy, I and the bus driver are all on Valium, blissfully unaware. We fly out in 24hr hours, plenty of time.

Firthy to me, 'Let's get a few whiskies in, we've got ages.'

23 hours later.

'Fuck, fuck, drive we give you fifty Baht,' throw money at Tut-Tut driver. He's on one wheel screaming through Bangkok on the way to the airport, smoking three fags, chatting happily away on the phone. Shit, we're going to miss the flight.

'How is that fucking possible? Firthy, how?'

'Well, there was the time in Hervey Bay, Toowoomba, Brisbane, Stradbroke Island, now Thailand, need I go on.'

'Damn it, we have so much prior history!'

Out of the countless airport journeys I have attempted, I had always been curious as to how people ended up being driven through the terminal on those golf cart buggies. I had assumed it must be white privilege, royalty or had the driver's favourite daughter been kidnapped? Now I bloody knew. You had to be a complete idiot.

Amber light flashing and the Thai driver making a Formula 1 car look slow, we hurtle through departures, absolutely intoxicated. When we arrived at the desk, the security had seen the state of us and in true beautiful Thai style, instead of ending up in the clink, we had been escorted via the buggy to the plane. They had actually held the plane back for 20 minutes so we could board. They wanted to make extra sure we left Thailand for good, start the process of rebuilding its shattered reputation.

'You leave Thailand now! You NEVER come back!' The security guard scolds both of us! The guard was making absolutely sure we got on the flight; save his people.

The dirty looks that we got as we made our way unsteadily down the aisle, I will never forget. Firthy and I fasten our seatbelts and summarily pass-out to 600 angry staring eyes.

In my dream, I can see Chris, Firthy's anxious mum, tossing and turning in her restless sleep, a cold sheen of sweat on her brow. It was either the rabies taking hold or the beginning of a niggling doubt. 'Safe hands,' she murmurs, 'safe hands,' rolls over and starts to snore.

Bahrain: next stop.

19
Bahrain: Safe Hands, Act 11

Arriving from Thailand, Firthy and I regain consciousness as the plane makes its final descent. The 600 still angry eyes follow us off the aircraft. There's just no pleasing some people, I tell Firthy.

As soon as we enter the airport, I feel a sense of paranoia. Every CCTV camera has swivelled and is pointing at me accusatorily. I knew Colonel Jones was behind those controls, growling ominously. We would be displayed on a large monitor with a big red target on both our foreheads. The Colonel had been following my moves (around different airports) ever since "that incident" with the shorts. Jack's goal: to forewarn his security mates; keep mankind safe.

It was a bit tricky for the Colonel and his global team of elites, as I had two passports British and Australian. So in the old days (with old technology), I could leave one country on one and enter the next country with the other, with no one any the wiser. Handy if I needed to disappear. Jack Jones had really taken that aviator Top Gun jibe so personally, I mused, looking up at his cameras.

I was annoyed. He HAD bloody looked like Maverick's dad!

We jump in a taxi, knowing my parents would forget to pick us up, head to Dad's headquarters (the British club sports bar). Meet up with Mum and Dad.

'What are you doing here, Brian?'

'What do you mean dearest parents? Firthy and my good self are over for a few weeks, show him the sights and generally behave ourselves. Remember?'

A few moments silence, a quick sip of their pints of Gin… 'Of course son, fancy a few coldies?'

'Too bloody right, we're parched.'

A couple of days later, Dan has turned up too, unannounced. Taxi from the airport to the Brit club bar later, we catch up. Ivan's* in town too, says Dan. One of his good mates, and a certifiable lunatic. Ivan had a guest membership courtesy of her majesty's prison service. You could never tell whether he was on parole or not. This time he was and had escaped to Bahrain. Excellent, give him a phone, let's hit the Town!

Ivan on the phone, 'Yes, I've borrowed my mum's car, come and pick you boys up.' Ivan arrives in his bright pink mother's Avon lady car.

'Fuck off Ivan, we are never going to get laid with that dayglow piece of shit!'

'Shut up, I got it up to 112 mph on the way here. Look I took a photo of the speedo.' Sure enough, the pink crap-mobile did indeed have an engine.

'Ivan, this is Firthy, my Ozzie mate,' intros over. 'Right, where we going?'

'Let's hit that dodgy Filipino bar in the old souk, cheap drinks.' Even cheaper dates no doubt, we all agreed.

'Sounds delightful, let's go.'

Ivan handbrake turns into the parking place at 40mph. 'What speed did you reach that time?'

Looks at the camera, '123 mph.' We leave the smoking Avon lady car and head into the bar/club.

There's a Filipino band in the corner and the rest of the audience are Arabs. Proper dodge, just as Ivan had promised. Firthy and Dan grab a table. Ivan and myself at the bar-counter when he tells me, 'Let's have some fun with your mate, proper introduction to Bahrain.'

'Righto, what you thinking?'

'Let's spike his drinks,' looks at the top shelf. 'Every drink we buy him, we'll work our way along that shelf; see how far he can go.'

'Ivan, you are truly a son only a mother could love.'

Ivan the big scouser with broken nose replies, 'Thanks mate. Better let Dan in on it too,' we agreed.

Right, Firthy starts on Bacardi and coke plus 100 proof Tequila. We are going to cover the globe's finest alcoholic beverages, think of it as wine tasting with a "twist of meths". Firthy, blissfully unaware of the *World alcohol tasting championship* we had organised, gets stuck in. About two hours in and nearly halfway through the top shelf, we drag Firthy away from the 40 dancing Arabic men.

'Wow, super friendly these Bahraini men,' he exclaims delightedly. We all throw each other a sharp look and roll our eyes. I would explain later to Firthy how friendly they could get if you weren't on your fucking guard.

Two-thirds of the shelf consumed, Firthy at 17 stone and six foot two is dancing on the table. 'Fuck,' I say to Dan, 'if he swings off that chandelier the whole roof will come down.' *It's too bloody late now, we have created a monster.*

Next thing, Firthy jumps off the table and rushes the Filipino band, the four-foot three group scatters all high heels and eyelashes, screaming in every direction. Big Firthy, 'Come 'ere, I just want to give you a big Aussie hug and say G'day, it's my first week in Bahrain.' Security, huddled in corner terrified, starts to become brave as one of the Filipinos band members goes over to scold them. Pointing at us angrily and getting even more hysterical, time to leave. We rescue Firthy from the microphone as he starts to sing *I come from a land downunder* and make a run for it.

The four of us are at the top of the solid marble stairs. Firthy suddenly trips and rolls down over and over again down the 40 odd steps, lies in a crumpled heap at the bottom. We look at each other, fuck I think we've killed him! I knew who was dead, me, when Chris (his mother) finds out. Safe hands and all. I would have to use those two passports go into hiding again.

Suddenly, Firthy springs back onto his feet. We look at each other, no fucking way!

He looks back up the stairs and yells, 'Where's the party at bastards?' trips over the lip of the door, falls backwards and crushes a four foot Filipino flat.

'Right, that's it, let's go right now!'

Outside, Firthy is leaning on a stranger's car when he staggers and rips off the wing mirror. We grab Firthy and bundle him into the bright pink Avon car, still holding the little mirror.

Then the three of us jump in. Ivan is making his own version of "room" by crashing it into the front car and then the back several times. As the bumper fell off and the exhaust became loose, we rattled off into the warm Bahrain night. We could just see through the back window, the angry Filipinos waving and yelling after trying to resuscitate their lead singer, Angel May.

'Well Firthy,' we said, 'welcome to Bahrain, have a nice day.'

'Ivan,' I said, 'you know you're fucked, right?'

'Why?'

'Well, we are in a bright pink Avon Lady car that was visible from outer space, with your mum's address and phone number blazoned all over it. Wouldn't take a genius to figure who the owner is?'

'Damn it, lucky I stole it, she doesn't know.'

'Well, when the Bahrain SWAT team raid her house she soon will. Isn't she also dating a Major in the BDF (Bahrain Defence Force)?'

'No, a General,' Ivan clarifies.

'Ivan, my good man, you are so dead. Not by the General by the way, but your mother. She has one of the worst tempers ever witnessed by mankind,' we all shudder.

'Shit, you're right and I've only just arrived, it's her birthday tomorrow. I will take it out to the desert and torch it. Say it was nicked by someone with a vendetta against the company's hair products. Anyway, it's a shit car, doing mum a favour. It would only be worth £500 if there was a £450 hooker in the boot.' Dan and I throw each other a look, 'I really hope that trunk is empty?' I whisper over to Dan.

Anyway Ivan, 'Kill two birds with one stone,' I offered, 'You could pick up a jerry can of gasoline AND a birthday present at the garage; save two trips, one on foot. But first, you can drop us off, before you get pulled and Firthy bleeds to death.'

As the image of Ivan torching his mother's only means of making a living vivid in my mind, I bandage Firthy up and escort him to bed.

'Everything all right dear?' Mum shouts from the master bedroom.

'Couldn't have gone any better, Firthy's had a ball. He's been dancing all night with the locals. He even bumped into a lovely Filipino lady.'

'Aw, that's nice dear.' Covering Firthy's mouth as he starts to sing *Once a jolly swagman,* I manage to drag him to his bed.

Two hours later, must be about 4 am I can hear what sounds like a small waterfall. I roll over and see Firthy, who should be in the next single bed is standing in the corner having a massive piss, whistling to himself. Once the *Waltzing Matilda* tune had finally stopped.

'You all right Firthy?'

'Never better mate,' jumps back into bed starts snoring.

I would phone Kenmore pharmacy, Queensland, first thing in the morning, where Firthy's mum picked up her usual prescriptions and inform them of the immediate change: from Horse to Elephant tranquilliser. Safe hands Brian, safe hands...

*Catching up with Ivan a few years later...I had another one of my infamous complete judgement fails. Insanely, I would invite Ivan along, as I was meeting up with an ex-girlfriend near where he lived. We could all go to the pub together. Ivan, being Ivan, then decided to flood the small Cheshire village's three pubs with several hundred pounds worth of counterfeit money. The dodgy notes made monopoly money look and feel like legal tender. It even managed to end up in the collection tin the following Sunday. My ex couldn't show her face for two years and suffice to say romance wasn't rekindled. Sorry, Nicola.

20
Making a Meal of It...Dinner's in the Dog

'Right,' says Charles, 'that's the kettle on. Isn't it funny how Man really strives day in day out, so that they can spend their weekends giving all their hard-earned money away to drinking establishments?'

God, 'They have to let their hair down sometimes. Look at you, your hair and beard are touching the floor!'

'Yes, but to escape reality, it's strange.'

'Maybe that is their reality,' God sighs.

'Look even animals like a drink, look at the wasps in summer, running amok, completely inebriated on cheap cider.'

'Amazes me they can find their way back to the nest,' Charles counters.

'Centuries of practice no doubt and a healthy fear of the Queen's wrath,' God replies.

'True, right let's play,' they both look nervously at the door. Nothing happens, they both sigh and relax.

Suddenly, there's a galloping noise, a neigh and they can hear squelching. Darwin now excited looks down at his bright yellow Wellington boots, starts tapping them together. 'Charles will you stop that, it's irritating. Here he comes.' A man in full red regalia enters, his right arm is tucked inside his tunic, a vast array of medals adorn his red jacket. Looking down his immaculately pressed white trousers there are a pair of bright pink Wellington Boots. The Iron Duke has entered.

'Well, well, what have we here, my lord, Charles, the rumours are true then? Chess, by Jove. You weren't playing that when I beat that trumped up pipsqueak Napoleon were you?'

God smiles enigmatically, 'What do we owe the pleasure, my great Duke?'

'Well, by Jove, I'm on a mission. I have heard a rumour that the Frenchies are about to launch another raid on one of ours, the damn cheek. So I'm sending in an expert that comes highly recommended.'

God, now suspicious, 'Recommended by whom?'

'Well, funny you should ask but a couple of nights back we were having the annual barracks bash when Loki came over for a chat.'

God, 'Not again, you better take a seat.' The Iron Duke squelches over. 'Charles, I love your Wellies.'

'Yours too,' Darwin replies.

Sitting, White Castle takes Black Rook. The Duke hollers, 'ATTACK!'

I wake up. I have the worst hangover I've ever experienced, yet again.

The hangover of death was nearly on par with the time that I had foolishly accepted a drinking challenge from a 70-year-old retired French Foreign Legionnaire. The result, an unscheduled visit to A&E.

I had accepted the attempt on my life with gusto. I had nailed 18 Tequilas in a row before; I would drink this 70-year-old French geriatric under the table. Think Waterloo I said to myself, channel Oli Reed, I would destroy him. Wellington could rest in peace; this victory against the French was in safe hands.

As the phrase "famous last words" started to cast doubt on my imminent triumph, the ex-foreign legionnaire began to order. 'Une, deux, trois,' pauses…to get his breath…

Hah, I've got this; even his medal of valour for saving those 312 orphans couldn't save him now. Wellington would have been so proud.

'Quatre, cinq, six,' all along the top shelf, points at a jug, the barman pours the six random spirits in. The soldier picks up the half-litre jug, smiles. 'Salute,' downs in one. 'Bon!'

Now suspicious, the voice in my head is getting louder. *I told you so, you're fucked!* Shut up, inner voice damn it…think Oli. I swig down the vile purple mix. The chances of my liver ever clearing this through departures to my pancreas were zero.

'Bon. Une, 'now' Deux, d'accord?'

'Oui,' I whimpered, now wait a minute Jimmy, I've been had. Barman places another jug. 'Salute,' the jug disappears. Now I'm in deep "merde". I just manage, trying not to gag, get the last drops down my gullet which is now in full revolt.

'Bon. Trois,' repeats the challenge. No fucking way, it's not even 2 pm yet. Every piece of organic matter that has a vested interest in me living is protesting in vain. My liver, pissed, has started singing, the room is swirling. Even the Iron Duke himself has raised the white flag and has galloped off back to blighty on his trusted steed.

I manage three, walk out of the bar into the bright daylight and summarily face plank into the gravel. An ambulance was called and I received six stitches for my complete lack of judgement.

So, today's learnings: if a French 70-year-old ex-special forces or the like challenges you to a drink-off, you politely decline and while their back is turned, scream 'KILLER SQUIRREL!' and flee.

Back to the present. The current hangover, however, is murder. I'm still fully clothed, I groan. I go into the bathroom (not my house) and go to wash my face. There is grease on my sleeve and shirt, on my chin too. I seriously need to floss. What the hell happened? We were heading out to celebrate the New Year? I look at my watch it's the 3rd of Jan. WTF?

So I get a phone call, it's Matt, 'It's New Year's Eve. Let's party big style, take some spirits up to the Tron (Edinburgh) and see in the New Year. Let's do it!'

Head up to town Tequila, Whisky, Vodka all consumed, we get trashed and see in the New Year. Dancing, people on each other's shoulders, a good time had by all into the early hours. 7 am, Matt, 'Hey let's keep the party going head up to mine in Glenrothes (Fife).

'Matt,' I said, 'isn't that twinned with Chechnya?'

'Yeah,' replies Matt, 'the Chechens were so disappointed when they found out?! They felt safer being bombed by the Russians, than coming to Fife for a day visit.'

'Sounds perfect, my good man!'

Holding each other up, 'Fife, it is!'

As we were manhandled off the train by the transport police, we had arrived. I thought to myself, *What could possibly go wrong again?*

We head to Matt's house. His mum is there, takes one look at us, has a little shriek and starts cooking with vigour. We have some life support food, a few drinks and a good laugh. At 8 pm we hit the town.

In the nightclub, Matt and I are on the dancefloor, literally on the floor. Doing the caterpillar and trying to breakdance…

As we leave, single yet again, we look at each other incredulously, where had we gone wrong? We so had that; resistance should have been futile. I would call for a public enquiry when we sobered up the following week. As Matt got his mojo back and started to chat up a lamppost, I made a break for it into the nearest rose bush, try and catch up on some much-needed sleep.

As I took my boots off to get comfortable in the -3 Scottish winter, Matt dragged me out by my ankles; his chat up lines to the inert object of light had been rejected. 'She's just playing hard to get,' Matt informs me, nonchalant. Picking myself up, I had no escape.

Matt wobbling exclaims, 'The party is not over yet!' Matt and I stagger and leave the boots in the hedge to sleep it off. Matt to me, 'I told you this was a brilliant idea.'

We have not slept in 48hrs. We head back to Matt's on foot, me literally. No taxi in their right mind will stop for us. We eventually get back to the sound of a cockerel.

Matt, says 'We've come this far, let's keep going. Get the Jack Daniels out.' I was in the future going to be Matt's best man (see "best man's speech") at his wedding, so to trust his sound judgement was folly.

Day 3, no sleep. Matt gets a phone call from his cousin Jimmy…who is having a party.

'Matt, how early can we go around?'

'3 pm.'

'We can make that.' I pick up my boots from the hedge first as we make our way to the party.

Arrive at the party, I'm starting to hallucinate. Matt is trying to chat with friends and relatives. About two hours in, I've been drinking whisky to keep the engine running but I'm fading fast. I'm also starving…ravenous.

I make beeline for the fridge; no one is in the kitchen. I open it. There is this massive roast on the bone, perfect. I don't want to look rude, so I subtly in my own eyes and inebriated mind keep going back time and time again, when the kitchen is free until I pick it clean.

Satisfied, I catch up with Matt, who is telling one of his elderly relatives a joke about prostitutes that should be exclusively reserved for hardened sailors. As the 80-year-old Auntie went into cardiac arrest, I rescued Matt. It was time to leave in a dignified manner, show some decorum. We stagger out, Matt wobbling looks at me confused.

'What is that on your face?'

Me, 'I have no idea? I can't even see.'

We both head back to Matt's home. Eventually, after three days, we crash out.

I finish in the bathroom and start to remember bits and pieces of our 72-hour binge, my serotonin completely stripped I feel death is fairly imminent. It's about 4 pm. I head downstairs. I shuffle into the kitchen where Matt and his mum are.

'What a state you two rocked in at!' Matt's mum scolds us. 'You'd better have a coffee and some paracetamol.

Anyway, I was just telling Matt, Jimmy's mum phoned earlier and you won't believe this! Seriously, the sick people out there. Utterly SICK! I was nearly ill when I heard it the first time!

At the party, some absolute animal went into the fridge and ate the dog's bone, stripped it clean! There were even gnawing marks where the monster had chewed it! The dog is furious.'

Me, under my breath, 'Oh crap!'

Matt looked at me, 'What do you mean, oh crap?' Matt groaned, 'No, seriously Brian you didn't?'

Matt's mum is also looking at me as well.

As I squeaked, 'I thought it was a leftover family roast. I was starving, it was a bit chewy but I managed.'

They both looked at each other, then at me and burst into hysterics. 'No way, Matt get the phone; wait until I tell the whole family. This is gold!' Matt rushes off to find the phone.

'Well, that's final then,' I said indignantly. 'I'm leaving Scotland for good, AGAIN!'

21
Great Escape. Kidnapped Morocco

Charles and God are contemplating death. 'It's all part of the cycle Charles, dying is as much a part of life as life itself. Intrinsically connected my good man. Also Charles, what about all your awards you are so eager to hand out? The cupboard would be empty and covered in dust. So you would definitely lose out on all your fun.'

'That's true,' says Charles subdued, 'just seems so final that's all.'

'Don't worry Charles, let's play, see if we can't cheer you up? Get that award handed out.'

Looking down, suddenly the room darkens. A Black chess piece, a King, starts to move...takes the White Queen.

God looks concerned, 'That doesn't bode well,' he murmurs. Charles lets out a slow whistle, 'Oh dear, that's a very "Ouija-board" like move, is it the "One that cannot be named", Voldem...'

God interrupts, 'Don't be so silly Charles. But yes, the dark one is amongst us.' They both shiver. A hissing sound starts from the corner. Hades shrouded in black glides over. They both look at each other, 'This is not good.' The three of them look down at the chessboard. God whispers, 'I'm not sure he is going to make it this time.'

We're both lying in a double bed sweating, it's hot...40 degrees plus. I need to make a potential life-changing decision. Mark, hyperventilating next to me, in total fear, bordering on abject terror. I can smell it, it's a familiar smell. I put my arm over him on his chest and whisper 'Breathe, be calm, relax, let me think.' I need to operate quickly, it's dire. Morocco, kidnapped, 1995.

If I get this wrong, we are both going to die, we both know this.

So I get a phone call, it's Mark. 'Fancy a trip around Spain, we can camp and see all the great places. Go for three months.'

'Mark mate, that sound great. Let's book a flight.'

Arrive in Madrid, we are going to head south through Seville, then across to Granada then up the East coast catch up with an old friend, Carlos from Australia (see Hervey Bay story).

Two months of sleeping on rocks with no sleeping bags and only the innards of a tent that collapsed every night, we were knackered. We had even resorted to using rocks as pillows. Freezing at night we just wore all our clothes, then by 8 am we had to remove them all as the pretend tent turned into an oven.

We were now in Cadiz, in the south.

'Hey Mark, you ever been to Morocco?'

'No.'

'C'mon, let's go. It will be fun and our rapidly depleting cash stock will last much longer; more beer money!'

'OK, sounds good.' Marks desire for beer was a strong one.

Right, Morocco it is! 'At least we can find some cheap 'digs' rather than sleeping on rocks in desert-like conditions every bloody night! I never want to see another rock for as long as I live!'

'Me neither, or that bastard tent!' an exhausted Mark growls.

That was my first mistake.

We take the short journey over to Ceuta by ferry and cross the border into Morocco. It's classic Arabic style mayhem, everyone is shouting, chickens are flying everywhere and every car horn is beeping in an angry manic state. We see some other tourists (Dutch) and ask if they want to catch a taxi with us. We all get in the taxi. Then *what we thought at the time* was an Arab, got in too.

'Hi, my name is Hamid; I will be your guide, very cheap.' The Dutchman starts going mental, swearing and yelling, gets out of the car with his two female companions, hails another taxi and leaves. *That's odd*, I thought.

Mark and I now have Hamid the guide as a travel companion. At this stage, we thought nothing much of it. He asked if we had ever been to Morocco and had we read the lonely planet guide. I thought it was a bit unusual but he was selling himself as a guide, it kind of made sense. Later we found out, there were warnings in the book of so-called "guides".

We are travelling to Rabat, in the clapped-out hot and dusty taxi. I'm exhausted. The lack of sleep in the last 60 days has finally caught up with me.

I fall asleep, that was my second mistake.

We all arrive and Hamid leads us to a Pension (guesthouse), which he obviously has permanent residency at. We enter a large fortified metal gate then walk along a thirty-foot walkway with 15-foot walls on each side, which are all part of the Pension complex. This would become very important later.

We drop our kit off, relieved to finally recognise a bed that isn't made of igneous rocks.

'Hey, you guys like seafood? I know a great place, by the sea. Let's go.'

'Sounds great, I love seafood,' I said.

On the way, we are walking through little alleyways, when suddenly Hamid grabs a young boy, about 8 years old and gives him a tremendous kick, sends him reeling. We look at him, my alarm bells are starting to ring. Hamid looks at us, smiles with crooked brown teeth.

'Pick-pocket, many thieves.' Spits on the floor, 'I look after you.'

We arrive at the restaurant, exactly as Hamid described. He is obviously well known to them and we are led to a table by the sea. The food is excellent, the staff, however, are very hostile. They keep looking at us and especially Hamid.

I'm starting to get a really uneasy feeling about our so-called guide and his true intentions. I start to find out more. It turns out he is not Arabic, but a Berber. This little bit of information is very important and will act as a lifeline later. I now know, we have an advantage point because if he had been an Arab he probably wouldn't drink alcohol, but Berbers do.

I start to test him. I'm being deliberately obtrusive, needling him. Seeing his reactions, my gut is telling me I'm on the right track. Hamid is a very dangerous individual indeed. Mark hasn't picked up on the subtle signals yet and is enjoying himself. I start to speed up the drink intake; beers first and then some local spirits. I know we can handle them but I'm betting Hamid can't.

I go to the toilet and pretend to pee. I need to think. Outside I can hear the staff muttering. I hear them mention Hamid but I can't work out what they are saying. They are definitely not happy. I can't believe I've got us into this situation. I was damn well sure I was going to get us out.

We finally finish up, it's about 11 pm. Hamid is shooting me dark looks, he knows I've clocked him. Our problem is that when dropping our kit off, we had foolishly left our passports. We have to go back. I can't believe I've fallen for it. What the hell was that conversation I missed in the taxi? Falling asleep, you fucking idiot Brian! I was cursing my stupidity. I should have smelled it a million miles away.

Mark, still oblivious, 'Let's hit the town.' Hamid seems delighted by this.

'No, I'm not feeling too well, must be a dodgy prawn. Let's head back, get some much-needed sleep (and our fucking passports, I thought to myself).'

We all head back enter through the 10-foot gate, along the walkway. It's dawning on me, that even the Pension has been deliberately chosen, escape would be very difficult. Think Brian, think.

We enter the bedroom; all three of us are staying in the one room. There is one single bed and one double. Hamid now drunk becomes agitated, 'Why you not want to go out, why?' Starts yelling, 'I take you to drugs and whores, we party.

'No, I'm not going! End of.'

Hamid is now raging.

Mark has finally clicked that shit is going down big style.

'Hey Hamid, we best friends, you and me.'

Hamid back 'Yes you, not him.' Now we are in a dire situation, there is no escape and Hamid is playing out a well-rehearsed routine, he's a "pro" at this. He has no fear of taking both of us on, which meant he was "pretty handy". I am 100% sure he will be carrying a blade and has probably been using it since he was a kid. He makes a move from his back then front kicks me onto the bed. He hasn't pulled the knife but the threat has its intended consequences. Mark bargains with him, 'Look, take our clothes, we give you some money, I'm your friend.'

The cat and mouse game goes on for at least an hour. Good cop (Mark) bad cop (Me). Hamid now has most of our possessions. His anger hits a new crescendo; I'm sure he's going to attack me with the knife.

Mark tries one last attempt, 'Look we will go to the bank in the morning and give you cash, lots of cash.'

Mark's tactic has worked, Hamid starts to calm down, he's swaying. The alcohol has caught up with him. Satisfied he has scared us into submission, he lies on the single bed, looks at his new watch and falls asleep.

Mark and I are in the double bed.

'Wait Mark, just wait,' I start to calm him down. I can hear him hyperventilating.

'You've done your bit, brilliantly. We're still alive,' I whisper. 'Now it's my turn. He's out cold, Mark. I knew he wouldn't be able to handle the drink.' Mark whispering back, 'What the fuck are we going to do?'

'Just wait.'

About 2 am, just before I am about to operate, we can hear a boy's voice outside the window. We are on the first floor. 'Hamid, Hamid?' Silence…then a small stone rattles off the window, then another shout of 'Hamid!' This continues for about 10 minutes but seems like a lifetime. If the street urchin wakes Hamid, we are screwed. Mark starts hyperventilating again, 'Be calm if he wakes, I will have to rush him, be prepared.'

One last desperate call, 'Hamid!' Then there is silence, the boy has left and Hamid is snoring, the alcohol, our saviour has worked.

Right, I need to move fast. 'Mark, I'm going to go out and have a good look around. You stay here, stay calm.' Mark looks at me, wild eyes stare back wide as saucers. 'Don't worry,' I reassure him. I move silently, keeping a close eye on Hamid. I open the door and go out into the dark corridor. I have to be careful the Pension owners are sleeping somewhere and goodness knows who else. I know they are all involved in this little money-making treachery. *Goodness knows how many poor sods have had the misfortune of Hamid's "guidance",* I thought to myself. I started to get angry but I needed to stay calm, be silent.

I eventually find the roof and climb up. It's a beautiful sky; millions of stars are twinkling back at me. All I can see is white rooftops but none are reachable. Even if we do escape over the roofs, there would be another hundred "Hamids" out there ready to prey. The place was a snake pit; the cops would be bent too. I look along the 30-foot alleyway from the roof and notice the large metal gate is slightly ajar, by about an inch. If closed there was no way out; before it had always been locked. The young street urchin may just have saved our skin but it was too close to call yet.

Back next to Mark, 'Any movement?'

'No, he's totally passed out.'

'Good, I've found us a way out but it's still too early. We have to wait,' I whisper.

'Wait?' Mark looks horrified. 'Be calm Mark, fear is our biggest enemy now.'

It's about 6 am, I'm unsure as Hamid is wearing my watch. I thought about retrieving it but it was too risky.

'Right, let's operate, you start to pack the rucksacks, get the passports. Don't be too quiet but not too loud.' Mark looks at me quizzically. 'If he wakes and thinks we are trying to escape, he will attack us and we won't make it. By packing normally, we can fool him, buy us some more time. I will stay in bed, so it looks like we are not trying to make a run for it.'

I'm waiting fully clothed in the bed as Mark starts to pack. If Hamid wakes, we have no choice but to attack. I'm on a knife-edge ready to pounce.

Mark finishes packing. Hamid rolls over, mutters something. We are both staring at him; I can feel the sweat trickling down my temple and back. We wait, he starts snoring. We silently leave, I've explained to Mark our get out route and the open door.

We are right by the pension door, just about to turn the handle. When suddenly, this woman comes screaming out of an adjacent room.

'Hamid! HAMID!' She shouts at the top of her voice, 'They escape Hamid!'

'Mark, see if you can buy some time while I get the first door open, now quick!' Mark goes up the stairs, not 10 seconds later Mark has leapt down the stairs in two giant leaps.

'Run, fucking run, he's pulled out a massive knife and he's coming! Run!'

Fuck, I've managed to get the first door open, but Mark's momentum hasn't stopped and he crashes into me, and we pile out the first door into the 30-foot walkway. Mark has got in front of me, that's bad. One other life-threatening slip up is that I hadn't told Mark that if he pushes the main gate, we will be locked in. I sprint like I've never sprinted before – Mark is still ahead. Mark reaches for the handle, I make at last ditch effort and dive for the door.

I just manage to get my fingertips on the gate and before we could both crash into it and lock ourselves in a fight to the death. I wrench it open.

We pile into the street, it's early and not too many locals are about.

'This way, follow me,' I start to lead Mark down a multitude of alleyways just like Ali Baba and the forty thieves.

Mark is running, 'No slow down, slow down!' I grab his arm. 'We need to walk, act natural.' We were both white as sheets. We both slow down, start walking.

'OK, we need to get out of this town, fucking right now.'

We found a local café with some local taxi drivers drinking tea in the sun. Mark and I, jumped in the nearest taxi. I shouted, 'Yalla, Yalla, we go!'

'Where to?'

'Spain!'

I never did find out what the original conversation in the taxi had been but I could only blame myself. All those years of misadventure and I had fallen for that. I was furious with myself. I had nearly gotten us both killed. Even leaving the passports at the pension, *you twat*. I berated myself.

Mark talking (when we were safely back in Spain), 'Wait until I tell the all the boys back home, that's the scariest thing I've ever seen and done. I thought we were both dead. He was definitely going to kill you.'

'Yes Mark, I'd gathered that.'

I took a sip of my ice-cold beer, 'Anyway Mark…I wouldn't bother telling anyone.'

'Why not?'

'Because they won't believe you, they never do.'

Over more beers, 'There is one consolation prize though,' I said to Mark.

'Really?'

'Yes, he did steal your only boxer shorts that for the last two months have been rubbing lovingly on your sweaty bollocks all day and night!'

We both laughed and heaved a very long sigh of relief… 'Fuck me, that was close!'

22
Saving the Basking Shark, Cousteau's Last Stand

God, 'Charles, that is a great cup of tea.'

Charles, 'I know; anyway as I was saying, when I discovered the theory of Evolution.'

God 'Ahem, you discovered?'

'Yes, me, it's my book so I wrote it already, Origin of Species, the greatest book ever.'

God groans, *here we go again.*

'So in the 19th century you discovered what was already there, and what had always been going on? Hmmm, really Charles?'

Charles flustered, 'Well yes, obviously.' God smiles reassuringly. Charles musing to himself, 'It's all a big jig-saw puzzle isn't it. Mankind's reality is that it all exists, they just have to find it; everything is 'in situ' patiently waiting to be discovered, found out, figured.'

God smiles, 'Just like chess Charles, let's play. It's your turn.'

Rat a tat tat…

'Was that the door?'

'Sounded like it,' God sighs…

A man in full 1930s deep sea diving suit enters, dripping wet. Unscrews diving helmet, 'That Marianna trench, just amazing,' he mutters to himself.

'Bonjour milord, Charles, ça va?'

'Bonjour Mr Cousteau, what do we owe the pleasure?'

'Well, as you know I invented the Aqualung.' Charles shoots God a sharp look, gets a smile in return. Charles rolls his eyes.

Jacques in monologue continues, 'Off the coast of Cornwall, each summer the glorious basking sharks arrive, to feed on the burgeoning plankton bloom. So I am sending in two expert divers. One that comes highly recommended, to monitor the sharks' behaviours and health. The recommended one sirs, you are playing chess with…so with your blessing, I would like to play.'

God, 'An expert? Really? Recommended by whom?'

'Well, funny you should ask. I bumped into Loki in one of the corridors last week and he was most convincing.'

God, 'Err…you do know he is the Norse God of mischief?'

Jacques stares back, a few second's pass.

'Mon Dieu, what have I done! My poor sharks.'

God, 'We better find out…'

White Pawn moves, takes Black Pawn. They all look down.

So I get a phone call, 'Hey Brian, it's Allan' (aka Al), expert diving instructor, BSAC with five trillion dives under his belt.

'Hi Al, (PADI open water diver, swimming pool expert, five and one quarter dives under my belt), what's up?'

Al explains, 'It's basking shark season, off the Cornish coast. We could go down this weekend, do a few dives, swim with the sharks. I know the Dive shop owner down there, he's a mate of mine.'

Conveniently forgetting that the last instructor had to rescue my air tank from the sea bed, I assured Al that I too was an expert.

'Sounds great, let's do it.'

10 plus hours later, we arrive at 7 pm, drop all our kit off at the Salty Mariners Guest House. Off to the pub we go. Local band playing, song lyrics *If thy love thy showed for me, was as grand as thy love of a Cornish pasty, eternity our passion would ever be…*

'Just beautiful,' I said to Al, wiping a tear way.

We perused the famous Cornish ales. Now, we had heard of the stories but we were hardened Scots. We ordered Cornish Knocker Ale, what could possibly go wrong again?

Two hours later, after the band managed to recover their accordion, we were thrown out into the warm Cornish night. Dignity intact, we bade the angry locals goodnight. Staggering, holding each other for support, we made our way back to the… 'Al, what was it called again…Salty Dog? Sailors Shores…or was it Whore? Mermaids Rest or was it Breast?'

Three hours later, we finally arrive back from the 10-minute walk. Like zombies swaying, we go to bed.

The stories are true, every single one of them. I have the worst hangover ever. I'm flat-lining, I can't even move my head off the pillow. Groaning, I cry for help. Al is also crying in the bed next to me. 40 minutes later we manage to extract ourselves, get dressed and stare at the full English breakfast for 30 minutes.

Turning a deeper shade of green, we leave for the Dive shop. Both in tears, we explain to Al's mate, Mark the owner, that we had drank a few local ales last night. Hugging us he commiserated, we looked around several other tourists were also crying and being comforted by staff.

One American, 'Why, why, only two pints…' sobbing hysterically, collapses on the floor.

'Right you two, pull yourselves together, dive boat leaves in forty, get kitted up.'

What seemed like three days later, we had our wetsuits on ready to hit the sea!

On the inflatable rib, bouncing along, my green pallor reached a whole knew as yet undiscovered spectrum. We arrived at the site. Al, feeling better, backward somersaults into the water. My good self, full sea sickness in tow, crumbled in.

On the surface, like a jellyfish, I'm floating. The instructor still on the boat, has a pole and is trying to push me under the water, then starts to use his foot, several people join in. I'm bobbing like an apple, utterly ill. 15 minutes later and after the cry, from the skipper 'Throw a rock at him!'…as the rock bounced off my head, curtesy of two Devon boys, I submerged.

Al looks at me with a WTF look. We descend; it's only 20 foot down, I could have saved the hassle and just worn my speedos. A fish swam past, shaking its head. My mask starts to fill with water; the diving curse was striking again. After clearing it a few times, I take it off to inspect forgetting that I'm underwater. As the saltwater bit, I lost the mask.

Sod this! I think I'm going to be sick. I head to the surface. Dragged back onto the rib, one look at my ashen face the instructor says we better get you back to shore.

30 minutes from the start of the trip, I am back on land. Dignity intact, I head back on foot to the dive shop. As I arrive, I have cast off all my kit, fins, wetsuit, belt et cetera…I leave a trail of kit carnage across the village. Then, I dragged myself semi-unconscious back to bed. Groaning, I fall back asleep.

Two hours later I wake, still wrecked. Survival hair of the dog required, off to the pub for a couple. Al, still out diving. Couple of non-Cornish, non-ales later, I start to feel like I'm part of the human race again.

By now the word has spread, the whole village had heard of the floating Scotsman…the green man that couldn't be sunk. I could hear whispering…strange looks.

Folk tales were being created. Parents in the future would scare their kids to sleep, with tales of the fateful weekend when the green Scots came to ravage the village.

Give Al a phone, he's back on land and in desperate need of the same medicine. Ashen, he arrives, followed by kids throwing rocks at him with shouts of be-gone evil.

He sat down, 'Strange lot these Cornish folk? They keep making weird signs at me like they are warding off evil or something?'

'You too? Must be a cultural thing.'

As we started to consume the whole coat of the dog, we caught up with Mark and his mates and a couple of Devon boys who were guilty of my submersion on the dive trip.

Mark to me, 'Wow that is one of the worst dives I've ever seen. I've never seen such buoyancy.'

'It's a skill I perfected in the pool, PADI y'know, full open water,' I boasted. Impressed he rolled his eyes and ignored me for the rest of the night.

Last parting words, 'Oh and your kit is still being found all over the village, might be on e-bay by the morning.' Thanking him with a curse, I saddled over to the Devon boys. Not understanding a word they said, I mentioned the insanity of drinking Cornish ale last night. They ooed and ahhed, 'Cornish knocker, that's bad, very bad, locals don't even drink that. Only for hardened criminals, the women and gullible tourists,' they both grin.

Mental note, I would phone the tourist board in the morning to inform them of this "threat to life".

One Devon boy, 'Explain the surface diving though. I never have seen a man float like that.'

'Ahem, it's a skill y'know, swimming pool, PADI,' they both nod sympathetically. 'Anyway, what do you boys normally drink for poison?'

'Well, let's see,' the Devon boys peruse the Ales. Excited, selflessly I call Al over. I knew he would thank me in the morning.

Four hours later, after the 10-minute walk home, we stagger back to the Captains Cock or was it the Barnacles Bum…chased by the locals shouting 'Out with Ye…beware the Scots…' We waved them goodnight and staggered off to bed.

Groaning, we wake up, the worst hangover take 2.

'I can't move.'

'Me neither,' wails Al. 'I feel so ill.'

'Are we diving today?'

'Yip, I'm afraid so,' Al whimpers.

'Why are we here again?'

'The Basking sharks, remember.'

'What sharks?'

Staring at the breakfast again, we head off to the dive shop. I have to hire all my kit, as mine is rapidly travelling the country via Parcelforce. At least the locals could be thankful for something on our visit, I mused. Baying mob outside, we joined the dive team.

On the rib, déjà vu decided to revisit. Sick as a parrot, the hangover arm-wrestling with the seasickness, both won. I tumble back into the sea. I look up to see the Devon boys looking down, grinning, bright as daisies. Bastards…I would show them with my superior PADI skills, I was on top of my game. We all knew this.

I got down this time, with not even a prod or a thrown stone. Hah, 10 minutes later I resurface being strangled by my own kit, the squid, or was it called the octopus, was trying to drown me. With one fin and no weight belt, I was nailing this.

The instructor manages to snag me with a gang hook to save his company's reputation and clean mortality record. Another early return back to shore for me. That was seamless, I congratulated myself. I'm going back to the pub. On the way, people are screaming, picking up their children, covering their eyes and running in all directions. Someone shouted something about a priest…Ye gods, I realised it was Sunday and time to leave. The pub would have to wait.

As Al finally came running and dived into the car, chased by the pitchfork-wielding mob. We bade them good health, farewell and left.

2 hours into the 10-hour journey, that would take 23 hours at 23mph, with matchsticks propping up our eyelids. The heads on full hangover Cornish Ale thump. Me to Al, 'You know I have the weirdest scrapes, almost like a burn mark on both elbows?'

'You too?' Al looks confused, pulling up his sleeves.

One hour later, 'Bloody HELL! I've figured it out. We were bouncing off the walls in the Guesthouse after that bloody ale. The wallpaper had taken the skin clean off! What was its name again?'

'The Saggy Tits Rest, I think?'

'Yeah, I think you're right,' I said confidently.

Five hours later. 'Y'know what Al? That was such a successful diving weekend. Flawless, I would say!'

Al groans…

'We should up the stakes. Do an overseas dive holiday next?'

Al looked at me with the utmost respect and rolled his eyes.

23

The Wedding Planner. One Fool, Best Man's Speech

'Wow, that's some attire Charles?'

'Yes, 'Sports Direct' had a crash sale on, I went a little mad. I even bought an exercise bike.'

'Well, I guessed that, considering you are peddling like a Lycra MAMIL. Charles, be careful, your beard will get caught in the spokes. What is this all in aid of?'

'I need to lose at least six stone and smarten up big style.'

'Why?' Asks God intrigued.

'Because, I've only scored a hot date with Venus.'

'No way, isn't she a bit racy for you Charles? You fainted the last time, remember?'

'Yes, she's a cracker, but apparently, it's not about looks. She likes a keen mind and a good book.'

'Bit of advice Charles, please don't bore her to death with "your book". Especially since it's about 30,000 pages long. She will have evolved into another God by the time she has read it!'

'Relax, I've got this, my lord. Let's have a quick game before I have to shave for half a day.'

'Excellent idea, looks like a wedding is going to take place?'

'We love a good wedding,' they both smile.

White King takes the Black Bishop. God and Charles look at each other, both groan.

Matt ecstatic, 'I'm getting married, I'm getting married…and I would like you to be my best man.' As I digested this request, I wondered whether my good friend was either drunk, on drugs, both or had forgotten to take all his morning meds. 'What about the riot team the last time?' I tried to dissuade him.

'What riot team?' came the baffled reply. In my head, 'I rest my case, Your Honour…' *As the battering ram was about to swing and tear Matt's mum's door off its hinges (his parents were away on holiday), I opened it. To be greeted by eight heavily clad riot officers. Wearing only my boxer shorts, I looked quizzically at them, 'Can I help you officers?' I was surprised as I had been expecting a paramedic, as Neil not forty minutes past had fallen off the roof. The first two officers enter to find Matt, Neil and Rob passed out in various positions of indignity on the living room floor. He looks at me incredulously, 'We have had multiple reports of a full-blown riot? We were expecting 40, not 4.'*

'No officer just the four of us and as you can see definitely in no fit state to cause a riot.' After a quick check, they left shaking their heads. They had turned up with two riot wagons. To this day Matt, Neil and Rob were oblivious to their close encounter with tear gas.

'Are you absolutely sure about this Matt, mate?'

'Yes, 100% bulletproof.'

'It would be an honour then, but ONLY if you are 100% certain my choice is the right one?'

'Absolutely, what could possibly go wrong again?' Matt beaming with delight.

I thought to myself, *Wait until his mother finds out!*

Matt overexcited, 'Excellent, I have arranged to meet the chaplain next Wednesday. It's going to be a church wedding. The vicar likes to meet the groom and best man beforehand, make sure everything runs smoothly.'

Wednesday arrives, we open the large wooden church door. Big Booming voice, 'GET OUT!'

Me to Matt, 'I knew this was a bad idea.' The vicar "shoos" a cat out. We both breathe a sigh of relief. That was close. I thought it was the big man himself.

'You must be Matthew?' Looking at me, he makes the sign of the cross.

Eyeing Matt again, 'You look much more like marriage material and you must be the uh "best man", Brian.'

Bowing, 'Yes, your Excellency, always the bridesmaid never the bride.'

Under his breath mutters 'Remember they are all God's children, Father.'

Sighing, 'No, I'm not referred to as his Excellency, that's a Bishop and please stop bowing.'

'Sorry, your Eminence.'

'Nor that.'

'Your Holiness?'

'Nope.'

'Your lordship?'

'No.'

'Matt mate,' I said perplexed, 'this is so hard…Governor?'

'No.'

'Any chance we can have a clue?'

'No.'

Exasperated, the vicar, shaking his head, 'Ughhh this is going to be a really, REALLY long day. Right, where to start (with you two). Please sit, no don't kneel.'

We start praying. The man of the cloth motions us to rise, we both get up off the floor, start to bow again. A little tear has welled up and is running down the Pastor's cheek.

Sighing again, the Padre exhales, 'Let's begin. This is going to take much, much longer, than normal.' Shouts over to Deidre (his secretary), 'Cancel all of today's appointments.' She looks back concerned. 'Right, where were we? Ah yes, Marriage...

Marriage is a holy communion between two blessed persons who agree, before the eyes of God, to enter a loving contract. That will last till the day they meet their maker.'

One hour later, I whisper to Matt, 'The pubs will be shut at this rate.' His lordship continues, 'Morality and righteousness will guide you and show you the path of divinity.'

Another hour later, Matt whispers, 'My bum has gone numb.'

'Mine too,' I whisper back. 'Do you think there is any communion wine leftover? I'm parched!'

'God, I hope so.'

We knew that the Padre also knew that this was one of the very few chances he would have to hold us hostage and save our infidel souls from the devil's grasp. With our ears on full bleed...

'The lord crusheth thy enemy downeth,' the man of God drones on with vigour. It was going to be a long day, probably miss that happy hour after all.

With the cold beer slipping away. The lecture continued, 'Hell, fire and brimstone, the lord God will smite down any UNBELIEVERS!' He glared at us. Damn it, does he suspect! I thought I better try kneeling and motioned to Matt. His Grace had picked up a gear and was becoming fanatical. He finishes.

'I bid you good night gentlemen, and I will pray for your redemption...' he leaves muttering to himself. 'So much work...so much. Total lost cause' and something about Satan.

Me to Matt, 'I think that went well.'

Matt back, 'Yip and if we hurry we can still catch last orders.'

'Nice one,' we run off.

Matt's mum, 'WHAT! You asked Brian to be your best man, have you completely lost your marbles?'

Matt back, 'I have every faith. The Archbishop was really impressed with him, I could tell.'

Mum back, 'He's a vicar dear, you were supposed to call him Father.'

'Father, hey, who knew? Damn it, we were so close (later on, when Matt recaps the conversation with his mum).'

'So, your mum's OK with this?'

'Sure is, matey.'

'Y'know what Matt, (I was thinking of the previous day) that Cardinal should have worn a name badge or at least handed out a business card, avoid all that confusion and name calling. I'm sure their elderly congregation would appreciate it.'

Matt, in quiet earnest, 'Now you won't fuck this up?! The missus (to be) will kill me (and you).'

'Matt, safe hands mate, safe hands. I have it all planned out.'

Matt, 'Phew thank god. You won't believe how many people have questioned my sanity over this. One even asked if I'd stopped taking my meds.' I stifled a cough, 'Don't worry, like I said Matt safe hands mate.' In unison, 'What could possibly go wrong again?'

The big day arrived, all in kilts we rocked. Matt, pacing up and down the corridor, off the chart nervous. A slow creeping dread had begun to set in for myself. I had insanely, deluded myself that I could "wing" the best man speech. After all our crazy escapades I had so much material. Surely by divinity, I could improvise and do the married couple justice. I confided my genius to my horrified brother and sister on the drive up to the wedding. In unison, 'Oh crap Brian!'

When we arrived. 'You better get some drinks down you,' my siblings tell me as they both hand me a double whisky.

Matt at the altar is so nervous. I thought he was going to faint. He didn't. Ceremony complete, we retired to the reception room.

I'm now absolutely scared shitless, the enormity of my stupidity has now fully sunk in. I'm having a panic attack that no amount of whisky is going to cure.

Everyone is seated; it's intimate. I can see elderly relatives of the married couple everywhere. I can see my brother and sister sitting straight in front of me. Smiling encouragingly, with concern written all over their faces.

I begin by thanking everyone for turning up, then I panic. Every bit of wit is lost, my mind has gone and I need either an earthquake or an outbreak of Ebola to save me. I wait, neither happened. Over a hundred eyes are looking at me waiting…

Shit, shit, Brian think. So I begin by telling the audience of Matt and his new wife's finest relatives about the time that I quote "Matt slept with a prostitute in Thailand". As I dug myself further into the pit and to make sure Matt would never speak to me ever again, I continued on.

My story, staggered, faltering, but unwavering, I finished. I had to be resilient, Matt was counting on me. Only by the silence and absolute shock on the audience's faces, I realised I had delivered a masterpiece. The pain in my right leg was intensifying. I looked down to see Matt's mum stabbing me in the leg with a fork, in a vain attempt to try and get me to shut the fuck up. My leg finally ran out of blood, I took a small bow and collapsed into my seat. Looking sideways at Matt's mum, I nodded to thank her for her support.

My sister was just looking at me, shaking her head in disbelief. I could tell Dan was in stitches as he hid under the table. However, Matt's elderly relatives were being ferried away in ambulances. Stunned silence, a pin dropped and everyone heard it.

Matt afterwards, 'I chose you because I thought you would be funny.'* I couldn't look him in the eye. 'Oh and by the way, I have never even been to Thailand, let alone shagged a street hooker!'

Matt, under his breath, 'Could you not have at least made it a high-class call girl, rather than a crack addicted, street whore!' And Matt hisses, 'What was that about the hooker desperately needing the money for one of her kids, needing a fucking heart transplant!'

'Well,' I said Matt, 'firstly you couldn't afford a high-class call girl, so a crack whore is much more authentic. Secondly, I told my good friend, I thought the kid transplant story would be more emotive for the guests.

Matt, mate, I thought it would spice it up a bit!'

'A bit, a bit!' yells Matt in a shrill voice incredulously.

'Yes, I acknowledge it was a little bit of car crash.'

'"A little" Brian! Think full-on 60 car pile-up with no known survivors FFS,' Matt fumes.

'Calm down Matt, more like a small tap on the bumper. Anyway, we all know someone slept with that prostitute,' I countered. 'Probably half of Germany no doubt,' I told Matt.

Matt mate, I reassured him, 'I would investigate first thing in the morning; get to the bottom of this disgrace!'

In my head, on the phone to the German embassy the next day, 'Hello is the ambassador there?'

'No sorry sir, he's on a family holiday?'

'Where?' I queried.

'Thailand,' the receptionist replied. DIRTY BUGGER! Wait until I tell Matt.

Growling, Matt utters furiously, 'Thanks mate, thanks a fucking bunch. The new missus is devastated. You know her elderly grandmother was in that room, you just nearly killed her off. Mum's going around apologising to everyone, most are in tears. Safe hands, remember! SAFE HANDS BRIAN!'

Sighing, 'Matt you only have your poor judgement and misplaced faith in myself to blame. Remember our history together, the "bone incident" as exhibit A, the riot police, the 72-hour booze binge, need I go on…And you really thought my appointment was a good idea? Really, Matt?'

Matt, 'That's a fair point, damn it! Still not fucking happy though.'

He storms off to find his new inconsolable wife, muttering 'Safe hands Matt, safe hands…Just what the FUCK was I thinking!'

So disaster averted, the party could begin in earnest now.

*Total car crash. I'm so sorry Matt, I will take the guilt to the grave with me.

24
Three Fools Feeding the Chickens, Gambia

So I get A phone call, it's Big Neil (a Scottish mate the size of a house), 'Fancy a trip to the Gambia?'

'Yes, sounds good. I have another mate, Firthy. An Aussie mate of mine, living in London. I know he will be interested too, loves travelling.'

'Excellent, let's book it.' *Firthy delighted, makes his way up to Scotland, for the trip.*

The chartered flight over from Edinburgh would have been a tight squeeze even for a family of fleas. On one side I had Neil, six foot five, 24 stone and counting. On the other, six foot two Firthy, a mere 17 stone. As we finally came to a stop on the Gambian runway, I rummaged in my washbag, here it is! My emergency tin-opener. I then, with a bit of effort, managed to extract myself from the ashtray. Putting my thumb into my mouth, I blew until my one-dimensional body became three again (with a popping sound for confirmation). Delighted at been crushed for the last 5 hours, it was time to enjoy ourselves in "The Gambia".

We headed along a makeshift road on the charter bus, crushed once again between the two brutes. There is a tour guide on board, who starts to orate. Suddenly, super excitedly, he points at a set of traffic lights.

'These are the first and only traffic lights in the whole of The Gambia,' he exclaims clearly delighted. The tourists on board, 40 cameras pointing at the traffic lights, that are in plague like proportions back home; start snapping ferociously. I say to big Neil, 'Get a picture mate.' He gives me a fuck off look. 'Neil, when in Rome mate, you have to get into the spirit?'

He grunts, 'We're not in bloody Rome!'

That's definitely not in the spirit of The Gambia in my opinion, the big bastard.

Suddenly, another massive squeal of delight, the tour guide can't contain himself. 'Our very first and only Shell garage, with a shop,' he exclaims proudly. 'With a shop,' I say to big Neil, 'that's worth a photo?'

Neil growls back, 'We may as well be in Weston Super Mare!'

'Neil, their Shell garage doesn't have a shop, definitely worth a photo this one. I'm taking one.'

'Me too,' says Firthy caught up in the excitement. 'I wonder if they have a BP station,' say's Firthy thrilled. 'Shut up! If it has a shop too! I'm definitely getting a photo,' I elbowed Neil enthusiastically in the ribs. Neil has lost the will to live, puts his head against the window and ignores us for the rest of the traffic light and petrol station tour.

The guide overhears our conversation, 'Sadly just one garage in the whole of The Gambia. We only have three cars.'

We arrive at the hotel; there's a pool and a bar, looks good. Sorted, dump the bags, get a few beers in. A couple of hours later, let's hit the town of six and a half people!

First place, small bar. We pay £5 to the policeman, who's the brother of the classic sting we have just fallen for. What the Hell! We have only been in town for 20 minutes. Handing back the "doobie" that is clearly more "Tea leaf" rather than "Sweet leaf," he beams, 'Welcome to The Gambia, have a very nice day.'

Set up by his brother and his Gambian mates, Big Neil also beaming, 'I told you so.'

'Shut it Neil, you big bastard, at least we got some decent snaps of that traffic light.'

Few more beers, rejecting another five stings, sorry boys we have no more "extortion racket" money left, disappointed they grinned back.

'Welcome to The Gambia,' they waved the three fools cheerily off, 'Have a very nice day.'

Trying not to correct the horological mistake, we headed back at 2 am.

Lovely people these Gambians so trusting, all three of us agreed, as we crashed out.

Next morning, lying by the pool, we are met by Denby, who will be our waiter/guide for the duration of the holiday. Over the next couple of days, we become friendly with Denby. We ask him if he could organise a tour for us. He says he hasn't done that before but yes he could arrange. We could go meet his family too. Perfect, tour with Denby it is!

Next day, Denby beaming, 'I have tour, we go.' Meanwhile, I have one of the worst hangovers ever, again. Feeling that death would be a mercy, we get picked up in an old open Land Rover circa 567 BC. Denby's cousin, massive big friendly grin.

'Welcome to The Gambia, have a very nice day,' he greets us.

We ask Denby to stop off at the Shell garage. We would go to the shop and buy his family some groceries and presents, as a thank you. In the shop, there is only Indian spices and food, served by Mr Singh. Gambians must like curries, I assumed. Must be their staple diet, considering every shelf was full of various curry powders. We fill a box with various Indian food and spices. That should do it, last the village a good six months.

Now sitting in the back of the Land Rover, we head off to meet the family. We have to stop for three days, whilst we wait for the only traffic light to turn green. Firthy and I, excited again, use it as a perfect opportunity for another photoshoot. We'll fill the album at this rate, I tell a delighted Neil. Denby and his cousin are very happy that we have acknowledged the importance and beauty of this traffic control system. 'We should celebrate,' they inform us with big grins.

They stop two miles down the road.

'Try this,' they say as they hand us a DIY bottle, 'palm wine,' they say. It's about 160 proof, it's like snake bile. Turning yet a new shade of green, I take a tiny swig. I really need death to hurry its arse up, I feel so ill. Firthy and Big Neil, without the hangover, get stuck in. Next, they try an un-ripened cashew nut. Denby tries to grab the fruit the nut hangs off. Too late! Down the two boy's hatch it went. Now, they have this weird dry mouth sensation, they can't shake. Their tongues are the size of a small watermelon. At least, I would get some peace from the big bastards; enjoy the bone-rattling tour now.

After 16 breakdowns, the three now green foreigners finally arrive at Denby's parents' homestead. The whole extended family has turned up, including 401 chickens and every goat in The Gambia.

We offered the box of food, full of curry powders, to Denby's mother. She thanked us with a quizzical look of happiness; and left for the kitchen. We are all sat under a tree, it's very hot. The family is delightful, very chatty and very friendly. Neil and Firthy have recovered from their culinary mistake and alcohol poisoning. A massive rice platter arrives full of large chunks of fish still on the bone, followed by a hungry retinue of flies. The chickens started clucking ecstatically, my hangover reached a new crescendo.

Firthy and Big Neil, get totally stuck in, the family are delighted. Now, I'm no genius but eating fish this far from the coast in 40 degrees, with that many excited flies in Africa for a tourist, isn't going to end well. Plus, the hangover wouldn't allow anything passed my lips anyway. Not to be impolite, I would distract the 83 eyes as best I could and every time the chickens came past I would flick some food off my plate. Quickly becoming the chicken's new best friend, I managed to clear my plate and have some chance of surviving until my serotonin could return. Stop the suicide.

We bade our new found friends goodbye. 'Welcome to The Gambia, have a very nice day,' the 452 Gambians waved us off.

Denby is now getting angry. After the 18th breakdown, he is yelling at his cousin. The cousin looks shocked but I told you on this tour breaking down 432 times is normal. There's no mechanics in The Gambia he tells Denby, we only have three cars remember. They would face starvation or die of boredom. Fixing the jeep, we head off to our last location, the fish market.

We arrive at about 6 pm, the market is just starting to close. A massive six-foot-seven local is pulling one of the fishing boats in by hand; the rope stretches 200 metres out to sea. It's very impressive but not as impressive as the fish hauls lying all over the shoreline. Little mountains everywhere, all un-refrigerated, baking in the hot sun all day. The flies are going berserk. The smell is palpable.

'So Denby, my good man, how long would it take for this fish to reach your family?'

'Oh about a week, then they cook next few days, very fresh.'

Delighted, I look over to Firthy and Neil, 'It's going to be an interesting "Welcome to The Gambia" for you two tonight. I think I will stay at bar; get hair of the dog in, stay safe.'

Travelling back to the resort, after witnessing the only other two cars in The Gambia crash into each other at the traffic lights intersection…the first rumble starts.

'Neil was that you?'

'Yeah, I don't feel too well!'

'Me neither,' pipes in Firthy. The two big bastards on arriving back, make a break for the loos.

Off to bed they went, 2 am the projectile vomiting starts, the two big fellas are having to tag-team each other as every orifice is screaming for attention. Worst bout I had ever seen, each would weigh about two stone in the morning, that's if they survived. All night the chorus continued.

I thanked my lucky chickens that I hadn't touched any. Thank THE LORD for hangovers, I congratulated myself. Good job I'd had those 43 beers after all.

Next day by the pool, a very worried Denby hurries over, 'Brian sir, we have big problem back home.'

'What is it Denby, an outbreak of Ebola?'

'Well, food you brought in box, we not know how to cook.'

'You don't eat curries?' I was dumbfounded.

'What is curry?' came the puzzled look.

'Well,' I explained it's Indian food. 'You just put a small spoon of the extremely hot vindaloo powder into your fish, chicken or goat, from one of the packets. That makes a curry of your food.'

'That's the problem, we put whole box in fish dish now everyone sick, need to go toilet all day, very long queue many people angry.'

'That's 40 packets,' I said!

'Yes, we count. Even the chicken's line up for toilet, little hut full all day!'

'What is this burning sensation?' he asks as he grabs his bum and runs off to the loo screaming.

'What's wrong with him?' Big Neil and Firthy have finally surfaced, both walking like John Wayne.

Firthy, 'That was some fucking curry yesterday. Ferocious vindaloo, if ever I've tried one, gave me the shits all night.'

'Me too,' says Neil, 'I need some bum cream urgently.'

'Try lemon juice,' I offered Neil some sound unproven medical advice.

I explain the curry powder mishap. 'Shit, that'll explain it, 40 FFS!'

However, it looks like that shop purchase has poisoned Denby and his family too. That's a bit ironic, we all agreed. Normally the visitors get the "rumble in the jungle". Not the locals. Most holidays with the boys had ended up in at least one fatal food poisoning episode. We generally didn't end up poisoning the hosts that often, especially not in Africa.

I could just see the local headlines: *The Gambian Daily: Mass poisoning of local village; 41 chickens and 2 goats dead. 3 tourists arrested. Authorities are calling it "fire-bum disease". Indian Shell shop owner, Mr Singh, denies all knowledge of sale of the virus or even being an Indian national.*

Seems like Denby and his family were not having a very nice day in The Gambia after all, I mused. However, their undies were definitely having a ball. It was time to catch that flight. We bade Denby, still groaning in the toilet, a very nice day and left. Denby one last scream as the volcanic vindaloo made another guest appearance…

This time I was going to be prepared, get some legroom. Avoid a blood clot and having both legs amputated on the plane. A quick stop at the local bar first, have Big Neil and Firthy trafficked in a classic people smuggling sting. The

S.I.C.B.U.M (Stop Insane Christians Bombing Us Militia) in Mali, could deal with the two of them from now on. Pay the extortionists £5 a piece, the pair of proper big bastards.

25
Stairway to Heaven, The Mighty Buachaille

Charles, in a contemplative mood, 'Why does mankind always want to conquer everything they see?'

'Well Charles, it is good to get out and get some fresh air. Get those pins and lungs working!'

Charles, 'Yes, I do like a good walk,' he looks down at his new leather walking boots. Sees God admiring them, 'Crash sale on at 'Blacks' he pre-empts the question.

'Ah,' says God 'might pick up a pair too.'

God, 'Well good news Charles, I've put an "out of order" sign on the front door, so we can finally play in peace. I've got a really good feeling you'll get a booking for that Awards ceremony this time. Get the fandangle award handed out posthumously. You should see his guide, couldn't be more perfect. Doesn't take surviving too seriously at all.'

Charles eyes the award cabinet nervously, 'Is it the "unhinged" one?

God nods, a little smile forming on his lips.

'Excellent,' Charles super excited does a quick bit of dance "flossing".

'Charles stop that, it's quite disturbing. Let's play.'

Black King checks White King. Ouch, that is a very, very, powerful move. They both look down, expectant.

So I get a phone call, it's Bruce (an old friend from school-Colditz).

'Hi Brian, feel like a climb this weekend?'

'Where, dude?'

'We'll go to Glencoe, in the Highlands, do a couple of hills.'

'Hills?'

'Yes, nice and easy,' Bruce replies with a deliberate nonchalant tone.

'But "Highlands" might suggest that they are not hills at all Bruce?'

'Don't worry Brian, all good. You're in safe hands matey!'

'OK, sounds nice and safe. I will bring my brother along, he like a nice stroll in the hills.'

'Cool, Damien will meet us on Sunday. He has a climb in mind too.'

'Damien? Are you sure Bruce?

He's insane you know.'

'That is a matter of speculation for the doctors Brian, we'll be fine.'

We arrive first thing Saturday, set up our tent not realising the annual midge festival is in full swing. Every square inch of skin has about 300 bites on it, we run for our lives. Save yourselves. I can see Bruce running off into the distance. Nice and easy! I've already lost eight pints of blood.

However, the drive through the valley is spectacular. I say to Bruce, 'What is that monster over there,' pointing at a massive rock angrily protruding from the ground.

Warning any (idiots) who dare to trespass of imminent death.

'That's the Buachaille Etiv Mor,' says Bruce, admiration and awe in his voice. That looks insane, thank all the saints and their mothers we are not climbing that big prick!

We drive to the car park and begin the ascent of Bidean Nam Bian, translated from Gaelic as "Peak of the Mountains". It's a really hot day and we haven't taken enough water, cigarettes yes, water…no. The stats on it are as follows: Distance 11km, time 7-9 hours, ascent 1316m. That, in my mind, is not a nice and easy hill. The guide book, just to add to my anxiety: steep, rocky and complex terrain. I would pencil in later; "big monster-bastard too", best avoid. (In the footnotes).

Several hours later, we arrive at the top. We have to cross a ridge with massive drops on either side; it's only about 20 foot. However, it may as well be the Grand Canyon. I start crawling on my stomach. Bruce hissing angrily, 'Brian, what the fuck are you doing?'

Me hissing back, 'What the fuck does it look like? I'm trying to save myself from instant death! I suggest you crawl too Bruce, save yourself.'

'Stand up Brian. Stand up it makes it easier. Just walk normally.'

Bruce surveys the mountain to make sure no one can see this total embarrassment. I eventually get on one knee, then two and finally stand holding back a scream. The urge to throw myself like a lemming off the cliff is palpable.

'Just walk Brian.' I comply now feeling like the idiot that Bruce has pictured in his mind.

'What the hell was that?' Bruce says when I got to the end.

'That, my good man, was me showing what a rationale human being would display when suffering from abject terror. I absolutely hate heights. Sharks I'm good, heights I'm not.'

Bruce raises his arms in the air, 'Now you fucking tell me!'

'I would have told you earlier but I have been holding in an internal scream for the last four hours. Hill you said, nice and easy you said! Are we training for Everest, you should have said! Look, I can see the Sherpa base camp below those clouds over there. Hi Everest,' I waved at a smaller mountain eight thousand foot down.

Bruce, rolling his eyes, 'Man up princess,' walks off.

We eventually reached safe and horizontal land by about 6 pm. I cradled a flat piece of ground, I love you flat piece of land, don't ever leave me. I looked up at the monster we had just climbed, bad rock, I scolded it. It just looked back, bored.

We set up a fire and lost another three pints of blood to the midges. By the time Bruce had put the first sausage on the BBQ, Dan and myself were both unconscious.

Bruce woke me a couple of hours later. 'Right, let's go to the pub.'

'Bruce, I hope this is not a mountain top pub on a small safe hill?'

'No, it's over there, you can see it,' he retorts.

'WHAT! Why didn't you say so?' We have lost two hours of valuable drinking time, with all that fooling around burning sausages nonsense.

We go into the Clachaig Inn, it's full of climbers all wearing the latest kit. Crampons, ice picks and ropes everywhere. I saddle along to the bar to discuss my extensive climbing experience with some bored looking free climbers. I'm telling you, great-grandson of Edmund Hillary, that crawling is a perfectly acceptable form of traversing a death-defying ridge. Bruce quickly scurries over, bows to the man.

'Do you know who that is?'

'No, but he needs a safety climbing masterclass. No ropes! What next? Living life to the max again by getting killed no doubt! Health and safety really needs to be dramatically improved around here. I will draw him a diagram of Survival Mountain Crawling. That should help! Do you have any paper? Pen?'

Bruce groans. The Scottish country dance music is playing. A traditional song starts…

Donald, where's your troosers? If that wind blaes high, then wind blaes low then surely your Claymore would make a show, then Morag and her 8 ginger sisters would surely say hello, Donald where's your troosers?

I thought, *Good luck to you Donald, you would need it. Arm yourself with a tent peg, fight off the pesky ginger horde.*

Next show starts. Some young girls in Tartan are dancing around swords. I said to Bruce, outraged, 'That is definitely a health and safety issue. I will go have a word. Where's the manager?'

Bruce quickly tackles me as I cross the dance floor. Deeply disappointed at his lack of safety procedures and compliance training, he quickly diverted me to the bar.

'Let's get some Malts in, stay safe.'

Four hours later with the sword in my mouth and security running after us, we headed back to the tent.

The following year Scott (Bruce's brother), would be car surfing on my dad's new car, down this very same dirt track at 3 am. Impersonating the beach boys, I would not inform Scott of the time that Dad's car keys were stolen in Zambia. As a precautionary measure, he wired the car up to the house electrics (see Zambia story). Not looking forward to my chat with Dad, I would inform him that the surfing damage was a most unfortunate accident. Whilst driving at a completely respectable time of the day, with not even a surfer in sight; a large family of squirrels had obviously over-eaten and fallen from a tree branch.

Landing squarely on the new car roof. Fortunately, none were hurt, not even suffering mild indigestion. That should pacify him, he loved squirrels. I would add in that they were "Red" too, make the story more emotive.

Back home, *Poor choice of vermin,* I thought to myself, as the bullet ricochet's off the wall next to my head. He had been attacked by a rogue squirrel as a kid. Bloody Red one too! Hated the little pricks, who knew? It was Dalmatians that he loved.

Imagine a family pack of Dalmatians falling out of that tree, so unbelievable. Damn, I wish I'd thought of it though. Also, the car repair bill would have been much, much, higher too. He should have thought of that before he took aim again, so ungrateful.

We wake up early, Damien has just arrived. He's only managed to kill four people on the journey up and is clearly disappointed at the low score rate. I have the hangover from hell and so does Dan. Whisky is the devil's juice, all that "water of life" nonsense. Damn lies! Groaning, we wash in the river.

'Right, boys are you ready?' Damien is starting to do press ups. I wondered if he was related to Lippy, same imbalances and unsafe constitution.

'Where are we going?' I asked Damien suspiciously. After Bruce's "small hill" soiree, trust was at a premium. 'Don't worry nice and easy,' came the nonchalant reply. Nice wee hill. I shoot Bruce a hard look of betrayal. Bruce yawns in response.

We arrive at the carpark, Dan has already been sick. We start the ascent of HELL.

Me to Damien, 'Where are the ropes?'

'Ropes,' he just laughs manically. 'You know what forget ropes, where's the fucking elevator for fuck's sake!'

There are three ridges (Curved Ridge, is the official route name) you can free climb/scramble. Unknown to Dan and myself, we were about to find out how terrified one can get without simply imploding. Dan didn't even have proper climbing boots on. His Saturday night dance clogs would be no match for this beast. Up we went. I have never hung onto a piece of rock so hard in all my life. My knuckles were white, years later my finger indents in the cliff face would be mistaken for some long-lost dinosaur fossil trail. As we ascended, I roughly translated the meaning of The Buachaille in my head; simply the "Big Bastard Rock that is going to murder you". Now feeling even more confident about my immediate death, we carried on.

About halfway up, on another crazy steep section. Damien was leading, Dan was in Damien's backpack crying, I was next and Bruce last. I start to overthink my survival chances and get what's called a "sewing machine leg". It starts juddering up and down uncontrollably. Bruce grabs my foot and starts to steady it.

'Calm down, don't think, Brian.'

'Bruce!' I hiss back trying not to look into the abyss. 'If I survive this I am going to kill you, there's a thought for you!'

Thinking that Bruce was giving me a foot up to the next ledge, I pushed off and carried on with my internal scream. We all managed to get on a five-foot wide ledge. Bruce face completely ashen. Bruce is shaken, 'Brian you fucking idiot! You nearly just kicked me off the cliff. I was steadying your foot, not giving you a leg up.' Bruce had just managed to grab the ledge, as I had pushed down from the obvious "leg up" and carried on.

'Err nice and easy Bruce remember? Safe hands remember! If you had paid attention to my diagram on survival crawling last night, instead of apologising to that Edmund fella you would have been perfectly safe.'

Last stage and it's got even steeper. I'm sure these gradients are defying physics. We have to shuffle 20 foot along sideways, facing the cliff on a two-foot ledge. With a sheer certain death drop egging us on. *Do it, jump! DO IT!*

I was channelling a lemming again.

It was terrifying. Dan got to the end and was climbing up a 15-foot ridge. I was directly below, still on the ledge. I could see Dan's rubber soles bending and slipping. If he slipped we were both dead, no question. Dan just managed to scramble over the top after one last slide. My turn next, I managed it and was talking to Damien who was looking down at me. Bruce voice from below, 'Brian I am getting a little bit tired now.' I looked down and Bruce was hanging on for dear life to the cliff face, 1000 foot drop below him.

Right, keep moving, breathe, this is insane. Feeling like I had just been resurrected from death on loop for the last three hours. Shit, I looked at what was left of Dan's boots. Now looking very much like Gandhi's hand-me-downs.

We finally get to the top. Also looking at Dan's exposed toes, Damien is joking about the bollocking we would get if Mountain Rescue had been called out. I didn't think it too funny, that this certifiable lunatic might not have questioned the sanity of taking us on this monster; with the wrong kit, no ropes, a whisky hangover and no fucking HELICOPTER!

Damien starts to do some press-ups. I'm going to kill him.

26
Red Sea Adventure. Two Fools, Eyeball Challenge

Charles talking, 'You know I once took up jogging, all the Victorian rage back then. 5k theoretical evolution race beat that Alfred Wallace fair and square, AGAIN! Anyway, halfway round I swallowed a fly, it was utterly disgusting. However, if I had been a bird that would have been a delicious win. Please explain?'

God, 'Oh dear, running shorts Charles? Really! Anyway, for nature, consumption is about survival and reproduction. Consumption for mankind is insatiable and is no longer about either of the above…it's all part of the great equation. Man vs. nature, nature vs. man. Mankind has disconnected from nature and through a mixture of arrogance and ignorance will pay dearly but they have yet to figure that out.'

Darwin, 'I'm not holding my breath.' God sighs, 'Me neither.'

'Wow, what is that smell?' A little bell tings, a voice hollers, SERVICE! One of the greatest Chefs, Alain Chapel (3-star Michelin) founder of Nouvelle cuisine enters the room, two dishes in each hand.

'Voila. Sheep's eyeballs al a Mer. Lovingly plucked from the finest sheep, marinated for 2 years in the tears of a hundred virgins, pickled anchovy caviar with a touch of Tabasco. Enjoy.'

'Sounds exquisite,' both Charles and God agree.

God, 'Fabulous. Now to the task at hand. Mon Chef what do you have in mind for the award?'

Greatest Chef responds with Gallic flair, 'We could try to kill him by food poisoning if he fails to drown himself first.'

'Yes, Yes,' they all high five, 'this is so, so exciting. Closest we have come yet to that award. Allow me, Mon Dieu, Monsieur Darwin,' Chef leans over…

White Bishop takes Black Bishop. 'Oh no! That's messy,' they all look down.

So I get a phone call, it's Allan again. 'Rounding up some boys for a dive trip, Sharm al Sheik. You in?'

Me, 'After the triumph of Cornwall, I most definitely am. I will pack my speedos and my handwritten notes on how to dive in a swimming pool in an expert fashion.'

Al delighted, groans. 'You know Brian. The Mayor of Cornwall is still sending me hate mail, something about tourist numbers being decimated, local children going hungry.'

'Well, I'm baffled,' I said indignantly, 'they were so hospitable, and our diving was flawless. That Cornish tourist board should be paying us after that trip.' Al groans again. 'Get your shit together Brian, we are leaving in two weeks.'

Me back, 'I will pack my kit, just bought a new Squid.' Al, under his breath, 'Here we go again, Octopus.'

'And some flippers.'

Al, rolling his eyes, 'Fins. Flipper was a Dolphin Brian!'

'Sorry Al, pretty sure it was a killer whale, both part of the Dolphin family, did you know that Al?'

Al under his breath, 'FFS.'

'Y'know last bit Al, if you're desperate, I could teach your mates a few of the expert tricks I have learnt with my Open water PADI certificate.'

Al deep sigh, 'We really need to talk about that...'

We catch up with Al's crew at an airport bar in Heathrow; there are 10 of us together, nine boys and one girl. The poor girl didn't take long to realise that she had made a fundamental holiday booking error. Getting the tequilas in, we introduce ourselves. Al's main mates were Johnny and the "Beast". I quickly inform them of my diving credentials and my special swimming pool expertise. Utterly impressed, they left to talk amongst themselves.

Arrive at Sharm airport, it's 1 am and there's not much there, passport control is a hut. The delightful Arabic passport controller took one look at us and spat some green phlegm on the floor. 'Welcome to Egypt, infidels' he proclaimed with unbridled joy. Four hours later to travel five feet, we cleared passport control. What a lovely man we all agreed, an absolute delight.

A neutron bomb must have gone off recently. The whole town has been newly built but it is completely empty, not a soul. Built on the expectation of mass tourism, wrecked by the reality of the local Jihadis.

We shouted down two taxis. 'To the hotel, garcon!' The infidels had arrived.

So in the expedition, we have three qualified BSAC diving instructors the rest are made up of dive masters, advanced divers and most importantly for survival a PADI open water diver with expert pool experience. The guide diver for the trip is an Australian advanced diver (PADI). He is unaware of the experience of the dive party and currently has a full set of brown hair and a look of complete boredom. I could read his mind, *not another boat full of whingeing Pommie Bastards,* he perused us disdainfully.

On the first dive, we kit up (2-3 dives per day for five days), backwards somersault into the sea. The reef is amazing, untouched. Lionfish abound, we are followed by a large Grouper. Suspicious as to our intentions and why air-breathing monkeys were invading his underwater kingdom yet again. A beautiful bright yellow sea snake swims by, uninterested.

We follow the Australian. Looking behind, I can see Johnny straddling the "Beast" like a Broncho cowboy, snorkel out and is using it like a whip on the Beast. The Australian finally realises that the only person he is guiding is himself. As his "flock" have all stopped to watch the spectacle. Quickly swims over, with his knife out, bangs his air tank furiously. Underwater shrug, Johnny hops off. We continue the dive.

Back on the boat the Australian has lost his cool, 'Look you bloody Po…I mean tourists, no more acting the GALAH. Diving is dangerous and should be taken seriously.' We all concurred that from now on we would be very serious, especially when diving but also generally in life. From now on, very, very, serious with no exceptions.

Suspicion averted he went up to the captain's cabin, muttering to himself about bloody Gallipoli and betrayal of some nature.

'Woah boys what was all that about?'

Johnny explains, 'It's called Beast riding. Tomorrow, lift the masks onto the top of the head and you have a jockey's riding hat, use snorkel as the whip.'

'Wow, that's bloody genius,' I said impressed.

'Oh, I so want a go.'

The Beast clears his throat and announces with some importance, 'Tomorrow we will have a Beast race.'

Excellent, the group all high fives each other.

Only if it is taken very seriously though, we all agreed, sombre.

Have a dip in the pool, a few drinks and ready for the night out. Off we go, two taxis, no headlights on. It's getting a little bit dark. Must be a local thing?

We have a nice meal. Smoke from the Hukkah pipe, a few more beers and tequilas, time for home. We pitch up to the makeshift taxi rank, with a massive gilded 14-foot-high cage, with a monkey in it. Swearing in Arabic, to anybody who would listen. I translated for the group. The atmosphere was such that I would not have been surprised if Indiana Jones passed by shooting at bad guys on a horse drawn carriage. Disappointed at the "no show" of the hat-wearing, whip cracking, snake-o-phobe. His horse must have broken down, we waited. God willing, we would get one.

Two taxis turn up, no lights on. However, looking inside the taxi, there are hundreds of fairy and Xmas lights all over the dash. We all pile in; you couldn't see a bloody thing. I had a strong desire to sing a Christmas carol and open something wrapped. Resist bursting into "Rest ye merry gentlemen" we ask the driver about the blackout. 'Lights on very bad, very bad, run battery down. We no fix, very expensive, no good.'

So for the last 20 years, tourists could only safely travel between dawn and dusk, battery life was a very serious business in Sharm.

We acknowledged his concern. But in all seriousness we now had two taxis, nine fools and one sensible girl. A taxi race back to the hotel, double time was inevitable. 'Yalla, Yalla, let's go!'

Delighted, he shouted at the other taxi driver, they lined the taxis up.

'Yalla…Yalla…!' The ten of us sped off into the night, unable to see a bloody thing. "Hark the Herald Angels sing" …the little fairy lights jingling everywhere. We make the 40-minute trip in 15. Rewarded handsomely for their rally skills and pure night vision, we thanked them and went to bed. The car batteries saved for another day.

Day 2. The Australian instructor confident that he now had a compliant, very serious diving group led us to the next dive. Unsmiling, we entered the water. We have hatched a plan. Al will divert the instructor while we practice for the race. Each one rides the beast and gains experience. Masks on top of head, snorkel out. I'm beast riding about 25 metres down. The fish stop to marvel at the spectacle. Unimpressed at the tomfoolery of the underwater apes, they swam off…Meanwhile, the tour guide is oblivious, bored he instructs on with only Al in tow.

The second dive, the race is on. Al and Johnny will occupy the Australian, while we will line up for the race. Go for 20m down. It's going like clockwork we have eight divers, four jockeys and four Beasts. Just about to start, the instructor becomes suspicious. He doubles back, swims around a reef ledge and catches us at the line-up. Incredulous, eyes wide open, knife out banging his tank like a lunatic. Motions for everyone to surface.

Disappointed at the premature disruption of the race, we head back up.

On board, he's developed a twitch. He's trying to control himself. No longer bored, he starts to lecture at the very serious nature of diving. No longer hiding behind congeniality, 'You Pommie Bastards could die down there and worse than that I will lose my fucking license. I will have to go back to Tasmania,' he shudders. 'Have you seen the bloody Sheilahs in Tasmania!'

Silence, I was shocked. I had no idea the lady situation was so bad in Tassie. Strike that island off my travel plans, I took a mental note.

Now convinced of his right proper bollocking, he storms off to the captain's cabin, muttering something about the Anzac sacrifices and Churchill being a fat bastard.

'Right, boys and girl, this is the three BSAC instructors (with several hundred dives all over the world between them) talking, if anyone is up for it we are going to show you bouncing. We'll do it, you guys just watch, it's unconventional to say the least. Could die, but remember diving is a very serious thing.' We all laugh, let's get back and have a drink.

That night the word has spread. The taxi drivers are fighting over who will give us a lift into town and how fast they can do it. A local bookie has set up shop and bets all over Sharm are taking place.

We arrive in town in 13 minutes. Dusting ourselves off, we head to a local bar. Few tequilas later we go to a restaurant. Al is opposite me, 'You know Al, I spent 20 odd years in the Middle East and I've learnt a thing or two.'

Al, staring back admiringly, sweat on his brow.

'One of these things is a deep understanding of Arabic cuisine and the surrounding culture associated with it, it's like a ritual.' I continue in full monologue. 'So for tonight, I will choose a dish for us to share. Remember Al, sharing is the very fabric of Arabic culture.' Al enthusiastically agrees, wipes more sweat away. Unconcerned frown, all over his face.

I head to a makeshift counter with a wide selection of two fish. Now, we're on the coast, fish is the natural choice. I expertly chose the green one.

The local chef, swatting a few hundred flies dead on the fish with his hand. Spat on the floor and grinned. 'Good choice, infidel.'

I agreed but felt regret that the fly wedding party had been cut short, the honeymoon ruined. Mourning would start first thing in the morning, for the bride, groom and 600 guests.

I checked the eyes to make sure they were sufficiently cloudy and therefore fresh. Ordered the delicacy. Chef excited, barks to the cowering waiters, 'Feed the INFIDELS!'

Back to the table, Al opposite, heavily perspiring.

'So Al, I've ordered the delicacy, well known treasured fish, very culturally important.'

'What's it called?'

Me back, 'The Green Fish.'

Al back, 'Are you absolutely sure you spent 20 years in the Middle East?'

'Al, Al, my good man, oh ye of little faith; trust me. Have I ever let you down?' Al, stifling a groan, 'Here we go again...'

'Anyway, Al shush, I'm thinking of writing a cookbook on Arabic cuisine and culture. Did you know when a new guest arrives, in Bedouin hospitality, to offer them the best morsel is the greatest honour!

So tonight, in the greatest Bedouin tradition, after we consume this delicacy we are going to eat the eyes, one each,' I exclaim dramatically.

Al sighing, 'Brian I'm pretty sure that's a sheep's eyeball, not err fish?'

'Al, my good man, that's exactly what an infidel would say.' Al rolling his eyes. 'Anyway, the premise is the same, you both see out of them, don't you? Let's not get caught up in fact or any detail Al. That nonsense always ends in cultural misappropriation,' I informed my first culinary pupil.

Al under his breath, 'I can't wait for the release of this new culturally important cookbook.'

'Me neither Al, very important day indeed. The world will have their eyes opened at last. Not unlike these two grey ones staring back at us.'

Al hesitant, 'I'm sure they're supposed to be clear.'

'Al, yet again, that's exactly what an infidel would say!'

We consume the fish. Two eyeballs left. Order a shot. Pluck out an eyeball each. Salute (sihat jayida/good health), down the hatch...

Tomorrow we have a deeper dive, SS Thistlegorm. A famous sunken ship, super cool; on every divers wish list, 100% not to be missed. The SS Thistlegorm, built in 1940, was sunk in 1941 by a pair of Heinkel He-11 bombers with all military cargo still attached. Now a war grave about 30m down with jeeps, Norton and BSA motorbikes, even a locomotive still in situ. You need a minimum of 20 certified dives to be allowed down. It's on most divers' hit lists but not Al's, not on this trip.

The morning arrives, Al in bed next to me writhing in pain. Both of us were up all-night relaying back and forth to the bathroom. Even our pores are leaking toxins in a vain attempt to rid the ravaging food poisoning bugs. Between gasps and floor rolling, Al says, 'I told you it was a sheep's eyeball, not a fucking fish.'

Me back, 'Who knew? Damn it! I should have picked "The Red Fish"!'

Al, shrivelling up like a dried prune. He was being drained from every orifice. 'I can't dive today. I think I may be dying.'

This was a man that had speed-marched 60 miles for two days at a time when his feet looked like the insides of a tuna can. I knew he was screwed.

'Maybe next time, stay off fish. Try a halal chicken eyeball instead?' I mused.

Maybe, we should have taken a step further back. Start smaller and tried prawn eyeballs instead, build up our immunity? I would investigate on my return. Try one on Al, in between his death-throws. One more trip to the loo, no bodily fluids left. I was ready.

I crawled out of the room, time for dive day no.3.

I'm so ill. The dive is at least 2-3 hours on the boat. I'm on the front writhing in agony, accompanied by a new deeper shade of green. As the sea-sickness joined forces with its cousin, Ebola, the final assault on my mortal coil was underway.

I can see the Australian looking down gleefully. Cheered up at the thought of my toxic death. I could see him mouthing 'Pommie Bastard.' Revenge for being directly related to one of the Queen's Corgi's, no doubt. The corks on his hat jiggling all over the place…the motion makes me sick all over again.

We finally arrive. I am the size of a small shrew; so much liquid has left my body. We go through the dive plan, 'You all right mate?' The Australian shoots over, looking very unconcerned.

'I'm good, let's just get the fuck down!'

I crumble into the water. About 5 metres down, I start to puke. I'm vomiting through my regulator. The fish are ecstatic, the mayor has turned up. The "Green Fish" they had sent on the covert mission to poison the infidel had come through. The banquet could start in earnest now. His death had not been in vain.

15 metres down, I'm gaining control, still feel really crap. 30 metres then bit more below, I start to recover. So finally, I have discovered a new cure. The world's press would be waiting. Nobel Prize for Medicine, a surety.

Not only will eating fish eyeballs in Egypt make you wish you were dead but you can solve this by deep diving. The bugs utterly confused as to how they have ended up 30 metres under the sea, press the panic button and abandon ship. I knew I had to get back and inform the medical world and Al.

However, I was still not feeling great. The botulism was playing hardball.

Back on the boat, I had to expel the last of my virtues in the boat loo. However, as much as I tried with buckets of water it wouldn't flush down. Five buckets and still feeling like death, I gave up. Only to open the door to the only female group member. Pretty, petite and private school educated but no education was going to protect her from the aftermath of a fish eyeball challenge.

I bade her good luck, shouted 'squirrel' and dived over the side; to be attacked by a 'herd' of passing dolphins.

Avoid the poor girl like the plague for the rest of the trip.

2nd dive of the day; bit deeper, I start to feel almost normal. The deeper I go, the more it dissipates, 40 metres down, I feel good. Before I Narc out, I rise. Nitrogen Narcosis (Narc'd), is where nitrogen gas bubbles form in the blood, due to pressure and you start to feel stoned. It's a great killer of many a happy diver.

Just as well the hippies hadn't found out. The sea would be littered with floating guitars, tambourines and hairy, dyed jean wearing corpses.

Dive over, I arrive back on the boat. The first fool had survived. Back to shore, see how Al is getting on.

Day 3 nearly over, Al is the size of an amoeba. Still writhing, I ask him what on earth was he playing at, lazing in bed all day! When not only was the dive of the century on, but I even managed to mouth-feed the fish, like a pro.

Beast and Johnny had been demonstrating bouncing too. I scolded his lifeless form.

'Man up princess,' I encouraged Al. 'We have a taxi Rally to win. Followed by Hukkah pipe smoking. Then there's the halal prawn eyeball challenge (keep it safe this time). All to be finished off, by a lesson in Arabic from the swearing monkey.'

Al feeling apologetic, in no uncertain terms, told me to go enjoy myself!

'No pleasing some people,' I retort. 'I gave you an intricate cultural education on Arabic cuisine and this is how you repay me…INFIDEL!'

Al groaning, 'You nearly killed us both.'

'Al, Al, my dear chap, food poisoning in Egypt, you can't get much more authentic than that? You can thank me later. I'm off to the bar.'

Day 4. Al lives, time to "bounce". The Australian, now with a full twitch and greying hair is murmuring to himself. Smears himself in vegemite to ward off the Pommie Bastards and starts to feel better.

Backwards somersault, we all drop into the warm water, the reef is looking spectacular. The Australian has given up all idea of control. Al, Johnny, and Beast start to bounce. Which basically means pinging from 30m down to 50m super-fast, this is so not recommended and I waiver all knowledge of said events.

The Australian instructor by now has completely lost it. Knife out, tapping his tank like a mad man. We get our knives out and start tapping our tanks back in unison. We all surface. Fun over, he runs off sobbing, back to the captain's cabin. Muttering something about flying home immediately and declaring Tasmania a Pommie free Republic.

Last night. The locals have decided that rallying at night with Xmas lights is an excellent idea and has become the new Egyptian national sport. The bookie turns up in a Ferrari with the lights off, thanks us for supporting 20 tribes and the upcoming local election fund. We head out, arrive 10 minutes later. Tequilas with no eyeballs, we have a great last night, as top mates.

Dive 5, the Australian incoherent, full grey hair, no longer bored. Al leads him on the dive. Now, 20 metres down, we display all the skills we have learned.

Johnny riding beast, Al is bouncing at 50 meters down. The rest of us have our knives out and are re-enacting a 17th century sword fight.

On the surface, we all look at each other. 'I think that went well,' we all agreed.

'At least no one died this time,' laughs Beast.

'What do you mean this time?' I gave Al a sharp look!

Back on board. We eventually arrive back on shore, where the local ambulance run by the local Jihadis quickly whisks the hysterical Australian back for reconditioning.

We need to rush, it will take at least five hours to get through the passport control hut. But first, we have to wave the "Starting flag" for the first: All Night, Fairy Light, Sharm Al Sheik, inaugural Taxi Rally. Sponsored by Duracell.

How many participated or watched or even who won? No one knew.

Walking past the passport hut, the same large Egyptian passport controller is truly delighted that the non-believers were finally leaving his chosen land.

'Goodbye infidels, have a nice day,' he growls pleasantly and spits on Al's shoe.

We all look up from Al's shoe. What a genuinely lovely man we all agreed. 'An absolute delight!'

27
Diving the SS Breda: Life Insurance Claim No.1

The ink hadn't even dried on the life insurance policy Damien had secretly taken out on Shirley and myself. If you looked closely at the small print, a full pay-out was assured if no bodies were ever found or if we died horrifically in a car crash.

Damien, Shirley's old boyfriend, had been a deep-sea diver on the oil rigs and was not known to take survival too seriously. Damien turns up in his trusted Saab 900, otherwise known as "the Tank". He's wearing a crash helmet, which really should have given away his murderous intentions. 'Jump in we're going up the West Coast to dive the SS Breda.'

Built in 1921, sunk in 1940.

Damien only knew how to drive either in the middle of the road or on the wrong side. This depended on how recently he had visited his therapist. Blind bends were perfect overtaking opportunities. Damien (quite rightly) believed that no one else was foolhardy enough to attempt such life shortening skills, thus avoiding a head-on crash.

We drew straws. Shirley lost and took the passenger seat. Shirl wrapped the seatbelt around her neck, to make for a quick death, in the likely event of an accident. The three-hour trip took about 40 minutes. As our two screams finally faded, Damien cut the engine. At least we were awake now if not petrified. Damien switched on the windscreen wipers and the two elderly cyclists we had picked up 40 miles back slid off the windscreen. Disappointed at the poor body count and lack of life insurance on the two layabouts, Damien says we've arrived.

There was just enough adrenalin left for Damien to start the second attempt on our lives. What had Shirley done to have us both murdered? This needed investigating. If that "sticky beak" Miss Marple was waiting on the dive rib we were shagged. I would give her a good kicking this time, the witch. Phew! No sign of the vicious foreteller of death, bloody do-gooder. Probably off murdering some poor sod in Boston.

I was now feeling quite positive, surely if we were to die today that road trip from hell would have done it. I spoke too soon, Damien starts to do some press-ups; 20 this was serious. The last time it was 10 and we had ended up in the decompression chamber. I would have started sweating if the minus 20 wind-chill in this skimpy "wetsuit" would have allowed it. Damien had thoughtfully "commandeered" our kit from the school where he worked as the Dive instructor. It wasn't officially stolen if we returned it all in one piece. It must have belonged to a 12-year-old girl, as I may as well have been wearing a small plastic bag.

Damien grins back, professional full dry suit on, snug as a BBQ'd bug. Bastard.

We make a jump for the rib. Shirley just managing in her wetsuit, suitable for a small 8-year-old, flops on board. I'm counting: 24, 25, 26…The weather has picked up and white horses are galloping along the waves, racing each other. We arrive 20 minutes later. It's now hitting a gale force, much to Damien's delight; 124, 125, 126…

The boat is moored to the wreck buoy. We somersault in, and start our decent down the guide rope. It is absolutely Baltic and the Vis doesn't stretch past my retinas, we can't see a bloody thing. Hand over hand, we make our way down. The current is ferocious and is threatening to tear us from the line. I look up. Shirley's eyes are wide as saucers, just like my sphincter. 156, 157, 158…

The SS Breda rests at an angle; the top half is about 20m down leading to the quarterdeck 30 plus metres down. One tank would usually suffice unless you were going into the bowels. Then normal folk would take a guidewire, needed for safety and those with a keen sense of self-preservation. As Damien was far from normal nor keen on safety (especially ours), the idea of it ever being part of his constitution was an anomaly. He would have us both killed in the guts of the ship.

Rubbing his perfectly warm hand at the thought of the pay-out, we crawled along the deck. Any lifting up and the current would have swept us away. Shirley and Damien are about three fourth the way down towards the bridge, 201, 202…Boom! Shirley has removed her snorkel and is thrashing Damien, who is pointing to a hole that he wants to lose us in. Shirley is world famous at losing her temper. She has won the global Miss "effing furious" championships three years in a row. Damien is getting a bollocking at 30 metres down in the freezing soup. Even the current has stopped to enjoy the spectacle.

Bollocking and thrashing over, we crawl past the hole and enter one of the cabin doors. We have to be careful not to travel too far. Many a diver has become disorientated and joined Davey Jones's locker on the Breda. Damien's dive computer is starting to beep manically, alerting all non-certifiable folk to evacuate immediately. In our plastic bags, frozen solid with one tank each we press on…where fools feared to tread, Damien marched on.

We enter a couple of eerie rooms, careful not to stir the silt, any more non-visibility was unnecessary, it may as well have been a night dive in a tunnel. That's it, another sound thrashing, the knife will be next, I'm sure. Damien, at last, sensing his own imminent death at the frozen hands of my sister, relents and we turn back. Just in time as his dive computer is hitting a new state of alarm, desperately tries to unstrap itself from its unhinged owner and swim to safety.

We crawl back, I can't feel anything. I'm in full hypothermia, snap the toes off when, or if we make the rib. The current has picked up even more if that is possible. The silt has stirred up completely. I can see about a foot in front of me.

We miss the line twice before all three get a good hold, we make our treacherous ascent. The current is so strong we are heading up horizontally. I can see Shirley's snorkel and my fin disappearing into the deep grey swirling mass, now officially reported "stolen". I wondered if Damien had those insured too?

We finally scramble back onto the rib. Shirley and I are cuddling each other, to get the blood back into our blue bodies and avoid death by irresponsibility.

Damien, 'Wow, just WOW! What a dive, that was mental!'

'Damien,' Shirley snarls, 'when I finally get any feeling in my body, I am going to stab you in the eyeball.'

'Wonderful!' shouts Damien. 'Now that's what I call being ALIVE!' I stop Shirley's lunge, the domestic would have to wait. It was still minus 20 (in the wind) and my testicles had made an executive decision and migrated north, to seek refuge with my kidneys.

Damien, 'God, it's boiling in this suit,' he exclaims. I look at our frozen Asda bags, moonlighting as loosely described wetsuits. 'I think I will kill him first,' I inform Shirl. 'We'll draw straws,' we both agreed. How many times had I peed in the "suit" to keep my body at a life-saving 37°C? The warm insane Bastard, I looked over as Damien started to do some star jumps.

We get back to shore, pack the kit up. We draw straws; Shirley wins and takes the passenger seat. That's an ominous sign. Had I packed my diazepam? This could get rough.

Damien sets off at 143mph. 1, 2, 3…I immediately action my silent scream and find a safe place in my head, naked, chasing rabbits in the forest should do it. Ah, that's better.

Meanwhile, 4, 5…Boom. Shirley is wrestling Damien for the steering wheel. Screaming, that's it, time for him to die! The car swerves over the road, which ironically was identical to our trip up. C'mon Diazepam, work your magic my little beauties. Damien wrestles the wheel back.

'Are you trying to get us all killed?' says a muffled voice behind the crash helmet.

'Me, you BLOODY shit!' Shirley exclaims incredulously.

I lean forward. 'Right, can we leave the domestic, until we make it back to Edinburgh alive?'

Both fall silent, fuming inside. Damien runs over another elderly jogger, now feeling better.

Looks back at me for five minutes, 'Brian, you know what?'

I stop chasing bunny rabbits and re-enter my body. 'What?'

'We've got that mountain trip next week. I will pick up (commandeer) some ice picks and crampons from the school, go up Cairngorms and practice getting lost.'

Under my breath, 'God I wish that insurance company would just pay-out. Then he could stop trying to murder me.'

Big warm thumbs up from Damien. I would have given him the finger back but it was still frozen to my palm. The toasty proper mental Bastard.

28
Cairngorms Avalanche Training: Life Insurance Claim No. 2

'Isn't life wonderful?' Damien exclaims as he jumps up from 30 press-ups on the -30°C ice.

'Well, it was for those three charity race runners, just before you ran them over.'

'Yes,' Damien says annoyed, 'they really slowed us down.' Looks up, the weather is closing in. 'Let's go.'

We start to head up, passing the ski lifts, move higher over a couple of ridges. We attach our crampons, get the ice picks out and Damien teaches a masterclass, just in case of an avalanche. Hammer in both picks firmly in the ice to stop falling and make sure bend knees, so crampons don't hold and flip you off the precipice. I've got it.

We move further up to greet the complete white-out with utter delight. The visibility is shocking and everything is starting to freeze over. This time I had brought my own gear not trusting Damien's thieving instincts (from his old school). I probably would have ended up with a 13-year-old girl's blazer, necktie and skirt again.

I was confused, why on earth was I trusting "Damien the unhinged" again? Get us both killed, AGAIN! Maybe I could make a claim on that life insurance policy too, we could split the cash?

I queried Damien on our imminent demise. Damien, 'It's called "living life to the max", Brian!'

'What, by being killed, Damien?'

'Yes, of course, that's what living is all about.'

I knew irony was never going to form any element of Damien's thought process or belief system. We head up to a really, really, narrow steep ridge; we are traversing the sides like two frozen Yetis. Suddenly, no warning Damien dives onto the side of the ridge, plunges picks into the side and lifts feet off ground, the fucking side is giving way, its certain death.

Cursing my poor climbing buddy choice yet again, I instinctively dived on top of Damien instead of the ridge. 'Get off, what are you doing?' he tries to shake me off. 'Look prick,' I informed my demented guide, 'if I'm going to die, you are too ASSHOLE! What about the warning shout bit, Damien?'

'Err yes, it was just so quick,' Damien the assassin mumbles weakly.

Right, once the danger was over and I clambered off him, 'If you are not careful Damien, I am going to do a "Trotsky" between your shoulder blades.' I wave the ice pick menacingly at him, 'then my friend you'll be living "life to the max" on this very ridge.'

'Hah, all good fun, let's crack on. Now, where did I put that map?' Pulls it out from the side of the backpack just in time for the wind to whip it away across the ravine.

'Shit,' exclaims Damien!

'Yes, Damien thank you, we are now officially in the shit,' for once I got to roll my eyes.

'Damien my good man, when you said practice "getting lost", I thought you were being rhetorical. I didn't realise you fucking meant it.'

'Hah, don't worry Brian, we have a compass.'

'Can you even see it?'

The weather is in full gale, the snow is whipping like a sandblaster. You couldn't see one lousy foot in front of the other. One of my eyeballs had frozen solid.

'Let's build a snow cave ride it out for a bit,' Damien finally has a moment of reality.

We settle down, eat some food and drink from a flask; we wait for a couple of hours. The weather breaks, right we need to shift. The problem is we can't see a way-point to get a reading.

Let's head to the top and see if we can see any ridges that might give us a clue. On the mountain peak, we get a break in the cloud. The range which looks identical goes on for miles and miles and fucking miles. If we get this wrong, Damien won't be able to make that life claim after all, as either the weather or my pick imbedded in his forehead would have seen to that.

'Hey, what's that?' Damien says excitedly.

I look, just make out some dark movement. Look closer yes, it's definitely climbers; four of them. We start shouting and finally they spot us, we catch up.

'Christ, what shit weather?'

'Yeah, came in super quick, caught us out too,' the group replied.

'Hey, that's a Cumbrian accent,' I exclaim through the frostbite. The four Cumbrians' agree that indeed coming from Cumbria that would make it the correct observation. 'Do you know how to get off and reach safety?' we ask.

'Well, we would have but we have lost our only compass.'

I don't believe this, bloody typical! Only Scots and Cumbrians, my two trusted gene pools colliding, could and would lose their only navigation tools and think that was wasn't a complete fuck up. Under my breath, 'Fuck me!' We look at each other through frozen eyeballs. We need to move quick-time on this "certain-death" mountain in full whiteout. If we don't get the fuck off now, none of us will be "living life to the max" any time soon.

"Living life to the max", greatest non-exponent of life Carl, the group leader grins, 'Let's go!'

Christ! I would have to go along to the next life survival mountain training course; explain to the group the meaning of "irony". Being killed young is not "living life to the max". I would coin a new motto *"dying young to the max"*, much more appropriate. Especially with Damien as my heroic guide.

Carl, in monologue, 'By eck, me n't fella's been bivvy whacking fort week, back t' civilisation when caught on't small hill wid'weather, near death thrice. Great fun!' They all grin. Bloody Hell, only mad Cumbrians would consider this a nice relaxing holiday, in minus 30, with dying a good result! Damn those genes, it sounded like an excellent idea, I had to admit.

However, guided by killer Damien, next time I would take my own map, a working compass, and a Kalashnikov to kill him with.

'OK, let's get off this beast.' Between the two groups, now with a full complement of life-saving navigation tools (our compass and their map) we could maybe get off. Just needed way-points but they were hard to come by. The weather went rough a few more times. We traversed another peak and spotted a cairn that was popping out of the seven-foot snowdrift. 'Got it,' Damien whoops.

It was now getting dark, after nearly 10 hours on the range, we made our final descent.

We finally reach the car park and high fived each other with the ice picks. 'Now that's what I call living life to the...' whoops Damien, a crampon "accidentally" imbeds itself into his foot. Quick yelp, it's time to leave.

We bade the mad buggers a good (if short) life and hope never to see them or us lost in an artic whiteout ever again.

Damien contemplative, 'I think that went well?'

'First class, smooth as always Damien, my good man,' I congratulated him.

'Great! Now to get my *kill points* up, I make those last three joggers a good 60 pointer.'

'Oh Damien, you can do much better than that,' I offered. 'But first, we to have to prepare.'

Damien put's his crash helmet on and I uncap my pill tub and three shakes later, 20 diazepams swallowed and silent scream activated, we tear off home in the Saab 900 beast.

29
Hitchhikers' Guide to Ireland

King Brian Boru (978-1014 AD) enters the room.

God booms, 'Before you say anything your highness, can you put £100 in the "swear box", last time the room was blue. Charles needed counselling, as did the mimicking parrot.'

Parrot angrily, 'Fec…' God pinches the beak together, 'That will do.'

My lord, 'Tis the way of the Irish, be jes…'

God throws him a stern look, 'Make it £200.'

King Boru, does a quick calculation in his head, puts 260 euros into the box and sits down.

'I hear you and "Evo" boy are playing chess, you know he's one of ours, old Irish both sides.'

'Isn't everyone,' retorts God.

'Yes, very fashionable, Irish these days, top 'o the morn.' God sighs, 'Indeed, even Charles has Irish in him. Mainly a few Guinness's on a Sunday, then you can't shut him up. Just don't mention his book (with a few pints in him) or ironically we'll be here till eternity.'

'Well, won't that be a grand tale, the beardy boy on the good stuff; pure genius.' Pint in hand, 'Charles you pour yourself one too, top 'o the morn.' They all get comfortable.

'Potatoes, let's start.' White Pawn takes Black Knight.

'Slanj!' King Boru and Charles tap their pint mugs together. They all look down. The parrot looks down too, 'Oh FEC…!'

So I get a phone call, 'Brian, catch a flight over to Dublin, get the bus to Galway and we'll pick you up.' Pete hangs up the phone. Kiwi mates are travelling around Ireland. Big Pete, his brother Adrian, and Debbie (Pete's long-suffering girlfriend), who after camping with the two boys for several weeks, was about ready to murder every living organism.

'Excellent, see you tomorrow chaps.'

Arrive Friday, straight to the pub. 'Let's have some of this Irish "craic", says Adrian. Full of drink, we finally head back to the campsite. Big Pete, slurring, 'Did you get any of that Irish "craic"?'

'Didn't understand a bloody thing?' I slurred back. 'Me neither,' Adrian says, starting to hiccup. Deb, joins in yawning, 'Nope, not a single word!' Slight flaw in the plan, I had just come over with a duffel bag for a long weekend, so no sleeping bag et cetera. Alcohol and multiple clothes wearing would suffice. Three pairs of socks later and four boxer shorts on, time for sleep.

'What are we doing tomorrow, Big Pete?'

'We are going to kiss the Blarney stone. I've been practising.'

Debbie annoyed, 'Pete dearest, put that bloody rock away, let's get some sleep.'

Jump in a hired car and off we go to Blarney Castle. In order to kiss the Blarney stone, you hang backwards and give the big rock a solid "smacker". The legend of the rock is that by completely ignoring basic hygiene standards, kissing it gives you the "gift off the gab". Pete got carried away with his tongue. A grown woman screamed and a small child was taken ill. After security had regained their composure, we were escorted off the site. 'Practising, hey Pete?' I grinned.

I threw Deb a look of pity. Deb, embarrassed, 'He has been practising on rocks all week.'

'He hasn't improved,' I commiserated.

Pete suddenly exclaims, 'Potato, Feck!'

'Pete,' I queried, 'what the Feck were you doing, Potato?'

'Feck, Arse, I don't know?' he replies. Deb starts, 'Potato, arse too.' We all look at each other, 'What has happened to our chat?' Big Pete, 'Feck, Potato must be that stone, feck, arse. TITS!'

Now that we are speaking fluent Irish, we couldn't shut up. We were making "Spud's" job interview, *from 'Trainspotting,'* look positively tranquil. Back in the pub, I get chatting to a local girl. 'Feck, potato what's the craic with the stone?'

'Ah, that'll be the fecking curse, legend has it if you have Irish ancestry, kissing the stone will awaken your Irish.'

The Galway girl continues, 'One poor American tourist, a priest, had to be repatriated, every word he said was Feck, followed by bum, didn't go down well with his 85-year-old congregation.'

'How long does it last, Potato, Feck.'

'Oh, it fades when you leave Ireland.'

'Thank Feck for that. I will be writing to the Irish Tourism board, first thing in the morning to insist on a warning sign placed by the stone, Potato.'

Back in the tents, I relay the chat with the Irish girl to the Kiwis. 'To be fair Pete, that's your normal chat anyway.' Pete back, 'Arse, TITS!'

Right, let's get some sleep... 'Good night, "top of the morn", bum,' says Pete.

'Feck off, potato to you too,' Adrian murmurs.

'Sweet Arse dreams everyone,' I said. Starting to snore, we all fell asleep.

Day 3. We do some sightseeing, avoiding conversation so as not to offend the masses. We head back to the campsite. Deb wants some peace from boyzone, so Adrian and I will hit the town, they'll go see a movie. We all jump in the hired car, back to Galway. We get dropped off in town, they go off to the movies. Everyone's happy, especially Debbie's therapist.

After showing Adrian how to breakdance and body pop instead of his usual twerking; we were finally getting somewhere with the ladies. Galway had not seen dance moves like this, since Michael Flatley, high on crystal meth, had last come to town. Escorted out by the baying mob, we hit one last nightclub, it's about 2 am.

Couple more drinks, I'm chatting to some local girls. 'No, no, be-Jesus, you don't have to get a taxi back to your campsite. Everyone hitches over here, dead easy. Hitch, get some craic, go on, go on, GOOO ONNN!'

'Hey Adrian, the ladies say don't worry about a taxi, we can hitch, piece of piss.'

'Are you sure mate?' Adrian replies with a frown.

'100% bulletproof Adrian, trust me, can't fail!'

Not five minutes outside the club hitching, we get a lift from three gorgeous girls. I'm looking at Adrian, grinning from ear to ear. 'No flies on me mate!'

'Yeah, yeah, bastard,' he grins back.

'Sorry boys,' the driver looks back eight minutes later, 'the campsite is that way and we are going in the opposite direction.'

'No worries, was it the Potato chat?'

On the road, it starts to rain. Wearing our fluorescent Hawaiian shirts, I felt pretty confident we would get a lift. 'Adrian, have trust mate, when have I ever let you down?'

'Well,' Adrian sighs, 'there was the time…'

'Not that time again,' I retorted. 'That's so last week.'

'Then there was the time before that,' say's Adrian, now in monologue, 'and the time before that even…'

'So last month, Adrian…

Right, let's just move on, shall we?' I informed my untrusting hitching partner. 'Let's start walking, campsite can't be that far.'

20 minutes later, about 3 am a car comes along. Stops 20 yards ahead, we run to get in, it speeds off with an arse hanging out of the window. We start walking again; it's now 4 am, two more speeding arses later. We start to jog, a couple of miles later we come to our senses. Fuck me, if we sweat out all the alcohol, we would have wasted all that money putting it in.

Delaying sobriety, we start to walk again.

After a count of six arses and one pair of boots, I was delighted at this unexpected bonus at mile 13.

'A good sign,' I told Adrian. We finally arrived exhausted at the campsite. It had been light for hours. After what seemed like an eternity, a good 10 hours later and completely sober, with Adrian still shaking his head, we collapsed into the tent.

Adrian, 'I am never, ever, listening to you ever again! EVER! FFS!'

Me back, 'Potato.'

We crash till after lunch. Pete and Deb are in hysterics.

'It was so not funny, bloody Irish,' says Adrian.

'We did get one decent consolation "flash",' I said, trying to placate him. Adrian throws me a dark look…

'Well just saying, silver lining and all that.' Adrian, glowering, livid. I sighed, 'There's just no pleasing some people.' Adrian looks like he is going to kill.

'Right, I need to know how far that was. Let's all jump in the hired car and check on the speedo clock, get some supplies too.'

'18 miles, 18 fucking miles…18,' mutters Adrian.

'Well,' I said, 'at least the Irish has worn off!' He throws me an angry, confused look.

'You said fuck not feck…must have been all that walking, so I've actually cured us.' I grin, delighted with myself.

After Pete managed to unwrap Adrian's fingers from around my neck and I regained consciousness, I knew we were "besties" again.

Looking up at a passing plane, I suddenly realised I had a flight to catch and needed to go. 'I will see you all back in Scotland,' I said cheerily.

'Do you think I should try hitching?' I asked the kiwis.

Adrian makes another lunge for me… 'ARSE!'

30
Hunting Aliens, Lost in Dargo

Darwin, 'Mankind sure likes to fool his own brothers and sisters!'

God, 'Well, that's a sweeping statement, dear Charles.'

'Well, my lord, for starters, let's take the moon landing for one, are you seriously telling me they landed that tin-can on the moon in 1969? The average Trabant 601 had more technology.'

They both start laughing, 'Yes seriously funny, they may as well have sent a Banana.'

God smiling, 'Well, they certainly took humankind on a "Banana ride" that time. Truth is always the first victim when people are trying to invade with ideology.'

'Well, I'm glad we sorted out that little misdemeanour.' Pop, Pop! The toaster expels the little delights, 'Excellent that will be the crumpets. Charles be a good man and don't be too stingy with the butter.'

Both seated, 'Now down to the game, where were we?' Suddenly the doorbell rings in a very strange fashion; the odd tones starts playing, blue, pink, yellow and red colours light up the room "dah, daa, dah, dah, daa…"

E.T. enters on a small child's pushbike with his little finger in the air acting as a guiding torch. 'Home, home! We send him home!' E.T. repeats in a delighted fashion.

'Ah Eric,' God smiling, 'you have arrived at last, we are just about to start. Pull up a seat. Let's see what our good Alien friend has got in store.'

E.T. waddles over, sits on the chair with his feet dangling, childlike. Moves a Black Pawn which takes the White Knight. God intrigued, 'How interesting?' Eric, 'Now we send him home.' They all smile.

So I get a phone call, 'Mr Dawes that is your flight booked to arrive in Perth, Australia on Saturday. Enjoy your stay.'

Two of us, an old girlfriend and I. 'Let's travel around Australia for six months, then catch up with my old Queensland crew.' What could possibly go wrong again? Girlfriend, I to my life shortening escapades, grins back excited.

We see a campervan for sale, in the local backpackers for $1000, sorted. Two Dutch girls have just finished their travels and are selling their van. They turn up with long blonde hair dressed up to the eyeballs, obvious selling tactic that I was not falling for. As I drove off $1300 lighter, with girlfriend glaring at me, I knew it was a sound buy.

Off we went on our travels, in the 1600cc Toyota Hi ace van with the 1.2 million kilometres on the speedo clock, mattress in back and camp stove to keep us alive. I picked up some fishing rods, gas for the camp stove, 60 litres of wine, seven cases of beer, 300 packets of 2-minute noodles and 5000 cigarettes. Rough plan, pick up supplies and catch fish on the way around. Genius bulletproof plan, I assured my future ex with a weak smile.

Australia is big. Very, very, big. The van had a top speed of 60kph at a push, this was going to take time. One month later, another attempt on our lives is made, after being run off the Nullarbor Plain by yet another psycho road train (two-trailer monster truck). The "truckies" in general thought braking from their 120kph speed was for lesser men. Foghorn blast and the little van careered off into the desert bush once again, to kill the last remaining Roo.

It occurred to me that tourists practising life survival road skills were massacring what was left of the local wildlife. We stopped to take a few photos of the marsupials, all unmoving on either side of the road. A bit like ourselves, if we didn't get off this 1700 km stretch soon.

Travelled, camped, fished and drank warm alcohol, we arrived in Southern Australia. The journey led to one of the most isolated places I have ever been. Spectacular beach, fishing was going to be awesome. We camped up in a makeshift Rangers campsite. With one other campervan next to us, we went fishing.

A couple of hours later, back in the van, fish and noodles eaten. Big Knock on the side of the van (no windows).

Open up the side door, massive six-foot four bloke.

'G'day mate, I'm the local ranger. How you two doing? Mind if I come in for a wag, I haven't spoken to a soul for two months or so.' As the suspension dropped four inches, the big fella called Jack entered. I knew I had to be on my guard. *I had watched the Australian horror documentary, Wolf creek. Whereby (out in the bush), some mad Australian bugger exposed to too much sun and warm beer, went mad and started eating unsuspecting backpackers. As you do?*

We shared a smoke and a warm beer, just to make sure that any cooling from the 40°C heat was a virtual impossibility.

The three of us sweating and swatting mozzies, start wagging. 'Where you guys from?' We relayed our travel story so far. 'What about you, what's your story?' I asked the big fella.

'Ah mate, I've been out bush for 10 years or so now. I forget.'

'Shit mate,' I said concerned, 'are you lost? Do you need a lift back home, see your family?'

'Na mate,' humour lost on him from overexposure and general madness. So I said, 'How do you manage that, Toyota Hilux?'

'Na mate, on foot.'

'On foot, bloody hell, where have you come from?'

'Oh, I first travelled from Victoria over to Western Australia then up to the Northern Territory and I just kinda loop around, visit the tribes.' As I looked at him, he realised that we both knew he was obviously insane.

'Yeah, even the Abo's call me crazy, can't believe the places I travel on foot.'

Me, 'How do you survive, even the lizards are booking Easy Jet flights out, it's so fucking hot!'

He laughs, 'I slow my body and mind down, reserve energy, use bush-craft, eat berries, and I fish. I can survive off one fish a day and any roadkill I come across, that's good tucker. Oh and snake. I like snake.'

'Aren't they all poisonous?' I enquired nervously.

'Yip. Mate, I could show you how,' he offers generously.

'Y'know what, I'm good. We have non-roadkill 2-minute noodles (which now sounded delicious), if you fancy a change.'

'What and miss out on me Tiger snake, bloody Pommie Bastard.' Now in Australia any animal, even a dead one just has to look at you, instant death. Even the twigs, one look…dead!

Another warm beer another smoke; must be about 45°C in the tin-can campervan. As I dreamed of Jack and mine's fine dining experience:

> The Waldorf's outback bush tucker A 'la Carte menu. Violin Quartet
> playing. 'Haute cuisine' fine dining:
> Tiger snake gall bladder soup starter;
> Roadkill Roo with a medley of entrails for the main
> Finished with a flurry of Puffer fish poison paradise.

I was starting to salivate, 'Three months of 2-minute noodles' I started to repeat to myself. Jack heard my distress, he comforted me best he could. I wiped away a tear. 'The snake really is bonza mate, no foreign tucker out bush, all organic.'

Meanwhile, the van next door is going wild, drunk as arses. Stereo is screaming *I come from a land Down Under*, on full blast with two wild Australians singing their hearts out.

Jack, tosses a sharp look in their direction. 'I will have a word later.'

'No worries Jack. Look as you have so much time on your hands, I have just finished this book I brought with me. It's called *Custom of the Sea*.'

Jack big grin on his face, 'Nice one, I can read it before sunset, what's it about?'

Me, 'You sure you don't want a lift home, see the wife and eight kids?'

Custom of the Sea, was the unofficial code of the old 18th century and earlier tradition of eating your own crew when shipwrecked. In the old days, if your ship went down and you were on a lifeboat or make shift raft, as starvation knocked on death's door, you would start to eat the lower ranks. Starting with the cabin boy, that's why on a long sea journey the cabin boy was offered BBQ sauce as sun protection, while everyone else was on factor 50. Cabin boys not the brightest but very tasty.

As the cabin boy bit spilled out. It suddenly dawned on me that Jack was a serial killer. No man that size could live on one fish alone per day, *Wolf Creek* sprang to mind again.

Fantasy became reality, I wondered if I could reach the frying pan in time and bash his brains out. Or that all those years of studying Karate Kid's moves would pay off. I made my move and lunged for the pan. *I would explain my rationale to my hysterical girlfriend, after we buried his body in the bush.* Jack stood up and bade us good night and safe travels and he would have a word with the party van. As we waved him goodnight with the frying pan still in my hand and the van righted itself. I said, 'What a lovely chap.'

One curdled scream later and a muffled denial of never even being at sea let alone a cabin boy, we fell asleep.

Woke up, no van next door and no sign of Jack. I wondered if that book giving was such a great idea and that my next novel. *How I accidentally created a serial killer* would become a hit.

Next adventure, quick stop at Melbourne, four months into travel. Let's have a nice meal for once. I had woken up sweating again, after being chased down another dark alley by an angry pack of 2-minute noodles. It was getting tiresome.

Vietnamese, really nice restaurant, combed hair we're good. Camper van hidden on a different street so as not to crash the local housing market. Order a sharing deluxe platter, it's flash, big flower on top, waiter hovering over smiling, anticipating our delight. Girlfriend grabs the large flower in the middle of the dish, starts chewing on it. After what seems like an eternity, the waiter rescues the plastic condiment from said diner's mouth. I knew then that she was a keeper. As the waiter rolled his eyes and became excited in Vietnamese, we left.

Back travelling. Avoid civilisation mode button…on.

Next stop…Dargo.

Five months in, my beard has an ecosystem all of its own. Travelling through Victoria along the coastal route, we see a sign, *Dargo winery-30km*. The little van takes a turn left.

Arrive in Dargo, it's a small village with a winery at one end and a hotel at the other, with an ongoing generational feud in-between. We stop at the winery and go for a drink. Served by a lady in her early '60s, true blue Australian. 'G'day, what can I do for you?'

'A couple of wines, please.'

'No worries.'

'The wine is fantastic,' I complement it.

'Yes, it's my husbands, he's originally from Austria, and his family has been producing wine for generations.'

'Yes, it shows.'

We have a few more, sod it, we'll crash in the van stay a night. A few hours later, at about 8 pm, a huge guy, six-foot-five wild staring eyes enters the bar. He looks proper mental, large booming voice… 'Ja you guys like the wine?'

'We love it.'

'Goot, Goot, long family history, come let me join you' (the bar is empty).

Sounds good. A couple of hours later, we have Hans' history, a family of Austrian wine growers, immigrated to Africa, was ex-special forces Rhodesia (another one, I checked no relation to the colonel) and completely insane.

I knew we were going to have a good stay. Hans talking, 'You know what, we are about to pick the grapes this week. Why don't you two help and we'll pay you in wine.'

'Perfect,' Dargo stay it is.

Meanwhile, another one and the only customer enters. Hans booms over, 'Hey Syd, come and meet these two, they are going to help harvest.'

Syd mid 50s comes over introduces himself, another true-blue Aussie. 'G'day.'

Syd, Hans and the two of us, have a few more drinks, we chew the fat. Tired, we head back to the van. 'Y'know what lovely people, completely normal. Just shows, you can't judge a book by its cover,' I say to my girlfriend.

Early the next morning, we start to harvest the grapes, it's 40 degrees of pure Australian heat, but the work is fun and everyone is enjoying themselves.

Hans, 'Lucky the snakes were not out today.'

'Snakes?'

Finish up at about 5 pm, we head to the bar, to drink our pay.

Four of us again, a couple of hours in, we have bonded. Syd, 'You know Hans was in special-forces, well I was a vet in the Vietnam War. Let me tell you a few stories.' About an hour in and blood completely drained from our faces, after describing, the horror, torture, necklacing and general destruction of all and sundry. They had gone feral and were out of control, the devil of war had entered their souls.

After the war, Syd became a long haulage trailer truck driver. I recounted being run off the roads along the Nullarbor.

'You were lucky we all took loads of drugs, amphetamines, speed, everything to stay awake. It had also been a hangover from the war,' Syd explained.

Great, so not just psycho drivers, but hallucinating ex-vets at the helm, that would have given Freud many a sleepless night. Hans pipes in, 'Tomorrow night you can come out. We are going hunting in the bush, plenty of rifles and ammo.'

I'm curious, 'Deer?'

'No, No, No. This is important business and crucial to Australia's and Dargos' national security.'

I am intrigued, 'Go on.'

'Yes,' puffs chest out proudly, 'we are hunting for (there's a dramatic silence) …Aliens.'

'Oh crap,' I said under my breath.

Tired and sloshing with vino, we return to the van. I say to my girlfriend, 'Y'know, what crazy people, completely insane, just shows you CAN judge a book by its cover.' I love it, it's mental we are 'defo' staying now.

Next morning, there is the biggest wild boar, must be 200kgs arrived overnight and housed in a pen at the back. Hah, I thought to myself, hunting Aliens, cheeky bastards. They are out hunting wild pigs. Hans is there, talking to a real true-blue Aussie, cowboy hat and boots. Classic stereotype.

'G'day mate,' he introduces himself. 'Yeah, we got this monster pig, we are having a BBQ wedding this Friday and he's gonna be the guest of honour.'

Me, 'Is he marrying one of the locals?'

They both roll their eyes, bloody Pommie Bastard. 'No mate you drongo, he is the tucker, but we have to boil him first, so the hair drops out. That's the bit me and the good old boys are trying to figure out, he's a big prick.'

Four more cowboys turn up,

'Nah mate, what about a drum?'

'Nah mate, what about an old bath?'

Nah mate…the conference goes on.

'What we do need is a great big fucking fire.'

'Agreed mate,' they said in unison. I left the Aussie senate to deliberate on their cunning pig boiling plan. I wished the pig luck, he was going to need it with their sharp minds.

Another day harvesting with interjections of SNAKE! As I stifled another scream and resisted the urge to save my life, we cracked on.

Back to the bar, I check on the pig. Still there, as are the cowboys. 'Nah mate, what about a drum, nah mate, what about…' I thought the pig might be safe after all.

Back at the bar, we have a few drinks.

Hans, 'I'm off out hunting with the boys, you want to come.'

'No, I'm good. We are going over to the hotel across the village tonight.' He shoots us a steely glare, walks off, taking his wild staring eyes and unstable disposition with him. I shrug, 'Let's go.'

We have a nice night. Walk back, it's a bit creepy. There's a weird feeling of being followed. Arrive at winery at about 11 pm. Syd's the only customer.

'Hey Syd, how's it going?'

Syd, 'Like bloody hell, no.1 there is a massive feud between Hans and those bastards at the hotel and no.2 did you not notice all those eyes following you.'

'What eyes, Syd?'

'Wild dogs' mate. Pet dogs, gone feral, very, very, dangerous. Especially to Pommie buggers. There are some real brutes, American Pitbull crosses, Alsatians, Rottweilers…you name it.'

Me, 'So even the pets eventually become Australian, and then set out to kill you!'

'Yip!'

'Oh FFS!'

Syd lightens the mood, 'I will take you on a tour of the bush tomorrow, show you the sights.'

'Excellent, good night Syd.'

'Good night Pommie travellers,' he bade us farewell.

As we are leaving for bed, Hans arrives back in, 'Wow that hunting was insane. We only just got away.' I said 'Lucky you weren't eaten by Cujo.*' Hans humour fails again… 'Not animals, I told you Aliens.' I stifle a foreboding guffaw as the six foot five ex-special forces started to relay his mission over the last five years of hunting Aliens out in the bush and the close encounters he had witnessed. I thought E.T. would have been toast cycling across that full moon; Hans was an excellent shot.

But only armed with his small team of cowboys, he had managed to protect the area, hold off the impending invasion. As I thought of the cowboys earlier, I knew that we had entered the twilight zone. Looking around, I was waiting for the music to start, oh there it is…when Syd pipes in, 'Yeah they're a pain in the arse those bloody UFOs.'

As I pictured Hans shooting at the Moon, Mars, Saturn, Jupiter, visiting meteors and the odd possum (collateral damage), we went back to the van to sleep. Followed by 40 hungry eyes.

In the Ute (pick-up) with Syd and his sheepdog in the back, Skippy. I ask Syd, 'You haven't taken any mind enhancing drugs today, the park is only 5km away.'

Syd puts his stash away, 'Old habits mate.'

It's really beautiful, stunning. Skippy is making a stereotype of a sheepdog, herding invisible beasts in a general state of intoxicated happy confusion. Syd is going mental. Constantly shouting at Skippy, 'Get out of there, get out of there, don't go in there, stay out of there,' on a continuous loop. I'm thinking it must be a training issue.

I ask Syd about this, as we settled down for a light lunch and a few beers, in the bush.

'Snakes mate.'

'Snakes?'

Syd waves his arm expansively, 'Everywhere, the place is riddled.' As I gained my composure for the 50th time that week, and curtailed the urge to scream. I asked, 'Poisonous?'

'Deadly, the bloody lot of them, lost three dogs last year.' I thought suggesting a lead might not go down well, or never ever leaving one's house as a practical means of pooch life preservation. As I resisted the desire to run and dive into the back of the Ute, screaming every man, woman, dog for themselves, we finished the last couple of beers and headed home. Skippy completely unaware of his master's futile attempts to have him killed, jumped in the back, off we went.

Meanwhile, the cowboys had stacked a massive pile of wood ready for the pig's de-coating exercise. As the fire took hold, and the (now dead) pig bobbed in the massive water-filled drum, I thought that the wedding party as a back-up might want to have the local Pizza Hut on speed dial.

The week seemed like a delirious eternity. Last day, it had been insane. Dargo, who knew of this village of madness? Under continual attack off rabid pouches, poisonous snakes and baffled aliens, proudly protected by the posse's leader, six foot five ex-special forces, Hans.

As I waved goodbye, I saw the pig's four upright legs poking out of the drum. The water still not boiling, 20 hours later…

I thought Dargo, would indeed summarily be invaded by extra-terrestrials, with the cowboys in charge of village defences.

Off the little van went, onto the next misadventure.

*Cujo was an 80's horror movie whereby a rabid pooch (rottweiler) with anger management issues ate everyone.

31
The Professionals, Batman Returns

Back in Scotland. Looking up from the dance floor covered in broken glass and beer, I couldn't help but admire Bryce's robotics. We were at the top of our game. Between my body popping and Bryce's pneumatic moves, we were flawless. The 30 hairy bikers behind Bryce growling menacingly knew this too.

Earlier that day, Dave our long-suffering manager at Bauhaus Pharmaceuticals was on the phone.

'So we can all catch the train up to Aberdeen for the team Xmas party.' He sighs, 'Just let's not have a repeat of last year or the year before that. HR and some of the spouses and their hungry children were still looking for some team members a week later. Maggie was eventually found on a park bench two days later cradling an empty bottle of Gin, snarling at passers-by.'

'Yes, I acknowledged she has form that one. Remember that conference last year with the photo booth?' Maggie and I were dragged by Cathy into a comedy dress-up photo booth. The three of us have our fancy dress costumes on. I'm in the middle, Cathy on the right, Maggie on my left (next to the booth exit). Next costume change there are only two of us. I look down to see Maggie's feet still in high heels poking through the curtain. The other 90% of her was sprawled outside. I start to drag her back into the booth by her ankles. As I'm doing this my head is poking through the curtains and I look up to see a massive security guard, his face incredulous.

'All good!' I explained, 'She's a drug rep, perfectly normal behaviour.' We continued with the photoshoot. The shoot over we receive our little strip of photos. First, there's the three of us, then two and a half as Maggie fell through the curtain, then just Cathy as I'm dragging Maggie back through by her high heels. Then, viola! The three of us again dressed as pirates and a pig, all in hysterics. Maggie would be rationed to just two bottles of Gin from now on. Make sure next time we get a full photoshoot and not scar the security team for life. Maggie concerned, 'Don't tell Jeff, he'll kill me.'

'Don't worry Maggie, my dear, discretion is my middle name. He can read it in my book.'

I gave Dave a sympathetic look, 'Then there's Victoria! Remember the time that she bit Bryce in front of that senior manager. We couldn't prize her off; she'd just had her new teeth put in.' Dave starts groaning... 'Anyway, Dave, it was just as well you intercepted Bryce's Email to the director of HR:

Dear HR,

I would like to make a formal complaint against Victoria. Last night the fucking bitch bit me. On reflection, the organisation may have a rabies problem.

Yours sincerely,
Graeme Bryce
Territory Sales, Bauhaus.

Dave sighs again and starts to look for his medication. 'Dave, you know I keep telling you. It's 100% your fault. It was your poor judgement in our good characters that has given you chronic hypertension and insomnia. You recruited us in the first place, remember!'

'How could I forget!' Dave retorts. 'All those promotions passed up, the disciplinary meetings…that fire.'

'Dave, don't worry,' I comforted, 'we will all behave impeccably at today's Christmas party. Just like the professional team you have always dreamed of.' Dave, 'It's 10 am, I think I will have my first drink now.'

'That's the spirit what could possibly go wrong again,' I reassured his shattered nerves.

A few weeks earlier, on conference, Dave has warned the team again! Under no circumstances are we to admit that we are the Scotland team. If anyone from HR asks after 2 am, we are from Gavin's, the South Wales team.

'Now get your accents sorted before dinner tonight,' Dave growls.

'You two,' he gives Bryce and I a "hard" look, 'make it by lunchtime, I really need that promotion.' Under his breath he mutters, 'Or Tracey will break my other ankle!' Dave agitated, 'You are not allowed to talk to anyone above the rank of bell boy! GOT IT!'

We had just finished the last afternoon session that would make smoking a crack pipe on par with watching paint drying. We look at each other, both sigh, 'That was so fucking tedious!'

I confide in Bryce, 'I keep hallucinating that a giant smurf is being rogered stupid on stage by Paddington Bear in stilettos.'

'You too?' asks Bryce. 'Maybe it's delirium setting in.'

'Probably,' I acknowledged, 'can't wait for the marketing messages tomorrow. Fuck me. Maybe up the game and add some BDSM with little Miss Piggy that should get us through the morning session at least.'

Bauhaus Ltd has booked a hotel and we are sharing with another Pharma company, Lil-Lets Ltd. Both companies are in a formal alliance to sell one of their joint owned products. Bryce and myself catch up with Sarah, who is waiting by the lifts. Sarah suspicious, 'What are you two up to?'

'Nuffing, maybe go for a quiet pint?' The doors open and we are greeted by four elderly folk taking the lift upwards. Sarah enters, turns and is looking at us expectantly (to get in the lift too). As the doors close, with a couple of inches to spare, Bryce says, 'Get the porn on love, I will be up in five…'

Sarah now has 10 floors to travel with three accusatory looks and one elderly gent quickly penning his telephone number down. Sarah, afterwards, 'The embarrassment will stay with me for the rest of my life…!'

'Right Bryce, let's go for a pint!' We enter the bar there is no one there. Fucking lightweights, probably at that awards ceremony…

We have a few beers and are nicely relaxed, when a tall gent comes in, sits in the corner. 'Bryce, let's introduce ourselves,' it's 6.30 pm.

Half an hour later, after describing another one of our career shortening escapades. The drink jackets fully zipped up, we were bulletproof. We tell the well-dressed man, 'God, what a load of "shyte" this conference is. That Alliance company, wankers the lot of them. You can tell.'

'How?' says the gent who was paling out in front of us. 'Well, look around the bar, it's empty. Wankers!'

'Ahem, look I have to be getting to my room. I have an important meeting tomorrow, that I must prepare for.'

'Yeah us too, but first I'm going to take Brian upstairs and shag him hard up the arse.' We both burst out laughing. The gent holding back a little bit of sick stands up and makes a break for the lift.

'Bryce should we hit him with the porn gag.'

'Nah, he looks stressed enough as it is. Must be that really important meeting.'

Well, what a pleasant start to the night. True professionals! We clashed our pints together.

It's now 2 am and PK has just been escorted off the stage for the 8th time. Saddles over, we hand him back his pint of whisky. 'Got to the 3rd verse (of *Mustang Sally*) this time,' he grins. 'Before the bastards got me!'

'Err,' I interrupted, 'bastards "boyo" remember? We are in disguise now.'

'Aye, err…I mean yes, boyo' came PK's reply.

'Is that Welsh, the "yes" bit?' Bryce asks PK, with a quizzical look.

'I don't know try "Leek" instead,' I offered.

'No,' cuts in Bryce again, 'that translated into Welsh is "goodbye", boyo.'

'I didn't know you were fluent in Welsh? Boyo.' I replied, impressed.

Bryce looks at his empty pint, 'I am now, boyo.'

Anyway, we have cunning disguises. We hand PK a daffodil that we had "borrowed" from the wake that had been droning on for hours next door. 'Stick that in your ear, fool-proof.' Suddenly, a man all dressed in black drops from the ceiling, rolls in front of us and springs catlike to his feet. Oh crap, it's an HR officer. Looks at watch, 'Morning gentlemen, are you from Dave's Scottish team?'

'FUCK OFF…boyo!' The three of us replied outraged. 'We're from Gav the Welsh pricks team over there.' We point at a team studiously pouring over the brand plans ready for tomorrow's meeting. Their table has an array of glistening awards. I can just make one out: *Outstanding Manager of the Year.* The HR Stormtrooper strolls over to have a formal chat about his poor leadership skills.

I say to the boys, 'We'll nick that award for Dave later. Stop his missus putting him back on crutches, after returning home empty handed 10 years in a row!'

I could just imagine the conversation, on Dave's returns home, without an award in tow. *Tracey, his long-suffering wife, sighs 'Empty handed again? Dear husband.' Dave, head bowed, 'Yes dear, I'm sorry. It's that bloody team! Have you met them? They couldn't win a prize in a one ticket only raffle.' Tracey, another big sigh, her shoulders slumped, in a resigned, disappointed fashion, 'Go get the sledgehammer and wood blocks.' Dave stifles a sob, 'But you haven't met them, honey, sweetie.' Tracey, replies, 'Just shush now. No more excuses, I will try for a clean break this time, but I can't promise. I'm VERY disappointed.'*

'Yes dear,' Dave whimpers back. 'But THAT team?!'

'No more dear,' Tracey interrupts. 'Just go.'

So with that in my mind, we needed to get a medal to rescue Dave's ankle from the chopping block.

Next morning, Miss Piggy is giving Kermit a blowie in the brand plan session. Bryce and I after a 3 am finish are not feeling too bright. Dave is giving us "you're so fucking fired again" looks across the table.

Next, there is flashing lights, music and the stage erupts in a fanfare. "Defo" not helping the hangover. The smoke parts and there standing on stage is the very chap we had accosted in the bar yesterday.

'Ladies and Gentlemen, it gives me great pleasure to introduce you to...' *more drum roll...* 'The vice president of Lil-Lets.' *The room erupts in applause.* Bryce and I look at each other, 'Oh fuck!' Dave clocks us! Hisses over, 'A word after boys!'

'Dave, look the descriptions may have looked and sounded exactly like us, down to Bryce's dodgy jumper, but I swear on your life, we were going over the brand plans all night. You hired us to be professional and using an old adage, you get what you pay for.'

Dave under his breath, 'I wonder if that contract team is still for hire?'

Presently, the team of highly trained professionals are on the train heading up to Aberdeen for the Christmas work party. Dave, due to past team history is on his second bottle of vodka; it's 11.30 am.

We arrive and immediately make sure the fine dining experience of the other guests and the coveted Michelin star would be destroyed forever. Noaksey is in a giant panda onesie, Cathy is gargling champagne, Mish is having an entrails eating competition with Bryce who has just turned green after snorting Sambuca through a straw. Mel and Hannah are dressed up as S&M Santa's, all whips and chains. Carolanne was twerking and Eileen, dressed as a naughty nurse was giving Niall CPR, after choking on a potato. Kaz is belly dancing on someone else's table. Hilda who has the right hotel chain is sitting alone at a table in the wrong city and Victoria has just bit someone again.

What an outstanding team I thought to myself, so proud. Scotland would definitely clean up at the awards ceremony next year. Perfect time for a bushfire methinks. Before I start, I have to dodge out the way as Ritchie, Will, and

Graeme go shooting past on the desserts trolley pushed by Lynsey dressed as a Viking in full scream (obviously didn't get the memo).

Eight hours in, it's carnage.

Dave, 'Let's get a drink in.'

Dave comes back with a pitcher of TVR (Tequila, Vodka and Redbull) each. Stands up, 'I just wanted to congratulate the team on a very successful year.'

'Did we smash the sales target?' I piped in! Everyone starts laughing. 'Hah! Hah! Brian, you're so funny.'

'No,' says Dave starting to well up. 'None of you got fired! Not even a disciplinary. First year ever. I couldn't be more proud.' There were a few tears at the table that night I can tell you. Especially after Bryce fell off it again.

The whole sorry episode is being photographed by Gordie. The only non-alcoholic team member with a steady hand and sound constitution.

Bryce, slurring, 'Let's hit the town!' *The rest of the team are catching trains back home.* 'Cool,' I said, 'I will crash at yours, head back to Edinburgh tomorrow.' *What could possibly go wrong again?* I thought to myself.

As I finally stopped spinning on my head, I looked past Bryce's shoulder at the Bikie gang. It hadn't occurred that the Grampian Growlers bikies club (that we had staggered into by accident) were not up to speed with the latest breakdance moves. Thrown out by security to save our lives and their image as a bunch of ruthless outlaw renegades. We headed home.

I wake up, it's pitch black. I have no idea where I am. Have I been kidnapped again? Are we in electricity challenged Cumbria? I smash through a door, to find Bryce in the sitting room watching *The Professionals* on TV, in his Batman pyjamas. Looks at my glorious entry and the door lying off its hinges. Quick as a flash says, 'You're only supposed to blow the bloody doors off!' in a very dodgy Michael Caine accent...

'Now go to bed Brian, it's your PTSD playing up again.'

'Yes, Batman.* Bloody PMT!' I stagger back to bed in my boy Robin boxer shorts. *Thank the lord, his missus Donna was away visiting relatives!*

Next morning, Sarah, who lives in Aberdeen has brought her giant kid along. Marauding Viking genes all over the young monster. Sarah is going to scrape me off the sofa and give me a lift to the train station.

'Who's the smelly man in the living room?' I could hear the bundle of joy enquiring of my hungover corpse.

On the train, I have a first-class ticket. The flies circling my head are annoying the other passengers by landing on their cucumber sandwiches. The usual looks and angry muffled coughing starts. The good folk of the world were starting to make signs of the cross, a small child started crying.

Fuck this! Dignity intact, I crawl on all fours back to cattle class.

Christmas party boxed ticked! Still in employment box ticked! Now there's an unexpected result!

I congratulated myself on another successful year as a true professional. First-class, Mr Dawes.

"DING" Oh, hold on that's a text...it's from the Director of HR.

*RIP my great friend, it was an honour. Bryce wouldn't make it to the age of 50, suffering an auto-immune condition, secondary liver cancer would take his awesome soul. To you my friend, we danced the life fandango together for too short a time. Mine's a pint in Valhalla…yes, it's your shout.

32
Great Balls of Fire: A True Professional

Charles exasperated, 'Just one award, that's all I'm asking, what does it take? Could you not just strike him down with a lightning bolt, my lord?'

God hands over a pamphlet, 'See life rule 9.' Charles looks down, *No.9 No lightning bolts (even if you are really, really, tempted).* Charles sighs, 'I have a whole cupboard of awards gathering dust, it's soooo unfair!'

God, 'Yes I know, but I have a good feeling this time.' Darwin now excited, 'Should I go and get one, my lord?' God, little smile, 'Go on then if you must. But remember Charles, if he escapes this attempt, we can play time and time again, in between cups of Tea and Mr Kipling's cake. We do have all of eternity after all.'

'Oh yes, of course, my lord.'

'Well, in that case, let's get on with it! Time waits for no deity.'

'Or man,' pipes in Charles, clapping his hands together in delight.

Back in Edinburgh. Out of the pub, home is right. Darwin's first move, 'Makes him go left.' Black Knight jumps the Pawn and checks the White King, on the left-hand side. They both look at each other ecstatic.

Professionalism (noun) definition: the skill, good judgement, and polite behaviour that is expected from a person who is trained to do the job well.

I look in the mirror, suited and booted. *I look sharp, just like a true professional should,* I thought to myself. I had an important dinner tonight and a presentation to deliver to a distinguished clientele of Charity chiefs. Nothing could possibly go wrong again, I assured myself. Let's face it, that last incident, with the fire, I really don't know what all the fuss was about, it was eventually put out, after two days. It's not like anyone died!

Smiling to myself, I was growing in confidence. Let's do this Mr Professional.

Right, I better phone a taxi, these clients like a few drinks.

Important clients, clapping politely: presentation over. What a true professional. I heard one audience member say, ELECTRIC! Proud, I sat down next to Anne (the organiser and a good friend).

'Well done again, true pro Brian. Definitely food for thought,' Anne wipes away a tear.

'Thanks Anne, should we go for a few drinks, bring some willing clients too?'

'Cracking idea, my son is just back from Afghanistan and wants to catch up tonight.'

'Anne my dear, what excellent news. We should celebrate his safe return. I could re-do my presentation for him? Think of it as an excellent education and learning practice piece.'

'What an opportunity for him!' Anne agreed, rolling her eyes.

One hour later...Anne's son and myself in deep conversation. 'You see Steve, hiding a slide pane in a "Window's presentation" when in front of important clients is fraught with danger, anything could go wrong. Need nerves of steel, just like Afghanistan.' Steve frowning, acknowledges the danger. 'Uncanny similarities,' I suggested knowledgeably. Now in full monologue, 'Just like when you saved, under fire and threat of IED's, those 20 orphaned children from imminent death by the dreaded Taliban.' Anne's son agreed the parallels were quite striking...more Tequila is drunk.

We start a dance-off, on the 4-foot square pub floor. He's super fit, battle-hardened but no match. I have years of standing in front of screens presenting...quads of steel. Afghan village dance versus Edinburgh street dance. Suddenly, I feel the urge to twerk, I'm on it. My work shirt is covered in sweat, my tie, now a makeshift bandana keeps the sweat from my eyes. We collapse on the floor, both exhausted, it's a draw. The earlier clients who had joined us, look on horrified.

Anne holding a pint of Jamieson Whiskey wipes away a tear. 'You boys make me so proud. You as my son, a soldier fighting dark forces, risking life and limb to protect the innocent.

Brian, err we'll talk, maybe come up with something later.'

'Anne,' I said puffing up my chest, 'what about my expert "presenting" skills?'

'Yes, about that, the topic tonight was supposed to be; *How to fund, motivate and inspire those on long-term sick to re-enter the workforce.*

Your title: *How to get the lazy Bastards out of bed and back to bloody work.* Needs um, a little bit more developing...'

'Pretty close Anne, that's mere semantics,' I reassured her.

'Well Brian, your idea of "Electric shock torture" was a bit extreme.'

'Electric Shock THERAPY, Anne,' I corrected her. 'I thought that was inspired Anne, 50000 VOLTS would motivate me to get out of bed...'

'Ughh, I think you're missing the point Brian.'

'Am I Anne, am I?'

Eventually, we get up off the dance floor, dignity fully intact. Must be time to leave, the security is coming over. Ejected for bringing African-American street dance into disrepute, I departed.

Now, home is on the right. Two miles away lies safety and a nice warm bed. I turn left…

I wake up hungover. I'm knackered, have a shower, try and eat some food. Sod it! I'm going back to bed. In the bedroom, I look down. What the Hell is that? I find some kitchen tongs and pick up the remains of a shirt, badly burnt, still smouldering. One arm completely gone, no back or collar, the other arm still attached and the front still intact with buttons. Smells of BBQ chicken?

Oh, hold on a second. So as I turned left, onto the high street, there was an entertainer, with fireballs on a chain; the Edinburgh festival was in full swing. I watched for about 10 seconds and convinced the young man that I too was an expert. '10 years mate, in the Bahraini circus,' I informed him. 'I once even ate a burning lion. Oh hold on, was it a Tiger? I forget, anyway it was one of the Panthera genus.' I enlightened the admiring Russian, who spoke no English. '*Zalupa*,' (dickhead) he replied.

'Agreed my good man, now step back and be prepared to be amazed!' I checked for any wild cats. Nothing.

As I wrestled the flaming Nun-Chukkers off the good Russian, I nodded reassuringly to myself and waved at the growing crowd of tourists.* I begin my well-rehearsed routine. The crowd screaming in delight! One more mass duck, they shouted encouragement, 'Someone call the police!' One idiot tourist got too close and had to be patted down, screaming. What an inconsiderate scoundrel, I thought to myself. Bloody Japanese tourists and their over-enthusiastic photo-taking and general miscomprehension of the world at large behaviour.

An artist, even a pissed one, must be able to create unimpeded. I needed more space. I was a professional after all and this audience would damn well know it!

Stunned the crowd looked on unable to run, like rabbits in the headlights. They were mine! As my confidence grew, I had that recurring feeling of being on top of my game again. Nothing could stop me now, not even the blaze on my back. The ensuing dread on the previous owner's face, after demonstrating my swinging prowess, should have been a warning. One more swoop and the collective crowd took a massive step backwards, a woman fainted. I had this baby all sewn up.

As my years of training and watching Bruce Lee took hold, just like the back of my shirt. I remember thinking to myself, *Brian, look at these adoring fans, running screaming all over the place. There is absolutely no doubt, you truly are a professional.*

As the tourists fled in terror, the owner, muttering in Russian had to roll me on the floor several times, before the flames finally died out. Recovering his flaming balls, we exchanged pleasantries as he chased me down the road.

It would be a 15-minute sprint to get home. I was hungry; the smell of burnt BBQ chicken filled the air. I looked for the source, it was very close but every time I turned around it disappeared. No matter, I knew there was a cold pie waiting at home. Credibility intact, I waved to the few last remaining fans as I sped past, some still crying. It was very touching.

Back home after losing the Russian down the 6th alley, I thought that could not have gone any better, my good man. First class.

What a successful night! Great presentation, good customer relationship built. I was polite, showed skill and good judgement at all times. Delighted, I had even learnt a new skill.

I would demonstrate the new fire training with Nun-Chukkers at the *Annual Fireman's Health and Safety Conference* in the New Year.

I knew I was a professional; I had pulled it off. I would write a glowing report to the management team in the morning. The promotion was assured. One eyebrow left and not much of a shirt with a strange smell of BBQ chicken still in the air.

The smell began to make me feel hungry again, now where had I put that cold pie?

* Initially the gathering tourists thought that I was part of the street act, then as my swinging became more erratic and the fire took hold, they soon realised the error of their ways.

33

Three Amigos, Captain Sensible Rides Again

God speaking in earnest, 'Family is so incredibly important, the love, support and guidance is so crucial in making a good, solid, decent human being.'

Charles, 'I totally agree; all that wonderful evolution can be destroyed in an instant if the foundations are poorly planted and un-nurtured. A trusted mentor is an absolute must.'

'Yes, well we definitely have one here, truly dependable! Can be a bit too sensible sometimes, but solid none the less.' Granny Dawes with a tea trolley laden with cake enters the room.

God, 'This cream scone is marvellous! Granny Dawes's special strawberry conserve is a treat.'

She's such a dear, they both agreed.

'Well,' says Charles emphatically, 'Granny certainly knows how to bring up a respectable, stoic and very sensible son.'

'Indeed,' God acknowledges, 'safe pair of hands for sure. Now to the task at hand, Charles my good man.'

White King takes Black Pawn.

'That's very unusual, he looks so incredibly sensible?' they both agree baffled? Granny Dawes looks over, 'Oh bother, I better boil up some gooseberries…'

Some years earlier…As I landed in Bahrain, from Australia, my excitement was palpable. Dan was flying in from Scotland and for once Dad had remembered to pick us up. Probably because his partner in crime, Mum, was back visiting her own mother in Scotland. The parents' party "folie a deux" broken, we should be safe for a short while.

I was looking forward to a long relaxing holiday. The Cowboys in Toowoomba had been using my liver for Footie practice, jaundice was setting in. I needed to dry out badly and recharge for next season's play-offs.

Now, I knew that Christmas holiday would be fun but sensible and the alcohol consumption in proportion. Nothing would go wrong. After all, Dad was a relatively quiet, stoic individual, liked a beer for sure, but as everyone knew, a very sensible man. As a Managing Director, he was well respected and could be safely said to be a "pillar of the community".

In terms of the sensibility scale, Dad is an easy 10, Dan is about 3, my good self a hard fought 2; after all Dan and I were in higher education, which added the two extra points.

I felt a sense of calm as Dad suggested we go for a beer. Dad was definitely a safe pair of hands. The three of us enter the British club, catch up with old faces.

We finish up nicely intoxicated, we grab a shawarma as was to become our nightly ritual and head home.

Next morning, Dad is up at 6 am, goes to work. Dan and I, sleep off the small hangover. I'm 22 and Dan is 19, we're both pretty fit. Me, from playing football in a furnace and sprint training from Queensland's unreported snake epidemic. Dan from being beaten half to death most nights by his psychotic Martial Arts instructor aptly named "Mad Tam".

Dad being a dad, was considerably older, and had retired his football boots a few years back.

I just hoped he could keep up with a couple of hardened students like ourselves. I looked over at him, concerned. It was 1 pm we were travelling to the sports bar for a couple of beers. We join the familiar faces. There are now about six of us in the round, all Dad's good friends. Big Frank, an enormous Glaswegian, enters the bar.

He's a good friend of Mum and Dad's; he's a lovely man always kind and courteous. Frank runs the national Bahrain prison and is also the Chief Executioner and our annual Christmas dinner guest. Frank was ex-special forces of a company long forgotten and never really known about, originally operating in the Far East.

What one in modern times would be referred to as a black-ops outfit, Frank was doing the dirty work for Governments. Un-thanked and un-known to the wider community.

Dad and Frank, as was form, go to the end of the bar and are talking in quiet earnest. Probably some political mess that needed sorting. The local Shia had been kicking off again lately. Storm clouds were brewing.

Round 4, the ice-cold Fosters are going down a treat. Dan and I are getting stuck in. Amir, an old Bahraini Pearl diver and good family friend is regaling us with past dive stories. He was missing a finger, which he always swore had been taken by a shark. Thanking Amir for (yet again) ruining my beach bathing experiences in the Gulf forever and any saltwater swimming in general. I look over to see Dad and Frank have finished their conversation.

Dad walks back over. 'Frank is joining us for Christmas dinner,' Mr Sensible informs us.

'Do any of us look capable of cooking a Turkey?' I enquired. We all look at each other. 'Nope.'

Right, the Brit club it is for Christmas day.

Another case of Fosters consumed, we head off to "Shawarma land". Drunk we head home. Dad doesn't seem affected at all, damn it! True bloody "pro". All those years in the Navy and cutting his teeth in pubs, he was destroying us. I started to think we had been duped, was that the smell of a rat?

My liver was starting to pen a formal letter of complaint to my medulla cortex.

This carries on for a few more days, Dad up for work bright as a daisy at 6 am. The two drink hardened students are starting to slip, the earliest we can manage is 1 pm. My jaundice is gaining ground. Dan is groaning in a foetal position in the bed next to me.

Christmas Eve arrives we are off to the club, it's day six. We are on average drinking twice our own body weight in Fosters. The sessions are starting at 2 pm and not finishing until the early hours. Dad is averaging about four hours of sleep on a good night. The rounds are now consisting of 12 people.

The three of us are all inebriated, even finally Dad is showing wobble signs. We hear on the vine that there is a party at Paddy's house (an Irish mate), just behind the club. The three of us decide that being Irish they wouldn't mind with their famous hospitality being gate crashed.

As we entered through the front door the sword *Seamus of the Gaels* was quickly put back on the wall. When the IRA chanting finally died down, we felt most welcome.

Dad, 'It's like a Catholic, Irish masonic lodge meeting, let me try a handshake?'

'No, DAD, No! Wrong club!'

Being the only non-Irish IRA members, we had forgotten to bring our spoons to thrash on our knees. We quickly search the kitchen for appropriate utensils. Danny (Paddy's dad) strolls over, 'Top of the morn, be a grand night for it.'

Danny, between clenched teeth, 'Evening Tony, I see you have brought your sons along too!' Scowling, pours us all a Guinness.

'Slanj! Invading British colonials,' he welcomed us warmly.

'Cheers old chap, here's to the Queen.'

Muttering in Irish, rolls his eyes, grunts 'Feckin 3 Amigos!' Danny makes a jig like dance to the kitchen, with panpipes in tow, singing 'I'm a little leprechaun. So I am, so I am…'

Paddy stands up to recite a poem he has written…finishes with 'Down with the murderous British scum.' How delightful, the hosts could not have been more hospitable to their uninvited invaders.

I sing a Rugby song, finishes 'Stick your pole in a mole boys, stick your pole in a mole, shag a wallaby.' I take a bow and sit down to dark stares and Irish folk making signs of the cross. We could hear mutterings of devil-worship and something about the three amigos being let loose and the upcoming apocalypse.

Dad, who would normally slit his own throat than make himself the undivided centre of attention at a party, stands up and clears his throat. The crowd growls with delight, the spoons that were manically being tapped on knees have fallen silent.

Dad starts to sing, 'Maggie, Maggie…' then silence. We are all looking at him expectantly. Starts again, clears throat, 'Maggie…MAGGIE!' I start to cover for him by playing a knife and fork on my knee. If Dad was going to kill a famous song, I was going to give him breathing space with cultural misappropriation. Maybe, just maybe, we could escape before the Irish nationalists lynched us.

One more Maggie and Dad sits down, there is stunned silence. Damn it, I will have to up the game, I now have a wooden spatula and a salt shaker playing on my knee. Look over Dan has a whisk and a potato peeler drumming away on his elbow.

I nod at Dad, still in shock. He gets the drift, grabs their 17th-century priceless Celtic sword off the wall, wraps himself in their rebel flag and starts swinging wildly in the middle of the room. With a new found wind, he starts to sing again… 'Maggie, Maggie…MAGGIE…'

Paddy, emotional, crying in the corner after re-reading his poem, his spoons had fallen silent. I offered him a meat tenderiser if he was going to emotionally self-harm, in for a penny in for a pound I say.

Paddy finds a new source of inspiration looking at Tony swinging the claymore into the chandelier. Paddy starts to scribble with gusto, all over the pubs in the Republic, a new poem would be recited in honour of the martyrs. The night of a thousand cuts, a poem about a madman slaughtering heroic rebels with *Seamus Sword of the Gaels*.

As the sword got stuck in a lampshade, Dad was rushed by three burly Irishmen, screaming freedom or death.

Dad is rolling with the three rebels trying to retrieve the sacred sword. I spot our chance and grab a case of Guinness; Dan has a wooden ladle. Dad has now broken free clutching the remnants of the sword handle.

'Aw, must remind him of his old sea marauding days,' I say to Dan.

'Dad was a pirate?'

'Isn't it obvious!'

We gingerly make our way to the exit, followed by a cacophony of banjos, spoons, poem recitals and emotional renditions. Last image is of Paddy's large wracking sobs, feckin three AMIGOS!

Off the three of us go into the warm night. 'You know what sons! I think we will definitely be invited back next year' (we weren't or the year after that).

'Yes Dad, they must thank their lucky stars the entertainment turned up. Next time we should bring a stereo.'

Dad contemplative, 'They must be really poor to have to sing all night.'

'Keep the boredom at bay I guess,' Dan offered. What a horrendous way to live, we all agreed.

Paddy's poems had affected me, 'Yes, we should donate to their cause, sounds like a worthwhile charity indeed. Buy them some instruments too, using spoons? Tragic, not even having enough money to buy a triangle.' Dad and Dan both nod in agreement.

'Dad, you know what,' I said excited, 'I will write a poem for Paddy next year! I will call it "The Potato".

Cheer him up, so melancholy all the time, it's not good for his health.'

Dad, 'Aw, that's so thoughtful son.'

Yes we would definitely be back next year. Bring a golf club next time too.

Off to "Shawarma land", the three new found philanthropists staggered on. 'How does that song go again dad?'

'Maggie…Maggie…' Dad concentrating and then one more MAGGIE…the voice only a mother could love.

'Eat your Shawarma, Dad.'

We get up just in time to catch Christmas dinner at the club; we are now both in a foetal position crying uncontrollably.

Dad skips in, 'C'mon, we are going to be late!' He has his dodgy pony Christmas jumper on and has never looked better.

'We'll meet Frank and have dinner together.'

'Here, this will sort you out,' he hands the bedraggled hungover heaps two ice cold Fosters.

'I've already had breakfast,' he says as he empties the last of his can. 'Let's go!'

I look at Dan, 'I'm not sure I can handle much more of this, I'm fucked.' Dan a faint sheen of sweat on his brow, 'Me too!'

Dad is a machine, we finally acknowledged. He's going to kill us. Groaning, my jaundice and Dan's pancreatic failure were taking their toll.

Back at the club, I swat a fly dead, that had been feasting on one of my necrotic eyeballs. Frank's big booming voice, 'I see your father is taking good care of you,' he grins savagely. I'm looking frantically on the floor to see if *the hair had fallen off the dog*. Sod it, why fight. I would be wearing the whole coat again later if "Fostinator" had his way.

We start to consume Frank's body weight in ice cold Fosters. We have dinner and hear some details of prison life according to Frank. Thank God, we would never all end up in there…ever again?!

Later on, there is 18 in the round now. I've had to move onto vodka as the beer is making no difference at all. My liver is scribbling furiously again. Dad, 'Let's have an impromptu party at ours. We have loads of booze and batteries for the stereo. No need to bring your own cutlery or singing voice, just a gas mask.'*

Four of us in the car, "Drunk Driving" was a national sport in The Gulf. We end up stuck in a ditch. 'Right everyone out,' says dad, 'we'll bump it free.'

Dan, Dad, myself and Frank the Chief Executioner of Bahrain, are bouncing the car to get it back on the road. 'Hurry up!' says Captain Sensible.

'Why, the cops?'

'No! No one will be at the house to let the party guests in.'

The irony of us being arrested alongside the Prison Chief had not dawned on us. Frank would have to let himself in, with his own keys. Arrest us, then himself. A cop car did drive past, they must have recognised colossal Frank and pretended not to see. Putting their car sirens on, they sped off in the opposite direction with their eyes closed.

Back to the house just in time, as the other cars bumped out of ditches, removed from tree trunks and the "pulled out of the sea" intoxicated stragglers arrived.

Everyone into the bar room, the music starts. Dad, Dan and I (wearing gas masks) are behind the bar serving. 'You three look like the three Amigos,' Angie* says.

Yes, everyone agreed the three Amigos it is. Angie on the lunatic Richter scale, was off the chart. She was a classic Jekyll and Hyde. Lovely, until a few drinks had bypassed the grey matter, then she became a certified psychopath from Govan, Glasgow. One of the roughest areas in Scotland. Angie, now Mrs Hyde, after another drink, tonight has decided she will become a temporary lesbian. Just for the duration of the party.

She informs the three Amigos of this transition by revealing her 55-year-old breasts in one quick motion. Angie, swaying but proud, 'Look at these beauties!' Perception had tripped up the construct of truth yet again in Angie's mind. As the half-century boobs hit the floor, so did the three Amigos behind the bar. There wasn't even time to scream!

All three of us on the bar floor, Dan has fainted.

'Boys? Boys?' The thick accent searches for us. 'Do you think another woman would like these beauties?' Angie tells her own reflection.

I squeak from behind the bar, 'Maybe you should buy her a drink first?' Dan has regained consciousness next to me, 'Shush, shush…' Dad, looking very sensible in his pony jumper, has a tear running down his cheek.

Angie is now chatting her own boobs up in the bar mirror. But getting no visible "c'mon" signs, gets bored, spots an obvious lesbian kissing her husband. Wanders over. Last words, 'Look at these beauties, I'm a lesbian too.'

The husband screams and faints, thankfully caught by his adoring pregnant wife.

The next day, 4 pm feels like day 4001 AD, the sun must have surely burnt itself out by now. Dad has been at work for 10 hours already.

'I'm serious Brian, he is going to kill us.'

'I know Dan, should we subtly check for machinery or mechanical components?'

'He can't possibly be made of organic matter?'

'Maybe it's sorcery?'

Must be, says Dan, 'He hasn't even been for a piss yet! How do you even do that?'

'Anyway Dan if you'll excuse me, I'm going to be sick now.' Snap! We both rush to different loos.

Both in a cupboard cowering, 'Shush I can hear him. We should call for help…Mum?'

'No way,' Dan whimpers, 'she's far worse.'

'Your right my liver would never speak to me again.'

Dad enters the bedroom whistling. 'Boys? Boys? C'mon it's happy hour at the club. What are you doing in the cupboard? You won't find any cold Fosters in there, I drank them all this morning.' We fall out of the cupboard, hair and teeth everywhere. Flies circling around our heads and I'm thinking of throwing myself out the first-floor window. Dan makes a move first.

Dad catches him, 'Wow you boys are so keen to get drinking! Even jumping out of first floor window with no rope ladder. Now that makes me so proud.

You should have said if you're that desperate! We can pick the pace up.' Shaking his head, he laughs. 'Boys just like their dad.' Rubbing hands, 'Let's go, the bar awaits…'

I think I'm going to start crying…

Dad chorales us up and bundles us into the car, in a flood of tears. 'Remember we were burgled last year, I put a security latch on that window.* We'll drive instead, arrive there faster, get more drinking time in.' I whisper to Dan that I need a lifesaving drip, could he steal away at the club and call a doctor. Next time hide in the washing machine. Dad knew we were allergic to laundry cleansing equipment, he would never suspect. Be sober and safe for a little while…

There are 26 in the round now, average age 56. I'm not sure which country or interstellar planet I'm on. Try whisky, the vodka has no effect now.

Dad is telling a story of how last year when Daniel and himself were in Mansouri Mansions steak house, they had nearly been blown to pieces by a Jihadi bomb. I'd obviously heard the story but at least I could keep one interested eye open as I suffered organ failure silently. I nudge Dan, one eye opens up.

'Yes, it really was a great steak!' Closes eye and starts snoring again, on his feet.

Dad and Dan had been having dinner, it really did have a good reputation for fillet steak and baked potato, that restaurant. Just about to get stuck into their steaks, whilst sitting by the window, a bomb had been planted and detonated. Fortunately, it had been placed in the wrong direction and had blown outwards. The Japanese table next to Dad and Dan, disgracing their Samurai heritage, had sprinted out in every direction, screaming.

Dad, after they had finished their steaks, (after all you had to book to get a seat, demand was outstripping supply) was furious at the security forces trampling all over the evidence. Colonel Jones turns up, aviators on. Daniel can hear them outside conversing…'Bloody amateurs!' they concur.

Dad was livid, he had been looking forward to that Crème Brule dessert all week and one little incident…they just had to shut the kitchen down. Jack Jones to Dad, 'The Ship Ahoy has a very good Crème Brule, you can still catch it if you hurry.'

Dad to Dan, 'Jump in the car, let's go!'

I was so jealous! A steak literally to die for! The pair of lucky bastards.

Last night of the three-week marathon, we are at the club there is 43 in the round, I order a pint of bleach. Nothing else works. Martin finally turns up in a Korean Gama (human carriage) carried by his 12 bodyguard girlfriends.

Reminded me of that caring, non-sharing legend, Mick from Toowoomba. They had the same gentlemanly protective disposition. "Marvellous Martin", one swoosh of his long brown locks and the left flank of bodyguards fainted, another glorious flick and the right troupe collapsed, righting the carriage once more. Martin's locks would never recede, just like his unquenchable libido.

He stepped out dressed in a magnificent deep velvet robe with solid gold lapels his famous moniker MM, embroidered in the finest silk. You could see the legend was exhausted after being carried around all over the place by his adoring entourage. Buy my good friend an ice-cold Fosters, perk him up. His throat must be as dry as a snake's eye, barking orders all day long. His girlfriends were not known for their map reading skills, so Martin was forever getting lost in the old Bahraini souk, the desert and lingerie shops. His nerves were at wit's end, poor chap.

George and 'H' have also arrived (Dad's mates) wearing t-shirts with the logo, three Amigos wanted 'Dead or Alive!' 50 Dinar Reward (on the back). Picture of the three of us behind bars on the front. Our family's past penal discrepancies were finally coming home to roost.

The three of us? I was baffled, Dad was so incredibly sensible.

Dad, 'George is organising a Hash run tonight in the desert if you two fancy it?' The thought of finally sweating out some poison on a 5km run was irresistible, every organ, tissue and cell was in agreement. This might just save us. However, it was George, so I was suspicious.

The Hash is a 5km fun run with multiple false trails. There had been people lost wandering aimlessly in the Bahraini desert, often dressed in completely inappropriate outfits, for years. The Bahraini Bedouin had reported seeing Gorillas, Werewolves, Dracula, Bugs Bunny, Scooby Doo and even the Queen *which had caused widespread panic amongst the Al-Khalifa Royalty. Had their PA misplaced Her Majesty?*

So I should have realised, as I sat with my buttocks out on a large block of ice with a pretty girl on my shoulders, pouring a bucket of ice-cold beer over our heads, that I was never going to dry out in "expat world".

The Hashers are chanting 'Here's to Brian, he's a blue, he's a Hasher through and through…he's a piss-pot so they say and he'll never go to Heaven in a long, long way.' The bucket empties, and my internals all start complaining again. 'Dear Brain…'

Last day, Dad annoyed in airport departures. 'Right! I want you two to learn a song off by heart! Before next Christmas, when that Irish party invite is sure to drop through the letterbox. We'll show them! But no more rugby songs about molesting unsuspecting animals! Got it!'

'Aw Dad! Just one?'

'No!' Walks off, fresh as a daisy, singing 'Maggie' to himself.

'Thank fuck that's over! I'm going back to Uni to bloody dry out.'

'Me too!' says Dan.

'Dan bro, did you see that wire poking out of his neck? Next time bring some bolt cutters, short wire his circuit board. Stop the "Boozinator" in his tracks.'

'Do we have to come back? I'm scared.'

'Christ, I hope not! First stop: AA rehab, when I get back to Australia.'

'Yeah,' Dan replies, 'I'm putting the Scottish Samaritans on speed dial on my return.'

He looks so damn sensible?! We both agreed, scratching our hungover heads.

'Later bro!' Utterly shagged, we have one last cry and sweating alcohol, we flop into different planes.

The stewardess takes one look, grabs the speaker phone and frantically screams '…Is there a MEDIC on board!'

Another look over, another squeal, 'Scrap that! Is there a PRIEST on board!'

*Robbery. Dad by himself asleep gets woken by a robber and molester trying to get into bed with him. Quick sort out and he was assisted in exiting head-first from the upstairs bedroom window.

*Gas mask, during the first Gulf War, all expats were sent gas masks as a precaution against an attack by Saddam. So, in true expat style, the only sensible thing to do was…have a gasmask party. All perfectly normal.

*Frank would be "disappeared" a few years later. You didn't get to retire to Florida and draw a nice pension in his "sensitive" line of work. Another inconvenient truth, long forgotten.

*On reflection, I wonder who that bomb was intended for. Who knows? Dad did indeed wear many hats.

*Angie a few years later would drag four victims along to Radio Bahrain at 8 am after an all-nighter, New Year's Eve party at hers. The reason, the DJ had refused to play her radio request. At the barrier, a Pakistani guard came out of a little hut, 'Yes madam how can I help?'

Angie, 'I've Come to Kill the DJ!' the soon to be fired (and repatriated) guard looks at her and us, 'OK Madam, you can go in,' unbelievably opens the barrier. Inside Angie, has stormed the live show and is explaining to the desperate DJ the intricacies of temporary lesbianism, on New Year's Day, in a Muslim country. That was Angie, through and through…a completely normal expat.

34

Ode to Tony Dawes; Tinker, Tailor, Soldier, Sailor...Spy?

God sighs, 'Is it that time already?' Looks up at the clock...which has stopped ticking.

Neptune, God of the Sea, 'I'm afraid so, my old friend. As you know, no one escapes, that's the rules.'

Black Queen takes White King, the only two pieces left.

The King falls across the board lifeless. CheckMate! Neptune, with a heavy heart, 'I will go and get him,' picks up his trident from the umbrella stand. King Dunmail, the last of the Cumbrian kings and last Briton to rule the tribe (circa 530-590 AD), moves out of the shadows to look down at the board. Saddened, 'Wait, your lordships. What a life! One of life's greatest adventurers, this one.

Before you leave Neptune, Lord of the Sea, let's look at one of the most intricate games ever played.' They pull up another chair.

'Sit, King Dunmail, last of the Britons, he is one of yours, as well as ours.' They all look down, the Chessboard resets itself.

White Pawn moves forward, by itself...

It's Mum on the phone. 'I'm worried about your dad, he was supposed to return home yesterday?'

'Don't worry Mum, I will go and check. He's probably tinkering with his boat again or the pub might have got in the way.' Mum, laughs nervously, 'No doubt.'

I drive over to the boat club; it's starting to rain and the very last leaves have fallen in the October chill. I can see his blue car in the carpark, take a peek through the window and everything looks normal. I can see one of his trademark caps on the back seat.

A couple of days earlier, Dad, Dan and myself, had a day's sail in the Firth of Forth. I had just come back from Australia so it was great to catch up and see their new boat too. It was a great day, very relaxing, Dad was in his element. Since his Navy days, he had always loved the sea. Everyone was on form. It was a great laugh telling all the old stories.

We moor up and head to the pub, have a great time. We have to head back into town but Dad has decided he is going to stay and sleep on the boat. The boat needs lifted out of the sea and stored for winter, so there's work needing to be done.

As we are leaving, I can see Dad seated, 'Dan go and ask if he wants a pint.' Dad puts up his hand, you could never buy him a round. So typical of this kind and generous man. Dan comes back over. I look back and smile, not knowing it would be the very last time any of us would see him alive again.

I walk over to the jetty where all the boats are moored on small pontoons, the rain is getting heavier. As I make my way to the boat, I have to "duck" under a small underpass. Just before I do this, I can see the RNLI team further down the jetty, they have a dummy that they are leaning over. I just assumed it must be a training drill.

I head to the boat, something isn't right. There's a carry-out fish and chip box un-opened and a bottle of red wine just sitting there. I go on board and check the cabin, the door is wide open his laptop and personal effects are all there. I can see his favourite book, Treasure Island (a book that as a kid, made him yearn for overseas adventure). The full realisation starts to dawn on me. I head back to where the RNLI team are.

On the jetty, they make way for me, I can see my dad, there's been some trauma to the side of his head. His eyes, once sparkling, now lifeless are half-open. My world collapses. I throw myself onto his body. 'Dad, what have you done? What have you done?'

They eventually pull me off and I'm escorted back to his boat. I'm back in the cabin, emotionally shattered. I can smell him everywhere. I pick up his treasured little book and start to weep. The police arrive, I explain all the events of the last two days and the phone call from my mother this morning, hence my search. They console me best they can.

My confidence, like a glass bottle falling in slow motion onto the hard floor, shattered into a thousand pieces. Creating hairline cracks of emotional imperfection from that day on. Always present if you looked close enough. He was my rock, my soul.

Oh God, what am I going to tell them, Gran too, her first born? This is going to kill us, and for Dad, a life cut short. I start to shake with the shock and enormity of what has happened. The police take me home, the longest drive of my life. Everyone is devastated, utter disbelief and shock. The next few days are a blur. We are walking around and talking but inside there is just a vacuum. I start to drink heavily, that would last years...

John, my cousin comes up with his guitar and songs to help with the pain, which was much appreciated by all. We sang our hearts out.

After the post mortem, the verdict – drowning. I can only assume that as he came back, he had slipped, knocked his head and unconscious entered the freezing water.

Mum, Shirley, Kate (Dan's wife) and myself are watching Dan. He is on the little pontoon where their joint owned boat is still moored. He is cross armed looking out to sea, completely silent, deep in loss. The sea, that was totally still not one minute before, starts to rise enough to make white horses appear, there doesn't appear to be a wind. It's a strange occurrence but one that we all saw and took some solace in.

The days and weeks and months blurred into one another. We all needed a break and a log cabin was booked.

It's around 11 pm. Mum, Shirley, Dan, Kate and I are sitting around the table. Mum is starting to get upset again… 'Just show me a sign Tony,' she starts to weep. Suddenly the double doors burst open…Mum looks down and exclaims, 'My watch has just stopped!' We all witnessed the event, which along with the jetty experience has always made me wonder.

Who knows?

The pain has travelled for many years. Time is a great healer but it is not a cure. I don't know if spirits, Gods, deities or other entities exist, but I really hope there is a Valhalla. So that one day we can all have at least one last story together.

I salute you, the greatest Dad and adventurer, never far from our thoughts. It was always an honour, with so much fun and laughter.

35
Girls' Night Out, Glasgae Girls Hit the Toon

'Glaswegians aren't they just the best,' Charles is speaking. 'They are just so funny, chatty and bonkers, especially with a few drinks in them.'

'Yes,' God replies, 'we definitely broke the mould when we made those crazies.'

'Look there they are,' Charles says excitedly, 'this is going to be too much, have they had a drink yet?'

God, 'I could almost guarantee it Charles, usually in their Cornflakes for breakfast. Start the day off as they mean to finish, two days later.'

'Oh wow, yes they've definitely had a tipple.'

'More like a reservoir,' replies God. 'This is going to be a good one!'

*Many years earlier, Bahrain...*Dad's secretary pops her head around the door, 'Mr Dawes, I'm so sorry to interrupt your board meeting. The British club are on the phone and there is a situation that needs your urgent attention.'

Dad, 'It better be very important, we are just discussing the upcoming visit from the Crown Prince.'

'Hello, this is Tony Dawes, Managing Director, a Very Import...Yes? Really? Oh no, you can't be serious!'

Elias *the club superintendent*, 'Yes Mr Dawes sir, we have a situation here at the British club. Mrs Dawes, Mrs Simpson, Mrs Hunter and Mrs McDonald are intoxicated and have barricaded themselves in the Britannia Arms bar. The Madams are refusing to come out until someone re-opens the bar. They have been here since last night! It's now 11 am, sir.

Oh and they haven't stopped singing.

Can you help, as Chairman of the British club and husband and friend of the ladies in question, we desperately need your assistance! The staff are very scared.'

8 pm the following night.

'So let me get this right...if I sing a song and you like it you will give me money, so I can go "on the town" with my mates.' Four 'Aye's' back.

'Well, that's got to be the easiest money I've hustled yet.' Posh restaurant called the Concorde in the British club. Mum out with her Glaswegian friends all dolled up. I only know rugby songs. So as I finished off my last one about bestiality to the sheer disgust of all the fellow diners and with rapturous applause and whistling from Mum's table, I walked away with 50 dinars (about £80).

Drinks on me, catch up with the crew. I left them to it, what could possibly go wrong with a group of decent law-abiding ladies from Glasgow, enjoying a quiet drink. Oh, hold on a second…

Caught up with the crew, had a blast, went to bed. Next day got up late, nicely hungover. Go down to the Brit club, go for a swim and sweat the poison out. Sorted. Sizzling in the 40-degree sun, full baby lotion Factor 50 smeared on, making sure future skin cancer was inevitable. It's 11.30 am.

Freddy Hunter, a mate of mine and son of one of the mum's comes over. 'Brian, shit you're not going to believe this. They are still here!'

'Who is still here, Freddy?'

'Our bloody mums! You have to see this, they have barricaded themselves in the Brit Arms bar. They have refused all negotiations until four bottles of Gin are delivered safely.'

This I've got to see. We rush over…

A crowd of superintendents and staff are surrounding the bar, chanting from inside, *'Oh flower of Scooootland, when will we see you're likes again.'*

Yip, that's Mum and her pals all right.

'Look Elias, I will go in and have a word.'

'Thank you, we are very scared. I have phoned your father at work, he is on his way.'

I wedge the door open. A chair clatters across the room. It's dark. I can see some bodies in the back where the Scottish wailing is coming from. 'Shut the door,' they all start cackling hysterically.

'Shut the door, don't let the light in. Aggghhhh! We are vampires and will turn to dust…' giggling insanely together. It's like a car crash; bodies strewn all over the seats, one passed out snoring. The others are cradling the last of their drinks, snarling protectively over the last dregs.

Mum *slurring*, 'Oh, it's you! I thought you had gone out?'

'I had Mummy dearest, 15 hours ago. Have you been here all night?' I asked the once human posse.

'No, no, we got asked to leave the *Concorde* just after your singing, then we went to the *Londoner* bar and got asked to leave there too. Then we went to *Sasha's* nightclub at about 11 pm and you know how snobby they are in there…

They took ridiculous offence at us dancing with their decorations and swinging off the big disco ball hanging from the roof. Look here it is…' Mum says showing me a five-foot mirrored sphere that's glistening back at me; terrified, it's future uncertain.

Sighing, 'You do realise you are all over 55?'

'Shush, we were escorted out by security and the cheeky buggers gave us a lifetime ban.'

'AGAIN?'

'Yes, so we got a taxi back, got over the 10-foot wall and gate-crashed the bar.'

'Yes, I hear Superintendent Elias has been negotiating over the "loudspeaker" all morning.'

Mum, 'Is that what it was? We thought we were hearing voices. Anyway, fancy joining in a song…'

The group starts up again, *'Oh flower of Scooootland…'*

'No. I'm good. Anyway, I will leave you vampires to it. Dad is on his way to sort you lot out.'

Mum conspiratorially, 'Tell him to bring some Gin. We're nearly out.'

I go back to the pool, leaving a frantic Elias to wait for Dad.

Dad arrives. 'Yes, Mr Dawes, Managing Director, Very Import…'

Elias is in tears… 'Sir, we are very tired now.'

'Where are they?'

'In the bar sir.' Dad goes in.' RIGHT you lot! What? No, I haven't brought any Gin.'

'Give us a song Tony? Tony, Tony, Tony,' they chant…

Dad clears his throat, *'Do ye ken John Peel with his coat so…* Oh hold on a second, I'm not falling for that again. I've got an important meeting to get back to. I am rounding you up and taking you back to the flat to sober up and stop terrorising the club and staff.'

Dad sighing, 'Is that a giant disco ball?'

Back at flat, they pile in. Dad, 'Right, behave. I will let the other men know.' Dad sighs, 'I can safely say, my chances of selection for Chairman of the club next year are zero.' Walks off, whistling another hunting song, catches himself. 'Damn it Tony, they get me every time.'

Dad goes back to work. Problem solved. Starts to prepare for the Royal visit.

'Hello, this is Tony Dawes, Manag…under his breath, *Hells fire!* What! Again! I have just locked them back in the flat, how did they get out?'

'Yes,' confirms a distraught Elias, 'they have snuck back into the Brit Arms, barricaded themselves in and have brought bottles of Gin with them this time.'

Elias, 'I am very scared, sir.'

'Right, I'm on my way again.'

Dad arrives, 'How did you get out, I locked the apartment door!'

'Easy, we tied some sheets together and climbed out of the bathroom window!'

Dad, 'It's on the first floor!'

'Aye' came the four replies.

'Well, that's your fun over, George and Billy are on their way from work to separate you lot and lock you away for good. I better warn them about the sheets and escaping bit.

Elias looks like he will need to go into therapy after this drunken caper and I better take that disco ball back to its rightful owner and apologise yet again.

Right everyone out!'

They look at each other, start giggling… *'Oh flower of Scotl…'* Dad's foot starts to tap…

36
Goan, Goan, Gone. Shirley's Wardrobe Malfunction

I wake up, peel myself off the bed. Groaning, I look down there's my rucksack, packed…looking expectant. I head downstairs, Shirley has made a coffee.

'You must be excited?' says Shirl.

'Why?'

'You don't remember, do you?'

'Not a thing,' I reply holding my hungover head.

'Well, you better phone this number,' my sister says enigmatically. Hands me a small piece of paper.

I head through to the lounge, I look at Jeff crashed out on the sofa. What's Jeff doing here? I knew something was wrong, as he hadn't been stripped naked and set alight. Shirl comes through, 'You two turned up at stupid o'clock carrying that four stone onyx chessboard. You then started conversing in a new as yet undiscovered language.' Interrupting, 'It was probably Greek,' I told her.

Bloody Ouzo! I cursed my poor drink choice yet again.

'You better check if your passport is still valid.'

I look at the phone number that resembles hieroglyphics, obviously created by a 3-year-old with a crayon addiction. There's also a name scrawled on it but I can't make it out. I phone the number.

'Good morning STA travel, Deidre speaking.'

'Hi, this is a bit embarrassing but can you help? I had a knock on the head last night and suffering from a mild concussion and have forgotten the details of my err…booking?'

'What's your address? …Ah yes, we have you booked on Flight 457.'

'Flight? Err…OK, Tenerife? Dubai?'

Deidre sighs, 'I have a Mr J Hunter, Miss S Dawes and Mr B Dawes, booked on a week's holiday to Goa.'

Thank fuck for that! The last time it had been Mogadishu.

'Yes, booked at 3 am online, all paid by your credit card. Leaving tomorrow at 9 am.' Shit, better check my passport and inform work of my spontaneous holiday leave request. Check diary, cancel all client meetings and cross-out any chance of promotion this year.

'I hope you are going to buy a nice suit for our special event,' the operator purrs down the phone.

'Sorry?'

'Oh don't be all coy now, remember we were on the phone for over two hours this morning.'

'Really?' A small sheen of sweat appears on my brow.

'Yes, you proposed to me.'

'I did?'

'Yes, you promised a honeymoon in Kabul on your return, you romantic devil.'

'Good price too,' I offered...

'What did you say your name was?'

'Oh you joker, it's Deidre of course,' came the husky reply.

'Hah, just kidding my love. Well, I better look for a suit in Goa while I'm out, my call centre cutey.'

Deidre giggles, 'My cataract operation should be out of the way by then.'

'Excellent news.' *I would not be stood up at the altar this time! Always the fucking bridesmaid Brian, I cursed myself.*

Deidre, with a tremor in her voice, 'So call me?'

'I have your number and you have my booking reference.'

Deidre excited, 'We can use my pension money for Kabul.'

'Yes my love, we may need that for the ransom exchange.'

I give Jeff a kick. 'Oh Christ, it's you!' Quickly checks his eyebrows, big sigh of relief. A bank manager with no eyebrows was not good for business, it broke customer rapport. 'What are you doing in my house?'

'Jeff, this is my house.'

Jeff, juddering with alcohol withdrawal syndrome, 'Fucking ouzo!'

'Anyway, get excited, we are going on Holiday.' Jeff groans, 'I'm not going back to Somalia, EVER!'

'Hah, don't be so dramatic, we are going to Goa, perfectly safe. No marauding armed rebel group this time, no sir!'

'Goa? Wasn't that where those rampant sex pest Hippies went in the '70s?'

'Precisely, may still be a few left if we hurry.'

Jeff yawning, 'I doubt it, most of them will be sectioned under the Mental Hippy drugs misuse Act 1973, by now.'

'Damn it to hell Jeff, that useless legal system. Can't even have a psychotic episode without intervention these days. Bloody do-gooders.'

Jeff looks over at the chessboard. 'HAH, beat you again, that "Benko Gambit", never fails.'

One day, I promised myself after my "Sicilian defence" had failed, I would buy Jeff a lobotomy voucher from Groupon. Finally, win a game. Just one small victory that's all I wanted, selfish clever bastard.

Quickly check phone, no deals today, damn it!

The removal of Jeff's brain would have to wait. Excited, we are going on holiday, hope it's hot. Get a tan for the wedding pics.

Go and repack as one pair of undies and a teaspoon wouldn't suffice. Two pairs of undies and a decent supply of cutlery, I was ready. Head downstairs.

'Hey Jeff, you better pack, phone your work too and cancel that promotion.'

'When are we going?'

'Monday.'

'But it's Sunday today!' Jeff exclaims.

'I know, exciting hey! We'll phone our respective Head Offices from the airport. Try and undo the damage this spontaneous career shortening break would cause. Tell work it's a vital humanitarian trip, save the last surviving group of sex-mad Hippies from extinction.'

Jeff, 'Oooh that could work,' rolls his eyes.

'Shut it, you skinny Bastard!'

The three of us fly out, pit-stop in Bahrain Airport. Avoiding Colonel Jack Jones's cameras, we all hide out in the toilets. Avoid being re-arrested for past misdemeanours. Back on the flight as free men, land in Goa. The bus running on spirituality rather than a solid engine eventually stops at our loosely described "hotel".

Shirley fainting at the sight of our glorious accommodation had to be revived with a splash of Perrier water. Finally gathering what fashion sense she had left, stepped out in her Gucci dress. We walk up the crumbling steps avoiding the falling masonry, and head to the plastic reception table.

Shirley, quick as a flash with her new Prada bag has swotted a fly dead, which had landed on the receptionist's forehead. We waited for what seemed like an eternity for her to get up off the floor. Shirley impatiently tapping her manicured fingernails on the counter…the receptionist conscious again, we were finally booked in. Shirl annoyed, 'I hope their service dramatically improves, that took forever.'

'Goan time Shirl. Everything is on a different time scale, 63-hour clock malfunctioning every 3rd day on the sub-continent,' I informed her.

'Ughh, let's just get to the room. I hope it has an en-suite, marble Jacuzzi and decent room service? First thing order some Bollinger, I'm parched.'

Opening the door, we enter what can only be described as Tesla's laboratory. There is electricity dancing all over the roof. Wow, so pretty! It's like our own light show. Shutting the door, which falling foul of its rusted hinges, collapses into the corridor.

Ducking and diving to avoid the random lightning strikes, we inspect the stained bunk beds. Shirl starts to weep softly. Jeff sighing, 'How much did you pay for this again?'

'Well, I have no idea! I didn't even know I was getting married to Deidre?'

Right before we are BBQ'd to death by a 10000 volts, let's head to the pool, get some beers in.

Actually quite a nice pool, there are more Brit families and we get chatting to a few. One large family comes over every year. They go fishing most days and believe the cost of living more than makes up for being electrocuted most nights. We become temporary holiday friends.

We head out, Shirley in Armani. There seems to be only one dish available and that is lobster. There is an industrial scale massacre going on, people are wearing them as shoes, loincloths, and even hairpieces. Some eventually found themselves on a plate. The local crabs eyeing the decimation of their cousins had already migrated across the sea to Oman. Therefore avoiding the pot, being a fashion accessory and genocide.

I thought some of those hippy chemicals must have escaped into the local water supply; the place is all a bit mad, disorganised and hectic. The formula for a good cheap holiday. Jeff and I, after visiting the local market are £10 lighter, now with flowery shirts and flares. Blend in perfectly with that elusive hippy commune. We felt confident that "Free love", if there was any left, would be ours if we paid enough.

Few more drinks, we put our rubber crocs on and "earthing" the beds with a coat wire. With the electric show acting like a night light, we fall asleep.

Next day, we head to the beach. We are lying on loungers when an 80 something year old, wizened local man comes over and starts prodding in Jeff's ear. 'Must be a cultural thing,' I say to Jeff. 'Probably major insult if you fob him off. You'll be run out of town by the villagers.'

Jeff, so as not to be burned to death by local farmers, says, 'May as well enjoy the local customs. Let the witchdoctor do his thing.'

'Sensible move my good man,' I offer encouragement. The Voodoo practitioner seems happy that he has found two willing patients. Shirl swatting another 30 flies dead with her Burberry Bag on a passing ice cream seller, is not going to be exorcised, no fucking way.

Putting large rubber gloves on, a little vial is opened and then with large forceps quick as a flash turns Jeff's head to side, pours liquid into his ear. Jeff stunned, can hear crackling, then a pop as the sulphuric acid went to work on his wax and grey matter. The little auditory system cleaner then pulled out what can only be described as a coat hanger and goes to town trying to pick Jeff's brain out. I thought excitedly, that I might just win that next chess game after all. For some reason even after witnessing this snake-doctor's activity, I became a willing victim too. I wasn't going to miss out! I'd forgotten to pack my earbuds.

It would take two days before our hearing eventually made a re-appearance. Jeff spots a jet ski with makeshift hire sign. 'C'mon, let's do it.'

'What?' I cup my ear.

'I said c'mon,' starts shouting. I look at him puzzled. 'Oh forget it,' points at the Jet skis, gives thumbs-up and runs off.

Finally, the three lifeguards in an inflatable dinghy jump on Jeff, who for the last 40 minutes has been jetting at 40 mph through the safe swimming zone, sectioned off with bright buoyancy aids and rope. Jeff, completely deaf, couldn't hear the desperate shouting from the dinghy…that had been chasing after him all this time. He was also oblivious to the multiple hospital visits, via air ambulance, that his insurance company would have to pay for if he was ever allowed home. Back to the sun loungers chased by the lifeguards, time for another cocktail.

Shirley has just attacked another beach vendor with a Vogue magazine, when another local man comes over, 'You like fishing?'

'Can you shout please, we've just had our ears cleaned!' Repeats so the whole beach can hear. 'Yes, sir, I love fishing.'

'Good you come tonight at 12 pm here. We take you out on boat, catch big fish, BIG,' he bellows!

Back at the pool, I inform the family of the midnight fishing trip, initially confused as to why I was shouting at them, I explained. Kindly accepting the earbuds they had brought with them, play safe from now on avoid local customs, witch doctors and brain surgery.

I had my sixth sense radar on, it was perfectly feasible that Jeff and I after being robbed, would be thrown to the sharks thus ending our dream holiday. So I really, really, wanted to catch that "big fish" but was not keen on being murdered. Of course, lightbulb moment. I would invite the family, safety in numbers. We could use the pregnant wife as a shield, give us the precious time needed to catch that fish. I inform Jeff of my cunning plan. 'Bloody genius,' he confirms.

I extend the invitation, three men accept. I inform them of the "big fish" guarantee. They were so grateful after running in zig-zags from the local crocs every day at their favourite fishing site. A murderous robbing crew would make a nice change. I said they could thank me after, if any of us survived.

Now with four men and Jeff, there was a good chance we could fight off the murderous crew long enough to catch the "big fish" that I had been 100% promised. Suffice to say, seeing our numbers and not being able to murder that many men successfully, at 12 pm the man and his posse ran off into the night! Disappointed that the fish had got away, we promised each other we would try the people traffickers next, much more reliable. That big fish would be mine, even if I had to be smuggled into the "jungle" at Calais.

On reflection I told Jeff, we were lucky really, we had dodged a posthumous lecture on our return…from two very angry mothers.

Another night out and Shirley has devastated half the Indian insect population with her selection of priceless hand-made bags. We order anything but lobster. The three lobsters duly arrive. A few hours later, after releasing the crustaceans back into the sea, in a desperate attempt to save the species from extinction, we head to a bar. The whole time another murderous crew of robbers are eyeing Shirl's open handbag crammed full of local money.

'That's it! I'm going to put your money in my pocket keep it safe,' I tell her stuffing it in my pockets.

Few more whiskies, two hours later at the pool, about 1 am, sozzled. With one more "see the little Goblin" song, I dive fully clothed into the pool. Do a few lengths, the local staff have had enough and shoo me off to bed. My pool hopping training would have to wait until the next night.

About 30 minutes later, in bed, I bolt upright (not from electricity this time). Sprint over to the balcony. I look down at the pool. The local waiters have a large net and are scooping out Shirl's holiday money, floating all over the pool. Oh crap, if it wasn't enough that her Gucci dresses were starting to fall apart in the monsoon and her luxury items were being used as fly swats…I had just funded a down payment on two local families' new bungalows with her holiday money.

I would placate her by telling her I had been savagely robbed by a wild pack of hippies. Rolling her eyes, 'You jumped in the pool, didn't you?'

'Maybe.'

The next day after Shirl sold one of her Pradas in the local market to avoid malnutrition, we took a day trip to the Elephant reserve. Shirley has got elephant riding confused with a fashion shoot and her Chanel Safari shorts are being shredded by the hyper dermic needle-like hairs poking out of the top of the elephant's head. There is a small baby elephant following behind that is making the mother very agitated, she keeps turning and making grunting noises.

The mother is also completely unimpressed as to why three idiots had decided to come along for the ride, especially on the school run. She was running late and pissed. One last blast on her trumpet and Shirl's nerves completely shredded, we arrive at the river.

The magnificent beasts were being washed in a waterfall. We asked the local guides if it was OK to sit and paddle in the waterfall above and watch.

'Yes, yes, no problem.'

The elephants are playing away and enjoying getting a good scrub. Shirl starting to finally relax, 'Maybe it wasn't such a disaster "holiday" after all,' she tells me. 'See, nothing to worry about,' I reassured her.

I start to feel a tingling sensation and like the elephants below I am also being involuntarily body cleansed. I stand up covered in leeches, as is Jeff and my sister, who is now in a horrified silent scream. Her Dolce Gabbana swimsuit, a seething, writhing mass of black.

'That's the final fucking straw! You are never booking a holiday for me EVER again! Especially at 3 am…EVER!' Swats another fly and storms off with her retinue of blood-sucking friends hanging on for dear life.

'No pleasing some people,' I say to Jeff, who is now in urgent need of a blood donor.

A few days later after receiving several pints of blood from the local hospital, I rope Jeff into helping me beg on the street to pay for Shirl's last dinner: Three courses of extinct lobster. It was definitely time to leave, Shirl's favourite Jimmy Choo heel had just snapped after swatting a fly dead on a carpet sellers head; she was in a rage.

Suddenly fizzing with excitement, I couldn't believe I'd nearly forgotten. I was getting married in three days' time.

'Jeff mate, we have a wedding to organise and you're my best man.'

Jeff, 'Didn't you nearly marry that lady, Edna, from the British Gas Customer Complaints department after your boiler broke down last year?'

'Ah Yes, Edna, just dreamy, call centre chicks, just the best. Edna's voice was so sexy, those 40 pack years had really worked for her. Real shame she missed the big day…that double hip replacement couldn't wait!'

37

Brad's Stag, Saving Mankind from the Apocalypse Twins

Charles speaking in earnest, 'Marriage, the ring signifies eternity.'

'I wish they would stop using my name in vain, sober up then break up,' retorts God. 'It's supposed to be an institution, not a festive break.'

'I think,' Charles replies, 'looking at some of the car crash ones, it's more of a prison term.'

They both look down. Charles, a smile forming, 'Is that a stag taking place?'

God excited, 'Wow Charles, there are potentially so many awards here! I don't know where to begin. You're going to need to stock so much more metal polish. I better give John the carpenter a tingle too, we are going to need a much bigger podium.'

Loki bursts through the door, 'I just heard, is it true? Are they having a stag? This I've got to see!' Loki leans forward.

God quickly, 'Oh no you don't, it's my turn.'

White King takes Black Pawn. Loki, 'I can hardly contain myself…'

So I get a phone call, it's Chad, 'Brad's wedding is in a couple of weeks, we have to send him off in style.'

'Cool, where are we going? California, Seychelles?' Silence…

'Hello, are you still there…anyone?'

Chad, 'I'm still here. Yes, we are going to, wait for it…I know you will be so, so, excited.'

'Just get on with it Chad, FFS!'

'Dounreay, de nah, de, de, dah!' Chad exclaims dramatically.

'What the HELL Chad? Isn't that in the North Pole?'

'Close! It's where the nuclear reactor site is! I knew you would be excited. Yes, we've got a cottage, amazing price.'

'Well, that's OK then, are you trying to bloody kill us? I hope it was 50p?'

'Hah, we get to be test guinea pigs for their radiation trials. Just kidding, it was £1.20.'

Chad mate, 'We've been robbed.' I was now deeply suspicious. Should we be wearing hazard suits? 'Chad, how close is this cottage to the fusion core reactor?' Chad, now excited, 'Stone's throw Brian. Dress as Vikings, blend in with the two locals.'

'When is it?'

'Friday, old chap.'

I groan, 'OK, let's do it. I will have to dig out my drinking horn and leather armour again.'

Six hours drive into the bleak Scottish tundra, we arrive. There's nothing there except an old pub. All the seagulls flying about are fluorescent green, as are the sheep and the two locals. Jock, the last remaining Viking and the bearded Morag. Who, in a gnarled fist, is holding a big stick behind him, growling menacingly. Their distaste for those lucky enough to have one O Level and a general grasp of the alphabet, was palpable. That ruled out 108% of the stag.

I opened the cottage door to be greeted by some crew. 'Who in the HELL came up with this location for a stag?'

John, 'It was my missus's idea, she booked it. Lucy said that after the last stag, we should all be isolated. Keep Scotland safe.' Damn it, she did have a valid point, that last village was still on fire.

However, dressed as Vikings, we should be perfectly safe, except from the police, fire authorities, marauding Morags, the radiation fallout and human morality.

'Right Vikings arm your spears,' I shouted.

I was curious, 'Where are the girls at for the Hen party?'

'Burj Al Arab Jumeriah, Dubai,' replies John.

'Damn them to hell, isn't that like a 400-star hotel?'

'Yes, it's so posh you can even beat the staff and urinate everywhere, it's actively encouraged,' John reliably informs us.

'That's so cool but my Viking warriors…we have been bloody had, those witches!' I'm starting to glow a faint shade of green.

'What's that smell? It must be Italian, let's go see!' *The twins are in the kitchen. The twins! Oh my lord, we're screwed, no wonder they put us in isolation.* Italian operetta singing starts… '*Just one Cornetto, give it to meeee…DELICIOUS ICE-CREAM FROM ITALLLLYY!*' the twins are in town. We're fucked!

I enter the kitchen, there they are, the two brutes. Rutter-Rotter's, evil twin geniuses. Named by Satan himself as Anti-Christo and Dani-omen. The twins, born of three mothers, a jackal and four different dads, were smiling back at me.

I smiled back pleasantly, avert suspicion. I knew how that jackal story ended, I'd seen the documentary. I looked for the Rottweiler, nothing. Must be in the car? Anyway, I would check for the mark later, once they had suffered liver death at 2 am. I failed the last time, after shaving half a head and one testicle. I wouldn't fail this time, no SIR! Humanities' whole future was at stake. I would arm myself with a fork for now, keep safe.

'Hey Brian, looks like you're hungry already?' Pointing at the fork.

'Yes, I'm bloody starving, the local pub only serves live sheep and scampi fries.'

'Yuck, that's gross, scampi fries are shit!'

Anti-Christo (the more evil twin), hands me a plate, it smells delicious.

'What is it?'

'Oh, it's Lebanese lasagne[1].'

'Wow, isn't that culinary misappropriation?'

'Probably,' says Christo nonchalantly, 'try it.'

'That's amazing! I didn't know you boys could cook.'

'Yes, it's our speciality, would you like some "*red*" sauce with that?' The two grown men start giggling.

'You know you should send Mary Berry this recipe.'

'Yes, we did; that's why she only cooks with chocolate now,' they start giggling again.

Disconcerted, they had obviously gone insane. *Poor sods, must be the radiation*, I thought to myself, my green glow emanating back at me. After going back for fifths, along with the rest of the crew, I was still ravenous. The more I ate, the hungrier I became. It made no sense. With the 40kg lasagne half-finished, my need to save mankind from the apocalypse twins was dwarfed by my need for a chocolate bar.

'Right boys, let's go to the pub get a few pints in. Leave the Rutter-Rotter's and Chad all giggling in the corner to their mad selves.'

Jock, the bar owner and only light source, glowing green behind the bar, greeted us with a grunt.

'Kind sir, we'll have eight of your finest chocolate bars, please.'

'Och aye, what nae whisky?'

'No, chocolate is good, make it quick my good man.'

'Aye laddie!' the bartender looks under the counter.

Now sitting at the table, the stag, "Brad the Impaler" has a full Viking suit on, horns and small wooden sword, looking very confused. Too much lasagne no doubt. Now satiated with grouse babies dipped in chocolate, it was time to get drinking, Viking style. Getting to the bar was easy, being in the radiation fall out zone and the only customers for forty years had its advantages. I was starting to feel good, a little giggle escaped. What the HELL!

Back to the table, random giggles are breaking out. Suddenly, we look at each other, the Tsunami breaks, all out giggling ensues. 'Right boys, let's get back before Jock calls the local policeman 400 miles away.'

Quick bar stop first, 'Jock, my good man, 120 bars of chocolate to go.'

Sighs, 'Nae whisky then?'

'No Jock, just the chocolate, my good green man.'

'Bloody mad city folk, bonkers the lot of 'em,' he mutters with a green glow.

Rutter-Rotter's talking, 'Right lads, you up to speed with us now,' smirking.

'Yes, you pair of bastards.'

'Excellent, what should we do, it's stag time!'

'What about musical chairs,' pipes in Dan.

'Not enough room.'

'What about Sardines?' John giggles.

'No.'

---

[1] magic ingredient half a kilo of the finest Lebanese red hashish.

'Pass the parcel,' I suggest.

Silence.

Then the Rutter-Rotter's master plan unfolds. *Hide and seek.* Yes, we all agreed, Vikings would definitely have played that. Christo lays the rules down, make the kitchen the base, get there you're safe. That's bloody genius the twelve 30-year-old men agreed, horns nodding back.

'Right I will start,' says Christo. '1, 2, 3…'

'Hold on a second! What number are you counting to?' Gerry asks.

'Four and a half,' replies Christo. The proper evil bastard, son of a jackal, once removed…then returned. It's a long story.

Ahhh, runaway, runaway! As we fled to hide, Christo, shouts, 'If you start giggling…I will find you!'

'That's so Liam Neeson! The shittest Irish dad ever, after losing how many teenage daughters?' Giggling hysterically, we all go looking for hiding places.

I'm in the living room, the lights are off. I can just see Brad's horns poking out from behind the curtains. Chad, after way too much lasagne, has covered himself in cushions and is sitting motionless in an armchair. Gerry has rolled himself up in the carpet and John is standing in the middle of the room with a lampshade on his head. I'm under the couch that is now three foot taller on a slant. We are all telling each other to shush, stop giggling. 20 seconds pass, we're totally quiet. Brad is snoring.

Christo comes in, switches the light on. All busted, 'WTF? Christo, you satanic prick, you can turn the light on?'

'I thought that would be the obvious idea, it's not murder in the dark boys.'

'Damn it, you're making it up as you go along! I demand to see the rules. They wouldn't have had electricity, let alone a nuclear power station when the original game was created in 710 BC,' I protested. I would google the rules and historical evolution, when we reached civilisation again, 4000 miles away in Angola. Prove my point. Proper Beelzebub bastard.

'Right, my turn, 1, 2, 3, 4 and a half.' No turning lights on this time. I go searching. It's bizarre. Chad was on the loo giggling hysterically wrapped in toilet roll.

'WTF Chad, an Egyptian Mummy?'

'Don't be so bloody stupid, I'm disguised as a roll of toilet paper.'

Sighing, 'Yes of course you are, definitely no more lasagne for you. Not unless it's been cooked by an authentic Italian.'

Gerry, with another lampshade on. 'Let me guess, a standing lamp?' I say looking at his silhouette in the dark. Gerry outraged, 'Don't be so bloody stupid! I'm changing the bulb! Switch the light on when it's my turn. Catch you bastards.'

Dani-omen has managed to get himself into the washing machine on a 40 degrees, white cotton cycle. I would have to wait 50 minutes before he could be caught. Dan was in the fridge and we had to pull John out of the freezer.

I'm guarding the base when suddenly a massive Christo dives through the serving hatch and crash lands on the kitchen table. I look at Christo and the tiny serving hatch, 'How the fuck did you do that? That defies all laws of physics.'

Christo grins back, 'Lebanese lasagne, remember?'

'Nope not a thing. Whose birthday party was it again?'

Christo, 'That's the spirit, you did eat 3 kilos.'

'Is there a chip bowl going around?' I reply.

Proper evil bastard twin, I thought to myself. The "mark" had to be found. I don't care if it ruins the birthday party or not. Was it my birthday? Whose bloody birthday was it? Why was Brad dressed up as a Viking and what was the meaning of life? *Did Bubbles really cheat on Michael?* And the most important question of all…where the fuck had I stashed that last chocolate bar?

After shaving the other side of Dani-omen's head at 4 am, I was getting frustrated, no sign of the devil's mark so far. Trust my luck, it's probably on his bollocks. In for a penny in for a pound, I switched the electric razor up to "pubic" cut. It was to save mankind after all! Dani (16 stone of solid muscle) grunted, 'I love you Brad' and rolled over. Phew, start with his arse first then. Maybe, Dani and Brad were getting married? This was all very confusing?

Next day, anti-Christo has made Brad a "special" coffee. We watch as he became horizontal. We inform him of Christo's misdemeanour, Brad sits up, starts giggling. 'Is there a chocolate biscuit to go with this coffee?'

As the sun rose, we marched off. Dressed up as Vikings yet again…The stag party heads 100 miles to the nearest town. The only entertainment other than marrying a sheep or a cousin, is ten-pin bowling. We arrive, chanting Viking songs. Skol, Skol, Skol…Skol, to arrive at the aptly named *Viking 10 Pin Bowling centre.* Fate is as fate does, operates unexpectantly. John with blond braids and dodgy moustache… 'I thought Vikings were more rape and pillage rather than bowling?'

Dan, orange beard on, 'They need their down time too, must be exhausting all that conquering and unregulated sex.'

'Dan,' I countered, 'I'd imagine when they arrived in Scotland the local women were marauding them. Six-foot four blonde six-packed blokes, they didn't stand a chance. They must have shat themselves!'

The Viking longboat (a thousand years earlier) off the Scottish coast, Sven is peering through a Narwhal horn looking glass, 'Ah there I see one on the hill!'

Lars excited, 'Let me have a look! There she is, what a ginger beauty! Oh, hold on a sec…is that a beard…ahhhh! Row away, row away!'

'Don't mess with Morag and her 40 sex starved ginger cousins. More men for the "Me too" march next month, poor pillaging sods!'

Commiserating for the Viking's plight, 'I don't know how many times I've been jumped by Morags in the last week,' I sighed.

'Me too, they're a proper ginger nuisance,' says John. 'Yes,' we all agreed, horns wagging. 'Carry a can of mace from now on, stay group safe.'

'Right you lot, you can't come in,' says the burly bouncer.

'Err, why not?'

'There's a strict dress code,' points to a notice.

NO MARAUDING VIKINGS ALLOWED.

'Oh FFS.' Back to the cottage we go, 'Skol, Skol, Skol…'

'You know what?' I said to the group of misappropriations. 'What the fuck have the Vikings ever done for us?'

Dan, 'Improve the gene pool for starters! Did you see Morag? What a beauty, magnificent ginger beard, she even stood up to pee.'

'Fuck off, that's impressive' we all agreed, jealous.

Those Vikings were proper lucky bastards after all!

One last round at Jocks, we can hear whimpering coming from the cellar. I ask Jock.

'Shushhh, she'll hear,' he points over his shoulder. Morag is not two feet away, glowering. Holding a massive rolling pin, which she is bashing into her calloused hand.

Jock, 'She's stolen four Vikings. Ships have been rowing over looking for them for years…

Send help, "Erik the Red" must come!'

'Don't worry I know the Rutter-Rotter's have Viking connections.' Whispering, 'I will let them know when they both stop giggling.' Jock nods back grateful, a tear rolls down his cheek. Reaches under the counter…

'Here, take two chocolate bars for them.'

38
Chad's Stag, Creating the Naked Man

'Where are we going this time, Brad? My jaw is still aching from all that giggling, bloody evil twin bastards.'

'Chad, is getting married in two weeks, give him a good send off,' says Brad. 'We have booked two log cabins at Crieff Hydro.'

'Well,' I said relieved, 'that sounds much better, less life threatening. Let's do it. I'll bring the "Wasp", get proper mashed up.'

Brad now nervous, 'Do you think that's a good idea?'

'Yes, best one I've had in the last five minutes. Completely sound, 100% bulletproof. Don't worry Brad, we'll all be as good as gold, behave ourselves. You'll see,' I lied.

'Err, you know the Rutter-Rotter's will be there?'

'Damn it to HELL, those evil twin bastards!' Right, I will be on my guard this time. Not catch me out this time, with their dodgy food. Grab a fork for safety.

'Hey Brian,' Christo looks down at the fork in my hand, 'you hungry again? We've made Moroccan Cannelloni[2], with crushed "*black*" pepper.'

'Oooh! That sounds delicious, but I'm not falling for that again! Brad is still eating his own body weight in chocolate, and I had to work nights to pay for those confectionary costs. 627 bar wrappers I counted after the last stag, even my dentist is refusing my calls. Anyway, I have brought the "Wasp," that will be my fun.'

'Ouch, do you think that is a good idea?' Christo looks concerned. 'Absolutely the best idea I've come up with ever, completely sound. 1000% bulletproof.'

Everyone has now arrived, there are 16 of us fully grown, very mature men. One man seemed especially sensible and therefore was sticking out like a sore thumb. I introduced myself to this anomaly.

'I am Edward, Chad's older brother and an Accountant don't you know.' Impressed, I bowed. Wow, a potential crew member with a real job. Now that was a turn up for the cards! Edward perused the cabin, looking horrified at Chad's poor choice of friends. 'So is that like maths?' I enquired. 'Sort of, more accounts, profit and loss.'

---

[2] made from 4 lbs of outstanding Moroccan black hashish.

Right, quick as a flash, 'Why is the world spinning at 2000 miles an hour, yet I don't feel dizzy at all? Please explain in detail. I'm open to a drawing if that would help?'

Edward with a total look of exasperation, 'Are you on DRUGS?' The affronted accountant spluttered. 'No, but you should try the Cannelloni, I hear it's delicious.'

'I think I will!' Edward runs off, making signs of the cross on his chest and trying to ward off the other chaps with his crucifix necklace.

I thought he will fit in just fine. I could use a religious man. We could join forces to fight the evil bastard twins. I need to find that "mark" tonight, mankind's plight was getting desperate.

The first night, we go to the only local nightclub, called Scorpios. It was a bit rough, the local Morag's were hunting in packs again. Fortunately, we had all armed ourselves with forks. It would hold them off for a bit until we could get a drink. Edward is trashed, dancing like a man possessed. Tie now a bandana, shirt buttons all undone, just like the zip on his trousers. 'This is the best FUCKING party ever!' Stumbles over to me, 'That Cannelloni amazing, I ate six plates. I want this never to stop,' piles onto the dance floor. Four Morag's spot their opportunity, Edward disappears under a sea of ginger. Not to be seen for another 24 hours. Chad seems unconcerned, 'He really needs to get out more,' he confides in me.

We head back, no one can find Edward; he's completely vanished. I wondered whether it had been an alien abduction. Judging by some of the locals in that club, alien activity was obviously at plague-like proportions in Crieff. It was the only conclusion. Looking at the sky to see if we could spot the guilty space ship we headed home.

Now some idiot has decided to book two cabins that don't sit next to each other. We have a family in the middle of 16, now 15, completely intoxicated, mature men. What could possibly go wrong again?

We are in the kitchen, I'm on the kitchen table in my boxer shorts and I have the "Wasp" out. It's a beer bong, a long black tube that I decorated with yellow tape to give it an evil look. Holds 2 litres of booze, which can be downed in less than five seconds. In front of me, I see a new face, a teenager about 16. 'Who the hell is that? Don't tell me we have kidnapped someone again?'

'Yes, he's from the family next door, wants to come and party, so we grabbed him.' Came Christo's reply.

I can hear his mother calling his name frantically outside. Anyway, down to business. I go for the down, the "wasp" is pushed to the ceiling. At that very moment, the two Rutter-Rotter's on either side of me rip my boxer shorts to pieces, one half in each of their clawed hands. I'm stark bollock-naked, the 16-year-old screams and runs off.

Next thing the chant goes up, *'Naked man, naked man, naked man...'*
started by the twins. It's quite catchy and would stick as my moniker for the rest of my life. Now realising my new calling, moving forward…I would perform at Bar Mitzvahs, christenings and the odd funeral (by special request).

I would become the "naked stripper", wiping a tear from my eye. Mum would be so proud of me right now. A proper job at last! Start by cutting my teeth at poor Edna's funeral next week…cheer everyone up.

I had packed my electric razor, I hadn't forgotten my real mission! To save Mankind from the apocalypse twins! I would wait until the Rutter-Rotter brothers had passed out. Find where the mark of the beast was hiding. I was annoyed, Bloody Edward! Where was that "God" man? We had our calling! Many hands make light work, especially when tackling Beelzebub's offspring.

"Pubic buzz cut button, 'on'".

I wake up in the morning. I'm crashed out in the car, a woman hysterical, is screaming and banging on the car window. I don't even remember my name, let alone why this crazed woman is going mental. I get out, she's yelling at me. 'What did you do to my son? What did you do!' Starts sobbing…'He's barricaded himself in the room and won't come out. Say's he saw the devil last night; totally naked.'

'Ah,' I said 'that will be one of the twins, very evil indeed. The local priest should be able to sort it,' I would inform Edward.

'Also, one of your buddies came into our cabin last night with a tray of sandwiches and then we found him passed out on the sofa in the morning!'

'Oh praise the lord, that's a result. Can you wake him up, tell him to bring the sandwich's over, we're all starving.' I was annoyed, *'I told the lads we should have booked half-board.'*

'That's it,' the unreasonable lady screams, 'I'm calling the manager! Right now! You utter barbarians.'

'Seems a bit extreme,' I tried to placate her. 'Your son should be thankful he's had a free show. My very first, and what were YOU thinking, booking a cabin in-between two stag cabins?' Sighing, 'You really didn't think that one through, my dear.'

The lady looks incredulous, 'But…'

'So I think we have all learned something from this,' I patted her shoulder. 'Good talk,' I entered the carnage.

'Wow, that is proper destruction. What the hell happened?' One of the twins crashed upside down on an armchair, the other is slowly going in circles attached to the ceiling fan. Dani-omen, 'Strangest thing, I keep waking up with different parts of my body looking like they've been shaved by a madman. Even one of my bollocks, smooth as.'

'Dani mate, it might be the local alien activity or maybe it's an "Omen",' I throw him a hard, accusatory look. *I was half expecting the classical horror music to start from that infamous apocalyptic documentary.* It didn't. Dani yawns in response, 'Yeah probably.' *God, he was so evil.*

Suddenly the door bursts open, it's the manager looking furious. 'I want you guys out now, right NOW!'

Brad, saunters over, 'I've got this boys. Look sir, we are the guests, I've worked in some of the highest establishments in the land even "THE" Glencockeral Hotel, and the guest is always right no matter what. Always!' Brad starts to monologue about his life history as a kids swimming pool instructor. Stops for a breath, 'You look hungry have you tried the Cannelloni, it's really very good.' The manager is shaking, indignant. 'I'm not HUNGRY!'

Now, I'm sure that famous hotel was named after a raptor not domestic fowl? No matter, Brad had gorged on that Moroccan dish all night, good chance he was still hallucinating.

I thought Brad would really have had this if he hadn't been standing in three inches of alcohol, covering the entire cabin, dressed only in his underpants. The manager, shouting, 'You have one hour to get out, before I call in…not only the police but the DEA!' Looks around disgusted.

'Just no pleasing some people,' I said to Christo twirling on the fan. 'Wow, some folk are so uptight. Speaking of which, where is Edward?' Suddenly, the door crashes open again. It's Edward, covered in scratches and bruises, his nose looks broken. Babbling, starts to explain that he had finally escaped the Morag's but had face planked outside and had been picked up by the cops. He had been placed in a holding cell to sober up, as he couldn't remember where he was staying.

'I told you that Cannelloni was delicious,' Dani-Omen put's an arm around Edward's shoulders, gives him a little squeeze.

'Well, that's fantastic,' Christo pipes in, 'we have created "Naked Man" and now "Eddy the Unsteady", that my boys, was worth the carnage and the full lifetime ban.'

They all start chanting, *'Naked Man, Naked Man…'* I begin to get undressed, may as well start practising for that world tour.

Couldn't wait to tell mother, she would be so proud.

39
Meeting the Mother of My Children: Part 1

I wake up, look over at my bedside table. Several books are piled on top of each other: 101 Hangover Strategies for Parents; Valium for the New Parent; Preparing yourself for Bankruptcy a Parents journey; and Alcohol Self-medication Survival Tips for Dad's (Volume 8).

I lean over Heather, snoring happily to herself, and grab her Parenting for Dummies: an unpractical guide for new mothers, off her side table. I would skip to the back page as I was not one for reading instructions, as was demonstrated by the magnificent chicken soup, I had made last night.

Placing the whole chicken in the cooker, I turned the dial to cycle 3, which had a roasting tray symbol with little vertical lines, which were obviously heat rays. I waited for the swooshing noises to finish. The soup was marvellous, I would try a whole pig next time.

I told Heather of my culinary intentions, only to be informed that it was, in fact, a dishwasher and not chicken or pig safe. Damn it! What the hell had I put those dirty dishes in then?

I flicked to the back of the book, therefore avoiding several years of grinding parental tuition and sleeping routine instructions, which purportedly are essential for a confident and well-rounded child. Last page: The Conclusion, two words;

You're fucked!

Well, I didn't need to read the whole book to know that! What a waste of money!

Heather is mumbling in her sleep, 'Hello sailor, that'll be £10.'

Her dreams were becoming ever more disturbing…

The door suddenly splinters into a thousand pieces, both kids pile in. Start to use my groin for trampoline practice. Great financial strategy, I commended them. Make sure no future siblings are born. Not have to split the inheritance when that mysterious fatal "accident" took place.

The kids could then buy that solid gold Barbie dollhouse and own the Pony stables down the road. That every birthday had been denied. Unlawfully, as we were often told by the 3-year-old.

Unfortunately, for our chances of reaching pension age, they had been watching Bear Gryll's, survival of the fittest. Taking volumes of notes, they had been plotting their inheritance ever since.

Heather groaning from the hangover and Valium fog, rolls over. The flash of blonde hair has triggered a memory in me…

That's it, (several years earlier), single at the time, I need a holiday badly. I book a week's adventure package in Turkey. That should do it.

It's hot, we are outside the airport, four of us waiting on two more who are now officially missing in action. Peter our tour guide, is getting irate. Suddenly two blondes turn up, smoking six fags each. 'Whye aye man, we're not going till we finish these, off and shyte the knoo!'

Damn it bloody Geordies, this could only mean one thing. Trouble with a capital T. They could shame the Pope these two! Finishing school had been a complete waste of money.

Heather and Philippa (Phil), jump in the front seats of the tour bus. Throw us, a 'c'mon and try say anything look' and fall asleep snoring. Reminded me of a certain plane journey out of Thailand with Firthy, except we had a valid excuse that time.

These two chancers unscheduled fag break didn't cut the mustard.

We arrive at the motel and get unpacked. All head down to the bar, to start to become what Peter would coin "the good time gang". Alcoholics yes, athletes not so much.

The first adventure, we get driven to a gushing river full of trout, there are small platforms over-hanging the torrent that act like comfy seating areas, lie on huge pillows. Have a few cold beers, bizarrely there is a makeshift open-sided lorry full of hideous baby dolls. Why the trader thought that the location and the type of product was a winning formula, was a mystery to me. But his shrewd business mind was better than mine, so I purchased our new team mascot, Chucky. Place a cigarette in its mouth, hang it out of the backpack, now Chucky was a member of the good time gang. We head off to "kayak" down the river in rubber rings. After nearly drowning in the torrent, we got covered in miracle mud for good health and poor hygiene. However, one of the enthusiastic local guides got carried away on Heather's boobs. Couple of slaps to realign the guide's cultural misunderstanding, back to the Motel for drinks we went.

I'm having a drink with Heather, go off to the loo, next thing Turkish waiter saddles over within two minutes has propositioned marriage that needs to be consummated, before I can get back from my pee break. Heather informs me of the impending wedding.

'God, does that chat actually work?'

'Heather,' I said, 'you go to the loo, see if he proposes and try's to shag me. I'm going to accept his proposal and demand to meet his family in the morning.' *20 years of marriage later, that'll fuck him!*

Heather in some ways had a similar upbringing to myself. She had learned to hustle from a young age, after being dragged over to Greece by her permanently irresponsible hippy mother aged 5. Who after marrying a local Greek man, had lost all pretence of interest in her daughter's existence, let alone welfare.

We had a loving mother but we needed an endless supply of sweeties, that was our hustle. Heather had to fend for herself and hustled for food to survive and baby dolls that she would get tourists to buy for her ever-increasing collection. She spoke fluent Greek, which years later came as no surprise to me.

Next day, Samuel another tour member, was absent from breakfast again; must be all that man training he was going through. The poor sod was mentally exhausted. He'd tried to circumcise himself last night and nearly bled to death. I should be more sensitive about the "Rights of passage" initiations, he was really struggling with level 1.

Day of mountain biking ahead. Jason, one of the tourists from "Saarf Engerluund," had gone mental in the lycra shop back home and had purchased all the latest cycling kit in the brightest pink. He now looked like a proud male peacock, that had taken one too many LSD tabs. Dazzling in the sun, he was giving me a cataract. Off we went, it was hard-core stuff for this group of budding "Tour de Turkey" alcoholics.

I would keep the good time gang image alive by drinking Raki, a local 80 proof aperitif, as we made our way through the numerous local villages. By village eight, I was starting to hallucinate. Heather, in a rage up ahead, had picked up her bike and was swinging it over her head about to toss it over the ravine.

Trying to wrestle, the terrified inanimate object from Heather's steely grip, with the chorus of 'Why-aye Man, and Fook off Man, this bike's dead man!'

I knew instantly that she was a keeper.

Storming off into the support van with her helmet at a right angle, I knew Heather was the modicum of demure and sensibility. She would be a good fit for the family.

Cycling along, village nine, how fucking much longer? I'm starting to flag and my water bottle full of Raki is nearly empty. Peter, the guide is waiting up ahead.

'Follow me,' he says, belting off at an insane speed through the forest. I didn't even know you could reach those maniacal speeds on two wheels. The Raki flowing through my veins and the "Out of Order" sign back on brain's door, I sped after him. Not five minutes later, after rising off my seat to put more power in, I have ripped my board shorts, the front of the seat is now firmly positioned through the gaping hole. I've been impaled to the seat.

I'm stuck-fast, hurtling down the hill. Peter oblivious, (if possible) has picked up a gear. I had the image of Peter flying off like E.T. into the stratosphere. I manage to survive and reach the bottom, naked from the waist down. Bloody typical! Just when I really needed that Raki, I had run out!

The support van, skidding to a halt, finally catches up with Peter and I. Heather and Corinne, have been on a bus-tour for most of the ride, which was just as well with Peter's life-shortening bike guiding.

Later that night, few beers. Peter, 'Yeah we had a family couple of weeks back. A mum and her son, he rode off the side of the trail and died.'

'What?'

'Yeah, there was an enquiry, still going on. Definitely suicide.'

'Suicide?'

'Yes, no other way,' says Peter.

'That's one hell of a way to kill yourself. How do you even plan that and make sure it happens? You sure his shorts weren't attached to his seat?'

'Nope, suicide and that's the company line.'

I now knew my shorts had been tampered with, it was either a life insurance job or a snuff movie. I would tell the others to be on their guard. Peter was out to kill us, I was waiting for Poirot to appear at any moment, interfering Belgian bastard.

Next day, we go paragliding. I went over my straps and interrogated the Turkish instructor about life insurance policies and any connection to video equipment. The look of confusion signalled the all-clear. Satisfied, so far so good, no murderous attempts yet. But Peter was probably biding his time, plotting. Due to that previous earlier shorts sabotage and dodgy suicide cover story, he knew that I knew, that he was a murdering bastard.

I was sharing a room with 18-year-old Samuel. Sam was on his first holiday away from his loving mum and dad and in desperate need of man-training. Assuring Sam, I would be stepping up to this very responsible role. I would graciously offer my years of knowledge, training and experience as an adult. I would be his mentor and reluctant idol. Over his dead body, Samuel would be a man by the end of the holiday.

'Right Samuel, we need to shave an eyebrow off and set you alight. Don't cry,' I give Samuel a gentle slap, 'I was only joking. You're no way near that level yet.

Anyway, you millennials need to man-up. Before your 19th birthday Samuel, I expect you to be either: murdered, run over by a horse and cart, become an expert cliff-diver or at the very least have a lady-boy sexually assault you. Join Firthy and myself on the "Me Too" march next month.

Now stop crying.' I look around nervously. The QES were known to travel overseas on rendition jobs and I was still on parole.

'Right, let's go to the bar, start your training.'

Pointing at the top shelf, 'We'll start at that end and see how far along we can get,' Sam starts crying again. One more slap, 'Good man,' I encouraged him, 'let's begin.'

We have a few drinks. 'Samuel, y'know, you're lucky! The "Right of Passage" is often fraught with danger, take the Maasai Mara for starters. From 12 onwards, you could expect to be circumcised (hence Sam's self-inflicted bleed-out the other night) without anaesthetic, which must be endured in absolute silence. Any screaming and running off into the bush, holding your bollocks, would bring dishonour and a hungry hyena. So crying is a no no,' I give Sam a hard look. 'Then a spear was placed into your hand and off you went to kill a Lion.' I look at Samuel, starting to well up, his Pina Colada trembling in his hand…

I thought even if we sharpened his pink umbrella cocktail stick, armed, he would still struggle to take out the local 20-year-old moggy, asleep in the doorway.

'Right! Down that yellow beauty, soon have you acting like a man.'

Next mortal attempt: White Water Rafting. The journey there, on an old rickety bus, could have been included under "death by fright" clause in Peter's insurance policy. Teetering off cliffs with the back wheels hanging off the edge, we arrive several years older.

Now, like many places around the world, health and safety are words that have not yet been discovered in Turkey and that threat to life is likely to continue unabated.

Health and safety brief, consisting of: get in the raft and hang on. We sped down the Grade 400 rapids, along with Russians and a British group. The Brits were doing an excellent job of trying to kill themselves, even without their guide's assistance. One lady got crushed between the raft and rocks after falling out and was carted off to the local hospital. Thus reducing her chances of survival, permanently.

Peter at one stop, 'Right, everyone jump into the (angry swarming torrent) river.' He will meet us further down. Like lemmings, we jump in. Heather, whose body has decided to live today, has grabbed onto the side of the raft.

As I entered the water, the shock of the cold (funnily enough called cold shock response) has made me gasp and suck in water. I start to choke and inhale more, meanwhile being bashed around, as if trapped in a pinball machine. Along with the others, we hurtle down the rapids.

Eventually, the river calms down. Phil the only athlete in the motley crew, is whooping with joy. Her Geordie mad genes had taken control again. Heather, has made safe passage via the iron grip she had, on the side of the raft.

Samuel is choking, bent over, on a small pebble beach. Starts crying, 'I don't want to be a man any more! I just want to go home, be a student again.'

I vomit the last of the river out and finally retrieve some air. I shout over to Sam, 'Congratulations you have now reached Level 1.'

Corinne has now decided, after another day of trying to stay alive, that she is no longer talking to Peter, or ever leaving England, ever again! Jason has his new canary yellow lycra speedos on and is oblivious to all of the day's events, as he has gone blind.

Peter delighted, 'Wasn't that GREAT! It's called living life to the max! I've got it all on film.'

Hah! I knew it, snuff movie! The tour guide bastard.

Sam, is absent from breakfast for the fifth day in a row. He can't be hungover again? I go look for him. He's rummaging through a bin. Bloody students! They can't break old habits, not even on holiday! Student survival tactics were ridiculously difficult to cleanse.

'Sam, what are you doing and why are you avoiding breakfast?'

'Err, I'm a bit broke, and can't afford it (I had been subsidising his man-training alcoholism).'

'Samuel, you pillock! It's half-board, the breakfast is already paid for.' Samuel's emaciated face a look of horror, quickly runs off to gorge on the cold leftovers.

It's bloody lucky, I've poured all that alcohol down his neck. Otherwise he would have died of malnutrition. That's what responsible mentoring is all about, I congratulated myself.

Last night, before we all fly back to our respective homes. We are all having a delicious meal. Singing starts from a local bar across the street. Peter informs us that the Turks, after a few drinks, have a lively chat and then the melancholy songs of the old Ottoman Empire begin then they all start wailing and have a mass cry off. Suddenly, I felt homesick, that's exactly what happens with my mum and her Glaswegian pals. Although the crying is usually when the Gin has run out, not the yearnings of a long lost Empire.

We all say our goodbyes. Samuel comes racing over, 'Look I shaved my own eyebrow off,' he says ecstatic. Sighing, 'Samuel that's not how you do it, that's cheating. You have to pass out. Then your best friend, and this is the key Samuel, unbeknown to yourself, shaves it off.'

Samuel indignant, 'Yes but you set yourself alight on a regular basis!' I looked hard at Samuel, a few seconds later... 'Y'know I think you're onto something there. I will do some research when I get back.' *Consult "The Orifice" or was it oracle, I forget. Damn it! It definitely began with an "O." Hedge my bets and seek spiritual guidance from both.*

'Here,' I put a pink sticker on his T-shirt: Man Level 2.

'You really deserved it!'

Clearly delighted, he skips off to catch his airport bus, hollers back, 'I'm going to set myself alight as soon as I get back to Mum and Dad's.'

'Good luck!' I waved back. 'Send them my love.'

I hoped Samuel would check his parents building insurance before he torched their house down.

I catch up with Heather, not knowing at this stage she would be the future bearer of my children.

'We should catch up back in the UK?'

Removing the six fags, that would get her through the flight, 'Why-aye Man!'

Excited, definitely a keeper this one. Wait until I tell Mother!

40
Two Fools Attempt Croc Suicide, My Favourite Flip-Flops

Darwin to God, 'This is getting ridiculous!'

'Charles, my dear hairy friend, don't worry I've been playing chess with Neil for years! This time we can get two fools for the price of one.'

Darwin, now excited. 'Two awards to polish?!'

God and Darwin high five, 'Yes Charles, it's all sorted, these two need no help at all. Perfectly capable of planning and executing their own demise.'

Black King moves across the board. 'Watch this!'

Bagpipes start playing. Darwin looks at God…they both groan, 'Oh no, not the Scot's!' Big crash, the door splinters into a thousand pieces. God under his breath, 'The day that those visiting deities ring that door-bell!' The Celtic Gods pile in, big ginger beards all round. Followed by a distinct smell of whisky. 'Hah, you moved the King, watch this! We own these two.' God looks at Darwin, rolls his eyes…

'Open a window Charles, that smell of haggis and whisky is nauseating.'

So I get a phone call. Big Neil, 'Fancy Uganda?'

'Sounds like a plan, my good man.' I reply (knowing Heather would kill me again).

'Aye good, short arse.' says the eleven foot Highlander bastard called big Neil.

Big Neil continues, 'One slight problem?'

'Yes, go on.'

'Have you heard of the Lord's Resistance Army (LRA)?' A shudder runs through me. 'I thought they were in CAR or the Congo?' Neil, 'Well, they have been active in North Uganda, so I guess we'll see.' *The LRA, run by a psychotic nutter General, thought chopping childs limbs off was a kin to a mild misdemeanour, like a parking ticket.*

'So we're going south right?'

Silence…'Oh crap.'

'When we going?'

'Next Friday.'

'Shit, that's Heather's birthday again, I'm so fucking dead.'

Neil says, 'If the missus find out about the LRA, we are both dead.'

'Well, why don't we tell them we are going to Benidorm?'

Neil sighs, 'They'll know. They always know.' Neil adds, 'I think our holiday video of crocodiles eating a wildebeest, narrated by David Attenborough, might be a bit of a giveaway too.'

'True. Damn it to HELL! We could try a Spanish voice over?' Neil, 'They'll know.'

Right better pack my favourite flip-flops, this could get rough. We arrive Uganda, stay long enough to be able to recite the non-stop 24hr evangelical church hymns, off-by-heart. Constantly being sung all around the town in little churches, run by charlatans, blissfully robbing the poor.

Stay with Neil's uncle and aunty, medics who work in a local hospital for free and live in the local township. Very poor but very safe. There is a Ugandan newspaper on the coffee table in English. I begin to read. There was a very disturbing story of the rich folk burying human bones in the foundations of new office buildings; for good luck and mainly prosperity. I didn't think it had been very lucky for the poor sod who had involuntarily "donated" their bones for capital gain.

One story catches my eye. *Villagers still looking for man's penis.* I read on, a man was caught trying to molest a mother's daughter, she cut off his penis with a machete. Then a local dog with said penis in mouth had run off into the bush with the tasty morsel. The local villagers had been looking for the dog for two days but no luck. *I thought if they re-attach it now, the result might not be too appetising.*

'Welcome to Africa,' I said to myself, 'where justice is "severed" promptly!' With the image of the locals chasing after the luckiest dog in Africa, I fell asleep.

So as we left mortal safety to travel North, I said to Neil, 'What could possibly go wrong again?' As Neil had a similar propensity to shorten his life, on "safe" holidays, I was suspicious.

12 hours into the drive North, I warn Neil that our guide/driver is falling asleep (we are on a very dodgy African road). We are both watching him catch 40 winks, at least one of us will be well-rested when we arrive. Neil growls, 'Hey you OK there buddy, we would like to live today…' Driver's other eye opens up.

We arrive alive. The "place" is stunning, a National park with the awe-inspiring Nile running through it. 'Neil, you have knocked this out the park, matey.'

Neil, 'Aye.'

So we are in a resort, with luxury cabins, pool and our own herd of hippos directly beneath. Chatting away to each other, with grunts and coughs, in the mighty Nile. It's surreal, just stunning. Africa's magnetism is working its charm yet again. You can literally feel the continents' pulse, drumming away in a soothing, beautiful tone.

Having a few cold beers at the bar. Neil says, 'I've booked us a fishing trip called the Nile Perch Experience.'

'Neil, I've got to tell you mate, I'm so excited. I'm defo gonna wear my lucky flip-flops, get that award-winning fish!'

Safari first, our fabulous guide, the driver, is multitasking. We see fuck all, take photos of tanks protecting the park from the LRA. Bored, we snooze around the tour.

Up at 5 am, to do the greatest fishing in the world, on the greatest river. This became a truly remarkable day, with the threat to life as the icing on the adrenalin cake.

We meet our fishing guide, Zimbabwean, long blond hair, green eyes, square jaw. Indiana Jones came to mind. As he looked at the 6 foot 5, 24 stone Highlander Neil Macdonald, he knew his quarry. As I stepped out of Neil's shadow, Indiana quickly covered his disappointment. I knew he knew, he was dealing with a real man. As he looked down at my flip-flops and rolled his eyes, one man came to him: Hemingway.

As I wiped the tear from my eye, after Indiana told us he had to leave his devastated vogue-model girlfriend to travel around awe-inspiring Africa, my heart broke. Off, the three of us go…Quickly scrambling to the front of the 10-foot tin-boat, in a vain attempt to stop Neil capsizing us, we "wheeled" off along the Nile. Bait fish, first call.

The immense Nile is stunning. Hippo pods are everywhere, Elephants in the water. The Nile, untouched by the disaster of man. I ask Indiana, 'Is the rest of Africa like this anymore?' Sighs, 'No there's nothing left. I've travelled near and far, most has been wiped out. The savagery knows no bounds, the 'hunters' will spear a hippo with a rope attached to a large float (often a car tyre) and then wait for days, until it eventually dies in agonising pain. This park is protected, so everything here lives. Except what the crocs eat.'

'Err, about the Crocs?' *That are everywhere, I might add glaring at Neil, who is whistling to himself.*

So we go to one of the most famous waterfall passes, Murchison Falls, once visited by Churchill himself. On a little beach, just below the falls, we start to fish. Half an hour later big Neil catches big time. I'm so jealous, if only he was much, much smaller, I could take him, with a karate chop to the ankle…the big bastard. Huge Nile Perch caught, he can just lift it out of the water, it's so bloody massive.

Neil looks over and takes the "piss", 'What are you catching today Brian, jealousy?'

Cheeky big highlander "git", I would show him, channel Hemingway.

We're both on the water's edge. I knew the jaws theme played for sharks but what was it waiting for the imminent croc attack? Something quite snappy, I assumed.

Indiana, 'Ja, we try different beach now.'

Neil, 'Probably need an easier target for Brian, like a goldfish! Or a really, really, big net. We could always try the local fish market?' grins savagely. Metaphorically, I've already staved Neil's head in with the bait fish in my hand and fed the big bastard to the delighted crocs.

Quickly diving to the front of the tin boat yet again, we wheeled off at 45 degrees…to the next adventure. Neil smug, feather already firmly placed in his cap. He could relax and take his time with the insults.

I start to pray, *come on lucky flip-flops, don't fail me.*

We land on another beach. Neil dropped off and left (hopefully for good) with a local guide. Indiana and I with the boat on the right-hand side, moored off the small beach. I get a hit on the line it's big, fishing off the back of the boat. Bit of play, big catfish landed. Neil shouts over, 'That's not a Nile Perch!' I release the world record-breaking catfish and inform the big bastard 'That Perch was so yesterday. Catfish were all the rage now.'

I could just imagine in the *Catfishers Weekly*, a publication for true fishing professionals and world title holders, like myself. I could see the title on the front cover:

MAN-EATERS CATFISH WEEKLY.
Only for real men, 31p.

First Headline: *800lb Nile Perch are they really for men?*
New evidence, highlighted by a huge catch in the Nile last week, of a monster catfish. The heroic haul has drawn a shadow over the prowess of the now-defunct Perch. So yesterday, we can't believe we are even mentioning it. After the epic catfish fight (reported anonymously by a big Highland bastard) of four and half minutes, we can only conclude that Catfishing, due to the dangers and total fishing fatigue is to be crowned: Man-Fish, 2012.

Indiana to me, 'We need to catch you a Nile Perch mate. Let's go on the beach.'

On the beach I look to my left…the biggest crocodile I have ever seen is in the water estuary not 40 yards away.

Suddenly, a massive noise, Indy to the other guide (Big Neil has no boat and no escape), 'Hey man, is it a Buffalo, is it a fucking buffalo (quiver in voice)?'

Ugandan guide back, 'I don't know?' Shit, Shit! I look over, see Neil, we catch each other's eye, we wait…

If it is, we are screwed; it's the most dangerous animal in Africa! And we have no escape. We all know this. I for one was not going to make a swim for it. The sun is beating down and we are all sweating, none more than the big bastard.

We are silent, no movement. We wait some more.

Nothing happens. Indy, 'I think we're good.' I look back at the Nile, not 10 feet away, the biggest croc I've ever seen reappears, dwarfs the tin boat. Our only refuge.

Fuck this! I have to get a photo on the old camera. As I'm looking down, I realise I'm wearing my flip-flops, not Nike trainers with go-faster stripes. Bloody typical! How do you run from a croc with "flippies" on, zig-zagging, really? I tell Indy this. 'Hah, don't worry I've got your back, we're cool. However, that is a big female' say's Indy, 'so we are probably on her territory. Her young will be nearby.'

Marvellous, at least we won't have to worry about the LRA now.

Cue David Attenborough (posh sultry tone) … *'When the female Nile crocodile has her young threatened, she will do everything to kill the intruders by tearing them to pieces.'*

Neil on the other side, loud rustling noise again, starts to sweat even more. A massive croc rushes past him, not 3 feet away, into the river. Neil, immediate underpants change required. The monsters are everywhere; I'm starting to question Neil's poor choice of guide but excellent choice of getting us eaten.

The toxic mix of fear, adventure and beauty is making this one of the greatest days. I am so alive. I say to Indy, 'What do you think?'

Indy, 'If we run, we might not win.' We wait, the croc is not moving, just watching…waiting too.

Fuck, I'm still messing with the camera, I have no memory left. So as you do, when a large predatory dinosaur is looking at its lunch, I start deleting photos frantically. Skip the kid's ones or Heather would kill me too! Damn it, come across family wedding photos, that's five minutes wasted (and 30 years of their life too), then some holiday snaps, a christening. Oh for fucks sake, just come and take me now croc this is painful. What feels like two days, finally I can start snapping.

Slide show of the croc (when back home), 'You didn't delete any photos of the kids, did you?'

'No Dear.'

I have to get a photo of this beautiful beast; at least the authorities will know who ate us. Indy, hand on my shoulder, 'Don't worry it's all good.' I wondered how he knew this! Had he been eaten alive by a crocodile before? This needed investigating.

Damn it, Neil! Did you even check the trip reviews? Top review:

Yes, I and my pregnant wife were having a lovely time with Indy, when unfortunately she was eaten. Score 9/10. Dropped a point, as I didn't catch a Nile Perch.

Indy over to the other guide, 'Be very careful, we'll bring the boat over. We make our way silently to the Tin boat, which now looks even more flimsy. The croc could open it up, using its jaws, like a can opener. Finally scramble onto the boat, next thing monster croc, even more silent, is next to the boat and dwarfing it. "Super-cool" Indy says, 'What a beauty, must be over 16 feet.'

Sighing, 'Indy, about the crocodile infestation and beach fishing survival strategy? No wonder you take payment upfront.' Blondie back, 'Welcome to Africa mate.'

We pick Neil and the other guide up. We look at each other, laugh. Then a big sigh… 'Fuck me!'

Neil grins, 'I think we may need a few whisky's tonight!'

'Really Neil, REALLY!'

Any thoughts Neil, any? What about reading the 'Trip reviews' and the direct correlation of said advice and returning to our families alive, after being eaten by the local wildlife!

Reluctantly I ask Neil, 'So what's next?'

Neil grins savagely, 'White-water rafting down the Nile!'

'Are you fucking serious? What on, a Crocodile?'

'Aye!' Says the big Highlander bastard.

41
Meeting the Mother of My Children: Part 2

Heather and I had been seeing each other at the odd weekend, over the past year. I was in Edinburgh, Heather was working in Birmingham. I was having a BBQ at the weekend, so would extend an invite.

'Great see you then, Heather.'

'Why-aye, man!'

Invite next-door neighbour, Alfie from "Saarf Londuun", who generally speaking was insane. Delighted, he will bring his Bongos. Few more crew including my mum, Chad, Brad, Christo and others, there are 12 of us.

Set up the BBQ, we all start to have a good time...

Next morning, I am awoken by the doorbell and loud banging on the door. Which made a nice change from the one in my head...bloody Alfie's bongos! Hungover, I go and investigate.

'Open up in the name of the Law' or to that effect. I am walking like a Zombie to the front door; just catch a glimpse of Mum, facedown, snoring on the floor (in the living room). She must have fallen off the sofa sometime in the night.

'Hello officers, what can I do for you?'

They take my details, not falling for a pseudonym. I thought Martin Luther King, highly original. Unamused, as the freedom fighter had been dead for several years now, they give me a slap and sprayed mace in my face.

Impressed by their casual police brutality, I ask 'So how can I help?'

The officer sighs, 'We have had several million complaints.' He pulls out a notebook and the roll of paper hits the floor. 'Due to the sheer amount of paperwork that would be involved and lack of stationery,' smiles weakly, 'it's a funding issue, we have itemised the grievances. Rounding them up, we have three main ones.

Number 1, it is stated that on the Tuesday the 3rd of July, persons at this address, whilst engaging in nocturnal activities in said communal garden did indeed use the neighbour's 7-feet wooden washing line poles for firewood.'

Bloody Heather! 'Why-aye Man, we need more firewood, get this bonfire going. Generous these neighbours lend us wood without having to ask? C'mon give me a hand, man.' Jumps over the neighbour's fence.

'Yes officer, guilty of said crime. My mother, who is elderly and infirm, was getting a terrible chill. It was the only humane thing to do, burn that rotting wood. Keep her arthritis at bay.'

'Yes well, no real harm done. Get it replaced!'

'My mother?' I replied shocked. 'Ughhh no, the burnt wood!'

'Yes, sir!'

'*Number 2*, at the same venue, said persons could be heard to be having what many have described as a "Caribbean" themed music party. We believe bongos were involved, as we have just passed one hanging off the light, in the hallway.'

Bloody Alfie. 'Awight Guvnor, you won't Adam and Eve it, got my bongos me old china plate.' Starts bashing the shit out of his terrified little bongos, for six hours straight. We all started wailing as none of us had any idea how to carry a Bongo tune.

'Yes Officer, guilty of said crime. My dear friend from London is completely deaf, mainly in the tone department. Thus, our only means of communication is through the harmonious beat of the drum. If not for this said vehicle of communication, depression would rapidly set in and the poor chap would kill himself, possibly at a level crossing.'

'Yes, well that is tragic. Try and get a silencer or muffler on those vehicles of communication, especially at 3 am in the communal garden.'

'Yes, sir!'

'*Number 3* at same address, there was said to be what can only be described as a "supermarket sweep" taking place around the block.'

Bloody Me. 'Alfie my good man, fancy a race around the block? I've got a trolley handy, that I was thrown out of the pub in last week.'

'Mate me mucker, awesome idea.'

'Right, let's race the dog, Jack my border terrier.' Round we went *maniacal* Alfie pushing, Jack barking wildly. We stop for a smoke-break and have a chin wag with three blokes heading home from the pub.

'Nice night for it,' me in the trolley. 'Yeah, it's a nice full-moon, what you boys doing?' The gents enquired of Alfie, Jack and I.

'Racing the dog.'

'Just as well he's not a greyhound,' one gent replies knowledgably.

'Not wrong, that's why I bought a terrier,' I replied.

'Can we join in?'

'For sure, the supermarkets over the road, grab a trolley.'

Now two trolleys and Jack (stratospherically excited) are rallying around the block at 4 am. Heather has the start and the finish burning washing poles in each hand, so we can see our way around the race track. Jack victorious again. I throw Jack a hard look, get a Gerbil when he passes, even the odds.

'No sir! I refute this allegation of truth. It was him,' I point down to Jack sitting wagging his tail excitedly. 'There is your guilty party.'

The policemen look down at Jack, then at me. Incredulous, 'Go on...'

'Well, gentlemen, did on the 3rd of July at 4 am, neighbours not hear consistent barking around the block "on loop".'

Checks his notes, 'Well, yes?'

'I rest my case, take him away.' I would not have any undue competition at the next race. I was sick of losing every weekend. It would be a resounding victory at last, at next Saturday's "Calypso" themed BBQ, with steel drums.

Sighing, thinking of even more paperwork and the on-going pen crises, 'Just sort the poles out, clean the mess in the garden, re-seed the burn patches and no more bloody bongos.'

'Yes sir, immediately sir!' I saluted.

Just before the officers of the law departed… 'One last question? Do you always answer the door naked?'

'Yes Sir! I'm rehearsing for a world tour!'

He looks at his notes, 'Hmm, ah I see.'

I'm curious now, 'Can I have a look at that?' In bold pen, "Naked Man" is written on his small pad. There was a little star next to it.

Damn it those evil twin bastards. They had friends in high places! These two coppers must be minions of the dark lord himself. They weren't visiting to temper my behaviour; they were here to actively encourage it! Just as well we had that misappropriated Caribbean party next Saturday. That was the last straw! They must have painted that pentagon star somewhere in the flat again. I had to use nail varnish remover the last time! I would check under the bed when Heather stopped snoring. An idea came to me. Sick of the twin's Voodoo, I would give Edward, a decent man of the cross, a phone. He could perform a flat exorcism.

I wondered if he was out of drug rehab yet?

The constables gave me one last hard look and shaking their heads, left.

'Well, Jack!' I said looking down, 'that was a close one! Especially for you, bad boy! That tail wagging didn't help!'

Now to investigate the bedroom. Moving the bed a couple of feet with Heather in full snore, I can see a pointy triangle. The start of the satanic star, drawn in crayon. *Those bloody apocalyptic twins!* Standing back up, I catch a glimpse of the back garden from the bedroom window. Oh crap.

I look out of the window. I knew those neighbours had been overreacting again.

Bloody HELL! 'Heather, HEATHER! You better have a look at this?' I better put some boxer shorts on first… "Answer the door naked?" The cheeky buggers! Proper police harassment in my books.

Heather and I go out to the once lovely communal garden that Mrs Miggins had been tending with great care for over 40 years. Which after "Bongo" night, was still smoking in places. Charred remnants of washing poles scattered everywhere, its absolute carnage. The 12 of us have partied like 120. There is not one piece of grass visible from a paper plate, half-filled drink, sausage or pork chop bone. Someone had even managed to steal the next door's baby slide and swing.

Christ, was that Ms Rose's wheelchair? Now on its side, with the wheel still spinning slowly.

'Why-aye man, that 'twas a grand party!' Heather nods her head approvingly, looking at the apocalypse.

I looked down at Heather's blackened face and burnt eyebrows.

I congratulated myself, my first instincts had been right...*She was definitely a keeper!*

42
Receiving the Certificate of Life

God stands up and taps the clock, nothing happens… 'That's odd?'

'What is?' replies Charles, distracted by the chessboard. One of the pieces, the White King, had just fallen over.

'The clock has stopped,' God taps it again, the clock starts ticking. 'Phew! That's very strange?' Starts to pace the room, stops at Charles' shoulder looks down at the piece. Picks it up and places it back on the square. 'He's been very lucky!'

'I thought we were trying to present that award?'

'Charles my good man, don't get upset. I have a better idea,' pulls out a large certificate, 'I need your signature.'

God and Charles stand up from signing the Certificate and look out…As far as the eye can see, there are glass cubicles with Gods, Saints, Kings and Queens to name but a few, all playing chess with their designated partner. Humanities misadventures, being played out for eternity.

Charles sighs, 'Always amazes me when I look at it, so many.'

'Yes Charles,' God smiles, 'everyone's life is a chess game. No matter how young or old, race, religion or sex, it's all part of the game of life.'

I was training hard, running with 20lb packs, gym and "HIT" training to potentially enter for a Tough Mudder race with my good friend Dougie, aka "THE BEAST". *A monster of a man and insane PT instructor, with a panchant for killing clients through physical duress and poor humour. Dougie currently has a life insurance policy on my head that threatens to mature every time we go kayaking in a tornado.*

I had finally matured. Quite keen to be electrocuted rather than set alight, it would make a nice change. The "Yang" of a misspent life, through general alcoholism and excessive partying, needed the "Ying" of counterbalance, through fitness. In the gym, while lifting weights, I felt a "pop" in my left temple, just like you would "pop" bubble wrap. I carried on and finished the session. One of the kids needed a lift to gymnastics. Bent at almost 45 degrees, I'm driving back from dropping Freya off. The pain is excruciating. I go straight to bed, with a playdate of 5-year-olds in full pandemonium, screaming up and down the corridor.

Next day back at work, I'm helping out a new colleague. I'm looking at emails but I can't understand the sentence, the words have a sheen over them. I can't make them out. I eventually, via the GP, end up getting scanned up at the hospital.

I have had a massive haemorrhagic stroke and would be told later that I should have died. The vessels on my left side had burst and there was a significant bleed on my back lobe. The scan confirmed there was a brain, much to my delight and the surprise of most. I had always been suspicious that the vacant room with a permanent "out of order sign" really housed a drunken hamster juggling on a unicycle, smoking a Cuban cigar.

The next few months were a blur of shock and disbelief; I was 46 at the time.

Fortunately for me, but maybe not for you, dear reader, I made a full recovery. I never experienced the classic stroke afflictions, however, four angiograms later through the femoral artery, up through the carotid artery into the "spaghetti junction" of my brain, was an experience I could have done without. But a blessing it has been, "lady luck" was on my side that day.

The door splinters into a thousand pieces. Georgia 5 and Freya 10 pile in. Fortunately, due to the usual trampoline practice on my family jewels, experience had taught me to sleep with a cricket box. Stay safe.

'Dad, Daddy, there's a large letter arrived, is it Santa?' asks Georgie, always hustling.

'No 'G' it's April, that's eight months away.'

'Is it a large cheque for the pony club buyout?' pipes in Freya.

'Ahem, let's see.' I open the envelope, the stamp (I notice), is very unusual. Looks like the Universe. A medal drops into my lap. I turn it over: Life Survival Award 2017. That's strange? There's also what looks like a large diploma:

Certificate of Life Achievement Award.

Signed, G and CD.

I wonder who that could be? Probably from the hospital team that cared for me or possibly the Stroke Association? How thoughtful!

I retrieve the little medal from Georgie's mouth, who had been testing to confirm whether it was solid gold or solid chocolate, both of equal importance in her 5-year-old mind. Both girls deeply disappointed at this worthless, unsellable certificate and medal, run off to terrorise the guinea pigs, dogs, fish, rabbits, pet mice and the unwanted "wild" mice under the kitchen units.

Heather finishes snoring, 'Y'know Brian, now that you have officially survived, maybe you should write a book of your adventures?'

'Hmm,' I thought about it for a few minutes…

'What a cracking idea. Nothing could possibly go wrong again?' Heather and I look at each other, both roll our eyes.

Heather, under her breath, 'Oh crap, what have I let loose on the world.'

So after a lifetime of trials and questionable tribulations, that's my life so far. There is just one last thing I would like to say…

'Technically…none of it was my fault!'

43
The Unmasking of Loki

The Gods are in a large meeting hall, all looking down at a massive chessboard. God is pacing up and down, 'So let me get this right. The whole time Charles and I were playing "that" chess game, you Loki, were playing a counterbalance one? And let me get this right, with "The Dark one!"'

All the Gods *gasp*, 'Voldemort!' God gives the shocked deities an exasperated look. Charles, sullen, 'See, I told you so!'

'Yes, my lord,' Loki with a strange smile on his face. 'Hades and I also had a game on. Hades was furious that he couldn't claim his prize after the Zambian snake incident. He doesn't like to lose.' God sighs, 'No death rarely does.

So that is why you kept interrupting us and making game plays yourself?'

'Yes, I was trying to stop you aiding and abetting Hades.'

'All that corridor chat too?'

'Yes, I was strategizing.'

'Why would the God of mischief do that?' God asks with a frown on his face.

'I can answer that.' Mother Nature "wisps" forward. All the Gods bow.

God, incredulously 'I don't understand?'

Mother Nature smiles. 'I was deep in despair at the wanton destruction of our beautiful paradise. My tears were causing monsoons and my anger, droughts. Loki came to me deeply concerned. He told me he could cheer me up and that the clock we all watch will eventually stop ticking. Thus life, as we first granted would return. But he needed me strong for the rebuild.

To cheer me up, he offered a game of chess. We had heard of Charles and your game, Loki decided to investigate. Seeing Hades' interest only sparked our curiosity. Loki, to stop Hades from claiming his prize, challenged him to a game of chess too. Loki eventually won the battle. The "Dark one's" rage can still be heard from the basement...'

Loki smiles, 'I give you two of the pieces that I played with, please enter.' The Zambian gardener Samuel and the Moroccan street urchin come forward and both take a deep bow. 'Mother Nature also helped...'

God intrigued, 'How?'

'Well, first of all, "our Mother" created barley, wheat and all the other necessary ingredients to make a selection of fine alcoholic beverages. Most of which can be attributed to the game moves. It confounded Hades every time. She also assisted in persuading the snakes, sharks and crocodiles that the fools were highly toxic.'

'Well, well, well! Bravo, BRAVO! What an absolutely delightful twist! But, why stop now?' Loki sighing, 'Well in truth, Hades had him with the stroke. He nearly took my King but it was a trap.'

Charles whispers, 'That's when the clock stopped ticking and the King fell over?'

'Yes, my good Charles. After that Hades was finished.'

'Fantastic!' God looks around. Starts clapping. 'Well done everyone,' nods at Boudicca, the Elders, Hemmingway and Eric, to name but a few. Granny Dawes enters with a tea trolley laden with cake. Followed by her son, Tony, wheeling a massive keg of ice-cold Fosters.

'Is it all over yet?'

'Yes, my dearest, it is.'

'Thank goodness for that! I've run out of gooseberries!'

44

Evolution, the Folly of Man

God is pacing up and down. 'I'm just outraged at man's ignorance and arrogance! Which are not only in abundance but in a perpetual battle for supremacy.'

'I know,' Charles says disappointed. 'Anyway, good news my lord! The clock has stopped. So their time has finally run out!'

God, feeling a bit chirpier, 'Good! The Gods are furious!'

God, now in full monologue... 'We gave them Paradise and they have been wrecking it ever since. Mother Nature, bless her, is in a constant flood of tears. They've exploited and slaughtered almost everything. They constantly kill each other! They have failed miserably. We all had such high hopes, programming intelligence and thought into them. These sentient beings have been completely irresponsible!...Rant over.'

Charles saddened, 'Remember that last mistake?'

God, deep sigh, 'Yes, we had to send a meteorite to stop those marauding dinosaurs! What a mess, they ate everything! Can't win Charles...we gave them too little intelligence and this lot too much! It's all about balance.'

God rubbing his hands together, 'Right, let's start fresh. What should we try and evolve next?'

They look at each other, 'Not a mammal that's for sure!'

God contemplative, 'What about an insect?'

'Couldn't be worse; let's face it,' says Charles.

Darwin starts to jump up and down with excitement, 'What about a Dragonfly? I love those.'

God, 'Perfect choice Charles. Call the other Deities over on the God-vine. We'll have a council.'

Sometime later...after the Norse Gods had nearly sobered up. 'Excellent! We are all agreed then.' All the Gods nod back, after watching Odin fall off the table again.

God presses the "Green Evolve" button that starts to flash. An outline of a Dragonfly appears on the computer screen. 'That's my program,' God states proudly, 'never too old to learn.' Points to a certificate on the wall: Basic C++ Award, Open Universe Diploma in Evolution.

Darwin, hopping up and down, super excited. 'Make it bigger. With loads more teeth...'

Then shouts with delight, 'Give it three brains too!'

The massive clock resets itself and starts to tick again... The Dragonfly at 40 metres, with 400 shiny, sharp teeth and keen intellect, (the deities look at each other now satisfied), flies off...

...to hunt the last breeding pair of White Rhinos.

God whispers under his breath, 'What could possibly go wrong this time...?'

The End